"Hollywood loves Wager…for good reason. His novels are plot-driven story vehicles maximized for narrative flow. [*The Spirit Team*] is no exception.…A top-notch, pulse-pounding, heart-racing thriller."

—*The Record* (Hackensack, NJ)

"Wager is really a wonderful writer, bringing you into the plot and keeping you there until the end. Once you're in, it would be hard to get out. And it's never like you think it will be."

—Nashville *Banner*

"An outstanding thriller writer. Wager is a master craftsman."

—Chattanooga *Times*

"Wager is a master storyteller. He has perfected the craft of suspense fiction."

—*The Tennessean* (Nashville)

By Walter Wager from Tom Doherty Associates

THE
SPIRIT
TEAM

WALTER WAGER

A TOM DOHERTY ASSOCIATES BOOK
NEW YORK

This is a work of fiction. All the characters and events portrayed in this book are either products of the author's imagination or are used fictitiously.

THE SPIRIT TEAM

Copyright © 1996 by Walter Wager

Cover art by Alan Ayers

A Forge Book
Published by Tom Doherty Associates, Inc.
175 Fifth Avenue
New York, NY 10010

Forge® is a registered trademark of Tom Doherty Associates, Inc.

ISBN: 0-812-55087-0
Library of Congress Card Catalog Number: 95-53079

First edition: July 1996
First mass market edition: January 1998

Printed in the United States of America

0 9 8 7 6 5 4 3 2 1

This is a work of fiction, and does not deal with real people or events. However, the imminent threat of bacteriological warfare is all too real, outrageous and frightening.

W. W.

To Stanley Gewirtz,
a wise and civilized man, literate lawyer, and
a very special friend

THE
SPIRIT
TEAM

1

Thick clouds masked the pale winter moon.

The night was black. The wind was cold.

3:10 A.M. . . . the mouth of the mountain rimmed Torat Valley in the Islamic Republic of Madesh. Though the temperature was only forty-six degrees, the husky young army captain was starting to perspire. He had never received an order like this before.

"All of them, sir?" he asked.

"All of them," Colonel Kebeer replied immediately in a voice as hard as granite.

The captain wondered who they were . . . and why every one of them had to die. Standard procedure called for a comprehensive briefing in which the terrain and enemy force were described and the battle plan explained. There had been no briefing tonight, and all questions had been brushed aside.

Captain Ahméd Aziz forced himself to focus on the colonel's extraordinary order. Killing them all wouldn't be easy. Whoever they were, they must be well armed and numerous. HQ wouldn't send a full colonel with an entire infantry company to deal with a few ragged bandits. There were no large gangs left in this sector. These *couldn't* be bandits, Aziz reasoned.

Then he looked past the tall colonel at the tank truck. As Aziz tried to guess why seven thousand gallons of military jet fuel might be needed here some sixty-one miles from any airport, there was a strange noise from inside the valley. It sounded like a distant rumble—plus something else. Barely audible, the *something* was shrill and quavering.

Colonel Kebeer stiffened.

He listened carefully. After a few seconds he nodded.

"They're coming," he said and drew a nine millimeter semi-automatic pistol from the brown leather holster on his hip.

Aziz suddenly realized that he was in mortal danger. Killing them all would be a *massacre*. That was a violation of the Geneva convention and—more importantly—a *capital* crime under Madesh's own Code of Military Conduct. If he obeyed Kebeer, Captain Ahmed Aziz could be hung.

But if he defied the senior officer's direct command in this combat situation, the hard eyed colonel might arrest or even shoot him . . . right here . . . right now. At grave risk either way, the young infantry officer hesitated.

"You have your orders, captain," Kebeer reminded coldly.

Then he checked the ammunition clip in the gun he held. Aziz stared at the weapon for several seconds, considering the counterintelligence colonel's reputation for total discipline and ruthlessness. Ahmed Aziz worried and swallowed uncomfortably twice—before he made his decision.

He saluted, turned on his heel and called to his men.

"Headlights! Turn on your headlights! Light up the valley!"

Bright beams from a score of military vehicles stabbed the darkness, illuminating the valley's narrow entrance like a theater stage. The soldiers peered intently. They saw nothing but patches of grey ground fog silhouetted against the inky March night.

The noise was getting louder.

The enemy would be here soon, Aziz judged. What enemy? How soon? How many? And why the secrecy? Controlling his tension, the perspiring company commander strode swiftly to a nearby trio of platoon leaders to prepare them for the imminent battle. He knew that he must be direct and brief. He was.

"No prisoners," he announced. "Pass the word. The colonel says kill everyone coming out of the valley."

There was shock in their eyes as he told them how the enemy must be destroyed.

"Why?" one platoon leader blurted.

"No survivors and no questions!" Aziz responded harshly to hide the fact that he didn't have any answers. Now he pointed twice, his stubby index finger thrusting like a blunt weapon.

"I want machine guns *there* and *there* to plug up the entrance with crossfire," he said. "Range your mortars to hit one hundred yards inside. Spread the rifle squads all through those rocks, and move the torch men forward—*fast.*"

As the three lieutenants hurried off, Aziz listened to the puzzling noise again. It was building steadily. Aware that time was running out, he concentrated on identifying the two very different sounds. Maybe they could tell him what no human would.

The rumble seemed too constant to be thunder. Nothing in it suggested metal or machinery either. Maybe this was a herd of running horses or cattle, the city-bred captain speculated as he watched his riflemen fan out to take cover behind a wide crescent of boulders.

Now Aziz noticed that the other sound was much stronger and clearer than it had been. Irritatingly high-pitched and insistent, the warbling literally demanded attention. Even the machine gun and mortar crews moving their heavy weapons couldn't ignore it. The soldiers listened, frowned and shrugged uneasily. They had never heard anything like this.

Neither had anyone else on earth.

Something new was loose on the planet.

The shrill quavering had a discordant splintered quality. Suddenly Aziz recalled the awful chirping of a million hungry locusts in a film he'd seen. He shook his head a moment later. There were no hordes of insects here in the winter. These must be some other wild creatures, he decided. Whatever the sound was, it wasn't human.

But it had to be.

Kebeer had made it clear that the mission was to destroy people, human beings whose location the noise pinpointed. That must mean that human beings were the source of both sounds. Aziz tried to imagine what sort of humans would make such nonhuman sounds . . . and how . . . and why. He couldn't.

Frustrated and worried, Ahmed Aziz stared at the tall slim colonel who stood twenty yards away smoking a cigarette. The son of a bitch *knew,* Aziz thought bitterly. Kebeer must have the crucial information that the company commander needed, facts that might save infantrymen's lives.

Why wouldn't Kebeer share it?

And why was a deskbound counterintelligence colonel running a combat operation anyway?

Aziz swore but no one heard him. The torrent of noise from the valley drowned out his angry oath. Then an edgy corporal squinting down the barrel of his machine gun at the entrance stood up and pointed behind Aziz. The company commander turned at once to look.

Someone or something was moving in the pass.

There were several of them, all too vague to identify at this distance. Leaning forward, Aziz strained to count the shapes as they advanced through the ground fog.

Six . . . seven . . . eight.

They floated through the clotted mist like ghosts.

Rebel tribesmen, Captain Ahmed Aziz told himself. It could hardly be anyone else in this remote dead-end valley over one hundred forty miles from the frontier. The opium smugglers' convoys crossed the border far south of here. These rebel tribesmen must have committed some terrible atrocity to provoke this fierce and total punishment.

A dozen other soldiers were pointing at the pass. The number of approaching figures was growing every second. There were at least thirty . . . no, more. Visibility was still poor. Even with the illumination of the truck headlights, neither Aziz nor his men could see the enemy clearly.

"Flare!" Aziz shouted to a sergeant over the noise.

The man raised a fat-barreled pistol, inserted a 12-gauge cartridge and fired it into the sky above the pass. Ten seconds later a dazzling light blossomed three hundred feet over the mouth of the Torat Valley. The soldiers gaped in shock at what they saw.

They were facing a nightmare. It wasn't a dream though. This was real. Hundreds of two-legged figures were walking, lurching or staggering towards them. Some plodded straight ahead. Others wandered as if befuddled by alcohol or drugs.

The shapes were human, but these creatures didn't resemble any people the soldiers had ever seen. They were startlingly different in two ways. Almost every part of them was covered with what seemed to be fur.

It wasn't.

And it was bright blue.

Men, women and children—bearded grandfathers leaning on wooden staffs and infants in their mothers' arms—were all bright blue.

And all screaming. It was their chorus of uncontrolled shrieks and yowls that made up the warbling. This was the jagged sound of raw terror, the animal cries of a mob in utter panic.

Their massed feet made the thunder, Aziz realized as they pressed forward. These were unarmed civilians, not fanatical rebel warriors. Not one carried a gun but that didn't seem important now. What mattered was the blue thing all over them.

The blue thing.

That must be what the colonel wouldn't tell him.

That was why every man, woman and child had to be killed . . . why the enemy had to be scourged by flamethrowers.

What could the blue thing be?

Baffled by what they saw, the infantry clutched their weapons and stared. The phosphorus beacon above was descending inexorably. When that powerful light was gone, Aziz thought, some of *them* might slip by the soldiers. Even one could be a disaster. The blue thing had to be contained.

"Flare! Flare!" Aziz ordered urgently.

The dazed sergeant didn't move.

Ahmed Aziz ran to him, grabbed the launcher and ripped a three inch long illuminating shell from the kit that the NCO held.

Aziz loaded and fired the phosphorus round skyward as fast as he could. As the brilliant glare of five thousand candlepower lit up the night, Aziz slammed the flare pistol back into the sergeant's palm. The impact jerked the man back to duty.

"I . . . I'm sorry, sir," he stammered.

Aziz looked into the kit and saw four shells.

"Are there more in the lorry?" he demanded.

"Yes, sir."

"Get them and use them. If you stop you're dead. We're *all* dead."

The noise was almost deafening now. The screaming mob was at the mouth of the valley. Captain Aziz felt a rush of pity for them . . . and suppressed it. He had to. The time for killing was at hand.

He glanced left . . . then right.

The mortar and machine gun crews were watching him tensely. So were the riflemen spread out among the rocks. Aziz drew his pistol, chose one of the blue targets and took a deep breath. He squeezed the trigger and he didn't miss. The enemy—still nameless—crumpled.

The rest of the soldiers began shooting. Mortar shells arched through the air, and automatic weapons scythed down the terrified civilians with short bursts of intersecting fire. Ravaged by machine gun bullets, scores of the blue people fell. The riflemen killed or wounded dozens of others.

But the awful legion kept coming. Shrapnel and searing white phosphorus exploding from mortar shells, rocket-propelled grenades and a hurricane of bullets ripped their ragged ranks—and they still advanced. They surged forward like some inexorable toxic wave.

And they never stopped screaming.

They were less than fifty yards from the soldiers now, moving ahead into the deadly barrage because what was behind them was even more frightening. The platoon leaders shouted and gestured, and the flamethrower teams emerged from behind the boulders. No living creature could stand up to fire, Aziz told himself as the soldiers with the strange looking weapons adjusted the twin tanks strapped to their backs.

Each pair held fifteen liters of a petroleum and aluminum mixture that burned to the bone.

Devastating heat that ate flesh . . . over one thousand degrees.

Would it stop them?

Hundreds of bodies littered the mouth of the valley. Stepping over their dead and wounded . . . staggering and stumbling . . . falling and crawling, the blue people were forty yards from the soldiers. Aziz and his men fired as fast as they could. So did Colonel Kebeer whose face showed no emotion as he emptied another clip and reloaded.

The enemy was still screaming and still advancing.

Now the gap was thirty yards.

It was barely twenty when jets of fire erupted with a roar from the flamethrowers.

Two-second bursts. Each weapon had enough fuel to hurl fire for thirty seconds. With a pair of flamethrowers the total was a minute. This would be a sixty-second war, Aziz thought grimly. If the soldiers prevailed, the blue people would be exterminated. If the troops failed, thousands of Madesh's fourteen million men, women and children might die.

Maybe all of them.

More spouts of yellow fire tore at the surging enemy. A score of the blue people were ablaze. It wasn't only their clothes that the flames were ravaging. Their flesh was being consumed too. Beating at the pain with ruined hands, they shook and howled and reeled wildly before they fell rolling to the ground.

The others behind them showed no interest in the human torches. Lurching between the burning bodies, they moved ahead steadily. Bullets and grenades cut down dozens but more came forward through the predawn fog. The flamethrowers roared again and again.

Then they fell silent. Their lethal fuel was exhausted.

And the nightmare enemy was still advancing.

The firemaking teams dropped their heavy weapons and ran. Panting frightened infantrymen and machine gunners flinched . . . hesitated . . . and stood their ground. They were firing at point blank range now—ten yards.

The blue people would break through in a few seconds.

They didn't. Instead they moved more slowly and stopped. They looked left and then right, staring blankly as if they could no longer see.

That was it, Aziz realized. Between the bright glare of the massed nearby truck headlights and whatever the blue thing was doing to them they were practically blind. Nobody killed blind people, the young captain thought . . . and knew he must.

The soldiers kept shooting. A few of the sightless foe made desperate rushes into the blackness. One staggered to within five feet of Aziz before the company commander's pistol ended the man's life. Aside from one glazed eye, the corpse was entirely covered with the bright blue thing. Whatever it was, the blue thing looked as if it were alive.

Aziz had to turn away. He continued firing at the enemy. So did the other soldiers until none of the blue people were left standing. Hundreds of them lay dead, and many bleeding wounded sat or sprawled on the ground. The smell of burned petroleum and flesh hung heavy in the air.

It was clear that the enemy was helpless. The shooting slowed and finally halted. With the guns silent at last, the only sounds were the cries of the crippled and dying.

Aziz walked forward to assess the battlefield situation as a company commander should. After a few seconds the last flare sank from the March sky, leaving the headlights as the sole illumination. That was enough for several curious riflemen who came out from behind boulders to examine the extraordinary foe. Fingering the triggers of their weapons, the soldiers advanced warily.

"Stay back! Stay back!" Aziz yelled urgently. "Keep away from them!"

The riflemen stopped. Then Ahmed Aziz saw the colonel gesture, and the sweat drenched young captain hurried over to join him beside the radio jeep.

"Finish it," the counterintelligence officer said.

"Colonel," Aziz began.

"Kill them *now*," Kebeer broke in harshly and pointed at the fuel truck. "Soak the bodies and the ground. Torch everything with phosphorus grenades. I want nothing left but ashes . . . not a blade of grass . . . not a bone . . . not a tooth."

At that moment a new chorus of pain surged from the pass.

There were others alive inside the valley.

It wasn't over yet.

"Come on," the colonel said and Aziz followed him to a gap between the boulders that were the front line. Kebeer walked past the defensive perimeter to halt a few steps beyond the rocks. Another wave of the awful enemy could come out of the fog at any time, the young captain thought grimly.

"How many more are in there, sir?" he asked.

"I don't know."

Aziz turned to face Kebeer and the headlights.

"But you do know what the blue thing is," Aziz said.

"That's none of your business."

Then Kebeer saw it. It was only the size of a thumbnail but he didn't have any choice. There was no point in discussing this, he realized and drew his pistol.

He shot Ahmed Aziz between the eyes. Aziz tottered back and fell, a corpse before he hit the ground. Kebeer wasn't aware that the bright blue spot had been blasted onto the junior officer's shirt by Aziz's own bullet—the one that dropped the desperately charging man at Aziz's feet. Kebeer wouldn't have cared. He had said "all of them" and he meant it.

Stunned by the execution of their company commander, the

infantrymen eyed his body and wondered why he'd been killed. Two platoon leaders walked slowly to the colonel, trying to word their questions as they approached him. Kebeer spoke first.

"Captain Aziz did nothing wrong," he said. "We came here to destroy the blue *matter* and anything it contaminated. The captain was somehow contaminated, so he had to be destroyed. Anyone who discloses how the captain died or what happened here tonight will also be destroyed—by firing squad. Is that clear?"

The lieutenants nodded.

"Forget the blue *matter*," Kebeer ordered. "You never saw it and you never shot at any civilians. Neither did your men. This was a realistic night combat exercise that called for firing live ammo—just training."

"Yes, sir," the intimidated junior officers agreed.

Then the colonel told them to massacre the wounded and burn up all the bodies and ground cover with the JP-4 jet fuel. The soldiers worked quickly. The last of the helpless civilians were dead within a few minutes, and the hosing was completed less than half an hour later. Keeping their distance from the blue corpses and using launchers to hurl in nine WP grenades, the infantry turned the whole area in front of the pass into a carpet of fire.

The sight . . . the smell . . . and sound of the corpses burning made Kebeer think of the seven terrible hells described in the Holy Koran. They were all fiery horrors like this, he reflected before he raised his gaze to the rocky cliffs that framed the pass.

Desperate cries were still echoing from the valley but the colonel hardly noticed them. His focus was on explosives—not human beings. Kebeer calculated carefully. Yes, there were enough demolition charges in the trucks to seal the only way out of the Torat Valley. Whether there were one hundred people within or one thousand, they would all be locked inside forever.

With the blue death.

They couldn't hide from it. It would find and kill every one of them before the sun went down again.

There was another crucial question to be answered. The tall counterintelligence officer raised his night binoculars and started to scan the nearby ridges and crests. He turned in a full circle very slowly. Kebeer checked and rechecked each hill and mountain for any sign of life. Then he studied them all meticulously again.

Nobody. Nothing. Zero.

It wasn't surprising for almost no one lived in these remote and arid hills. Now Colonel Kebeer let himself sigh in relief. It was going to be all right, he told himself, for no outsider had seen what happened.

He was wrong.

2

He swam steadily through the warm Caribbean water, a tanned muscular man moving forward almost effortlessly in the calm sea. With another fifty or sixty strokes he would complete the three miles. He did this several times a week but not on a regular schedule. Each week he swam on different days, and every day at another time.

Now he propelled himself through the water more rapidly, accelerating like a racer sprinting towards the finish line. After each ten or eleven strokes his head turned shoreward so he could scan the beach and the dark green hills beyond it. The bright mid-morning sun didn't trouble his wide grey eyes, for they were as strong as his powerful arms and legs.

When the hard-bodied swimmer finished the three miles, he made his way from the water to the wide strip of white sand. Once again he studied the adjacent slopes covered with tropical trees and vegetation. After a dozen seconds of this careful survey, he nodded.

He liked the small and unimportant French island. No hordes of tourists came here, and hardly any reached this part of the southern coast. The local farmers, fishermen, shopkeepers, mechanics and paunchy civil servants had paid little attention to him since he arrived more than a year earlier. Though ninety-five percent of the population—black and white—had never left the Caribbean, they were French to the core and had no interest in those unfortunate enough to be foreigners.

This indifference suited the man on the beach well.

It made the waiting a little easier.

He moved swiftly across the hot sand to pick up the Air Canada shoulderbag, take out the sunglasses and don them. His eyes searched the hills another time before he began the walk to the house a quarter of a mile away.

Half way up a slope, it was a simple and comfortable three room bungalow on a back road. Some fifteen yards from the clearing, he stopped to peer through the trees at the small house and the Peugeot 205 in the shade beside it. It wasn't easy to discern the car, for it was the same shade of dark green as the nearby vegetation. That was no coincidence.

He looked and he listened intently. Then he slowly circled the bungalow to approach the rear door. With his right hand in the open airline bag, he listened once more and entered the building.

After a shower, he put on Chino slacks and his wristwatch. The stainless steel Omega showed five minutes after eleven. No problem . . . there was still thirteen minutes.

Now he walked to the kitchen, enjoying the cool tile floor beneath his bare feet. Thirsty from more than two hours in the sun, he chose a Sabatier knife from the rack, bisected and squeezed enough oranges to fill a tumbler with juice. He turned on the shortwave radio and sat down in a big bamboo-frame chair, sipping the sweet liquid as the measured tones of a BBC "news reader" in London filled the room.

Utterly uninterested in the latest half-truths that the righteous prime minister had told the House of Commons, he twisted the dial until pulsing Afro-Cuban music from a Havana station materialized. Then he began to plan for tomorrow. He'd drive into town after lunch . . . buy shaving cream at the *pharmacie* . . . stop at the post office to mail the bungalow rent check . . . purchase fresh local vegetables and a fish caught that morning.

He glanced at the watch again.

Six minutes.

After returning from town, he'd put the perishables in the refrigerator and go to the beach. It would be a different beach, not where he'd been today. He wouldn't swim tomorrow. Instead he'd run as he did once or twice a week.

Most weeks.

Some weeks he didn't run at all.

Four minutes.

He adjusted the radio dial again. A gospel song poured in loud and clear from a powerful transmitter on an island to the south. The vocal group sang in English with audible piety and vigor. The station was owned and operated by an evangelical organization deeply devoted to the Lord's Work.

He listened to it every day between 11:18 and 11:40 in the morning. This had nothing to do with religious commitment. He was thirty-six years old and—aside from weddings and funerals —hadn't been in a church for almost two decades.

He was an agnostic, and he didn't expect to be saved.

3

A little less than thirty-one hours later.

A little more than twenty-four hundred miles northwest of the green French island.

"*Jeezus,*" Bonomi said softly. Then he rechecked the input settings and twin video monitors for the fifth time, and shook his head.

Bonomi, a graying wide-shouldered man who took his unusual work very seriously and did it well, was standing in a large room on the second floor of a building with no windows. Located eight blocks from the domed United States Capitol in mid-Washington, it was originally a warehouse twenty-nine years and 188 million dollars ago. *They* had spared no expense in creating and equipping this special facility.

Official designation: Federal Building 213.

The dull beige structure was ringed by a chain-link cyclone fence crowned with a double row of barbed wire. There were guards with guns at both gates . . . additional armed men at posts inside . . . electronic locks and torch-proof safes . . . a full range of the most sophisticated alarms and other state of the art defenses.

Security classification: Wild Dog.

Those protecting this operation were authorized to kill intruders.

A blue and white sign outside identified the ex-warehouse as the National Photographic Interpretation Center. Inside this building it was always cool. No one had ever told the guards why, and they hadn't asked. Questions were not encouraged here. This was a need to know operation. Security was so tight in

Building 213 that there were areas the guards couldn't even enter.

The Center's huge air conditioner worked around the clock—365 days a year—because of the need to cool the powerful computers and coupled equipment. Bonomi stood at the console of a computer that was linked to the two video screens. The monitor on the left was connected to a central data bank which held many hundreds of millions of pictures taken during the preceding three decades. The screen on the right was displaying newer images—photos of the same target areas made within the past three days.

This operation produced for the Department of Defense vital Techint—technical intelligence. Comparing the two sets of images on side-by-side monitors would show any recent changes in the target areas. New airfields, roads or missile bases, movements of ships or armored units and other differences could be detected by cross-checking the images that the satellites radioed down every twenty-four hours.

This was an excellent Center with a very good system—a time-tested one that always worked.

Almost always, J. G. Bonomi thought grimly.

It wasn't producing results today.

These pictures couldn't be compared, for they were images of two different places.

Something or someone had malfunctioned.

There would be trouble upstairs. Upstairs was the National Reconnaissance Office created secretly in 1961 at the peak of the Cold War. The huge and basically invisible NRO was totally covert from birth. For years nobody referred to it by name. All NRO programs were still completely *black,* so secret that their multibillion dollar costs were hidden in the annual budgets of other federal agencies. Perhaps one in a thousand U.S. taxpayers even knew it existed.

The NRO ran America's spy satellites.

These disturbing pictures had come from one of them.

Completing his nineteenth year of meticulous work in the former warehouse, J.G. Bonomi was a senior photo intelligence expert. He was also a realistic civil servant about to receive a well deserved promotion. That and his professional reputation, which he prized intensely, were now in danger.

Somebody would be blamed for this mess.

There was just one way to make sure it wasn't J. G. Bonomi. It was clear that the new pictures had been taken of the *wrong* place, he reasoned. What he saw on the right monitor bore no resemblance to the military air base on the left screen, and those *things* obviously were not jet fighter-bombers.

Where was it? What were they?

If he answered those questions, he would be all right. He might even get another commendation placed in his personnel file. Now Bonomi glanced at his wristwatch. The analysis of these fresh photos was due at the Pentagon at 0800 the next morning.

He had to work fast.

4

10:50 A.M. the following day.

A churning ocean east of Washington.

The streets of the old city were still wet from predawn rain, and many of the canals were half shrouded by chill mist in from the North Sea. The temperature was forty-one degrees Fahrenheit, about usual for Amsterdam in March.

Six blocks from the central railroad station, a buxom twenty-five-year-old woman was doing what she usually did. She sat waiting in a room on the ground floor of a weathered stone building on Spuistraat—Sluice Street. Comfortable in a well-upholstered armchair, she calmly scanned the pedestrians outside. Most strode past without a glance, but some of the men walking by looked at her through the big window that framed her like a picture.

She wanted them to look at her.

She wanted them to want her.

That was why she kept the filmy robe open to exhibit her full figure overflowing the black minibrassiere and bikini bottom. This was her professional uniform. Prostitution had long been legal in the Netherlands, and she was using a time-tested method of attracting customers.

A tinted bulb in the wall lamp behind her cast a wide red glow. Clearly visible from the street, the crimson beacon identified this building as a place where sex was for sale. Other local brothels also displayed a red light, historic logo of the industry. Practical and direct like the Dutch themselves, these electric invitations pierced all language barriers in a city with many foreign visitors.

The woman in the window didn't care what tongue the men spoke. There wasn't that much conversation anyway, and clients such as the dapper Japanese who came by each Friday afternoon at precisely 5:15 "talked" in gestures and nods. It was basic communication but it worked.

She had no major problems so long as she respected the rules. There were three sets of them, all important. The police didn't want window girls to touch themselves "provocatively," and they must not wave in solicitation or lick their lips "lewdly." Jaap, the owner of the business, was equally adamant about not stealing from customers or changing the way he'd arranged the furniture. Her own rules excluded men hurting her or smoking in her room, and she insisted on condoms.

Closed only on Christmas Day, the house operated around the clock. After several weeks on the 8 A.M. to 4 P.M. shift, she was looking forward to next month's change to more profitable hours. This was another slow winter morning, she thought as she gazed out at Spuistraat. When a trio of well-dressed males in corporate attire sauntered by without a glance at her, she realized that she might not get another customer until her "regular" arrived at noon.

Then she saw the black man approaching. Wide shouldered and tall, he moved with the air of someone who knew exactly what he was doing. He had money or power, she guessed. Maybe both. The fur-collared overcoat was no poor man's garment, and she had no doubt that the cigar between his lips was a five-dollar Cuban product—hand rolled.

He slowed as he neared the window, and she smiled.

The police didn't mind smiling.

She shifted in her chair, leaning forward just a bit to expose more cleavage. He didn't respond. He couldn't. He wasn't looking at her. He was eyeing the furniture in the room.

That didn't mean he wasn't interested, she reasoned. He might be one of the many cautious men who began warily—avoiding eye contact with the woman they desired. Even some males who weren't shy or uneasy with attractive females did that. So did the men who didn't want to face the fact they were aroused by a whore.

He'd look at her in a few seconds.

Then he'd walk to the door and ring the bell.

He did neither. He turned to leave. As he did, she studied his face and wondered whether he was new to Amsterdam. He had to be. Though she didn't pay much attention to clients' faces, she was sure that she would recall a man as handsome as this one. He was probably an American banker who had just arrived.

She would have been very surprised if he told her that his expertise was in machine guns and missiles—not money—and that none of the three passports he possessed identified him as a citizen of the United States. She would have been astonished if he told her that he had walked past this window almost every day for the past nineteen and a half months.

He wouldn't tell anyone that.

He was a very private person who was excellent at keeping secrets.

That's why he was still alive.

5

The night air was thick with humidity, and a wall of steamy heat jarred her as she stepped from the air-conditioned taxi onto Suriwong Road in front of the ten-storey hotel.

It was—depending on your point of view—6:34 P.M. local time in the bustling capital of Thailand or about two hours after the well-dressed black soldier gazed into the window on Spuistraat. Whatever your point of view, the temperature here was eighty-one degrees Fahrenheit and unlikely to descend significantly for months.

Returning to Bangkok now had probably been an error, the slim young woman in the perfectly fitted silk suit thought as she eyed the hotel's large glass door. Hong Kong would be twenty degrees cooler, she reminded herself and turned her head to scan the street.

Not for anything in particular.

For *everything*. This was one of her habits like drinking fresh orange juice for breakfast, reading the *International Herald Tribune* daily and paying for things in cash. No paper trail of checks or credit card slips told where she'd been or when. She wanted it that way.

After carefully surveying Suriwong Road in both directions, she entered the hotel and shivered. The big air-conditioned lobby was even colder than the interior of the cab had been. Tuning out the conversational hum of tourists, transient business executives and hotel staff, she looked around for *everything* again before she walked towards the newsstand fifty feet away.

As she approached it, the moon-faced clerk behind the

counter put down the new issue of *Vogue* he was studying and blinked in approval. Taller and shapelier than most other oriental women, she moved gracefully on legs as sleek as those of any model in the foreign fashion magazines he revered.

Without the horn-rimmed glasses she'd be almost as pretty as some of those models, he judged. While his own taste ran to thirteen-year-old girls—and boys—he could appreciate this woman who was at least twice that age. Though she wore little makeup and no jewelry, she had an air of subtly stylish self-assurance. It wasn't just the fine suit and absolutely right handbag. There was something about the woman herself.

When she reached the newsstand she picked up a copy of the Hong Kong edition of the *Herald Tribune*. He wasn't surprised. Her features were classic Chinese—and something else. She probably knew two or even three languages, the clerk speculated, and her speech would be coolly cultured in all of them.

The woman, who was fluent in Thai, French, Indonesian, both Mandarin and Cantonese, English and the tongues of the Meo and Kachin tribes of the Golden Triangle, did not say a word. She extracted a ten-*baht* piece from her purse, put the coin on the counter in payment for the paper and walked away.

In fifteen minutes she would be reading the "help wanted" listings on the back pages. Somebody might be advertising for an art director who spoke French and Mandarin to work on a new quarterly magazine in Geneva. If not today, then tomorrow or next month. It was just a matter of time, and she had plenty of that.

Though she didn't look it, she had been dead for more than two years.

General Hassan wasn't dead, but he was close to death.

He didn't know it.

Some 247 miles south of Sicily, Hassan stood on a sandy rise overlooking the Mediterranean with three of his senior officers.

They were his most trusted men. Of course General Hassan, who had named himself Supreme Leader for Life an hour after car-bombing Fozira's previous president into cat food, didn't *really* trust anyone.

That was why he went everywhere with an elite unit of eighty heavily armed bodyguards. *Elite* meant that he paid them much more than regular soldiers got, and that they knew their entire families would be dismembered—slowly—if a bodyguard be-trayed him.

Hassan, a charismatic orator and righteous butcher who made Attila the Hun look like Mother Teresa, had come to this coastal defense post for two reasons. The first was to check on the garri-son's readiness. The second was to discuss covert operations with his key commanders. Since his many enemies were undoubtedly trying to bug both his office and army headquarters, it was much safer to talk out here.

"You'll have another twenty million dollars immediately," Hassan said when the Chief of Military Intelligence completed his report. "If you need more, ask. This attack will make history, and it has to go off perfectly."

Due west . . . one hundred thirty yards.

Just over the crest of a low dune the prone man grasping the SVD rifle adjusted its telescopic sight. Drenched with sweat after hours under the camouflage cloth that concealed him, he sighed in expectation. He finally had a good clean shot. The self-awarded medals that the Supreme Leader for Life wore made Hassan's chest an excellent target.

They were right over his heart.

Perfect.

Then the marksman frowned. The son of a bitch might be wearing a bulletproof vest. No, it would have to be a head shot. That was more difficult but much more certain to kill.

Not one bullet . . . *two* of the soft-nosed nine-millimeter rounds. Nobody could survive two in the head. They'd blow away half his skull, and in the confusion the shooter would escape on the high-speed motorcycle hidden under another cloth fifty steps behind him.

Pleased by the thought, the sniper squinted into the four-power PSO-1 scope and raised the gun muzzle until Hassan's face was centered exactly in the sight. Now the rifleman's finger began to tighten inexorably on the trigger.

He leaned forward . . . about three inches.

That was a mistake.

The SVD's muzzle glinted in the afternoon sun, and one of the bodyguards saw the gleam of metal. Shouting a warning, the alert corporal ran forward between Hassan and the threat. The pragmatic Supreme Leader for Life dropped to the sand, and the soft-nosed round meant for him tore open the corporal's throat. Blood spouted from the terrible wound as he crumpled to his knees and began to die.

The hidden marksman grunted, squinted intently through the scope to pinpoint his target again and prepared to fire two more rounds. He·didn't get the chance. Half a dozen bodyguards were scourging the top of the dune with automatic weapons. None of these troopers was as fine a shot as the man who'd come to slay Hassan—but they were good enough. Collectively they were too good, and in seconds the sniper was a devastated corpse.

More guards began firing frantically. They raked the crest for a hundred yards on either side of the body until their guns were out of ammunition. Then they slammed in fresh clips to blast the top of the dune again in case other assassins were lurking up there.

Now the "alert" armored car that always accompanied Hassan rolled forward to shield the Supreme Leader with its steel-plated bulk, and shouting lieutenants led a score of the bodyguards in a ragged charge across the hot sand. Panting in the afternoon sun as they ran, they stumbled and cursed and sprayed short bursts while they bulled their way to the crest.

They stopped. With their hearts pounding and their throats dry, they looked around urgently for someone to kill. After twenty seconds, they turned and gestured to the senior officers below.

There was no foe in sight.

A colonel waved to them to continue the search. As they fanned out to examine the other side of the dune, General Tewfik Hassan got to his feet. He didn't speak. Brushing sand from his uniform, Fozira's absolute ruler studied the nearby ridge for several moments. Then he turned to eye the bodyguards.

They watched him tensely. Would he be grateful that they'd saved his life or in one of his murderous rages because the assassin nearly succeeded? None of them dared move or utter a word. After the deafening blasts of so many rapid-fire guns the total silence . . . the sound of fear . . . seemed eery.

"I want some answers—right now," Hassan finally said.

Nine minutes later the beefy post commander apologized for the delay . . . mopped his brow . . . and reported what the soldiers found.

"Just one man. He's dead. Regular army uniform and the ID of a sergeant in the Third Infantry. It could be false."

"*Of course* it's false," Hassan erupted impatiently.

"Had a Dragunov SVD sniper rifle. Standard Red Army weapon. The Russians sold us lots of them eight or ten years ago."

"*Seven*," Hassan corrected automatically. "A dozen other countries got them too. Allowing for thieves and deserters . . . the normal human corruption . . . half the commando units and secret services on earth probably have some now."

"Including the Israelis, general?" the edgy colonel asked.

Hassan shrugged.

"You think the Zionist infidels sent this man, general?"

It had been a long day, Hassan thought. The last thing he needed was some religious simpleton ranting about the fucking infidels. The Supreme Leader, who rarely prayed if there wasn't a television news crew or a crowd of the devout nearby, controlled his temper and shook his head.

"The Israelis would send a whole hit team," he replied. "Don't worry, colonel. The traitor will tell us who's behind this."

"What traitor?"

"The one who got the sniper onto this base."

Then Hassan waved to a hard faced officer who immediately ran over and saluted.

"This is a matter for specialists," Hassan declared. "Major Khadif here handles counterespionage for my escort unit. I think that he should confer with your security officer."

"Captain Blida, a very competent man," the colonel said.

"Fine. Major, why don't you have *a good talk* with Captain Blida?" the Supreme Leader suggested.

His tone was casual. The look in his eyes wasn't.

The major had seen it before and understood. He saluted and left to find the security officer. Without another word to the base commander, Hassan nodded to his three senior aides and led them twenty steps into the shade cast by a camouflage-painted concrete bunker.

"As I was saying before," he began, "this operation is to proceed at top speed. If we execute it properly, it should be a total surprise and they won't even know that we did it."

They were discussing the new timetable for the assault when they heard the sounds. The *good talk* with the security officer seemed to be going quite well. Captain Blida wasn't saying much yet but he would soon.

For the moment he was concentrating on screaming.

6

He went on screaming for a long time.

Some forty-seven hours after he began, a coded message on the attempt to kill Hassan reached Central Intelligence Agency headquarters in Virginia. That was an hour and a half before Working Group Six assembled in a secure conference room in the Pentagon.

It was a Monday morning, and Six met there every Monday morning. As usual, generals and admirals and high level civilian officials from several major US intelligence organizations ringed the big table to coordinate projects and policies.

There was nothing extraordinary about the agenda either. The Ajax operation in Nicaragua . . . Emily's report on covert Chinese arms shipments . . . improved distribution of information from the Caesar network . . . stopping this month's military conspiracy to seize power in Manila . . . debriefing the Cuban admiral . . . next week's gathering of mad-dog terrorists in Damascus . . . the Blue Fox timetable . . . it was all standard fare.

At five minutes to eleven the interagency meeting ended. Sounds of metal attache cases being closed filled the room like a fugue, and then everyone started for the door. Dapper Edward Reed, whose cunning and silk bow ties were much admired by CIA colleagues, was a few steps from the portal when Brigadier General P. J. Sherman of Military Intelligence nodded to him. Reed stopped.

"By the way," Sherman began in a casual tone and Reed immediately knew that whatever it was it was important. Sherman had one of the best minds in G-2 but hardly any gift at all for dissembling or other routine conference procedures.

"Our embassy in Madesh picked up an odd rumor about three weeks ago," the general continued in the matter of fact tone as he took a briar pipe and soft leather pouch from a pocket of his uniform jacket.

Madesh? No strategic importance, Reed computed.

No large airbases. No oil. No uranium.

The main products were dysentery and illiteracy, and its armed forces were third rate even by the standards of the region.

While Reed calculated ruthlessly, the lanky soldier facing him opened the pouch . . . grasped a clump of fragrant tobacco . . . and began to fill the pipe bowl.

"You got any folks there, Ed?" Sherman asked a moment before he struck a wooden match and lit the tobacco.

Folks? The CIA executive managed not to wince.

"In Madesh?" he fenced.

"Right. Torat Valley—near the western border."

"I'm not sure," Reed evaded automatically. Answering any question directly was alien to him.

"Might be worthwhile to check out that valley," the one star general suggested and puffed on the pipe.

"Terrorist training camp—if the rumor's correct," he added.

Terrorist training camp? Not bad, Reed judged, but not that good. The soldier had emphasized *rumor* just a bit too much in an effort to minimize the entire matter.

That meant something big.

"The valley and the area around it," Sherman continued. "I think there's an army base thirty-five miles south—near Jammur. Troops there might have heard something."

Then the general paused to suck on the pipe again. He wasn't going to mention those pictures taken when the satellite's timer malfunctioned and the camera started ninety-one seconds too soon. He wasn't about to share what the spectrographic analysis and Cobra scan at Fort Detrick had revealed.

And he certainly wouldn't tell the CIA man that dozens of

Military Intelligence investigators across the country were already working covertly on this—around the clock.

Not one of them knew what was really involved.

Why should the goddamn CIA?

Since he couldn't speak out honestly, the G-2 general did what any sensible senior officer or civil servant would do in such a situation. He nodded and blew smoke.

As Sherman did that, Reed was computing at top speed. The request to check out the valley should have come in writing . . . through proper channels. That was normal interagency procedure. Or Sherman could have raised it at the meeting just ended. That too was acceptable bureaucratic conduct.

P. J. Sherman was a disciplined, West-Point-trained, professional soldier who'd lived by the rules for almost three decades. Why wasn't he doing that now?

Instead he was lying to hide something . . . something big.

What?

Deciding that he would find out, the CIA executive coolly offered an imitation of a warm smile. If the general was a near-infant in deception, Edward Derry Reed was not. His fake smile was excellent. Now he glanced at his wristwatch . . . shook his head.

"Meetings," he pretended to grumble. "Another one at Langley in forty minutes. I'll look into that for you, Paul," he promised. "Torat Valley, right?"

Sherman nodded.

"Never heard of it before," Reed said truthfully and hurried off to his car.

The hard-bodied man listening to the radio in the bungalow on Guadeloupe had never heard of it either. Outside the Republic of Madesh, almost no one but geographers and crossword puzzle addicts knew that the valley existed. Indifferent to word games, the agnostic who listened to gospel music every morning could find Madesh on a map but had no significant interest in that country.

Since his wife died over a year earlier, very little had interested him. He had concentrated on what he needed to do. He ate healthily, exercised systematically and maintained a high level of caution and alertness to thwart assassins.

He was no paranoid. The danger was real. There were violent people who might want vengeance for things done in the past, and there were probably equally brutal groups or governmental agencies who might try to destroy him so he couldn't do other things in the future.

He didn't know what those things might be. The men who put eight thousand dollars into his Swiss bank account every month hadn't said. It was entirely possible that they didn't know yet themselves. They had given him no hint when the payments began some two years ago.

Whatever they would ask him to do, it would surely be very difficult and his life would be at risk. He wasn't one of those macho neurotics who relished the possibility of dying—but he no longer feared it. Since her funeral he'd been beyond that.

His world was smaller and simpler now. It was basically down to patience and honor. Sooner or later his waiting would end—abruptly. Tomorrow or next week or perhaps next year, they would start the operation.

Exactly when or what or where wasn't that important. Those things weren't worth speculating about, he thought as the gospel choir sang on, for he had made an agreement and they had lived up to their part of it.

That was why everything was simple.

He had given his word, and he would keep it.

7

4:20 that afternoon.

Room 3C116 in The Pentagon.

Major Sara Velez, a Houston dentist's daughter with the fifth highest I.Q. ever tested at the U.S. Military Academy, stood in the doorway. It was her efficient logic and practical wisdom, not her dark and substantial good looks, that had caused Brigadier General P. J. Sherman to make her his personal aide.

Seated behind the big wooden desk that came with his rank, he pointed at the folder in her right hand.

"You got anything?" he asked bluntly.

"Maybe, sir," she answered before she entered and closed the door.

Too impatient for small talk, the general simply nodded towards the armchair in front of his desk. She sat down, crossed her trim legs carefully and opened the folder.

"Three of the forty-one people in the Rosebud group are dead," she began. "One's in a mental hospital—again, and another's doing five to seven for knifing his lawyer."

"That leaves thirty-six," Sherman reckoned as she glanced down at her notes.

"Yes, sir. We ran the thirty-six names through Army, Civil Service, FBI and Social Security. Checked motor vehicle bureaus in fifty states, D.C. and Puerto Rico. Hit the credit card companies and the IRS—hard. The IRS didn't like it."

"Screw the IRS!" Sherman erupted.

"We did," she said coolly. "Fed them a bullshit story about the thirty-six working on nuclear tests, and appealed for help in

41

finding these poor people who might have radiation sickness."

Suddenly his mind's eye filled with the blowups of the photos . . . all those corpses . . . every one that bizarre blue.

Day-glo dead, he thought and forced the awful images from his consciousness. Then he pointed at her folder.

"Of the thirty-six," she resumed, "seventeen were scientists and nineteen support staff. As of an hour ago, we've located and interviewed ten of the scientists and fifteen staff."

She saw him tense.

"Did they say anything that could help us?" Sherman asked.

"Zero, but we're not done, sir. There are still eleven of the thirty-six we haven't found. Our investigators are hunting for them now."

"Full court press?" he demanded. "Around the clock?"

"Bet on it, General."

As he frowned in concern, she considered telling him about the bloody shooting in Detroit. She decided that it could wait.

"Where's your *maybe?*" he challenged abruptly.

"It comes in three parts, sir. Each involves probabilities."

"Probabilities? That's all you've got?"

She evaded the frustration and confrontation in his question.

"Shall I continue, General?" she asked in a calm controlled voice.

He glared, shrugged and nodded.

"Eight of the missing eleven have some special things in common," she announced.

"How special?"

"You judge, sir. Of the twenty-five Rosebud personnel we found, two-thirds are married. But none of these missing eight are. That's the first improbable thing."

"I'm listening."

"All of these eight took out or renewed a passport about two years ago. Only four of the other twenty-five have ever gotten passports. Why the difference? Such a disparity just isn't probable," she said.

Sherman leaned forward now.

"Keep talking, Sara."

"When do people usually get or extend passports, sir?"

"When they're planning to travel abroad."

"Exactly," she agreed. "General, there is *no* record of any of these eight—repeat, *any*—leaving the country. I'd say that's improbable too."

She was right, he realized. Right and smart.

"What else would you say, Sara?"

"I'd say they could have gone to Canada or Mexico by road or water. We don't log the names of all the thousands of US citizens who cross every day by car or private pleasure boat. Our border controls are aimed at travelers heading in, not out."

"From Mexico or Canada they could fly anywhere," he reasoned.

"And there'd be no way to track them if they switched to other passports, sir."

The worried general shook his head.

To Sherman's surprise, his aide didn't seem the least bit troubled. There was an odd half-smile on Sara Velez's face . . . a gleam of naked anticipation in her eyes.

She was onto something.

"Let's have it," he said.

"How they left isn't that important," the dentist's logical daughter told him as she closed the folder. "What matters is that the disappearance of one fifth of the whole Rosebud group *can't* be a coincidence."

"Bottom line," he ordered.

"General, if it's no coincidence then somebody organized it. They were good—but nobody's perfect. Nobody bats a thousand, so there must be Rosebud people who were approached by the organizers and wouldn't play."

"We can send our agents back to talk some more with the twenty-five they already interviewed," he thought aloud.

"On the double," she agreed. "And not only those twenty-five, sir. The woman in the mental institution and the man in jail . . . and anyone connected with the missing eight. Former landlords and nosy neighbors . . . hostile ex-wives or husbands or lovers . . . the full spread of of relatives . . . friends, enemies and accountants who did their taxes . . . managers at the banks where they had accounts . . . dentists who might have forwarded their X-rays . . . the whole number."

"What if talking doesn't work?"

"It'll work if it's done right, sir. It doesn't have to be *nice* talk. Just about everyone has some vulnerability . . . some secret. We're good at secrets," she reminded.

"Threaten them?"

"With everything and anything. Loss of pensions . . . freezing their bank accounts . . . deportation of a friend or lover . . . public scandal . . . prison . . . you name it. It's hardball time, General."

"And there isn't much of it," he said grimly.

Then he considered her plan for several seconds and nodded.

"Do what you have to do, Sara."

"Yes, sir."

"And be damn careful to maintain the cover story," he added. "Let's keep the name of G-2 out of this."

Now she had to tell him about the two dead men.

"One more thing I should report, sir," she began. "We've run into a little problem in Detroit. I think it's under control."

"What the hell has Detroit got to do with this?"

She stood up, smoothed her skirt casually.

"General, one of our teams went to an apartment in Detroit where a Rosebud scientist had lived. It seems that he'd moved out, and some drug dealer was in there—making a sale," she said. "When our people knocked on the door, the men inside must have thought it was a bust."

"What happened?"

"They opened up with Uzis, firing through the door. I'm sorry, General. One of our agents was killed instantly. The other died in the ambulance. That's the bad news, sir."

He managed not to curse.

"Is there any *good* news?" Sherman asked bitterly.

"Sure. The Detroit cops bought the yarn that our men were tracking down a deserter."

"Is that what you'll tell the next of kin?" he challenged in a voice edged with anger.

"Why not? It worked once."

"And what about the bastards with the Uzis?" the general asked. "Got away clean, right?"

She nodded, hoping that he wouldn't comment again on street violence and the awful state of American society. That was for those professionally outraged people on the television talk shows —the well-fed furious. It wasn't for Military Intelligence.

She waited in silence until Sherman sighed. He didn't say anything about law and order or public morality this time. Instead he commended her "excellent analysis" in what seemed to be a sincere voice, and instructed her to keep him informed of any developments.

After she left, the general thought about dapper Edward Reed and wondered what the CIA was doing about the Torat Valley. It might have been a mistake to involve Reed. Everyone knew that he was devious . . . *very* devious.

There was one other thing to be done, Sherman realized. Deciding that this might be the time to do it, he reached for the scrambler phone.

8

At that moment . . . some nine miles northwest in the CIA global command center . . . Edward Reed was proceeding by the book.

As a veteran bureaucrat, he always did.

Well, almost always.

There had been a few exceptions during his twenty-six years with the Agency. The big one involved five corpses . . . each in the wrong grave . . . thousands of miles apart. Reed had gone by his own book in that operation. He'd never told anyone about it.

This afternoon Reed was following standard Agency procedures. While the Army general in the Pentagon spoke on the scrambler-protected phone, Reed was in the office of the appropriate CIA specialist briefing him on Sherman's "suggestion."

The specialist was Evan Blackshaw, the highly intelligent, largely bald and often bored forty-three-year-old man who headed the usually unexciting Madesh Desk. Reed correctly and carefully reported what Sherman had said, and noted that it seemed to be a transparent fabrication.

"Why else would G-2 be interested in the Torat Valley now?" Reed asked.

"The new sat photos," Blackshaw replied immediately.

Then Blackshaw told him about the pictures routed to him because the target was in his area—Madesh. Blackshaw had also followed normal CIA procedures.

"I ran the blow-ups past our own photo-analysts," he said. "Their report reached me half an hour ago. *Red Stripe.*"

A red stripe on an Agency folder meant that the contents required immediate attention.

"Something's happened in the Torat Valley," Blackshaw announced. "Corpses all over the place. Over 380 inside the valley and at least five hundred . . . all jammed together . . . just outside."

Body count: approximately nine hundred.

Reed said nothing. His face showed no emotion.

He didn't seem the least bit bothered by the slaughter, Blackshaw thought. He was right. Edward Reed wasn't bothered. He was interested.

"There were also troops right outside," Blackshaw continued. "Our analysts estimate a force of about two hundred men. Trucks but no armor or artillery . . . probably infantry. They were spread out in a semicircle very close to the mouth of the valley."

Reed finally spoke.

"What else?" he asked bluntly.

"All the corpses were *blue.*"

Reed considered this news for several seconds.

"Camouflage outfits?" he reasoned.

"The analysts don't think so," the head of the Madesh Desk answered. "They ran color comparisons with the camouflage clothes and battle dress of every army within a thousand miles, and there's no match. It's not like any plants or vegetation our agricultural section has ever seen in Asia or Africa or anywhere else."

"Local tribal dress?" Reed pressed.

"Nobody in the area wears that color. It's a very unusual blue."

A dozen more seconds of silence.

Reed followed bureaucratic protocol again.

"What do *you* think?" he asked correctly.

Blackshaw pursed his lips before he replied cautiously.

"I think that General Sherman's suggestion merits serious consideration," he said.

Reed nodded, thanked him and left.

He had a lot to do. He did it all.

Reports . . . explanations . . . approvals . . . a coded message.

On Thursday morning, a battered and dusty Toyota minivan moved at twenty-five miles an hour along a twisting mountain road in northwestern Madesh. The bearded man behind the wheel had a driver's license that identified him as a sewing machine dealer named Ali Salif.

His name wasn't really Ali Salif, and he did not make his living selling sewing machines. He was an "asset" of the CIA station chief in the capital of the Islamic Republic of Madesh. For a monthly stipend of $450 . . . nearly half a year's pay for many Madeshis . . . he handled odd jobs now and then.

He didn't realize how odd this one was.

The station chief hadn't told him, and certainly never mentioned that this could be extremely dangerous. On the usual "need to know" basis, it would be inappropriate to mention these things to the "asset."

Now the minivan driver slowed his drab vehicle to read the sign beside the road. Peering into the sun's late morning glare, he saw that Jammur was seventy kilometers away. He had no map. Merely owning one could arouse suspicions in these mountains. He'd studied a map, however, and he had a good memory. If he was seventy kilometers from Jammur, he'd soon find a turn-off . . . to the right.

It would take him to his objective.

That side road would be worse than this, he realized, but he'd been promised a three-hundred-dollar bonus for the mission so he didn't mind. He was smiling a few minutes later when he spotted the crudely lettered sign marked TORAT. In less than three hours he'd be in and out of the valley, on his way back to the capital.

And his bonus. He had plans for that money.

According to the map that the station chief had showed him,

the mouth of the valley was six kilometers from the two-lane "main" road he was leaving. He covered half that distance before he saw the roadblock.

An army truck . . . one of the Dodges supplied by the Americans . . . barred his way. There were soldiers on either side of the big truck, gesturing with their US-made M-16 rifles for him to stop. Everybody in Madesh knew that one did not argue with soldiers for they angered easily and shot quickly. He had no choice.

He shifted gears and halted the van.

"This road is closed," a sulky faced sergeant said to him.

The driver didn't ask why. Madeshi citizens didn't annoy their soldiers with such questions. When the sergeant pointed back to the "main" road, the man in the van obeyed at once.

He could still get his bonus. He had a Plan B.

He'd been told that if he couldn't make his way through the Valley he was to proceed to Jammur. It was a city of fifty-three thousand . . . according to the latest and probably inaccurate census . . . with a military base nearby.

The army camp housed a full infantry division plus support units. Some of these thousands of men . . . at least a number of officers who got decent wages far exceeding those of ordinary troopers . . . must come into Jammur from time to time, the American had reasoned.

And among those who did a few might know something about current conditions in the Torat Valley. After all, military patrols went everywhere and anywhere in the region.

The station chief hadn't talked about hundreds of bright blue corpses. No one ever informed him about them. Reed did consider it, but decided this might be unwise. Edward Reed never was much of a sharer. Even his kindergarten teacher had noticed that.

The message from CIA headquarters did indicate that the situation in the valley "might be delicate or even somewhat hazardous." That's why the station chief prepared Plan B. And C.

Unaware of any of this, the bearded "asset" drove the weary Toyota into Jammur and rented a room in a small hotel near the bazaar. In this pious and puritanical Islamic republic, there were no bars or dance halls or streets lined with assorted sex establishments where one might hear things from garrulous customers or employees. There was only one place in provincial Madeshi cities where local gossip flowed freely, and he went there as soon as he finished a mediocre lunch in the hotel's ten-table dining room.

He wandered into the web of winding streets and alleys of the bazaar . . . commercial center . . . social center . . . heart of Jammur. He was looking for business people who fit his "cover" story, textile dealers or owners of small garment factories or tailor shops . . . men who might need sewing machines.

Meticulously observing the traditional amenities, he spoke with those entrepreneurs and drank tea with them and then talked some more. He listened very carefully, avoiding any direct questions. As an obvious visitor he'd be rude to inquire about anything. Guests didn't do that in this society.

He moved slowly and warily in each conversation. In the beginning he didn't mention the Torat Valley at all. It wasn't until his third "casual" exchange that he referred to a nameless cousin who lived there. When he drew no response to the reference, he spoke on for several minutes before he moved on to another merchant in another shop.

And then another. Each time he seemed to be the pleasant traveling salesman who appreciated good tea . . . who enjoyed the spring day . . . who respected tradition and prayer . . . and who had, by the way, some good deals on sewing machines.

He didn't seek immediate sales. He wanted to extend and expand the talk, and it would be improper for a stranger to rush things anyway.

They didn't trust outsiders here.

That was the way in this city . . . this nation . . . the entire region.

Aware of this, he insulted the "immoral devils" across the border. Hostility towards neighboring countries was a safe currency, a down payment on showing he too despised one of Madesh's traditional enemies. When a shop keeper cursed "foreign dogs and unbelievers" and spit, the asset spit righteously too.

And when the call to prayer echoed from a mosque beside the bazaar, the visitor joined the devout in solemn and correct religious observance. Afterwards he again mentioned a cousin in the valley. Once more he drew no information.

The hours went by. Listening more than he spoke, he heard the merchants talk about the price of cloth . . . the funeral of a rug dealer last week . . . the shameful decision in the soccer match with Pakistan . . . rumors of new taxes . . . the tasty spring lamb in a nearby restaurant.

Shortly before 8 P.M., he elaborately thanked the man whose tea he was sipping and set out for that restaurant. The meal wasn't very good. He was on his way to the hotel fifty-five minutes later, walking slowly through the dark narrow streets and planning his tactics for the next day.

Plan B would work. He'd make it work.

When he got to the alley where he'd parked the minivan, he decided to move it around the corner to the safety of a better-lit street in front of the hotel. There were thieves who might steal the vehicle or the sewing machines in its rear compartment.

He'd been professional and careful in the bazaar.

It was essential that he continue that way, avoiding anything that might bring him to the attention of local police or military authorities.

He glanced in both directions before he walked to the back of the Toyota. It made sense to check the cargo compartment, so he took out the keys and unlocked the rear door. As he did so, he heard a footstep and turned.

There were four of them.

Big men with heavy shoes . . . two holding knives and the others pointing automatic pistols.

Were they thieves or something worse?

He never found out. He opened his mouth to speak, and one of the men grasping a long-bladed dagger plunged it into the asset's chest. Now he tottered . . . reached desperately into his pocket to give them his wallet. The man who'd stabbed him jerked the blade free and cut the asset's throat. He began to die.

Trying to avoid the blood pouring from the wounds, the four men picked up the body . . . dumped it in the cargo compartment . . . closed the rear door . . . got into the battered Toyota and drove away.

They were military, the watcher in the shadows thought grimly. He recognized the automatic pistols as standard issue guns carried by Army Intelligence. He didn't know exactly what mistake the fake sewing machine salesman had made, but he knew those weapons.

On orders from the CIA station chief in Madesh's capital, he'd been cautiously following the dead asset from the moment he set out for Jammur. He was the backup man assigned to report on security in the area if the asset didn't make it.

He was another asset.

Plan C.

9

Where the hell was she?

Sara Velez was supposed to be here an hour ago, Sherman thought as he turned to stare through his office window at Washington across the river.

It was quiet in the Pentagon this Sunday morning. Only a small fraction of the thousands of men and women who worked in the huge building were at their posts. With the Cold War and Soviet threat melted, there was no reason for more than five or six hundred people . . . communications teams, security units and the battle staff that was always on duty . . . to be here on this day of rest and prayer.

There'd be a lot more praying if they knew, the G-2 general told himself and rubbed his tired eyes. He'd slept less than four hours . . . badly. For nearly a week, he'd dreamt of bright blue corpses every night.

Where was she, dammit?

The pressure had built from the instant that the strange blue was identified. Sara Velez's idea might not work, Sherman thought for the hundredth time. He wasn't used to making war by probabilities. As a professional soldier and staff officer, he was accustomed to battle plans and contingency plans—all kinds of plans. There was no plan for *this*.

This wasn't supposed to happen.

Now he heard his office door open, and spun immediately.

"Let's hear it for mothers!" Major Sara Velez urged as she strode into the room.

"Mothers?"

"Six of the missing Rosebud people . . . including one Harold F. Rice . . . have living mothers," she reported "and they've all got bank accounts. That's where we finally hit paydirt."

"What paydirt?" Sherman demanded.

"Edith Sue Rice paydirt," she replied and sat down on the chair beside his desk. "She's Harold's mother . . . age seventy-nine . . . and cozy in a nursing home outside Tampa. Every month twenty-three hundred dollars slips into her account in the First Dixie Bank to cover her bills. The money comes from an ask-no-questions bank in the Bahamas . . . gets there by wire transfer from a third bank over in Luxembourg."

"Cute," the general judged bitterly.

"And professional. There's more, sir. The Luxembourg account's one of those anonymous numbered jobs. We had to do some arm-twisting to get a name."

"I don't care if you broke legs," he said. "Whose account is it?"

Now she smiled and crossed her legs.

"A certain Hugo Reutter of Frankfurt . . . H. R. . . . Harold Rice."

"Son of a bitch!"

"Probably," she agreed "but he loves his mom."

The weary general rubbed his hurting eyes again.

"Is this cute and loving son-of-a-bitch in Luxembourg?" he asked.

"We may find out when the next ten thousand dollars enters the account," she answered. "It's come in every thirty days for the past twenty-one months. Always in the last week of the month . . . always in cash."

"Dollars?"

"No, sir. German currency."

Sherman considered the possibilities for several seconds.

"Aside from what's sent to Rice's mother, where else does the money from the Reutter account go?" he tested.

"It doesn't *go,* general. It *grows.* No other checks are drawn.

With ten thousand in and just twenty-three hundred out each month, there's now over one hundred sixty thousand dollars in the account."

Sherman shook his head impatiently.

"Okay, where the hell is Rice?" he challenged.

"Hear me out, general. The next deposit's due in four days," she announced. "We'll watch the bank . . . spot the courier . . . follow him, or her. That courier could be Rice or lead us to him."

Sherman nodded.

It might work.

But would it work in time? Yesterday he'd received the second set of satellite photos of the Torat Valley, the new pictures he'd asked the National Reconnaissance Office to make as a "special job." Things were even worse in the Valley than the first scan indicated.

It wasn't only the people who were dead.

All the animals . . . every horse, cow, chicken, goat . . . even the dogs . . . were blue corpses too.

And there was the other threat.

He certainly hadn't wanted to bring anyone else into this, but the situation was urgent and the CIA had many more covert operators in the field. The problem was you couldn't trust them completely. They were arrogant . . . competitive . . . and devious.

They had their own complex and peculiar agendas. That was especially true of Reed, the G-2 general told himself bitterly. A bastard like Reed was capable of *anything*.

All this pinwheeled through Sherman's mind in a few seconds.

Then the telephone on his desk rang, and he answered it.

"Hello . . . Yes . . . Yes . . . What?" he asked. "Yes . . . Alright . . . We'll be here."

As he hung up Sara Velez saw the shock in his tired eyes.

"Reed," Sherman said. "He wants a meeting at four this afternoon. He's seen the new sat pictures too, but that's not all he wants to discuss."

"What else?"

"Mr. Reed intends to talk about *Rosebud*," the general reported grimly. "Rosebud. How the hell did he find out about Rosebud, Sara?"

"And who else knows?" she added.

The situation was deteriorating.

It could soon be out of control.

10

Monday . . . Tuesday . . . Wednesday . . . Thursday.
11:30 A.M. on Thursday.

Aside from the hours that he slept, Reed spent almost every minute working on his next move. Even though he'd been planning this for years, he went over every possibility and dozens of scenarios again and again.

Each variation . . . every permutation in strategy and tactics . . . all the chances for success or failure . . . revolved around three key realities. Reed considered and reconsidered them day and night . . . the corpses in the Torat Valley . . . the capable, very cautious and quietly ruthless deputy director of operations who ran CIA's covert activities . . . and the even tougher man who would lead the mission.

There was no room for error.

This entire project was clearly *one chance.*

Edward Reed would have *one chance* to sell it to the deputy director of operations who rarely took *any* chances.

A lot of people might classify Reed's plan as *no* chance at all.

And if Reed did get a "go," there was a strong possibility that those who went would not return. That didn't bother him, for if they succeeded he'd be recognized as a genius in the world of bold men and clandestine operations. He wouldn't be a desk-bound bureaucrat anymore. That mistake he'd made eighteen years . . . eleven months . . . and thirteen days ago would be forgiven. It might even be forgotten.

Seated with the attache case at his feet in the reception area of the deputy director's suite, Reed knew that most people would dismiss his plan as too dangerous . . . bizarre . . . irrational. If he didn't convince the deputy director now, that very senior executive would probably consider Reed at least half-mad too.

And a criminal.

He'd never been good at making friends, and he had no strong allies to protect him. He'd go to jail for years.

It was worth the risk, Reed thought as the telephone on the secretary's desk six yards away rang. The forty-two-year-old and rather plain-looking woman, whom the deputy director had chosen because she wouldn't arouse bureaucratic envy, picked up the instrument and listened.

"Yes, sir," she said. "Go right in, Mr. Reed."

As befitting a deputy director, Carter Carling had a spacious office with a nearly new couch, a coffee table, four good chairs with arms, a big wooden desk with three phones and a top-of-the-line executive computer. The room's windows were filled with the latest high-tech glass that blocked even the most sophisticated listening gear outside the building from eavesdropping.

The look was just right too. Framed photos of two dead and legendary US intelligence leaders . . . Major General "Wild Bill" Donovan and Allen Dulles . . . and the current director of Central Intelligence adorned the cream colored walls beside charcoal drawings of the Lincoln Memorial and the Washington Monument.

Everything in this office was politically correct in the CIA culture, and nothing said anything personal about Carter Carling. It was safer that way.

The two middle-aged men exchanged perfunctory smiles and polite nods as if they were business cards. A moment after Reed settled into one of those good armchairs, he pressed the switch hidden in the handle of his attaché case. He believed in safety too.

Carling was already thinking about his next meeting in thirty minutes. Now the thin-faced deputy director scanned the digital desk clock and nodded again. Edward Reed got the message.

"I'll come right to the point," he said. "Western Madesh. Everyone in the Torat Valley . . . about nine hundred people . . . and all the animals are dead. They were wiped out by a bacteriological weapon."

"What have you got?" Carling asked automatically.

"Two sets of Grade A sat pictures. There's no doubt about it. The whole valley's a slaughterhouse."

"On-site reconnaissance?"

"We tried," Reed told him. "Sent in a man with a backup. Backup saw local security kill him before he could enter the valley. Between the first and second sat flybys the only entrance was sealed by a ninety-foot-high plug of boulders."

"Could an expert climber or parachutist get in?"

"In? *Maybe*. Dead *for sure*. Dead and *blue*," Reed said. "The weapon is spores that are still alive. They come from a blue fungus that spreads at terrific speed. Moves fast . . . kills fast. Two hours max."

Carling tried to imagine it . . . decided he'd rather not.

"What is it?" he probed.

"According to one of our own specialists and General Sherman of G-2, it's something new and nasty . . . a radical mutation designated Barcelona Delta."

The deputy director shook his head.

"That's not all," Reed announced. He enjoyed having information others didn't. That was a key reason he'd chosen this odd career, the pure . . . or impure . . . power. It didn't matter which to Edward Reed.

"Studying the sat photos," he continued, "we've identified a housing area with a few shops plus six other buildings. One is a BL-4 lab. Biological safety level 4, heavy duty . . . very sophisticated . . . a high tech containment facility for dangerous bioresearch. No foreign power attacked the Torat Valley with Barcelona Delta. The Madeshis were making this themselves, and something went wrong."

"Why?" Carling wondered. "They're not about to fight anybody. Why would they make it?"

"And how?" Reed added. "Where did they get the scientists and the cash? This setup in the valley cost at least thirty million dollars, I'm told."

"It doesn't make sense," Carling said. "They're dirt poor."

Reed blinked in pleasure. He was about to expose secrets other people had worked hard to hide. Those were always the best secrets.

"It's not *their* money," he announced.

"Whose damn money is it?"

"That's exactly what I asked," Reed said. "Then I remembered. The money's always the answer. Thirty million is a lot of money. Anyone who cares that much is going to try again. That means more money to finance replacement of the special equipment and biological materials . . . stuff you don't buy at the corner store. We flash-alerted a shopping list to all our stations and the intelligence services of several friendly countries."

"Yes?" Carling pressed.

"Definitely *yes,"* Reed answered. "In the past sixty-one hours we've had multiple reports of purchases of items on the list."

"By whom? I want a name."

"I've got nine names for you . . . companies in Germany, Brazil, Japan, Canada, Sweden, Taiwan, France and the USA. All dummy companies. All funded covertly by the same source."

"That's the name I want, dammit."

Reed coughed and cleared his throat before he spoke.

"It's Pariah."

The deputy director stiffened in shock.

Pariah was the US intelligence agencies' codename for General Tewfik Hassan, the lethal lunatic who ruled Fozira. Ambitious and extremely violent, Hassan was far more aggressive and vicious than any other head of state on the planet.

A germ weapon in Hassan's hands?

"He'd use it," Carling predicted.

"In a minute."

"Twenty seconds," the deputy director corrected grimly. "Got anything more on this fungus? Treatment? Antidote?"

Reed shrugged.

"*Zero,*" he answered. "That's why we gave up on Barcelona Delta three and a half years ago."

"What are you saying?"

"Back in '75," Reed explained, "the US and USSR and other countries signed a treaty to end all germ war projects. That sounded fine, but we suspected that we couldn't really trust the Sovs to comply."

"We were *right,*" Carling erupted. "The bastards kept nine different disease projects going. All big . . . all secret . . . all in direct violation of the treaty. Didn't surprise me a bit."

"Didn't surprise our Army people either. Aware this might happen, they knew we needed an effective deterrent," Edward Reed said. "There's just one deterrent to germ attack."

"The threat of instant and massive retaliation with similar or worse germ weapons," Carling responded automatically.

"Exactly. That's why our Army didn't entirely stop work on new bacterial agents. Purely for *deterrent* purposes," Reed said, "a few innovative research programs were begun . . . very quietly. One of the quietest . . . they were all max security . . . operated under the name Rosebud."

"What about the blue fungus?"

"The Rosebud team did that research and development," Reed acknowledged. "When they couldn't control the bacterial agent, the project closed down. The staff scattered to a variety of jobs in government, private industry and the academic world. Nobody kept track of all of them."

Now Reed described the urgent and covert search for the Rosebud scientists after the Torat Valley massacre, and the discovery that several of the "missing" Rosebud germ experts were banking in the USA, Switzerland and Cayman Islands money from Madeshi sources.

"We think they're in Madesh," Reed said flatly. "At least three of the Rosebud people . . . maybe as many as six."

Carling shook his head.

"*Our* weapon developed by *our* scientists in violation of a major treaty!" he said. "Of course, it isn't ours anymore. That homicidal maniac Hassan has control of it. Jeezus, I have to tell *that* to the Director and he's got to bring that nightmare news to the damn National Security Council."

"I don't think so," Reed declared.

The deputy director eyed him carefully. Reed seemed calm and rational.

"You got a better idea?" Carling asked.

"Much better," Reed said.

The deputy director nodded.

Edward Reed took a deep breath and began to explain his plan.

11

"**About seven years** ago," he said, "a lot of very experienced and dedicated people at the Agency were troubled by a whole series of new restrictions on covert operations. These changes came from pious politicians who didn't know anything about our work."

The deputy director remembered, but said nothing.

That was one way you got to rise in a bureaucracy.

"Those well-meaning amateurs didn't understand our world," Reed insisted, "and neither did the damn media or the clergy or the university crowd. They had no idea of our responsibilities. All they have to do is preach and condemn. It's our job to protect this nation . . . including their wives and kids . . . from terrible enemies around the world."

He was breathing hard as he paused for a moment.

"I could not . . . in good conscience," he declared solemnly, "let ignorant outsiders cripple this Agency and the defense of the United States."

Scores of covert action professionals had been "retired" or quit, Carling recalled. It had been a bitter time.

"I thought about this for months," Reed continued, "and I made a plan."

"Seven years ago?"

"Closer to six," Reed answered. "As a professional, I knew the time would come when our government had to do something violent and terrible . . . in the national interest. The challenge was how to do it without the operation being traced to us. A shocking covert action with total deniability."

It was an interesting idea, Carling reflected.

Not new . . . quite impossible . . . but still interesting.

"After a lot of careful analysis," Reed told him, "I decided that a small elite unit should be created. It had to be more than small to avoid detection. It had to be completely invisible . . . a ghost team. All very experienced and resourceful . . . all first class . . . none with any connection to the United States."

He paused to let the whole concept sink in fully.

"Yes?" Carling said.

"I did it."

"Did *what?*"

"I created that special unit. Not only are they all foreigners, but every one of them is dead."

It didn't make any sense.

"Dead?" Carling blurted.

"Legally dead. I arranged fake accidents and phoney heart attacks in various parts of the world . . . none of them here. Bodies were buried with my operators' IDs. There's a valid death certificate for each member of my unit. That's why I call them the Spirit Team."

The tradecraft was correct, but he could be lying.

He could also be telling the truth.

"Who are they?" the deputy director tested.

"I'm the only one who knows, and it's going to stay that way. I know where they are and their new names and their new faces. They all got plastic surgery and altered fingerprints. Each has several passports with matching ID."

He was speaking reasonably in a normal tone, but that didn't mean much. He might still be lying or insane, Carling thought.

"You won't find them," Reed said. "There's no mention . . . no record of these people in any US government file or computer bank. They're visible only to me. You asked who they are. Since they're the Spirit Team, I've named them Whiskey . . . Gin . . . Brandy and so forth."

He wasn't giving much away.

And so forth could be two or twenty.

"How many are there?" Carling asked bluntly.

Reed shook his head.

"You don't want to know. You don't need to know," he said. "They're mine . . . not yours. I pay them . . . quite well."

"Where would you get that kind of cash?"

"I broke the Agency payroll computer codes . . . and some others over four years ago," Reed replied coolly. "I've been stealing the money ever since."

"That's impossible!"

"You're absolutely right," Reed agreed, "but I've been doing it for years while the Spirits waited for my signal to strike. I've been waiting too . . . waiting for the time when the Spirit Team is the only solution."

"It isn't," Carling declared.

"Of course it is. Madesh is supposed to be our friend. We can't bomb a friend or drop in an airborne assault battalion," Reed reasoned. "How could we justify it? We certainly can't go public on this germ plant with our fungus and former Rosebud people . . . former US Army employees. There's no other way."

"There has to be."

"We don't have forever to play think tank on this," Reed said. "Now . . . right now . . . it's time for the Spirit Team to *total* this operation. How else can we keep the fungus from Hassan?"

The logic was as intolerable and inescapable as Edward Reed.

Total was the correct word, Carling thought. There must be nothing left. Every bit of the operation had to be obliterated.

"I'll talk to the director," Carling said ambiguously.

"You can't without compromising total deniability," Reed warned. "You can't risk delay either. The replacement lab could be ready in five or six weeks, and I hear Hassan might have his fungus in nine or ten more. He *really* hates us, you know."

"What are you saying?"

"His target could be Washington."

Reed saw the deputy director flinch.

"That's crazy!" Carling whispered hoarsely.

"So is Hassan."

Unable to answer that truth, the deputy director looked at the desk clock again. It was going to be a horror show, he realized. There was no way he could see to avoid it.

Whatever happened, *they* would blame the Agency.

The other US intelligence organizations . . . the creeps at State, the wise guys at the White House . . . would all dump the responsibility on the Agency. Jealous and fanatically protecting their turf and careers, they'd say the CIA should have detected this months or years ago.

It was really the damn Army's fault.

"I'll check this whole thing out immediately with General Sherman," Carling announced.

"Don't mention the Spirit Team. He doesn't know about it."

"I don't either," the deputy director responded irritably. "You could be making it up."

"Why would I do that?"

Carling gestured angrily.

"Why would you steal money . . . break laws . . . bust Agency regulations and go off on an I'll Do As I Please tear after years as a team player?"

"I told you why," Reed said.

"I don't believe that's all," Carling challenged. "I think you want something else . . . for yourself."

Reed hesitated to phrase his reply carefully.

"We can talk about that later," he said noncommittally.

The deputy director suddenly felt a bit better. It might be difficult to bargain with or manipulate someone who was purely ideological or principled, but you could negotiate with men or women who wanted something—anything—for themselves. Carling was used to the idea of people using each other.

Now a glance at the electrical clock on his desk showed Carling it was time to join the British MI-6 team upstairs. He rose to his feet. Recognizing this blunt signal that their talk was over,

Reed stood up too and they walked towards the door.

"I don't expect your official blessing on this," Reed said. "Silence will do. If I don't hear from you within seventy-two hours, I'll take it from there."

Carling didn't answer.

They reached the portal.

"One more thing," Reed continued smoothly. "I have a wideband jammer in my attache case. The microphones in this office didn't pick up a word of our conversation. There is *no* audio record of this meeting."

The two men stepped outside, and Carling carefully closed the door behind them.

"*What* meeting?" the deputy director asked coolly a moment before he strode off to his next appointment.

Half a day later . . . half a world east.

Ted Wheatly wasn't nearly as cool as Carling had been. The temperature in the Torat Valley was eighty-two degrees Fahrenheit. The wind sweeping over him as he flew the open-cockpit biplane made it a bit better but not enough.

The roar of the 650-horsepower Pratt and Whitney engine just yards away didn't help either. The wiry Australian had over twenty-eight hundred hours experience as pilot of this Grumman AG-CAT—and the *bloody* noise still annoyed him. Discomfort was part of the price you paid in flying a cropdusting plane. Danger that came in a single-engine aircraft operating at under fifty feet was another part, but the money made up for both.

That was certainly true on this job.

Because it was a short-notice and don't tell anybody deal, he was getting triple his regular fee. It didn't surprise him that they wanted to keep it quiet. Clients often did that to protect the reputation of their threatened or contaminated crops.

Squinting down through his goggles at the small valley, Wheatly wondered what blight or disease he was spraying. He'd never seen any agricultural infestation that was blue before. It must be something *nasty,* he thought and remembered the drums of pesticide the Madeshi had pumped into his spray tanks when he landed at the nearby military airfield.

He'd recognized those barrels.

They held an extremely powerful defoliant that killed all plants and trees, the notorious Agent Orange with two phenoxy herbicides that left no crop standing. He was uneasy spraying this dioxin-laced brew that US authorities had banned as cancer-causing, but he was wearing a top-quality mask and his exposure would not be great.

The valley was only a mile wide, less than two long.

He'd already completed three of the four sweeps they'd ordered. Just a final one now, and at double the usual altitude. He looked over at the Madeshi army helicopter that was circling at thirteen hundred feet outside the valley. It had guided him here from the military air base, and in a few minutes it would guide him back.

He'd already been paid half the money in advance.

Now he'd collect the other six thousand dollars from the tall, thin colonel and get out of here.

Wheatly didn't know that the colonel was watching him from the rotorcraft, and he had no idea of what had been done while he was in the air base office receiving his fee.

One last pass, and he'd be on his way home.

He turned the sturdy Grumman, swept in again to finish the job. Working methodically and leaving not an inch unsprayed, he guided the plane back and forth with the deadly defoliant drifting out evenly behind him in an acrid mist.

It was done.

Wheatly grinned . . . coughed despite the effectiveness of the excellent mask . . . and wiggled the plane's wings to signal that he was ready to return to the military air field. Colonel Yussuf Kebeer sighed, and shrugged.

He picked up the radio-control unit on his lap, flicked the ON switch and pressed the red button.

The Australian aviator was dead, blasted into many bits of flesh that didn't resemble human parts at all. The bomb they'd concealed in the spray plane shattered it into hundreds of fragments, hurling them in a wide arc like jagged razor blades. There was nothing that looked like a man or an aircraft on the floor of the Torat Valley.

Some chunks of the pilot that would decompose soon.

Pieces of bone that would blend in with all the skeletons already spread across the valley floor.

The metal scraps of the blasted spray plane would last longer, Kebeer reflected as the helicopter turned back towards the military airfield. The official report . . . there had to be an *official* report to keep the dead flier's family or insurance company from poking into this . . . would say Wheatly and his single-engine aircraft had both been totally incinerated in an accident.

Not here.

Not anywhere near here.

At least four hundred miles away on a job for a large farming enterprise.

That ought to do it, the colonel told himself.

That should do it nicely.

12

It was nearly midnight.

Amsterdam . . . five and a half days after Reed disclosed his secret and presented his plan.

The shift was changing in the brothel on Spuistraat.

The prostitute who'd noticed the well-dressed black man looking in her window was in fine spirits. There was less boredom and more money in working these late hours, and now she had whole afternoons for shopping. She was thinking about the bathing suit sale at Vroom & Dreesman as she entered the brothel's front room.

"I had fourteen—including a British couple. The wife wanted to watch," the blonde sex worker going off duty reported.

Then she yawned, tightened the sash of her baby blue kimono and left. The buxom woman coming on duty sat down in the armchair, arranged her flimsy robe carefully to show the right amount of cleavage and glanced around the room.

The electric coffee pot was plugged in . . . *good.* There were plenty of clean towels . . . *good.* A dozen condoms were stacked on the table beside the bed . . . *good.*

Then she saw something that might not be good at all.

Someone had shifted the floor lamp to the other side of the room. Jaap wasn't going to like that. The man who ran this house had made it clear that the furniture must not be moved. He was very strict on this point, and he had a temper.

At that moment she saw the reflection in the wall mirror. She turned her head towards the street. Standing out on the sidewalk and peering in the wide window was the attractive and obviously affluent black man.

The way he kept coming back so often clearly indicated that he was interested.

Perhaps he was finally ready to ring the doorbell and enter.

He didn't.

He scanned her room . . . nodded . . . and walked away.

Maybe he'd return tomorrow, she told herself.

That was not his plan. He had seen where the floor lamp was, and there was no reason for ever strolling past this building on Spuistraat again.

He'd be leaving this country in the next two days, and he had a lot to do. The first thing would be to buy the airline ticket in the morning.

Bangkok . . . six hours later.

The slim and elegant Eurasian woman who spoke so many languages and took so few chances was entering another tall and modern luxury hotel. She never went to the same hotel twice in the same week to buy her newspaper. Often she purchased a local daily and some magazine in addition to the *International Herald Tribune*.

Today the magazine was *Business Week*. As a responsible adult with over $290,000 in investments, she liked to see what the alleged experts were saying. With the two newspapers and the weekly under her arm, she left the hotel and took a taxi.

Not to where she was staying.

To a corner four blocks from that one-bedroom apartment.

After the cab vanished into Bangkok's tangled traffic, she turned the corner and zig-zagged to where she was living this month.

She took off her dress, hung it in a closet and sat down to let the air conditioning free her skin of the street humidity. Soothed, she kicked off the simple-perfect Italian shoes . . . crossed her legs . . . and examined the *Herald Tribune*. First she read the front page headlines. Then she turned to the classified advertisements.

There it was.

A new quarterly in Geneva wanted an art director fluent in French and Mandarin.

She immediately wondered who the others would be. People always interested her. People and music. She stood up and put on her record player a CD of the Juilliard String Quartet performing two of her favorite Mozart works.

The music and the performances were superb . . . satisfying. She realized that she might as well enjoy both while she could. She'd be flying out of Bangkok quite soon. There was no way to guess what conditions might be when the group assembled.

Or where she'd be next week.

Where she'd be next month was beyond speculation.

Half a world away, Eugenio Garcia Mendoza was doing what he did every day. A creature of habit, he checked his bank balance at least once every twenty-four hours. The fact he now called himself Eugenio Garcia Mendoza wasn't important. What was extremely important was the precise amount in his checking account.

Immediate access to that information was a matter of the highest priority. That was why he had an account . . . in addition to his numbered one in Switzerland . . . in a Caracas bank which offered a round-the-clock money machine.

Life was pleasant and easy in the comfortable capital of Venezuela where his US dollars went far, the restaurants were good and the local baseball teams even better. Despite those attractions, he wouldn't be here if there was no automatic teller machine with twenty-four hour service.

He usually came to the ATM during business hours when a lot of other people were doing the same thing. That way he was less likely to be noticed. Not being noticed was also important to him. Today he'd been delayed by a passionate and insistent young woman, so it was 10:50 P.M. by the time he got to the bank.

He inserted his card in the machine . . . punched in the numbers . . . pressed the button to summon up a display of the balance in his checking account. It had been the equivalent of $1,230 yesterday.

It wasn't anymore.

A deposit that would be $900 in US currency had been made. Exactly $900.

He'd been waiting for this deposit for a long time.

"Goodby, Caracas," he thought.

He would miss this sophisticated city, and he would miss Maria Elena too.

He looked at the numbers on the ATM screen, decided that he might as well punch out a withdrawal of two hundred dollars while he was here and pressed the necessary buttons. Then he put the currency in his pocket and began to walk to his car parked across the street.

Someone saw him get the cash from the machine. As he neared his car, *someone* stepped out of the shadows with a knife in his hand and gestured menacingly.

Eugenio Garcia Mendoza never found out whom the *someone* was.

Instead, he expertly kicked the stranger in the groin and stepped aside as the man gagged in pain. Sometimes they vomited when he kicked them in the groin. Then he seized the wrist of the hand holding the knife . . . and twisted very hard . . . very professionally.

The wrist broke. The criminal opened his mouth to howl. That was not acceptable. The noise would draw attention . . . perhaps police. To avoid that, Eugenio Garcia Mendoza knocked the man unconscious by ramming his head into the nearby building wall.

The whole episode was disgraceful. There wasn't that much street crime here. Mendoza decided that he shouldn't let this minor incident color his memories of Caracas. Having come to

that sensible conclusion, he was humming as he got into his
sports car and drove away.

Across the Atlantic . . . and the sands of North Africa . . . on
the east bank of the fabled river Nile which has nourished Egypt
for some six thousand years.

Cairo, a sprawling crowded city of over fourteen million . . . a
noisy bustling metropolis and a capital and a trading center
whose antiquities and very modern high-rise hotels draw each
year tens of thousands of tourists bearing cameras and warnings
not to drink the water.

Almost three thousand years old, this vibrant city is on both
sides of the Mother Nile. The slim man from Morocco preferred
the east bank for his observation post. A wide street called the
Corniche . . . the French had been here . . . carries a steady flow of
traffic along this shore. There are several good hotels on the Corniche. The man who watched the river knew them all, and his
favorite was the Nile Hilton.

It wasn't the newest hotel in town. It wasn't even the newest
Hilton here, but it was gracious . . . the kind of civilized establishment where Cairo society ladies of a certain age, women who
spoke French and wore white gloves . . . assembled for lunch.
The Nile Hilton had . . . to use an archaic term . . . class.

So each evening at 8 P.M. the man from Morocco . . . he could
speak Arabic in the accents of five countries . . . stood across the
Corniche from the hotel and looked out at the river. When he'd
first come to Cairo he'd taken a room on the hotel's seventh floor
and seen the pyramids on the horizon. He couldn't quite make
them out tonight from the bank of the Nile, but he knew they
were out there, and that pleased him.

Tonight was no different from any of the others. Still, he
wasn't the least bit bored. After all, this could be the one. His
eyes roamed up and down the river. He saw one of the big wide
ferry-like vessels that carried throngs of Cairenes and visitors on
air-conditioned dinner cruises.

No.

He was looking for another kind of boat. He really wanted to see it . . . and he didn't. Then he thought about the pyramids again, and he felt better.

He glanced down at his wristwatch in the growing darkness.

8:20 P.M. . . . he'd be off duty in another quarter of an hour.

Where would he eat tonight?

Suddenly he forgot about food.

Moving slowly up the Nile in the evening breeze was one of Egypt's traditional native vessels. They were commonplace on the Nile. There were thousands of these sail-powered feluccas, simple shallow-draft craft between thirty and forty feet long. Some had two masts, others three. They'd been basic and standard transport on this magical river for over a thousand years.

This one wasn't quite like the others though.

It was different in one significant way.

There were two red lanterns on the prow . . . a blue one and a green one on the stern.

The man from Morocco understood what that meant, and it didn't bother him. He'd updated the will under his new name only ten months ago.

Don C. Gould was studying a very different document.

It wasn't a will. It was a message form marked TOP SECRET— PRIORITY RED STRIPE.

Rereading it in his neat U.S. Embassy office in the untidy capital of Madesh, the CIA station chief felt uneasy about what the signal from Langley said . . . and didn't say.

It was brief and blunt.

PURGE FILES OF DATA ON TORAT VALLEY AND ASSET LOST NEARBY. IMPERATIVE YOU PER-SONALLY INCINERATE ALL THAT MATERIAL AND THIS SIGNAL WITHIN TWO HOURS.

CONFIRM COMPLIANCE WITH PHRASE "BUD-GET COMPLETED."

VICEROY

Gould wondered what could be so *hot* that even this signal must be destroyed. He didn't understand what was going on, but he knew VICEROY was the codename of the Deputy Director for Operations.

The station chief obeyed the orders swiftly, checking all the files three times before cleansing the computer records electronically and then burning the paper documents to a fine ash in the CIA unit's ultra-high temperature incinerator. It was nearly midnight by the time he finished.

Maybe Langley would explain the situation in a week or two, he told himself as he block-printed BUDGET COMPLETED on a fresh message form for transmission. Maybe not, he thought a moment later. These days it was oddly difficult to predict what they'd do.

The next day was April 9th.

It was hot in the Caribbean. On Guadeloupe the late morning temperature was eighty-six degrees Fahrenheit. There was nothing unusual about that.

In the bungalow up the hill half a mile from the beach, the man who had given his word was listening to his shortwave radio. There was nothing special about that either.

He'd been monitoring this station every morning between 11:15 and 11:40 for a long time. Though it was a daily ritual, he was paying careful attention to what he was hearing . . . and he was listening for other things.

Sounds outside the house. He always listened for those.

A car . . . a footstep . . . the click of metal. No, not yet.

He knew that a message or an assassin could come at any time . . . today . . . tomorrow.

Tomorrow would be a special day. It would be the thirteenth anniversary of his wedding, he thought as the radio evangelist deftly slipped in between the records to exhort and exalt with singsong sincerity.

No, *their* wedding. Her death hadn't ended that or the clear memories of their life together. Would they blur in time? He sighed and eyed his watch.

Eight more minutes.

Then today's monitoring would be finished. Now he heard the earnest man who wanted to save everybody's soul say something about "gospel classics." Five seconds later, the opening bars of "Good News, the Chariot's Coming!" filled the room. A powerful choir was singing the Reverend James Cleveland's moving work with talent and passion.

Their splendid performance wasn't what made the man in the bungalow sit up immediately.

It was this group singing this song that was the first part of the message.

Maybe not.

If it was not followed by the second part, it meant nothing and his waiting and listening would continue. He didn't want that.

Now the distant electronic preacher was offering a mailing address in Florida for purchases of religious books and a "truly wonderful" new series of sermons on cassettes.

"The Lord's work!" the evangelist declared.

Then the next record began.

It was a trio . . . *the* trio . . . lifting their voices in "Hide Me, Jesus, in the Solid Rock" by Thomas Dorsey. This was the second record. Then the third one—the final part of the message—followed.

The man in the bungalow stood up and felt a surge of strength.

It was time, and he was ready.

He'd be on his way before the sun set tomorrow.

It was important that he be there as soon as possible.

After all, he was the leader.

13

Those three gospel recordings did more than signal the start of the operation. The sequence in which they were broadcast set the time and place of the briefing.

Reed didn't want anybody . . . even his strike force leader . . . to know much in advance where or when it would be. He had to maintain total control and secrecy, Reed told himself. Not one of the Spirit Team knew Edward Reed's real identity.

He'd planned the rendezvous to leave no trace that he'd been there. It would be far from Washington but on US territory. He'd cross no border . . . show no passport . . . face no immigration or customs officials coming or going.

Minimum exposure. He'd be there only a few hours. In and out on different air carriers . . . tickets bought for cash under different names. Nobody would spot or wonder about the swift round trip.

He'd picked a busy city with half a million residents and a large number of visitors. San Juan, Puerto Rico, was a commercial and tourist center whose air terminal was crowded year round. With many airlines . . . scores of flights . . . thousands of travelers daily, it was unlikely that he'd be noticed in the human flow.

No one would be looking for Edward Reed anyway. He wasn't on any agency's "watch list." After his years at a desk in the Langley bureaucracy, the intelligence and security organizations didn't consider him worth watching.

They *would,* he vowed silently as the Delta jet from Atlanta

. . . he'd changed airlines there . . . landed at the San Juan airport. It was finally happening. His perfect plan was becoming a reality.

Caribbean heat and humidity enveloped him as he stepped from the plane, but Edward Reed didn't care. He was in the field again. He knew exactly what he had to do.

Some eighty-five minutes after his taxi left the airport, Reed stood perspiring on a sunbaked corner in Old San Juan. This was the historic section of the city founded by Spanish explorers over four centuries earlier. Buses carrying visitors to San Juan's sights and landmarks often stopped here. With a large photo-gear bag on a strap over his shoulder, Reed resembled a typical tourist as he looked up and down the street slowly . . . twice.

He repeated the inspection again.

He could see no threat.

Then Reed walked to the seventeenth-century Spanish church in the middle of the block, took off his silver-lensed sunglasses and entered the welcome cool of the colonial edifice. He'd come twenty minutes early as a precaution—standard tradecraft in the field. Tradecraft and proper procedures were important to Edward Reed.

Now he scanned the large chamber carefully and studied the dozen silent worshippers. Next he approached the worn stone font of holy water. The CIA officer wasn't Catholic, but he'd learned some of the rituals. After dipping his fingertips in the water and crossing himself, he advanced four steps before dropping to one knee briefly in correct obeisance.

Reed took a seat in a pew and lowered his head as if in prayer. The seconds ticked away, and he felt sweat beading at his temples.

Suddenly he heard someone right behind him.

"Don't turn your head."

Reed recognized the strong quiet voice at once.

Brandy, the strike force leader, had arrived.

"And don't say anything," the man from Guadeloupe continued immediately. "In twenty seconds I'll walk up the aisle to the front . . . turn right . . . then around to the rear door. Follow me, and don't look back."

A minute and a half later they emerged from the historic building into the miasmic afternoon heat. They walked down an alley . . . then left up a narrow colonial-era street to a blue sedan. The man from Guadeloupe had parked it there before he began scouting the church and adjacent streets for possible ambushers.

Applying his life experience, he routinely considered this possibility. That was why he left through the back door of the house of worship. He'd learned a long time ago that . . . in forest or desert . . . city or swamp . . . it was safer not to go out the way you entered.

They got into the car without speaking. The strike force leader slid behind the wheel, started the engine and swiftly guided the sedan away from the old part of the Puerto Rican capitol. The heavy traffic hardly slowed him at all.

He's an *expert* driver, Reed thought contentedly. And a first class paratrooper, underwater commando, desert warrior, mountain and jungle fighter too. His years with Britain's hush-hush and fierce Special Air Service had honed an arsenal of skills in anti-terrorist battle and urban combat. House to house . . . room to room . . . hand to hand, he'd done it all and well. He'd also been an effective intelligence agent on five foreign missions for London's secret MI-6.

This strong and versatile son of a Welsh father and American mother had mastered the machine guns, booby traps, sniper rifles, rocket launchers and other infantry weapons of the major powers. His greatest weapon was his mind. The man behind the wheel could think. He could analyze problems and swiftly improvise solutions.

He was more than imaginative.

He was *dangerous*.

Edward Reed admired . . . and envied . . . that.

The CIA bureaucrat didn't like to face this. It certainly wasn't something to think about now.

"You're looking well," Reed said as the car rolled east.

"Clean living," the tanned driver replied in a tone edged with irony. Reed acted immediately to assert his control.

"I don't have much time," he announced authoritatively, "and you don't either. The information you need's on the video-cassette in my camera bag. Know anything about Madesh?"

"Third World. Fourth rate. Poor people. Worse government. Army's equipped with US hardware because they're anticommunist. Is Madesh the problem?"

"The problem is a lethal blue fungus being developed in a lab there."

Then Reed described the legion of corpses in the now-sealed Torat Valley . . . the troops ringing it . . . and the equipment for a new fungus laboratory entering Madesh almost daily.

"Whole story's in the material on the cassette," he said.

That was probably untrue, the strike-force leader thought as he glanced at the rear-view mirror and turned the sedan left towards the coast. They never told you the whole story. One or two things were always held back to give them some kind of edge.

"Your mission is to destroy the new lab before it starts production," Reed said crisply, "and close down this fungus project permanently."

"Any suggestions?"

"Do *whatever is necessary,"* Reed ordered. "Going back to the cassette, it also has pictures of the renegade Russian scientists who're the brains of this operation."

He didn't say "kill the scientists." That was no surprise. Covert action executives who sent other people into the field shunned crude words such as *kill.*

What else wasn't he saying?

"As I promised," Reed continued, "you'll have first-class help. You'll command an elite team. In the camera bag there's a card on each one with skills, fingerprints and an individual identification—plus your countersign code phrase to confirm you're the team leader."

"Rendezvous?"

"You set it. They're on their way to the Athens area now. On the back of each card you'll see exactly where and how to reach that person after 6 P.M. on the day after tomorrow."

He'd chosen the Greek capital with the same care that he'd used to pick San Juan: a busy city where the team wouldn't attract attention in the international flow of visitors. Good location with ample air and sea service to the Near East, North Africa, the Balkans and turbulent former Soviet republics—places the team might be sent. And the long coastline and often relaxed border controls that made moving people and weapons in and out less difficult.

Reed wanted to explain all this but he couldn't.

The man behind the wheel had no need to know.

Instead of breaking the rules, Reed went on to tell him about the nine thousand dollars and five thousand British pounds in the camera bag for expenses and airline tickets in the next few days. In addition, deutschmarks equivalent to another three hundred thousand pounds or four hundred and fifty thousand dollars had just been put into the team leader's Swiss account for weapons and other necessities.

"I hear there are some good values in brand new Sov hardware available in Europe," Reed said. "Just a thought. I'm not telling you how to run your show."

The man from Guadeloupe checked the traffic in the mirror again and turned right without saying a word. Reed looked at him, expecting that David Lloyd . . . that was his name before the fake death and it was the one on the headstone . . . would comment on the comprehensiveness and excellence of the plan. He didn't.

"I guess that's *it*," Reed finally said, "unless you have some questions."

"Three," Lloyd replied immediately.

"Go!" Reed urged.

"Where? I didn't hear any mention of target photos or just where the new lab is."

The CIA executive cleared his throat, and Lloyd understood at once.

"You don't know where it is, do you?" he said.

"We're working on it. The damn Madeshis have tripled the security at their airfields and ports, so our people can't pick up the shipments as they move out. We'll find them though—and soon," Reed vowed.

"Where are you looking?"

"It's a big country, you know."

"And your satellites can't cover it all every night, right?" the team leader reasoned aloud.

Reed didn't answer. He wasn't about to acknowledge any connection with spy satellites. The whole program was supersecret even today, and admitting any link to satellites would certainly suggest a connection with US intelligence.

There was no way he'd do that.

"We're looking in many places," he said. "Just about everywhere except the Torat Valley area. They'll stay away from there now."

"That's what you'd do . . . and they know it," Lloyd announced and shook his head. "That's why they'll rebuild right in the area. Put your cameras up over there."

"What's your second question?" Reed asked in instant evasion.

"It's another one about pictures," Lloyd said. "Fingerprints are fine but I want to see what my team looks like."

"There are no photos. That's for your own safety."

Lloyd suddenly pulled the sedan to the curb and braked the vehicle to an abrupt halt.

"Games are over," he announced. "The pictures or get out of this bloody car."

"I don't have any."

"What you don't have is more than five seconds. One . . . two . . . three . . . four."

Reed reached into the inner pocket of his jacket and pulled out a small envelope.

"You can look at them but you can't keep them," he said.

Lloyd nodded in assent. Reed gave him the envelope, and the team leader studied the individual pictures carefully before he returned them.

Then Reed put them—one by one—in the ashtray and burned them. He stirred and crushed the charred residue with his pen.

"Third question?" he inquired coolly.

"Those men who were following you when you got to the church? Are they your people or somebody else's?"

Reed hadn't been aware of the surveillance, but he wasn't going to admit that. He forced himself to smile.

"Mine, of course," he lied.

Next they agreed on how Reed would deliver information about the new laboratory's location and where additional money needed would be sent in response to certain *"in memoriam"* advertisements in a London daily. Ten minutes later Lloyd dropped him off beside the taxis lined up at a beachfront hotel. An hour after that Edward Reed was back at the crowded airport boarding the jet that would take him to Boston on his way home.

So someone had been following him, he thought for the tenth time as he made his way to his seat.

Was somebody watching him now?

He looked around the cabin at the other passengers. They seemed to be ignoring him but that meant nothing. The surveillance had to be the work of the Deputy Director of Operations. It was just what Carling would do. He didn't trust anybody either.

That . . . and deception . . . were quite standard among the jungle creatures of the intelligence community. Reed had felt no compunction in lying to Carling that there weren't any pictures of the Spirit Team . . . and there were none now anyway. Carling wouldn't be any more angered by this untruth than Reed was at being followed.

Reed was bothered by one thing. He should have spotted the surveillance team himself. He didn't like facing the fact that his tradecraft and field skills were rusty. He'd have to pay attention to that.

Now the senior flight attendant was talking over the speaker system about safety rules . . . seat belts . . . oxygen masks and life jackets and evacuation procedures. The 747 was very safe, she sing-songed in her routine announcement, and there was only a tiny possibility that there would be any problem.

The CIA executive was only half listening, for his attention was focused on another possibility that still troubled him as the big jet rose from the runway.

What if the watchers were not from the Agency?

What if someone else had sent them?

14

It happened near Zurich at 9:05 the next morning. The entire incident took thirty-one seconds.

Plus several weeks of planning . . . half a dozen graduates of one of the more down-and-dirty courses in covert action . . . two bribes . . . a casual betrayal . . . and an indifference to human life.

Cruising along on schedule, the truck driver placidly hummed the melody of a folk song whose words he'd forgotten. This was payday, and he'd just heard that the plump Italian waitress was not pregnant. Everything would be all right, he thought as the vehicle moved through light traffic on the familiar route from the factory to the Zurich airport.

The waiting marksman had picked his spot carefully.

His goal was maximum destruction . . . total destruction.

The truck was rounding a tight curve when the concealed sniper gutted the right front tire with an explosive bullet. Now the heavy vehicle shook and heaved, almost instantly began to skid and lurch out of control with the driver shouting curses in a most un-Swiss manner.

The man-helper seated beside him yelled too but only for a few moments. That was all the time he had. Then the truck spun in a complete circle . . . slid across the road . . . and crashed into a big boulder.

The battered, bleeding driver was still shouting when gasoline from the ruptured fuel tank ignited. Both corpses were incinerated beyond recognition before the explosion.

Dental work let the Swiss police identify the driver, and they found enough of the other man's left hand to match fingerprints with his military records. Being Swiss and police, the dutiful investigators also had to put a name on the ruined metal thing in the cargo compartment—the fire-damaged machine that the truck had been carrying to the airport.

The bill of lading took care of that.

It identified the device and named the destination as Athens.

It didn't indicate that there were men waiting there with another bill of lading for the next leg of the journey.

At six that evening when General Hassan heard what happened, he simply nodded. Fozira's absolute ruler was pleased, but he didn't show it. He guarded his feelings as he did everything else. Hassan usually smiled only when he faced a camera. If he didn't like the still or television pictures, the man who took them—a woman was *unthinkable*—might have arms or legs broken.

That maintained the fear.

He realized that it was an old-fashioned management style, but fear was essential in Hassan's world. There were so many people in Fozira and other nations—nearby and far away—who were plotting against him. Or might be if he didn't paralyze them with terror or destroy them.

Like many other paranoids in and out of government everywhere, Hassan lived on hate and the conviction that he'd defeat his countless enemies because he was more cunning and more ruthless. He prized those qualities very highly.

He respected the Yemeni president who'd had all his ministers machine gunned at a Cabinet meeting because one might be disloyal. He admired the Syrian dictator who obliterated a whole city, dynamiting every building and ploughing the wreckage under with bulldozers after massacring the entire population of twenty thousand who dared oppose him. He applauded the good sense of the Iraqi and Libyan leaders who routinely dealt with dissent by eliminating hundreds of their countrymen and women.

Of course, Hassan hated those chiefs of state too.

They were his rivals for dominance in a vast region.

If they didn't submit sooner or later, he'd have to destroy them.

"You're sure the operation was a complete success?" he asked the plump colonel who ran the State Security Bureau.

"Absolutely," the covert action specialist replied. "That centrifuge will never help the Iranians make nuclear weapons, and our whole team got out of Switzerland undetected."

"Who do the Swiss think did it?"

"The Israelis, of course. It's the sort of thing the Mossad's been doing for years."

The absolute ruler of Fozira shook his head.

"They've mounted this kind of operation," he agreed, "but not this way. To minimize political fallout, they don't kill. The Swiss know that, and so does everyone else who's rational."

"Does that include the Iranians, General?"

"Probably not, but we'll still have to help the Swiss *and* the Iranians on this."

The colonel swallowed uneasily. He didn't understand what Hassan was saying, and he was afraid that he'd be blamed for some error in slaying the two Swiss truckers.

General Hassan was pleased to see the fear in his aide's face. He wanted them all to be afraid . . . to stay afraid.

"Look," the Supreme Ruler for Life reasoned calmly. "The Swiss want to find out who violated their neutrality so improperly, and the damned Iranians want to get even. We can help them both feel better by spreading the word in Vienna and Beirut, Algiers and Cairo that it was those terrible Iraqis who paid for this. The Swiss can quietly protest and the idiot Iranians can get their revenge by sending some of their pious action gangs to hit Iraqi targets."

"That's brilliant, General. I'll take care of it right away."

"Before you do, what's the word from Madesh?"

"Everything's moving well," the colonel reported with the enthusiasm of a man whose fear has subsided for the moment. "Most of the gear is in place, and they are training a new support staff. There's been no sign that anyone knows where the new facility is. It's absolutely invisible."

"And much safer than the Torat Valley?"

"At least a hundred times. There's no way that the fungus can get out of control there."

"I'm not planning on using it *there*," General Hassan said.

The colonel knew that it could be extremely dangerous to ask where or when or anything else that the general didn't volunteer. He volunteered very little. In fact, only Hassan and a handful of his senior officers knew what was planned. That was perfectly all right with the heavyset head of the State Security Bureau. When Hassan nodded for him to leave, the colonel departed immediately.

Now Hassan looked at the open calendar on his desk.

Six weeks? Ten?

Not much longer than that.

It would surprise a lot of people when the fungus was used, Fozira's chief of state thought contentedly.

At least a million in the first forty-eight hours.

In a week it could kill a whole country.

15

A clear sunny Athens morning.

Pleasantly warm, but free of the clotted humidity she'd left in Bangkok.

And the big and dramatic gold jewelry in the windows of the handsome Lalaounis shop on Penepistimiou Avenue was elegant, the Eurasian woman thought as she studied the fine pieces with just a touch of wanting.

She recognized the feeling, and she smiled. She wasn't the least bit ashamed of her eye for beautiful things, or the fact she might buy an unusual Lalaounis bracelet of twenty-two-carat gold. She didn't wear a lot of jewelry, but the imaginative designs of Lalaounis and classic creations in the nearby Zolotas boutique spoke to her in a strong sure way.

Her glance swung left . . . then right . . . as if she were absent-minded. She was totally alert, searching and waiting. She moved on to the next Lalaounis window, stopped and scanned the reflection in the glass of the street behind her. There was a steady flow of automotive and human traffic through this fashionable downtown artery.

Two very chicly-attired . . . all right, somewhat overdressed and heavy on this year's Paris *parfum* . . . society ladies chatted happily as they emerged from Lalaounis and headed towards the nearby Grand Bretagne Hotel on Syntagma Square. Their expensive scents lingered in the air as the slim woman from Bangkok admired a woven-wire dream of a golden ring . . . a lavish fantasy . . . in the style of this year's Lalaounis collection.

The door to the shop opened again, and she saw a tall, tanned man emerge. Muscular . . . well dressed in quality clothes that were not Greek . . . in his late thirties or a bit older . . . a face with even features and wide eyes . . . all this registered in four seconds.

For just a moment he glanced at her approvingly . . . without lust. She was used to being noticed by men. Now he was looking at the street as if expecting a car to arrive. His shoes were English, she noted automatically, then turned to a U-shaped gold neckpiece in the window. She wondered what the price might be.

"It's thirty-one hundred dollars," he said as if he'd read her mind.

Pick-up? Contact? Something else?

She studied him warily.

"We met at the museum on Saturday, Miss Celine," he lied.

"Of course, the reception at the Benaki," she replied.

Sign and countersign.

Contact.

The correct identification passwords had been exchanged, but she had no idea who he was. He knew that she wasn't any Miss Celine, and any name he'd give her would be equally false. Rules of engagement. S.O.P. on such a mission.

They were starting on an equal basis. *No,* he'd known what she looked like. In a maximum security operation like this only the leader would know that. What kind of leader would he be?

He raised his right hand, and a dark blue BMW sedan pulled up beside them. "Please join us, Miss Celine," he invited pleasantly. Then he reached for the car's rear door, smiling as he opened it.

Decent manners . . . slight Brit accent . . . good teeth, she thought.

He could still get them all shot to pieces or hung up alive on meathooks by the enemy. What enemy?

She entered the back of the sedan, watched him close the door and circle to the front of the car as the swarthy driver slid over. The leader took his place behind the wheel, checked both mirrors and started the vehicle.

The man beside him . . . the Moroccan designated Vodka in Reed's secret Spirit Team lexicon . . . looked left and right as the BMW moved slowly through the traffic of downtown Athens. On the rear seat the curious Eurasian woman nodded to the former Nigerian artillery captain next to her. The powerfully built soldier whom Reed had codenamed Whiskey nodded back but said nothing.

No one in the car spoke for more than three minutes.

Then the walkie-talkie on the seat beside the leader crackled.

"Acropolis . . . Acropolis . . . Acropolis."

Still no one said a word.

Another three minutes ticked away.

"Acropolis . . . Acropolis . . . Acropolis," the radio voice repeated.

"Clear," the man behind the wheel said.

"Back up van checking to see if we're being followed, right?" she said. "Grey Subaru?"

"When did you spot it?" David Lloyd asked her.

"Not *when,"* she answered. *"How many times.* I noticed it cruise by Lalaounis *twice* before you came out."

"I'm glad you did," Lloyd told her candidly.

She was as smart and skilled as the dossier he got in Puerto Rico reported. That was more than good. It was essential. Every member of this small assault team had to perform just about perfectly if they were to have any chance at all.

The African soldier beside her nodded again, this time in acceptance. He'd been told that this would be an elite group, but it didn't hurt to see her professionalism in action. Now the car moved away from the heart of this ancient city. Not directly to the destination, of course. Though they'd seen no car following them, Lloyd drove in a roundabout loop . . . sometimes turning down minor streets . . . sometimes doubling back altogether.

Always under the speed limit.

Always in compliance with all traffic rules.

It was almost half an hour before she realized where Lloyd was taking them. *Piraeus*. She was right. A few minutes later she caught her first glimpse of the capital's busy port, a great wide harbor dotted with tankers, cargo vessels and cruise ships waiting to take tourists to the eastern Mediterranean islands and Turkey.

The BMW paused to let a big trailer-truck pass in front of it, and Lloyd looked at her in the rear-view mirror. She was attractive all right. He could deal with that. It wouldn't affect how he dealt with her or the mission. Either would be both a professional and serious error he couldn't afford.

No excuses.

No mistakes.

No complications.

That was how you played this game for adults who never grew up and thought they'd never die.

The large truck rumbled away from the intersection, and Lloyd drove on for half a mile before turning right up a hill lined with private homes. This wasn't a neighborhood for budget-minded newlyweds. All these residences had three or more bedrooms, multiple car garages and gardens. Privacy mattered here with a number of homes hidden from the street by whitewashed walls seven feet high.

It was the driveway of one of those villas where Lloyd guided the BMW to park in the courtyard. They got out of the car into the warm sun, and she looked at the spacious three-storey house. Now the Suburu van pulled up beside her, and the driver emerged.

He was a theatrically good-looking Latin with well-tended hair, stylish sport clothes from some expensive tailor and an appraising look that evaluated every inch . . . every centimeter . . . of "Miss Celine's" face, hair and body. It wasn't the standard sort of undressing done by some oaf eyeing her with fantasies of carnal adventures, exotic intercultural experiences, and erotic miniseries. His examination was almost medical, she realized.

This aggressive attention didn't bother her much, for men and women had eyed her with appreciation or envy since she was thirteen years old. It did bother the strike-force leader whose urgent job was to build . . . as soon as possible . . . a strong team and total team ethic. What the man from Caracas was doing could cause stress or conflicts within the team.

It must be stopped.

She had the practical intelligence and cool style to do it economically and easily with minimum fuss, Lloyd judged.

But if she didn't do it, he would.

Right now he had something else to do.

He pointed to the house, and led them inside. They followed him through a foyer, down a short corridor and left into a large livingroom. It was comfortably furnished with big armchairs, a pair of wide leather couches, four sort-of-modern lamps, a deep rose carpet, an elaborately carved coffee table, several tired end tables and a couple of gilt-framed and truely mediocre water-color landscapes.

There was one more thing in the room.

It was a twenty-seven-inch television set with VCR machine attached.

"Each of you has been given a different recognition word to identify the unit commander," he began. "Here they are."

Studying his face, the other members of the Spirit Team leaned forward as he spoke to each of them in turn.

"Lion . . . Copper . . . Panama . . . Charlemagne."

His authority confirmed, they nodded and looked at each other carefully for several seconds before he spoke again.

"I'm James Trager," he told them. "From left to right," he continued as he pointed to the master burglar from Morocco, "Gamal Sharif . . . Eugenio Mendoza . . . Josephine Tan . . . and our heavy weapons specialist, Samuel Chibuku."

All the names were false.

Each of the Spirits knew it.

Legally dead . . . with altered faces and fingerprints . . . carrying expertly forged passports and other counterfeit credentials of the highest quality, no one on the Spirit Team had a past or a future. They were like holograms, unreal and temporary. The created identities would not exist after this smoke-and-mirrors operation.

Now the Spirits studied each other once again, wondering who these strangers really were. Lloyd saw that Mendoza wasn't staring at Tan anymore, and the team leader started the briefing.

"Ground rules first," he said and picked up the remote control device from the table near his armchair. "This is a maximum security job, now and forever. After it's done, it never happened. If anyone talks about it, I believe that the people who went to so much trouble to organize this team would go to even more trouble to eliminate the talker."

"Just take the money and run?" Mendoza asked archly.

"No, *walk*. Don't do anything to attract attention. There will be *other* people . . . numerous, well financed and angry . . . looking for the team that did this. If *they* get you, they'll kill you too —but a lot more slowly."

Since they were seasoned professionals, Lloyd didn't have to spell out the tortures that they faced if they were caught. He didn't.

"Let's get to the mission," he said. "We have two objectives. Target One is a laboratory that's getting ready to produce a new and secret weapon of mass destruction. It's a highly sensitive and deadly anti-personnel system."

"How deadly?" the Moroccan asked.

"Kill rate: one hundred percent."

"Holy shit!" Mendoza said softly.

"My view precisely," the team leader agreed in a cool even voice. "It's mean and it's fast. Within two hours every human or animal it touches is a corpse."

"Some sort of fusion bomb?" the Nigerian heavy weapons expert tested.

Lloyd shook his head.

"It's *alive*," he announced.

He saw her shiver.

Was it fear or revulsion in her lovely dark eyes?

"I don't like it either," Lloyd assured her. "I didn't ask for it. We all took the deal, and this is what we got."

Breathing deeply, she controlled her emotions.

"It might save time, Mr. Trager, if you told us exactly what it is," she reasoned in that soft French-tinged accent.

They had more than a right to know, the team leader decided. They had an absolute need to know, and that always prevailed.

"The weapon is a radically different fungus—bright blue and lethal in the smallest contact. It's like nerve gas. A single drop and you're history."

"I'm better at geography," Mendoza said. "Where is this lab?"

"We'll get to that," Lloyd evaded.

He wasn't about to tell them that the team leader didn't know the location of the targets. For planning . . . choosing and buying equipment . . . training and infiltration, he needed that information soon.

Within a week . . . at the latest.

Yesterday would be better.

"First I'd better show you the fungus," Lloyd declared as he changed the subject. "It's not pretty."

He picked up the remote control unit, turned on the video player and pressed the START button.

For twenty-nine seconds they stared at satellite pictures of fungus covered bodies . . . some sprawled alone . . . others in tangles and heaps of bright blue nightmare. Cocooned in the fatal embrace of Barcelona Delta, the dead people resembled grotesque snowmen and the dreadful corpses of two horses looked quilted . . . unreal.

The Spirits sat stunned as Lloyd stopped the machine.

"*No,*" said the angry African soldier who'd seen a lot of killed and maimed but nothing like this.

"Field test?" Mendoza asked professionally.

"I don't know."

The Eurasian woman had to swallow before she could speak.

"Who did this?" she demanded. "Who made this horror?"

"First class scientists, I'm told," Lloyd replied. "Former wizards in Soviet biological warfare programs who're freelancing."

Mercenaries like us, he thought, but he didn't say it.

"Here they are," Lloyd announced.

The VCR was rolling again.

Head shots. Close-ups of eight people.

Six men . . . two women.

All between thirty-five and sixty. One male looked oriental. The others appeared to be caucasian.

Each was on screen for ten seconds. The room was silent as the Spirit Team studied their faces. The strike force was eyeing the last one, a burly man with a thick mustache, when the woman from Bangkok suddenly spoke.

"Freeze it!" she called out urgently.

Lloyd stopped the machine.

She'd seen it, he guessed. That was good. It pleased him that she had an eye for small things.

"The clothes," she said.

"What about the clothes?" Lloyd tested.

"*Merde,*" she answered impatiently. "Those Russian scientists are all in *American* shirts, jackets, ties, blouses—and haircuts.

Lloyd nodded and smiled. She was right. Reed had overlooked those details.

"And eyeglasses," the Moroccan added. "Those are US-style frames."

"My compliments to both of you," the team leader said.

Samuel Chibuku shook his head.

"So we start this operation with either defective intelligence or a lie," he reasoned aloud.

"We've all had experience with both of those," the Moroccan burglar said.

The team leader nodded in agreement.

"Whichever it is," Mendoza declared boldly, "it doesn't chill me. Half a million dollars for one deal! That's too good to miss."

Lloyd nodded again, and looked at her.

"What do you think, Mr. Trager?" she asked.

"For better or worse, we're not ordinary people," he answered. "We don't do ordinary work. Any job we're offered is dangerous, and this one is particularly dangerous. I think we'll have to be particularly careful."

"I'm in," Mendoza said.

The Moroccan nodded his assent.

Samuel Chibuku hesitated for several seconds before he spoke.

"In."

"And you, Mademoiselle?" the team leader asked.

"Particularly careful? *Bien,*" she replied and wondered why she trusted this man she hardly knew. It wasn't his good looks. It wasn't anything but instinct. She'd always done well following her instincts, she remembered and crossed her legs.

Lloyd noticed that movement, and saw Mendoza was eyeing her again. This was no time for either of them to deal with him. Lloyd had to finish the briefing.

"Unless you have any other questions . . . ," he began.

He didn't finish the sentence.

"The eight scientists," she said. "Why did you show them to us?"

"I was about to explain that. I said there are two targets," he reminded. "The first is that laboratory. When we blast it . . . and burn it to cinders to cremate the spores . . . the immediate threat of production will be gone."

"For the moment," the Moroccan added.

"Only for the moment," David Lloyd agreed, "and we're after a permanent solution."

Gamal Sharif turned his head away, coughed and faced Lloyd again.

"We have to shut down the fungus project for good," the

Spirit Team commander said. "That brings us to the second target."

"What about the scientists?" she pressed.

"Tell her," Mendoza urged. He was smiling, and Lloyd realized that Mendoza had figured out what the second target was.

"Labs can be rebuilt. Heads can't," Lloyd said. "Our second target is . . . has to be . . . these scientists whose brains created the weapon. Those intelligent psychopaths are already mass murderers. They massacred nine hundred people, including children, in that episode on the tape."

"*Nine hundred* people?" she asked.

"Or more. We can't let them kill again," Lloyd told her. "If we don't stop them, they will and it could be nine thousand next time."

After several seconds she nodded in acceptance. Lloyd picked up the remote control and resumed the briefing.

In the global headquarters of the Central Intelligence Agency near Washington, Reed stood beside the desk of a senior photo analyst who was meticulously examining blowups of the latest satellite pictures. Then he did it again. That was the fourth time.

He sighed, looked at Reed and shook his head.

There was no sign of any laboratory.

There was no target for the Spirit Team.

16

At the other end of the big building . . . up on a higher floor with a better view . . . the well dressed deputy director of operations was having second thoughts. It was one of the things Carter Carling was really good at along with coming to work every day, taking few risks and trusting nobody.

Actually it wasn't quite accurate to say that Carling, who toiled diligently and did his job moderately well, was pondering second thoughts about Reed. Unless you saw the phrase "second thoughts" as generic, he was going over the situation for the 902nd time.

At least. He'd worried about this dangerous outrage again and again . . . day and night . . . since he first heard of it. Carling was used to dealing with weapons of mass destruction and sons-of-bitches like Pariah, but Reed threatened the Agency itself. With Congress still sizzling about the Ames mess, arrogant outlaw Edward Reed had created another vile scandal that could start a firestorm.

As a longtime player and winner-survivor in the jungle called the intelligence community, Carling knew what must be done. He had to take the initiative, not his favorite sport. He had to retake power and authority, for that was what it was all about. As a senior bureaucrat, he had experience in fighting such wars.

Control of both Reed and the entire situation had to be in Carling's hands when he took it all to the DCI. Reed's idea of hiding the whole operation from the director was a rogue adolescent's fantasy, Carling thought irritably. In the real world whoever brought the properly edited facts to the boss first could put the key self-serving spin on it and stay in favor.

What was happening out there right now?

The satellite pictures and G-2 confirmed Reed's account of the fungus, but how much of the other things Reed said were true?

And what did the bastard want for himself? Until Carling knew these answers, he couldn't control Edward Reed.

To grab control from Reed, Carling needed all the facts as soon as possible. So far he wasn't doing that well. The deputy director looked down at the blurred photo of a man . . . head half turned away . . . taken by the CIA watcher in San Juan before he lost Reed and this stranger. They'd checked this face against all their files. No match. Carling wanted to show it to the British, French and Israeli intelligence agencies but he didn't have the nerve to run that risk.

He wasn't desperate enough. Not yet.

He was trying just about everything else. Reed's home and office phones were being tapped, and there was a hidden transponder in his car to permit radio tracking. All his home and office mail . . . paper and electronic . . . and every computer use and his appointments had been closely monitored since the day Carling learned of the goddam Spirit Team.

Zero.

Surveillance around the clock. Nothing.

Records of five years of bank transactions, appointments and phone calls offered no leads. The only odd thing found was that Reed had reduced his credit card use and stopped making long distance or international calls on his home telephone three years and ten months ago . . . about when he said he began work on the Spirit Team.

He must have anticipated just such a scrutiny, and made the calls on other phones. Not near his house, of course. He knew the tradecraft, Carling reflected. Reed had handled the stolen funds equally warily. Where the hell was the money?

Of equal importance was how did Reed break into the supposedly impregnable computer system to get it. The Agency had to know so the hole could be plugged. If Carling could solve the theft and recover the money, he'd be safe. They'd put back every dollar recovered . . . add funds to match what he had already spent . . . so there'd be no trace it ever happened. They'd cover their tracks as thoroughly as Reed had after he built his Spirit Team.

What Spirit Team? A dozen of the Agency's shrewdest security investigators and top computer experts had checked and cross-checked and rechecked . . . and found no clue as to whom he'd recruited or when or how.

Or how much he'd stolen. It must be millions. Five? Ten?

The White House and Congress would go ballistic if they found out there had been multiple diversions of big sums over several years and nobody had noticed. This was the threat that egomaniac Reed, smugly confident that no one could touch him, held like a loaded gun. He'd made that subtly but definitely clear at a second meeting in which he'd reported about ongoing satellite sweeps.

Reed was trying to intimidate the Agency, Carling thought, but that was a two-way street. Now it was time for the Agency to push back. For three days Carling had been considering such a counterattack, an escalating program of step-by-step intimidation proposed by one of his senior staff. If Carling was going to seize the initiative, he could hardly wait any longer.

The deputy director picked up his phone, and dialed the aide's private line. Aware that the conversation was being recorded Carling spoke circumspectly.

"I agree with your suggestion about temperature control," he said. "We *should* turn up the heat."

"I'll speak to the janitor," the senior staff man replied.

Neither of the men he talked to in his office thirty-five minutes later was a janitor. They lacked the important skills of that honorable trade, but they had other talents. Carling's aide told the two field agents precisely where and how to apply them.

As they left the Old Headquarters Building with their tools, the deputy director was staring once more at the photo taken in San Juan. Even though it offered less than a full face view of the person with Reed, Carling could see that the stranger had the strong regular features of a handsome man and the look of clear confidence in his eyes.

He also had the moves of a professional, according to the watcher's report. He'd broken Reed free of the surveillance swiftly and expertly, slipping away with the effortless grace of someone who'd done it many times before.

Who was this stranger, Carling wondered once more.

Was he one of Reed's "dead" mercenaries?

Was there any Spirit Team at all?

17

David Lloyd wasn't an easy person to stop.

He never had been, which was a key reason Reed selected him to command the strike force . . . and codenamed him Brandy. Brandy had strength, style, and staying power.

The fact that he didn't know the location of the target did not prevent him from moving ahead exactly as he'd planned. They'd seen the entire cassette twice and discussed it. Now it was time to prepare for *insertion*. To some people the word had a sexual connotation . . . to others it was medical. There was a third meaning for the military and cloak and dagger communities.

Insertion . . . a typical bit of jargon that seemed ordinary to staff officers and intelligence paper pushers . . . meant putting a force of one or a thousand in some tricky place. If the force was not destroyed, there was another clinical and slightly pompous term that came into play in this weird game . . . extraction. Using this sort of fine language made all concerned feel scientific, well-educated and upscale in defense departments around the world . . . and, to be fair, in legislatures and insurance companies too.

Lloyd's immediate problem was neither linguistic nor sociological.

He needed to begin at the beginning by making a believable lie, a cover story that would permit insertion of the Spirit Team into Madesh . . . it goddam had to be Madesh, his reason and instincts said . . . without arousing suspicion.

"Now let's talk about a good *legend,*" he told the others, and they recognized the KGB term for false identity or cover story.

Josephine Tan wondered why he'd used this word.

Was it casual trade talk, or was he telling them something?

"Unless someone has a better idea," Lloyd continued, "I think we might enter as a video crew doing a respectful documentary . . . Fifty-two wonderful minutes on the historic sites and natural beauties of the target region."

"Where's that?" Mendoza asked.

"All in good time, my friend."

"Don't you trust me?" Mendoza challenged with a grin.

"I don't even trust your grandmother," the team leader replied truthfully.

Mendoza smiled again, glanced at her legs once more and nodded.

"A video crew moves with a van full of cameras and other equipment," the Nigerian thought aloud. "We might be able to conceal our weapons in among that gear by camouflaging them. Is that what you have in mind, sir?"

"Yes," Lloyd answered.

"And crews are often multinational," she noted approvingly. "I've seen them on fashion shoots . . . TV commercials . . . music videos too. We wouldn't seem that unusual."

"Now the question of who's funding this," Lloyd said. "If we're looking for a low profile, we must be totally minor and non-threatening. No link with any major power or any regime with international ambitions . . . no ties to any country that might run a covert intervention in some place smaller or weaker. That means the firm employing this multinational freelance crew can't be American, Russian, British, Chinese or even French."

"What do you suggest?" the Moroccan asked.

"Ireland. The peaceful and low-power Republic of Ireland which has historic castles and excellent drink but neither the money nor the muscle to play the world game," Lloyd answered.

"Green fields . . . fine tweeds and writers . . . but no aggression at all," she agreed.

"And a small army always ready to help in UN peacekeeping forces," the Nigerian soldier added. "Decent people."

"Whom nobody fears," the Spirit Team leader said, "and hardly anyone notices. We'll be working for a small film and TV production house in Dublin. It's a low cost operation that does a job now and then for the government tourist office or RTE . . . that's Irish Radio and Television . . . and for Swedish and Dutch stations."

It fit, she thought. Sweden and Holland were non-threatening too.

"If someone checks, I assume it's there," the Moroccan said.

"Has been for eight years," Lloyd answered, "and the owner's all right. He's always been good at keeping his mouth shut, and for three thousand pounds he'll be even better."

"Give him five thousand," Mendoza urged.

David Lloyd shook his head.

"Then he'd know that something very big and important was on," the team leader explained, "and that might not be healthy for anyone."

Turning to the pragmatic details of the fake video operation, Lloyd guided the Spirits into a discussion of which of them would be best for what role in the crew. The woman had expertise in handling eavesdropping and other electronic equipment, so she'd do the sound work. The slim Moroccan had done considerable videotaping of buildings he planned to burgle and the areas around them . . . planning his escape routes. He'd handle the camera. The Nigerian who had an intelligent, meticulous and practical mind, would be in charge of supplies and concealing their armaments. Mendoza, who could drive or repair everything from a Ferrari to a Harley bike to an armored personnel carrier, was both "Transport" and the Production Manager.

"I suppose *you're* the producer," Mendoza said to Lloyd.

"Absolutely. Divine right of kings," the team leader replied briskly. "If you want your half a million, you'll do exactly what I say, laddy. It'll also improve your chances of going home in a sports car instead of a body bag."

"I'd like that," Mendoza answered.

"So would I," Lloyd said. "You're a very talented chap, Mr. Mendoza. It would be a crime to waste all those gifts."

Yielding to the compliment and public approval as Lloyd had guessed he would, Mendoza decided that the team leader was both clever and insightful. And under those Brit manners he was tempered steel. That would come in handy too.

"About the weapons, sir," the veteran African soldier began.

"Next on the agenda. Very important," Lloyd assured him and looked past him at the clock on the sideboard. The team leader was relieved to see that he didn't have to end this abruptly. He still had nineteen minutes.

"We'll be acquiring both personal and team weapons quite *soon*," he announced. *Soon* was a nice flexible word . . . an elastic one with enough stretch to deal with the fact he didn't know when the target location would come.

"Since you've all got plenty of field experience in using US and British arms as well as Sov block hardware captured or stolen," he continued, "we should have no trouble in procuring high quality weapons. List both Western and Soviet weapons in each category . . . handguns, automatic weapons, sniper rifles, launchers, night vision gear and anything else."

Now he looked at the Eurasian woman.

"Write down all your needs in electronic and radio gear," he said. "We have ample resources. Whatever you want, you'll get."

He seemed completely cool and confident.

Edward Reed certainly wasn't either.

He'd just heard that other "customers" in the US defense establishment were pressuring the satellite people for the services of their eyes-in-the-sky. Those other intelligence organizations hadn't been told about Barcelona Delta and the slaughter in the Torat Valley, and they wanted their time on the satellites schedule for other missions.

Reed had used the satellite for thirteen sweeps.

All came up empty.

By bluffing . . . blustering . . . begging, he'd won clearance for two more. If they failed, he'd have to try to cover the 173,000 square miles of the Republic of Madesh with ground operatives. That was a large area, and the Agency didn't have a lot of people in Madesh.

Even more threatening, it didn't have much time.

Time was becoming a bigger factor every day. The reports on Reed's desk were showing a steady reduction in the flow of scientific equipment for Barcelona Delta development into Madesh. According to General Sherman and the US Army's biological warfare experts, just about all the material needed to go forward with the fungus had already reached Madesh.

Wherever the lab was, it would soon be ready for production.

How soon?

And where would Pariah strike?

18

9:20 the next morning . . . in a large hole in the ground.

It was the heavily guarded and blastproof Command Bunker under Fozira's presidential palace.

"Delivery project status," General Hassan ordered bluntly as the daily intelligence briefing began.

Colonel Malik eyed the notes on his clipboard before he started to report of how the weapon would reach the enemy.

"Our meteorologist confirms that wind patterns will be at their optimum for this operation from four to nine weeks from now," the head of the State Security Bureau said. "Assuming that you're still ruling out delivery by aircraft—"

"I certainly am," Hassan broke in impatiently. "A plane or pilot can be traced. A flier can be made to talk. No, there can't be any possible link to us. It *has* to be ground delivery."

"Yes, Excellency," the colonel replied at once. "When the weather patterns are appropriate, effective ground delivery can be accomplished by three cannisters equipped with delayed-action triggers. The containers will be the size of and look like those pressurized cans of shaving cream."

"Locations?" Hassan demanded.

"Carefully selected, Excellency. In each of the three largest cities one cannister will be concealed-in-plain-sight at a place where the air currents should swiftly disperse the spores as soon as they're released."

Hassan nodded . . . about half an inch . . . in approval.

"Estimated casualties?" he asked.

"Between 1.1 and 1.3 million in the first twenty-four hours.

The total should be above 2.6 million by the end of the week."

"What about the men who place the cannisters and set the timers?" the Supreme Leader for Life demanded.

"They'll be out of the country several hours before the spores are released," Colonel Salik assured him.

"And what's to prevent them from talking?"

"They're *our* people, Your Excellency," the State Security chief reminded.

"They're *our* people *now*," Hassan said, "but as soon as they're out of the country I want them to be *dead* people. Is that *clear?*"

The surprised colonel froze . . . absorbed . . . adjusted . . . and swallowed.

"Completely, Your Excellency. I'll take care of it myself," he vowed.

That was fine with Fozira's absolute ruler.

"Then we can proceed with the briefing," Hassan told him.

The "site situation report" was next. Almost all the equipment was in place, and work would resume within a few days.

"Around the clock," Hassan said. "Well, as soon as possible . . . without compromising safety. We don't want another mistake by tired people . . . How are they?"

"The Americans?"

"They're the key to the project," the general replied tartly.

"They seem to be all right, Your Excellency. The fifty-percent pay increase had a very good effect on the six who escaped from the valley in time," Salik reported. "They're not talking much anymore about the other two who died in the accident. They're saying the dead ones caused the accident themselves."

"Anything else?"

"They're not talking about all those dead Madeshi either, Your Excellency."

"They're thinking about money . . . not people," Hassan told him. "It's a common attitude in many countries."

The head of the State Security Bureau nodded in loyal agree-

ment . . . completed the briefing on three other intelligence operations . . . and departed. As soon as he was gone, Hassan moved
on to his second essential ritual. Like senior diplomats and chiefs
of state in half the nations on earth, he had his own satellite dish
and watched the world news on CNN at least once a day.

No one else in Fozira had such a dish.

It was a crime for anybody else to own one.

Whoever said knowledge is power was right, Hassan thought
as he turned on the set. He immediately grinned.

A massive car bomb outside the Iraqi embassy in Lisbon had
killed the building and nineteen employees including the ambassador. Looking at the devastation and corpses being carried
from the burning shell, Hassan was delighted.

Ignoring the sounds of the police and fire engine sirens pouring from the television set, the homicidal and virtuous ruler of
Fozira was confident that the false rumors he'd planted about the
recent Swiss affair had led the Iranians to "retaliate" against the
Iraqis . . . whom they hated anyway.

Everything pointed to the Iranians, Hassan reflected. After all,
car bombs were among the favorite weapons of the assorted
groups of pious terrorists funded by the zealots in Teheran. He'd
deal with them too in due course. He'd show them what *real* violence was.

Now the broadcast moved on to an account of the latest fam-
ine and civil war in central Africa, a subject of little interest to
Hassan. Since he despised the blacks . . . except in meetings with
foreign diplomats and gullible journalists . . . his attention moved
on too.

While images of starving children filled the screen, he thought
again about the half dozen US scientists on his payroll. The Supreme Leader for Life of the people, armed forces, oil wells, shift-
ing dunes and aggressive sand fleas of Fozira would soon be rid
of them.

But no one else could have them.

Even if they retired into obscurity it would be much too dangerous. Out of six, one or more would surely babble or try to blackmail him.

Sooner or later it would come to that.

That's why they had to die sooner . . . as soon as the laboratory had produced and packaged enough of the fungus for this operation . . . and, to provide for future contingencies, two more.

Maybe three.

19

David Lloyd had never been a morbid person.

Yet on the following afternoon he drove into downtown Athens just to read about death in a London newspaper.

Not even a recent death.

The Spirits were getting restless waiting, so he had to do this. He pulled up beside a newspaper kiosk that stocked *USA Today,* the *International Herald Tribune* and several British dailies including the *Times.* He'd done this yesterday, and he'd do it tomorrow if necessary.

He bought a copy of the *Times,* put it down on the seat beside him and drove a mile from the kiosk before he pulled over to the curb and stopped the vehicle. He'd checked the rear view and side mirrors a dozen times since he purchased the newspaper. Now he did it again.

All clear. Probably.

He began to scan the paper but not for news. Not for editorials, columns, indignant letters, reports on the royal family or even obituaries. He was interested in the columns of paid In Memoriam listings honoring both the recently deceased and the long dead . . . some devoted to men who'd died fighting for King and country in World War II.

This remembering in print is one of the many foibles and quaint idiosyncracies that make the British interesting, a flash of the national heart of gold, the decency that accompanies the sometimes stiff upper lip. Lloyd wasn't considering either the soul or social conscience of his homeland as he carefully read the In Memoriams. He was looking for a message.

For a few moments his thoughts shifted to his dead wife. No one was buying dignified advertisements to honor *her* memory. She wouldn't have wanted it. He couldn't do it anyway. It might be dangerous, for there could be enemies still looking for him.

Almost anything he did . . . ordinary things that ordinary people did casually every day . . . might be dangerous. Even with the new face and fingerprints, he might not be completely safe. "This is insane," he told himself, "and I'm not." He went back to reading the In Memoriams.

There it was.

Flight Leader D. V. Cuthbert, Royal Air Force . . . shot down over Hamburg . . . April 20, 1944 . . . had not been forgotten by his loving sisters Gillian and Elizabeth.

This was what Lloyd had been hoping for, and his heart beat faster. He might be on his way to his grave but at least the waiting was over. Lloyd drove back to the house in Piraeus, where he immediately assembled the Spirits in the livingroom. The slim Eurasian woman saw the smile in his eyes.

"Good news?" she guessed.

"The best. We are moving ahead," he announced cheerfully.

"Where?" Mendoza asked.

"On all fronts," Lloyd parried. "It is now time to acquire our weapons and other equipment. Check the lists you made. Last chance to add anything before I go shopping."

None of them asked where, for they understood he would have told them if he wanted to share that information. So they collected their lists, reread them and added one or two things before handing them to the team leader. He read each carefully, nodding as he recognized hardware he'd used or captured himself.

It wasn't that easy with her list.

He wasn't familiar with these items at all.

They were electronic, not explosive.

"I've got a problem," he told her quietly in a confidential tone. "Maybe you can help me."

"Of course, Monsieur," she replied.

"I assume that all these items are communications and listening gear," Lloyd said.

"All except the germ-proof suits," she answered.

"You're the only one who included them," the team leader said. "That was very thoughtful of you. Do you have any suggestions as to where I might buy them?"

He turned, forcing her to do that too . . . in a way that made it impossible for any of the others to hear or even read their lips.

He was as clever as he was handsome, she thought . . . and he treated her with respect. You could work with a man like this.

"I've never purchased such garments," she said, "but I know that Zurich has several biotech companies as well as the electronic supply stores I need. I *believe* you can get the suits in Zurich."

Zurich, that's where he had to make the pickup. What if he couldn't find some item on her list? He knew what to substitute for the weapons and combat equipment on the other lists, but his familiarity with field radios and basic SAS spike and wall microphones for listening into buildings occupied by terrorists wouldn't be enough if he had to buy some substitute for what she ordered.

Lloyd glanced at the window pane beside her, and saw Mendoza studying her again. It might be risky to leave her behind, the team leader thought.

"I'm going to need your expertise in buying your equipment or its equivalent," he told her. "I want you to come with me."

"Whenever you're ready," she answered.

"I'm ready now."

Then he turned to face the others again.

"Thank you for the lists," he said and held them up for a moment. "Miss Tan and I will be leaving within the hour."

"What about *us?*" Mendoza asked.

"You will gallantly hold the fort . . . under the command of Mr. Chibuku," the team leader announced. "Mr. Chibuku has considerable battlefield experience in commanding small units. We'll be back *shortly*."

He reached inside his jacket, drew out his wallet and extracted a half-inch thick wad of Greek currency.

"Here's the equivalent of three thousand dollars . . . a thousand each . . . of just-in-case money," he said to the Nigerian. "Consider this a safe house . . . an operations center. There's plenty of food in the house, and no reason to go out."

Chibuku was looking at him . . . listening intently.

Not only to the words . . . to the voice as well.

"No telephone calls or mail out, and no excursions to buy cigarettes or a newspaper either," Lloyd specified. "You take all incoming calls yourself. We can't afford any mistakes, and I know you won't make any."

"I'll do my best, sir," the dignified African soldier replied.

Lloyd started towards the doorway and saw the woman speaking with a smiling Mendoza. She was smiling too, and the strike force leader didn't like that. She was as intelligent as she was physically attractive. She ought to know enough to keep the man from Caracas at arm's length.

David Lloyd walked over to them.

"Half an hour. One bag," he announced bluntly.

She was packed and ready in twenty-three minutes. Mendoza was still smiling when she and the team leader departed in the blue BMW for the airport, and Samuel Chibuku was still considering Lloyd's voice.

In another time . . . in another place . . . he'd heard it before.

The Nigerian had a good memory as well as an excellent mind. He realized that it wouldn't be long . . . an hour . . . a day . . . a week at most before he recalled where and when. Then he'd know whom the team leader was/had been before he "died."

In certain hands, that information might get them all killed.

This time it would be for real.

20

Population: 363,000.

A city beside a seventeen-mile-long lake . . . a community scored by three rivers . . . a place of water.

Lenin lived here for years, and so did Einstein and Goethe. James Joyce sleeps nearby . . . restlessly no doubt . . . in Fluntern Cemetery. Composer and admirer Richard Wagner advised that "If you ever do retire, at least be so clever as to do it here."

David Lloyd and the woman who was now Josephine Tan were both clever, but they didn't fly to Switzerland's largest city to retire or see the sights either. They came to Zurich to shop for an assault and look at an extraordinarily expensive video.

They didn't know about the video as they got off the on-time-to-the-minute Swissair MD-81 jet from Athens at Zurich-Kloten Airport. That public facility was efficient and very clean, as was the train that carried them on the ten minute ride to the city's main and modern-with-all-conveniences railroad station.

Now the train slowed as the downtown rail terminal loomed ahead. She looked at him again for a moment. She hadn't spent enough time with this man to know him, but she'd learned some things about him. He was quick-minded, economical and purposeful . . . as a team leader should be. He didn't waste time or anything else. She liked that.

The train reached the station.

The Swiss are sensible and logical. The predominant tongue in the nation's economic and cultural center is German, and in that language *Bahnhof* means "rail terminal." When the team leader and Josephine Tan emerged from the bustling Bahnhof (the main one), they faced the Bahnhof Plats (Place). It was when he told the taxi driver to take them to the more than elegant Baur au Lac Hotel at the lake that she understood he (1) spoke flawless German, and (2) had taste and wasn't frugal.

Neither surprised her.

There'd be surprises later, she reflected as the cab moved from the Bahnhofplatz onto linden-lined Bahnhofstrasse—rail station street. Maybe sooner than later . . . there might be a surprise at any moment with this man. While too many men were . . . unfortunately . . . rather predictable, something about this one didn't seem to fit that mold.

Or any other she knew.

The traffic on Bahnhofstrasse . . . Zurich's Fifth Avenue, Rodeo Drive, Rue du Faubourg St. Honore and Ginza . . . was heavy. With only a few of the linden trees beginning to bloom, just a hint of the great sweet scent to come drifted in through the open taxi window beside her as she eyed the famed and fashionable stores of this celebrated shopping street.

She'd worked here on a modeling assignment, so she knew what to look for on this upscale artery. Once the cab passed the inevitable McDonalds . . . transatlantic totem of one fast world . . . she concentrated on the fine furs, luxury leathers, high style clothes, and jewelry in boutique windows. Even with the taxi going slowly she had to settle for glimpses.

She didn't pay much attention to the powerful banks . . . Swiss and foreign . . . nestled so discreetly among the retail-for-the-rich outlets. David Lloyd did. He studied the facades of these global financial giants carefully as he thought ahead to what he must do.

Suddenly he smiled.

He realized that he'd been . . . automatically and professionally . . . checking out the banks' defenses. He certainly hadn't come to rob a bank. He'd blown several vaults with assorted explosives in his career, but hadn't even thought about "doing" a bank since that assault in central Africa almost four years earlier.

More than forty-one million dollars in diamonds.

That's what they'd grabbed to prevent the local dictator from swapping the stones to European arms dealers. The bastard didn't get his tanks, and the tanks didn't roll over school children and other troublemakers.

Lloyd wasn't in Zurich to steal diamonds. He'd come to buy a book. The classy and classic Baur au Lac Hotel, which he'd phoned from the Athens airport, was luxurious, but Lloyd and his comrade-in-arms didn't do more than register . . . check into side-by-side rooms with a connecting door . . . unpack and hang up their clothes . . . before they were in another cab to a bookstore.

In the oldest section of the historic city . . . on In Gassen, a street paved with cobblestones . . . a bookstore named Daeniker's.

No, a "bookshop" according to the sign outside the 148-year-old outpost of works published in English. Lloyd and Josephine Tan were not here to browse but to purchase one particular volume.

"You say *The Scourge* by Thomas Dunne?" the bespectacled clerk asked.

"Thomas *L.* Dunne," Lloyd replied. "It's a novel."

"I'm not sure we have it, mein Herr, but I'll look."

The clerk was half right. The book had only been put on the fiction shelf the day before, and not by anyone who worked at Daeniker's. It took a few minutes for the puzzled clerk to study the price printed on the inner flap of the jacket . . . convert the dollars to Swiss francs . . . add the usual markup . . . and tell David Lloyd what he owed. As the team leader reached for his wallet, he saw Josephine Tan was turning the pages of a splendidly illustrated volume on Alpine flowers. There was pleasure in her eyes.

"May I get it for you?" he said. "Birthday present?"

"My birthday's not till July."

"The fourteenth. Bastille Day. I know. No harm in being early, is there?"

The surprises were beginning.

Why, she wondered, and wished she knew more about him.

She thanked Lloyd, and he paid for both books. It was a short walk from the shop to the outside cafe of the Zeughauskeller, one of Zurich's landmark restaurants. As soon as they'd ordered espresso and pastries, he excused himself and made his way to a booth in the men's toilet.

With the novel.

The inside of the back of the hardcover book was covered in fine blood-red paper. That was appropriate, the team leader thought while he took out his Swiss Army knife and used it to cut-peel off a piece of that crimson lining.

It was there. Working very carefully with the blade, he extracted the rectangle of deposit . . . the ticket he needed for the next step.

The coffee was excellent, and the ample pastries were highly caloric and delicious. The Swiss did excess so well without any of the errors of Beverly Hills or Tokyo, she reflected as she delicately applied the cloth napkin to her perfect lips without smearing the just right lipstick.

Next stop: the Bahnhof.

They could have walked the half mile, but a sense of urgency pushed Lloyd to flag a taxi. When they entered the rail station, the team leader guided her directly to the "left luggage" counter. There Lloyd gave a round shouldered functionary the claim check extracted from the back of the novel. Some fifty-five seconds later, Lloyd accepted a small and grey Samsonite suitcase that had been left the previous afternoon.

Not by a man or woman who knew David Lloyd.

Not by anyone who had the slightest idea of what was in the bag.

That didn't matter. What did was that *it* . . . whatever it was

. . . was happening. She could tell by the look in his eyes . . . by the way he held the handle of the hard-sided piece of luggage. She saw that it had a combination lock with numbers to be dialed. He'd know them, she told herself as another taxi carried them back to the elegant hotel.

His room . . . the suitcase rested on the coffee table.

Lloyd didn't know the combination, but he realized that the person who'd locked the piece of luggage was challenging him to reason it out somehow. It had to be the clever, devious and more than a bit arrogant man he'd last seen in San Juan. This was the sort of petty brain game he might enjoy.

That was an accurate estimate of the man who'd created the Spirit Team all right. Reed had hummed as he thought it would take the team leader at least half an hour and considerable tension to work out the answer . . . or give up and break the suitcase open by force. If Lloyd found the combination, that would confirm Reed's wisdom in picking him. If Lloyd didn't, the failure would identify Reed as the more cunning.

Eyeing the lock, David Lloyd sensed that the combination must be right under his nose. The odd father of the Spirit Team could not help playing games. The strike force commander considered . . . dialed three numbers . . . and pressed the catch.

It opened.

"Your birth date?" she asked.

"*Very* good, Mademoiselle," he complimented. "That's what half the world uses, and so obvious it would appeal to our founder."

"The dear Mr. White?"

"He told me his name was Green," Lloyd replied and raised the lid of the suitcase.

Contents: assorted and female.

Women's undergarments . . . running shoes, high heeled pumps and furry slippers . . . a makeup case and a plastic bag full of toilet articles . . . a week-old copy of *The Economist* . . . three blouses and four pair of sheer pantyhose . . . a pair of black silk slacks . . . a folded map of Paris . . . anti-allergy pills . . . a diaphragm in its plastic case . . . a videocassette titled *How to Tango* . . . a half-empty box of facial tissues . . . a short leather skirt . . . vibrator wand . . . and a paperback novel whose cover promised low bodices and high passion.

She scanned it twice . . . then looked at Lloyd.

He smiled pleasantly.

"Let's dance," the team leader said and picked up the cassette.

He put it in the VCR . . . used the remote control to start it . . . and sat back. Sensuous Latin American music came up as the opening credits appeared over a series of panoramic views of Buenos Aires, scenic capital of Argentina and the tango world. After half a minute of this predictable preamble, a good-looking man and woman in evening clothes blossomed on the screen.

Late thirties . . . lots of teeth . . . they appeared and sounded Hispanic. They danced . . . very well . . . for a few moments before they began to explain the glamorous history and romantic philosophy of the tango . . . the "magical" soul of the tango . . . and the first steps.

They were good teachers, and the music was hard to resist.

Six . . . seven . . . eight minutes of tango tutoring followed.

She saw that he was watching and listening very carefully, and wondered whether there was some coded message in the steps or melody. She didn't know that he was considering the same question as his head and shoulders moved in time with the syncopated surges.

It happened abruptly.

In four seconds everything changed.

The dancers vanished. There was no music.

Silence. The screen was filled with aerial views of a hilly, almost mountainous area. David Lloyd nodded. He recognized the place where so many blue corpses had been strewn.

Now three words jumped onto the screen.

TWO VALLEYS—EAST.

The broad aerial scan of the valley beside the Torat changed to a much tighter picture of a smaller area. There was something growing from or built at the base of what was a tall hill or low mountain. A narrow road led right to it.

Freeze frame.

Lloyd instantly stopped the cassette so they might study what the "something" was. He stared . . . puzzled . . . stared again. Then he recognized it.

"As your friend Mr. Mendoza might say, *Holy shit!*" David Lloyd declared.

"He's not my friend," she answered in a matter-of-fact tone. "Just somebody from the office. *Why* would Mr. Mendoza say that?"

"Because what's sticking out there shouldn't be there. It's the rear half of a bloody lorry . . . *camion* in French . . . *truck* in American. That's our target," he exulted and pointed. "That's it! We've found the fucking laboratory!"

"I didn't know it was lost," she said.

"Mislaid," he replied with a smile.

"It's inside the mountain?"

"Or under it. Some sort of preexisting installation. They couldn't dig it out and get it ready in a month or two," the team leader reasoned. "They probably only move the trucks in at night. I guess they don't expect invisible visitors with infrared cameras," the team leader told her.

She'd seen that the images were from above . . . high altitude . . . but she didn't even say the word "satellite." That would mean an unnecessary risk, so she simply pointed up. Lloyd shrugged, started the video player again and looked at another seventy-five seconds of the pictures taken by the spy-in-the-sky. Then the dancers were back . . . the music was throbbing once more . . . and David Lloyd stopped the machine.

"I have a question," she announced.

"I hope you're not going to ask where that valley is," he responded and began to rewind the cassette.

"Wouldn't think of it. If you were going to tell me, you'd have done it by now," she said and crossed her legs again. "I just wanted to mention that this charming hotel has three excellent restaurants, and to ask whether you'd mind dining in one to-night."

"Fine. How about the Restaurant Français off the lobby?"

"That's the one I had in mind."

Heads turned and blasé Swiss waiters smiled in appreciation when she walked into the salmon-colored dining room of the Restaurant Français with Lloyd a dozen minutes later. She smelled as fine as she looked, the team leader thought. He considered asking her what the special perfume was, but decided that might be too personal.

He couldn't afford that even if he wanted to, Lloyd realized. Arm's length and professional would be safer for all of them. That practical wisdom guided him as they were seated . . . ordered and sipped aperitifs . . . spoke about the fine restaurants and wines of Switzerland. It didn't surprise her that he knew a good deal about both.

The service and food that followed were refined and flawless, and the bottle of crimson Valois they shared left a warm glow within them. The colorless Kirsch liqueur that followed dessert kept the embers alive until they said good night at her door.

And afterwards.

She still felt it as she undressed. Standing straight and nude before the full length mirror, she thought about this strike force leader who wasn't like any other she'd met. The others . . . even the homosexual ones . . . had flirted with or pursued her. This man gave her a book on mountain flowers, and talked about Zurich museums instead of himself. She wasn't used to men who didn't speak about themselves.

Or tell her how pretty she was. She *knew* . . . she sensed it in her mind and body . . . that he was aware she was a woman. There was no sign that he was shy or scared or preferred men, but he'd said good night without the slightest effort to come close or kiss her.

Not that she was either aroused or offended. No, she was curious about this worldly, wary, almost surely dangerous man who said he was James Trager. He was actually good looking too, she realized.

What else was he?

Ten yards away in his room, he took off his clothes and put the jacket and trousers on hangers in the closet. He did the hands, face and teeth things in the bathroom . . . used the toilet . . . made his way to the bedroom and pulled back the covers. He turned out the light, got into bed and closed his eyes.

His mind moved to what had to be done the next day.

He carefully shaped an agenda . . . planned a route and schedule.

He went over it again, considering the priorities and dangers.

Then . . . quite suddenly and for no apparent reason . . . he found himself wondering about her perfume again.

He was still thinking about it when he fell asleep.

21

A crisp Swiss morning.

A fresh breeze was sweeping in off the lake . . . not a rain cloud in sight . . . a fine spring day. As they walked out the hotel's front door, she saw he had the look of a man who was en route . . . who was going somewhere to do something he'd planned.

Refreshed by a good night's sleep, she scanned the sun-dappled mountains on the horizon before she glanced at her gold wristwatch.

"9:40 A.M., and the war is on again," she said.

"It never stopped," he replied and nodded towards the main shopping street. Even with pausing to study window displays as did the buying-minded crowd around them, the stroll to the hunting and sporting-climbing gear establishment off the bustling Bahnhofstrasse took only eighteen minutes.

Their purchasing in this store required a minute less than that. Going down the list created by the Moroccan cat burglar and adding items on the basis of his own SAS assault training and no-holds-barred mountain combat experience, the team leader bought everything that seven climbers would need to ascend rock or ice . . . in duplicate. Clothing . . . ropes . . . climbing spikes and shoes . . . he had all their sizes, and the extra two sets were to camouflage the size of their group.

Deception came easy to him. He had a lot of experience, and it was automatic now . . . a reflex like breathing. They both kept him alive.

Now he took out his wallet. The sales clerk . . . half-bald but all-knowing about climbing and mountain gear . . . beamed as

Lloyd paid him in British fifty-pound notes. He was equally cheery when the team leader mentioned an imaginary Greek climbing team, gave the Athens address of a freight forwarding firm and handed over more fifty-pound notes for the air cargo charges.

"Anything else, mein Herr?" the conscientious vendor tested with the eternal optimism of sales folk around the galaxy.

Lloyd surveyed the shop abstractedly . . . "discovered" the racks of hunting rifles and shotguns . . . and pointed at them.

"A present for my brother," he declared enthusiastically.

There were nine different shotguns, and David Lloyd didn't think it would be discreet to reveal he wasn't interested in all the various features of each. He needed a self-defense weapon . . . this morning . . . and a shotgun was the easiest one he could acquire legally.

He would be . . . within the hour . . . in a potentially dangerous situation. A rifle wouldn't do, since it was best for distance shooting. If someone were to attack him, it would be from up close. He needed a weapon that required no government permit, and would do a lot of damage at short range. He picked out his shotgun.

It was an Italian weapon . . . big bore and 12-gauge . . . a semi-automatic model that carried six rounds. This wasn't exactly a refined weapon for a serious hunter . . . rather an expensive gadget for nouveau riche blasters. He didn't plan to blast anybody for that would instantly arouse police attention, but he'd shoot if he had to.

Swiftly and expertly. He knew a dozen shotguns well.

"Hugo will love it," Lloyd told her as the salesman listened, "and I think I'll treat myself to a new fly-rod case."

"You need it," she concurred as she wondered what he planned to do with the case. He wasn't about to explain, she guessed calmly.

He didn't. It took him several minutes to find the one fly-rod case in the shop that was big enough for the shotgun. They were wrapped separately, as was the box of two-inch shells. After the salesman gave Lloyd the three purchases and his very correct thanks, the team leader reciprocated just as properly and guided her out to the street.

He took a sheet of paper from his jacket pocket, scanned the rest of his schedule. First they bought a sturdy canvas shoulder-bag . . . the kind airlines used to give to first class passengers. He didn't say why. Next they made their way to the other bank of the river, found the modern building that housed an assort-ment of medical and scientific equipment companies and as-cended to the third floor offices and showroom of Hochsteller & Strunk.

Biological and bacteriological research gear was the major concern of this respected seventy-one-year-old firm. Money was also of genuine interest. This became clear when Carla Hoch-steller . . . a direct and well-nourished descendant of one of the founding partners . . . quoted a rather high price for ten sealed-and-bacteria-proof lab suits.

Of the best quality, of course.

Anything less could be *inadequate,* she explained.

She was too genteel to say *fatal.*

It was soon agreed that the required ten top-of-the-line suits would be boxed and ready when the two "doctors from Singa-pore" returned at 4:45 P.M. with an impressive number of Swiss francs. Josephine Tan was certainly impressed by the price. Lloyd was already thinking about where they had to go now.

The hotel. He still hadn't explained the fly-rod case when they entered his room. It was immediately show and tell time. Both surprised her. He unwrapped the three packages, and loaded a full complement of shells into the shotgun. He zipped open the fly-rod case, slipped the shotgun inside and tugged the zipper closed.

There was no visible sign of a gun inside.

Surprise.

Then he carefully felt the case until he located the gun's trigger . . . took out his Swiss Army knife . . . pulled out the scissors and cut a narrow slice in the fabric on either side of the trigger guard.

Surprise.

"I'm going to need a weapon very soon," he said, "and a pistol permit is out of the question."

"But no country requires a permit for shotguns," she reasoned.

"Exactly. I not only need a weapon," he continued, "but I want to conceal it and I must be able to use it at once if we're attacked."

"So you camouflage it as a fishing rod, and cut those small tears so you can just slip a finger in and fire. That's not bad, Mr. Trager."

"I have my moments," he replied wryly, "but you don't have your electronic gear yet. Shall we?"

He took the fly-rod case and the shoulder bag with him. She thought they were going to buy her equipment but they went to a bank instead. It definitely wasn't a place that offered consumer loans or gave out calendars at Christmas. This was much too serious and businesslike for that.

A Swiss bank with international clients . . . ten billion dollars in assets. Dignified . . . efficient . . . low key . . . discreet, like the other Swiss banks on either side of it on the Bahnhofstrasse. The neatly dressed staff wore dark clothes . . . spoke softly . . . and asked very few questions. They did their work well, and they obeyed the law.

Very reliable. Very sensible. Very Swiss.

The team leader had obviously been here before. He led her to the elevator that took them to the second floor where Herr Frohlich's office was located. The dark wood furniture was nicely upholstered. So was Herr Frohlich.

"Good to see you, mein Herr," the bank executive said.

A man of fine Swiss tact and manners, he didn't address the team leader by name. It might not be the one that the woman with him knew, or the one the client used in his home town. The great majority of the clients had but one name, but some . . . for various reasons . . . didn't.

"It's a pleasure to be here in this civilized city," Lloyd responded with mechanical courtesy. "This is my cousin, Herr Frohlich."

The banker declared it was an honor to meet her, and hoped she'd enjoy her stay in Zurich. The client hadn't mentioned her name, and Frohlich didn't inquire. It was not unusual for clients to arrive with comely young women who were cousins, nieces, administrative assistants, tax accountants or personal trainers. Frohlich never asked for their names either. He simply hoped that they'd all have an enjoyable stay in Zurich.

"We had a dreary flight," Lloyd lied and guided her to a couch along the wall. Then he strode to a chair beside Frohlich's desk near the window. It would be difficult for her to hear their conversation, the banker thought and admired his client's prudence.

"At least Zurich won't be boring," Lloyd said. "If you've got a minute," he continued, "I'd like to check on my *nine* account . . . get a balance . . . make a withdrawal."

He had two accounts. The one whose number started with a nine he'd created for money from Reed. The other account . . . the seven account . . . was older, and he didn't necessarily want Reed to know about it. Now Frohlich cleared his throat, and Lloyd gave him his passport . . . the one with the same name as the nine account . . . for identification.

Next Frohlich offered and the team leader signed a withdrawal slip. The fine dark wood furniture in the office was not modern, but the computer on the table beside Frohlich's desk was the latest model. The banker tapped several buttons . . . saw the client's signature . . . compared it to the ones on the passport and withdrawal slip.

Perfect match. This was part of the bank's procedures, all of which Rudolph Frohlich revered. Then he pressed other buttons on the computer keyboard, and the nine account balance was on screen. Frohlich carefully wrote the number on a page from his desk pad, and silently handed the piece of paper to the client.

The number was larger than what Lloyd expected.

There had been another deposit.

The number, which included that wire transfer from Monte Carlo yesterday, was in Swiss francs. In US dollars, the total in the account was now $3,492,100.

They had just put in three million dollars. That deposit was both money and message. It said that this assault was important, and must succeed. At what cost, the team leader thought and mentally "saw" the bloody corpses he'd faced at the end of his previous mission . . . and the one before that . . . ruined bodies of friend and foe.

This was no time for reflection. It would blur his focus.

How much should he take from the account . . . right now . . . to prepare for the assault on the goddam laboratory? He had only a general plan, but two things were certain. Getting out of Madesh would be infinitely more difficult and dangerous than entering . . . and he'd better bring more cash than he could imagine he'd need because there were always unanticipated problems and contingencies.

Three million . . .? No, he'd go with $3,300,000.

He pointed at the withdrawal slip. When Frohlich handed it to him, Lloyd calculated what $3,300,000 would be in Swiss francs and wrote that figure in the appropriate place on that form. He returned it to the banker.

"How would you like this, mein Herr?" Frohlich asked in the placid tone of someone quite accustomed to large withdrawals and deposits.

"Cash," the strike force leader replied.

In four different currencies.

All hard and widely accepted around the world.

Lloyd wrote more numbers on the slip of paper beneath the balance. These figures specified how much in Swiss francs . . . British pounds . . . German marks . . . American dollars. Then he put on the desk the shoulder bag. The banker understood immediately. It would have to be hundred-pound notes . . . hundred-dollar bills . . . all four currencies in significant dimensions so the whole $3,300,000 would fit in the bag.

It didn't.

"No problem, as the Americans would say," the banker announced pleasantly. Other clients had faced similar questions, so there were plain black attache cases . . . high quality plastic ones from Indonesia that looked like leather . . . and the bank would be happy to present one . . . a small souvenir of Zurich.

A gift . . . without the bank's name or any other identification. One must respect the security and privacy of clients.

As Lloyd packed the money, Frohlich glanced over at the very attractive niece seated near the door. A stunning woman . . . the kind respectable middle-aged ministers ran away from home for, the Swiss banker told himself. They'd be foolish, but they wouldn't be wrong.

What was she holding? It looked like a fly-rod case.

David Lloyd closed the case and the shoulder bag, thanked Frohlich and picked up the two money containers. They were not light, but that obviously didn't bother him at all. Admiring this fit and handsomely tanned client . . . and envying him for the cousin . . . the banker walked with Lloyd to the door.

She stood up, and he handed her the shoulder bag. In exchange she gave him a smile that wasn't cousinly and the fly-rod case. Now she put the bag over her shoulder. She seemed to be quite fit too.

"If there's anything else I can do," Frohlich said.

"Any thoughts on fishing places?" Lloyd asked.

Frohlich suggested two locations less than thirty miles from Zurich, and Lloyd thanked him again.

"Do you fish too, Fräulein?" the banker asked courteously.

"It's my passion," she answered.

"I wish you both good sport," Frohlich said, "and a fine visit to Switzerland."

"Why didn't you tell me fishing is your passion?" Lloyd joked as they left the building.

"I have *many* passions, Mr. Trager," she fenced slyly, "and I don't usually talk about them to strange men."

Then she asked the question.

"The video and the money? *That's* why we came here, *n'est-ce pas?*"

"You've just won lunch at the restaurant of your choice," he answered.

She chose the Zunfthaus zur Zimmerleuten . . . but she also chose to buy her electronic gear first at two establishments she knew. Then they proceeded to the restaurant for first-class chateaubriand steaks with perfect baby vegetables, splendidly sinful chocolate souffles and excellent coffee. No alcohol. It might cost him two or three seconds when he couldn't afford even one.

She saw his hand stray to the encased shotgun beside him.

He didn't look at it, and he wasn't thinking about it. He didn't have to, she realized. His body and mind . . . fused in the fire of so many assaults and ambushes . . . would respond automatically . . . and correctly. This man wouldn't shoot unnecessarily, she thought, and when he did he wouldn't miss.

He was treating her . . . and the other Spirits . . . correctly too, listening while maintaining a distance. This man had manners but he didn't want to get close to people, she judged. Minimum target or something else? she wondered as he paid the bill.

"We've got time for a walk before we pick up the suits," he said as they left the restaurant. "Let's go to Hell."

She understood, and she approved.

Some twenty minutes later they faced Rodin's powerful "Gates of Hell" beside the front entrance of Zurich's noted Kunsthaus museum, the big "art house" on Heimplatz. They studied the dramatic bronze . . . portal to Hades and the figures of the condemned . . . considering the nightmare-masterpiece silently for several minutes before they continued to the Hochsteller & Strunk showroom.

They were both in good spirits when Lloyd paid for the germ-proof suits and shipping charges to send them as air cargo to a freight forwarding company . . . not the one in Athens. This firm in the northern Greek city of Thessaloniki would receive the suits on behalf of a client whose name wasn't that of the buyer of climbing gear. Once readdressed, the protective clothing would go south by truck to the other forwarder in Athens.

There'd be no link between the two shipments.

Nothing to alert anyone . . . no easy paper trail to follow.

With the work in Zurich done . . . and without any desire to go around the city's streets at night with over three million dollars in cash, the strike force leader was content to play it safe this last night in Switzerland. They dined in their hotel. The duck breast in ginger sauce was rare and subtly flavored, and the maitre d' was much too gracious to say anything about the attache case, shoulder bag and tubular fly-rod case.

The good looking man with the stunning Eurasian woman had a slight British accent, the maitre d' reasoned, and the British were mad about fishing. This was one of their more charming eccentricities. It could be a mistake to suggest that the fly-rod case and other items be checked.

When Lloyd and Josephine Tan arrived at the airport the next morning, he didn't even think about boarding the Aer Lingus jet with the wrapped shotgun in hand. No country took the security of air passengers and planes more seriously, as metal detectors and body searches made clear. The shotgun was in his suitcase.

It came out after they cleared customs at the Dublin air terminal. Two exits . . . one marked red for those with something to declare . . . the other green for guiltless. Piece of cake. They cruised through . . . made their way to a pay telephone. Lloyd stepped close to make his call.

He held a coin in one hand.

The six-round shotgun—in its case—was in the other.

22

The appointment was for three in the chill, grey afternoon.

To be sure to be on time . . . it wouldn't do to be late to meet the Major . . . William Skelly left the offices of Brian Boru Video at half past two. Brian Boru was an ancient Irish king who fought the Vikings and some other Celts, and they killed him. It wasn't right, because he was praying in his tent at the time, but they did it.

The Irish have always had it hard.

The CEO of Brian Boru Video had endured his share of hard, and now had a glass left eye . . . a limp . . . several scars . . . and memories of dead comrades in arms slain in battle against "those fookin' lunatics." It was a generic term that covered terrorists of various nationalities, faiths, colors, politics, and sexual preferences.

He got to the shore of the Liffey . . . mother of foamy Guinness and a thousand poems by Ireland's abundant writers . . . and he turned left along the river bank as the Major had instructed. It wasn't simply that Skelly had been a lieutenant who always obeyed orders from superior officers. William Skelly, like everyone else in the Special Air Services regiment, took Major David Lloyd seriously.

He didn't see Lloyd watching him from the showroom-shop of Blarney Tweeds, but he knew that the Major would be scouting the Battlefield. Wherever the Major was, that was the Battlefield. Skelly sniffed the damp air, wondered when the damn sun would shine bright again and trudged on steadily.

Without sound . . . without warning . . . the Major was walking beside him. Skelly looked at the unfamiliar face. Lloyd saw the uncertainty in the Irishman's eyes.

"It's me, Billy . . . the same lad whose life you saved that black night in the airport assault," David Lloyd told him.

Skelly hadn't seen him approach. That was one of the things that the Major did well . . . suddenly being there beside friend or foe. It was beyond what the SAS training course had taught the elite commandos. Some kind of gift, Skelly judged.

There was something else Skelly didn't see.

A slim young woman was following them on the other side of the street. Following and watching . . . looking at them . . . beyond them . . . then behind them.

"Good to see you, Billy. How's it going?" Lloyd asked.

"Could be worse. This television's just as strange as our old trade, you know."

"And you meet a low class of people," the Major said.

"I'm used to that. The wife's a marvel though," he reported, "and now the damn leg only hurts when it rains."

"That's about four days a week here, right?"

"Five," Skelly corrected with a grin. "And you? Come over for some fishin'?"

He didn't . . . not for a second . . . believe that the fly-rod case sheathed fishing gear.

"That, and a new telly documentary," Lloyd answered. "I was wondering if you might help."

"Any way I can," Skelly said.

"You can . . . in more ways than one," Lloyd told him. "In fact, you already have. Don't you remember that you're producing a fifty-two-minute video on the scenic beauties, ancient culture and other wonders of Madesh?"

"It slipped my mind for a moment. Where the *hell* is Madesh?"

"Out east, Billy. *Marvelous* country . . . brave and noble people . . . beautiful mountains and mosques . . . all sorts of antiquities and exotic birds. Have you forgotten you're about to send out a fine crew to tape all this magic?" the strike force leader asked and handed him a slip of paper with the Spirits' cover names.

Skelly scanned it and nodded.

"That crew? Very capable professionals," he declared. "Capable of most anything, I'd guess."

"Anything and a half. It's all in your files, Billy."

Translation: make a file of fake documents to support this story with paperwork backdated three or four months.

"Anything else I can do?" Skelly asked as they neared the O'Connell Bridge.

"Well . . . if anyone should call to ask about this . . . you might explain it's just one of your documentary projects. Tell them *the truth.*"

"I always do."

Now Lloyd handed him a king-sized cigarette pack . . . empty of tobacco but filled with British hundred-pound notes.

"There's three thousand quid in there. Birthday present," David Lloyd told him. "All you have to do is what I've said. Keep it simple and basic. Don't get creative or spin elaborate stories. Oh, you *can* mention the Swedish client . . . it's in your file . . . that put up the money for the project."

Skelly nodded.

"You understand that this is a *private* thing, Billy. No connection with London."

His former comrade in arms nodded again.

"I realize that you may not have the time," Lloyd said. "If you're too busy with your work or family and can't do it, I'll understand."

It must be something grim, Skelly realized.

"I'll do it," he said and abruptly reverting to the old ways he glanced up and down the street for terrs . . . those bloody terrorists . . . or snipers . . . or God knows what.

Maybe God didn't, he thought.

Maybe God was too busy for this violent madness.

"There's a woman watching us," he told Lloyd.

"Hold your fire, Billy. She's on our side. Surprised you didn't spot her three blocks back."

Skelly shrugged.

"Maybe I'm out of practice," he said.

"Why shouldn't you be? You're out of the trade. One more thing," Lloyd said. "I'm arranging for you to get another birthday present . . . just like this one . . . if I can't deliver it myself."

If I'm dead.

"Jeezus," Lloyd sighed and put the cigarette pack in his pocket.

"Jeezus," agreed the Major. "Thanks for your help, Billy, and happy birthday."

"Happy birthday to you."

They shook hands, and Skelly saw him cross the street to join the woman. After he watched them walk away, William Skelly returned to his office where he looked up Madesh in his atlas. He ought to know where it was if somebody came or called to ask about this project and crew.

Who the hell was *somebody?*

It was probably better not to know.

23

So far . . . so good.

That's what Edward Reed thought as he systematically checked each drawer of his desk and file cabinet to make sure they were all locked. Then he engaged the security system on his computer, denying access to anyone without the three passwords.

It had been an ordinary day, he reflected as he locked the office door behind him. Some very devout people in Algeria had set off two bombs that killed sixty-three of their fellow citizens and maimed one hundred twenty-one others. Some patriotic young men in Afghanistan had fired eighteen mortar rounds and slain ninety-one other Afghans . . . the count on the mangled wasn't in yet. A couple of howitzer rounds in the former Yugoslavia had hit a school, making fifty-six children former human beings.

The body count was rising in the fierce fighting in one of the southern nations that cut loose from the USSR . . . the Myanmar Air Force had firebombed three rebel villages with fine results, mostly burned beyond recognition. Machetes were the weapon of choice in yesterday's tribal massacre of "about" eleven hundred in southern Africa.

To show their piety, some college students in Egypt had tried to murder the president. The more refined graduate students had attempted to disembowel a famous poet. That didn't bother Reed, who had considered poets pretentious since he was nine years old.

None of the bloodshed troubled Reed. Unlike many of his coworkers in the Agency, he wasn't concerned about other people. Edward Reed wasn't a co-anything. Aware this was unfashionable in the CIA's corporate culture, he hid that personality trait and got his reports in on time.

At precisely 5:50 P.M. he locked his office door behind him. Reed made a point of always leaving after the end of regular office hours. It caused those above him on the CIA food chain to see him as somebody who gave more than he had to . . . who really cared.

It was simple to fool them because they were simpletons, he thought as he made his way to the parking lot . . . simpletons like the security clods who'd followed him from his home this morning . . . who'd trail him now when he started his car. They belonged to the same group of simpletons who'd bugged the vehicle and his residence . . . who twice searched it clumsily so he'd notice and be afraid.

He wasn't the least bit intimidated, for he'd expected these moves and more. It was part of the Game. To play it well . . . to win . . . you had to project various scenarios, anticipate what the other players might do. Reed was determined to win everything. That had been his absolute principle since the second grade.

He knew that he'd win now . . . win big. He had to.

After all, he was smarter than Carling and the others and he had an ingenious plan. They were undoubtedly trying to figure it out, Reed thought as got into the car and carefully put on his seat belt. If . . . probably by luck . . . they did guess his plan, that would be no problem for Edward Reed. He had another plan, even more daring and dramatic.

That would definitely shake up small-minded Carter Carling.

It would really make the unimaginative deputy director of operations sweat.

Some 310 yards away, Carling was already perspiring.

It wasn't from his daily workout at lunch hour. It was raw fear.

He'd rehearsed . . . over and over . . . what he was about to do and say, and he was still sheeted with sweat. His throat was tight . . . his palms clammy.

He didn't want to do this. He should have done it sooner.

His sole goal had been the national interest.

Reed would probably say that too, Carling thought bitterly as he braced himself and entered the fine office of Sandra Jefferson Lynes. Sandy Lynes, who'd overcome the twin handicaps of a very rich father and a Princeton education, had later gone to the Harvard Law School with the President. *The* President, the one in the large white residence on Pennsylvania Avenue in swinging downtown Washington. Nine months ago she'd finished a decade as general counsel of the Air Force.

Gold-rimmed spectacles. Steel-trap mind. With the exception of congressional committees, she didn't suffer fools lightly. That's why this suite was jocularly called the Lynes Den. Since she had a quirky sense of humor in addition to three lovely children and a husband who collected radio stations, that phrase amused her.

Not much else did these days.

There were very few laughs in being Director of Central Intelligence. Noting the look on Carling's face, she realized that he wasn't going to add any. Cut right to the chase, her instincts told her.

"What's the problem, Carter?" she asked bluntly.

"Something has come up, and you ought to know about it. There's a policy question . . . a major one."

That sounded interesting, she thought.

"I'm listening," she told him.

"It's a mess," he said, "and an extremely dangerous one in many ways."

"What is it? Where is it?" she asked.

"In Madesh," he replied and took a deep breath. "I'd better start from the beginning."

24

Fine sherry.

Excellent Carlos Primero brandy.

Quality Spanish food that was discernibly superior to most airline meals.

The flight from Dublin on the Iberia 727 was comfortable, and the service in First Class better than that. It was after 7 P.M. by the time David Lloyd and Josephine Tan cleared immigration and customs at the Madrid airport . . . rented a car . . . and set off for the Spanish capital.

The sky was darkening as night took over the heavens. The strike force leader drove carefully with the fly-rod case resting on the floor between him and the woman. His eyes checked the rear view mirror at least once a minute.

"Expecting trouble?" she asked.

"Of course," he replied.

"Any special kind of trouble?"

"All kinds," he said calmly. "Enemy agents . . . those car thieves who've been robbing tourists . . . escaped mental patients . . . drunken bullfighters in Maseratis . . . frogmen . . . parachutists . . . Shiite suicide bombers who took the wrong turn . . . you name it."

"How would enemy agents know we're here? *What* enemy agents?" she questioned.

"I wish I knew. Think I'm getting paranoid?"

She shook her head.

"I wish I did," she admitted.

He glanced at the sign beside the highway.

"We'll be in town in twenty minutes," he said.

It took a little longer than that.

Some ninety seconds after he spoke, they heard a sound that told them a rear tire on the rented car was half flat. Then something flashed in his rear view mirror. The car behind them was blinking its lights, and a man leaning out the passenger side was pointing at the back of their sedan.

"Fifty-fifty," Lloyd thought aloud.

Those were the odds. He'd played with worse odds before, and he might as well find out now if he was right. He pulled the sedan off onto the shoulder . . . stopped. The other car whose lights had been blinking followed immediately.

The odds had changed.

"Seventy-thirty," the strike force leader estimated.

Two men got out of the other car, began walking towards them.

"If I say drop," Lloyd told her, *"drop!"*

She didn't ask him why or what. He had that look she'd seen before. It was a man preparing for battle.

The taller of the two men approached on Lloyd's side, pointing to the left rear tire. The shorter of the pair . . . a few steps behind . . . walked on her side of the sedan.

"Señor," the taller man said into Lloyd's window, "I think you've got a flat . . . and I've got a pistol."

He also had a mustache, a gold chain around his neck and a lot of teeth he showed in a smug grin. Lloyd ignored them. He concentrated on the nine-millimeter Star semi-automatic, an older model of the Spanish Army's current officer's handgun.

Spain had better guns than this, Lloyd thought.

Better armed robbers too.

This one still hadn't released the safety.

Careless, at best. Stupid, for sure. Possibly fatal.

"Nobody's going to hurt you," he told them with a smirk. "Just give us the keys and everything in the car, and we'll be on our way."

Lloyd looked across her out the other window. The shorter man held a short-barrel Italian Beretta pistol.

"Everything?" Lloyd asked.

"Everything."

"Does he have to point that at my wife?" Lloyd pleaded. "She frightens very easily . . . and she's pregnant."

"Of course. Alfonso, don't aim it at this pregnant woman."

His partner laughed . . . but pointed it away.

Suddenly she began to sob.

Very nice, Lloyd judged.

"You want the fishing rod too?" Lloyd tested.

She tensed.

"I said everything, dammit," the thief replied impatiently. "Come on. Everything. Now."

The strike force leader didn't keep him waiting. He picked up the fly-rod case, turned and reached to open the door beside him.

"Those bags in the back too," the tall man demanded.

Lloyd thought of the money . . . over three million dollars . . . and decided.

It took about four seconds.

Moments after that he stepped from the car, raised the fabric case and spoke one word.

"Drop!" he said.

Then he fired the shotgun . . . twice . . . at point-blank range. The first round blasted the Star automatic out of the man's hand. The 12-gauge pellets in the second shell hit his face as he opened his mouth to scream. He couldn't scream and he couldn't see and he couldn't breathe either. It wasn't just because his nose was ruined. The real problem was that he was dead.

Lloyd had already turned, pointing the shotgun at the other armed robber. Josephine Tan was flat on the seat, giving Lloyd a clear line of fire.

He hesitated for a moment.

"Any questions?" he asked the other carjacker.

When that man began to raise his pistol, Lloyd made up his

mind. He thrust the sheathed shotgun as far as he could into the car . . . fired another round through her open window. The man reeled back and spun around, badly wounded.

Lloyd ran around to the other side of the car where the thief was drenched in his own blood. Badly wounded . . . but still dangerous. Seeing out of one eye, he began to lift his pistol again.

Two more shotgun rounds . . . at ten feet . . . stopped that.

Lloyd looked down . . . saw the man was dead. The handgun was on the ground beside him. He had to leave one weapon so the police would identify these two as carjackers . . . and the taller man's Star was a better gun anyway. The strike-force leader walked around to the corpse of the taller man, picked up the Star, checked the clip, and put it in his jacket pocket.

He eyed the side of the sedan for a few seconds.

Just two or three drops of blood.

David Lloyd rubbed them off with a pocket handkerchief . . . and pointed at Josephine Tan. She got out . . . scanned her side of the vehicle for telltale red spots . . . and shook her head.

"Let's go," he said.

He drove half a mile to the next turn off . . . guided the car off the highway onto a side road and stopped the vehicle two hundred yards later. Then he changed the flat tire—just like the others that the dead duo had sabotaged on so many tourist cars . . . and never would again.

"I think I need a new fly-rod case," he judged as he studied the ravaged end of it. He opened his suitcase, took out a roll of tan duct tape bought in Dublin and sealed up the hole. She'd wondered why he'd purchased it. Now she knew.

He'd been anticipating.

A good team leader always anticipated, she told herself.

"That sobbing was just right," he told her and glanced over at her as they sat down on the front seat again. She was breathing heavily.

"They were ready to shoot us for the money, you know," he said.

"And you were *more* ready. I understand," she responded. "That was quite a thing you did back there. As you say, Mr. Trager, you have your moments."

He started the engine, and in ninety seconds they were back on the highway moving towards downtown Madrid. He didn't speak as he drove and evaluated the situation.

No witnesses.

He hadn't planned to kill anybody, but now there was no one left alive to talk about the shotgun or the money.

And he'd acquired a nine-millimeter Star with full clip.

It could have been a lot worse.

He glanced at her face . . . saw the delayed shock.

It was worse for her. He had to help.

"This is our last stop," he said as they saw the bulk and lights of the big city ahead. Telling her why they'd come to the nine-century-old and quite modern Spanish capital could distract her from the fear and violence and two corpses. She'd know in a few hours anyway, and if he shared the information now she'd see that he took her seriously.

Professionally, of course.

"We're here for some more shopping," he continued. "All those things our friends put on their lists for us to buy."

"Tools of the trade," she said.

"And agricultural implements," he replied. It was a running joke in the covert action world that weapons were often shipped by unimaginative arms dealers in crates marked agricultural implements. He had no doubt she'd know the joke.

He was right but she didn't smile.

It was too soon after the shotgun blasts.

It was time to speak about something else, he judged.

"I've booked a suite in a rather good hotel facing the Prado," he announced. "With *a little luck* in our shopping, we should have time to visit the Titians and El Grecos there."

She thought about the abundant masterpieces in the great and overstuffed museum . . . and the dangerous complexities of buying weapons and running covert operations.

"Are you really expecting *a little luck?*" she asked.

"All I'm expecting right now is an excellent dinner at the Palace."

It wasn't a royal residence. Across a wide avenue from the famed art museum, this Palace belonged to the commoners . . . the sophisticated ones who appreciated the amenities of a luxury hotel in the Sheraton organization. It was seven floors high . . . not new but grand in the classic sense.

It had old-fashioned style and elegance as well as the full package of modern amenities. Among these was the torch-resistant safety deposit box in which Lloyd placed fifteen of the hotel's handsomely engraved envelopes. They held $3,100,000.

He carried with him the remaining $128,300 left after the Zurich purchases and travel expenses.

He also carried the dead thief's handgun.

As the strike-force leader predicted, dinner in the large and gracious hotel restaurant was excellent. The traditional Spanish service was impeccable . . . the wines more than fine . . . and the chef quite talented. While they enjoyed the food and drink, David Lloyd considered telling her about his plan for the next day.

Tomorrow might be better, he reasoned.

Or it could be worse.

It would almost surely be much more dangerous than coping with those two left dead beside the highway.

He explained that after dinner when they got to their suite.

"About the morning," he began after she thanked him for the dinner.

"Yes?"

"We have a lot to do," the commander of the Spirit Team said. "It's going to be busy. Some of it might be *tricky.*"

Tricky meant life-and-death hazardous to this sort of British warrior, she realized.

Danger tomorrow morning.

She wasn't surprised.

"I assume we're dealing with the usual terrible people, Mr. Trager," she said calmly.

"A bit worse than that. I'm not Mr. Trager with the man who may sell us the tools," Lloyd said. "I just happen to have another passport with me. It's Australian . . . name of Gordon Robinson."

"Gordon Robinson," she repeated.

"Simply as a precaution, I'd like you to carry a handgun . . . if you don't mind."

"More firepower—is that the idea?" Josephine Tan asked.

He nodded.

"If I don't mind?"

He nodded again. He was being very tactful. They both knew that he wasn't really asking.

"I don't mind, Monsieur Robinson," she said. "I am not a total stranger to handguns . . . but you know that from my dossier, *n'est-ce pas?*"

"I know you're a special and valuable member of the team," he replied and smelled that perfume again. His face softened for a moment in response before he suppressed the reaction.

Suddenly she felt the fatigue *creeping on little cat feet.* That was a line by an American poet, she remembered. She'd had two drinks on the Iberia flight . . . the shock and adrenalin rush and let-down from the fatal incident on the highway . . . more wine and other alcohol at dinner.

It wasn't surprising that she was weary now.

There'd be more surprises with this odd man tomorrow, she realized, but that was tomorrow.

They parted, and she slept soundly without a dream.

Lloyd did not fall asleep right away.

Lying in bed in his room, he went over the sequence of what he had to do and he thought about the Romanian. Very rich . . . .

very sly . . . very dangerous. He did business with everybody, which was good. If not watched very carefully, he'd betray anybody . . . which was bad.

An equal opportunity son-of-a-bitch, Lloyd thought.

He could deliver a wide variety of *tools* though, and that was what the leader of the Spirit Team needed. Lloyd was dreaming about the cunning Romanian as he finally fell asleep. It was not a pleasant dream.

25

Before they ate breakfast, Lloyd changed one thousand dollars into Spanish pesetas and found a sporting goods shop's address in the telephone directory. He already knew where and how to reach the Romanian.

One didn't just show up at his "garage" . . . a weapons showroom camouflaged as an auto repair operation. Buyers came by appointment. David Lloyd wouldn't make the call from the hotel, of course. That could be hazardous.

Somebody could be "sitting" on the line . . . some Spanish police or foreign intelligence somebody . . . taping and tracing calls to the suave and spooky armaments merchant. There was more than one thing kinky about this rogue Romanian who was still wanted on a variety of charges by authorities in Bucharest.

As usual, the Spanish melon at breakfast was a fine beginning to the day. Then Lloyd consulted a terribly poised man in tailcoat behind the front desk about the best route for driving to the store where he'd purchase the fly-rod cases. He stopped on the way to use a telephone in one of his favorite tapas bars to call the weapons merchant. Ten minutes later they emerged from the burnished wood and high priced sports gear shop with a pair of leather-trimmed ballistic nylon cases for fishing rods.

"You think we'll need two?" she asked as he started the engine for the crosstown ride to the "garage."

"I should have bought three," he replied.

It took her a moment to realize that he was joking, sort of.

"We're going to visit an Argentine gentleman named Carlos Sontoya who moved here from Buenos Aires," Lloyd said. "His

real name is Nicolae Dionescu, and he's still wanted on a variety
of nasty charges in his native city of Bucharest."

"The Romanian?"

"So you've heard of him, Mademoiselle?" he asked.

"Several times, all bad. He was a colonel in the Security Police
when Romania was red, and he raped and stole . . . betrayed and
killed with the worst of them. In eighty-six or eighty-seven he
took off with some priceless religious treasures and a million dollars in Security Police funds."

"Two million six," Lloyd volunteered. "A gross and greedy
man."

"Un vrai salaud," she declared angrily. "A total swine."

"You could say that," he agreed and gave her the dead carjacker's handgun.

"What would *you* say?" she challenged as he removed the
shotgun from the ruined case to put the weapon in a new one.

"I'd say it might take two or three bullets to stop his rather
large bodyguard if things get dicey," Lloyd replied evenly. "I'd
go for a head shot if I were you."

"And what will you be doing, Mr. Robinson?"

"Feeding our host six flavors of shotgun shells," he said as cut
the opening to give access to the hidden weapon's trigger. "It
shouldn't come to that, of course. I think that I know how to do
business with these horrors."

She put the pistol in her handbag . . . didn't close it entirely.

"I see that you do too," he observed.

"Merde," she said. "I don't like this."

"Merde," David Lloyd concurred. "You'd be mad if you did."

She shook her head . . . took out the pistol . . . checked the clip
and safety . . . and put the weapon back in the open handbag.

"I just don't like it," she insisted.

"I'll get you a nicer gun later," he promised.

"You *know* I didn't mean that," Josephine Tan said irately.

He slowed the sedan . . . pointed straight ahead.

"That's *it,"* he told her. "Here we go."

Four minutes later they entered the arms dealer's icily modern office . . . wall to wall glass, stainless steel and leather furniture and a huge cactus plant. With his dead-eyed six-foot-five-inch bodyguard leaning against a file cabinet behind him, the slim and sharp-featured munitions merchant looked cool and rich.

Dressed wholly in Armani, except for a two-inch scar on his left cheek. The eighteen-hundred-dollar silk suit was so well tailored that Lloyd barely noticed the shoulder holster under his deftly cut jacket. His silk shirt covered a bulletproof vest, the strike-force leader realized.

Grand and assured in his black patent leather swivel chair, "Carlos Sontoya" flashed a caricature of a smile for two full seconds before he gestured to them to be seated. He made no move to shake hands. The gun dealer didn't like the touch of human flesh . . . aside from more-than-fat whores. It was one of his lesser foibles.

"Mr. Robinson," greeted the gun dealer.

"It's very kind of you to see us on such short notice, Señor Sontoya," Lloyd responded. "Our mutual friends in Algiers will certainly appreciate this."

The renegade Romanian was looking at Josephine Tan carefully. The big bodyguard, who was less given to subtlety, was staring at her and licking his lips. He'd clearly been brought up badly, David Lloyd thought.

He sat in a remarkably geometric and equally uncomfortable armchair . . . the fly-rod case across his lap. Josephine Tan gracefully lowered herself onto a twenty-three thousand dollar red leather loveseat created by a famous Italian designer who disliked people. Holding her open handbag, she eyed the bodyguard's face for a moment.

She wasn't being curious or sociable.

She was picking her targets.

The Romanian turned to Lloyd, waiting for him to introduce her. When Lloyd didn't, the arms dealer said something about the weather this week, and Lloyd made an equally insincere remark about the year-round charms of the "sophisticated" Spanish capital.

That pleased "Carlos Sontoya."

Sophistication was important to him. That was what his attire . . . office decor . . . all three cars . . . and lifestyle were about.

Something like approval flickered in his eyes, and he nodded benignly as he thought an Hispanic aristocrat would.

"I see you're a sportsman," he said and gestured one manicured hand . . . about three inches . . . towards the fly-rod case.

"Yes, I ride . . . fish . . . hunt too. A group of my friends are thinking about a hunting safari in Africa soon, and we'll need the right equipment," Lloyd explained.

"Big game, Mr. Robinson?"

"What else would be challenging?" Lloyd answered. "Large animals with thick hides. My friends might need armor-piercing explosive bullets."

"*Approximately* how many friends might be going, Mr. Robinson?"

"Ten or a dozen in the first group . . . they'd scout the beasts and the terrain," Lloyd told him. "If they find it interesting, a lot more would follow. They like to hunt too."

The message was clear. This person was buying for some sort of clandestine invasion force. A small number of scouts would go in first to reconnoiter the defenses and lay of the land. If an attack seemed feasible, the scouts would slip out undetected and brief the bigger force on where to land and how to strike.

Who would invade?

Where?

How could the terribly clever Carlos Sontoya make the largest profit?

Someone was probably trying to knock down one of the shaky regimes in Afrique Noire or Latin America . . . a group of exiles or political rivals. It wouldn't be the Caribbean because those control freaks in Washington still harbored the simplistic notion that they owned the Caribbean. It wouldn't be the Near East because the Big Players . . . major nations . . . ran the game there.

Who and where would affect the price.

The arms dealer decided that he'd shrewdly wile it out of the man . . . or the woman. She probably knew a great deal. Until the rogue Romanian got that information, he'd avoid quoting prices . . . as long as he could.

"What sort of hunting gear might your friends need?" he tested.

"Just basic things for the first group," Lloyd replied. "Since they'll primarily be locating the animals, their equipment doesn't have to be the newest or finest. As the Americans would say—"

"No bells or whistles," the munitions merchant offered smugly.

He was confident he had the right phrase. It was one of the cliches US military and intelligence types used all the time.

"Exactly," Lloyd confirmed. "Simple . . . proven in many climates . . . functional . . . with minimal maintenance required."

He didn't say old Sovblock weapons.

He didn't say *cheap* either, but the cunning fugitive from Budapest and all morality understood.

There'd be no problem.

Warehouses . . . official and illegal . . . in seven former Warsaw Pact countries and several other nations bulged with the full range of Red infantry hardware.

Russian designed . . . surplus, much of it still in crates . . . a glut on the international arms market. Too much . . . too cheap . . . too bad.

"I've got a list," the leader of the Spirit Team announced and took the folded sheets of paper from his inner jacket pocket. He picked out the Communist small arms, read those names aloud.

Semi-automatic AKM assault rifles, weighing a third less than the older AK-47. A dozen.

Czech Skorpion machine-pistols . . . Model 61 . . . only 10.6 inches long with the stock retracted . . . twenty-shot magazines . . . attachable silencers. Eight.

Red Army grenade and rocket launchers. Four each.

RPG7Ds, the light version for paratroopers of the RPG7V that hurls a 40mm anti-tank missile. Three.

SVD sniper rifles with high magnification scopes. Five.

A Chinese version of the Tokarev pistol . . . the Type 67 silenced to be an assassin's tool . . . eight-shot magazine. Ten.

China's silenced Type 64 submachine gun . . . Six.

The standard 1991 Red Army moonlight amplification and night vision units . . . two hand-held . . . ten sets of goggles.

Heat-seeking and shoulder-fired Strela anti-aircraft missiles . . . a dozen.

Czech CZ 9 semi-automatic pistols . . . 9mm . . . fifteen-round magazine . . . a dozen,

Soviet smoke and anti-personnel grenades . . . 30 each.

One kilo blocks of the odorless Czech Semtex plastic explosive . . . 25, with timers and fuses.

Concussion grenades . . . two dozen. Flares . . . a score.

Gas masks . . . a dozen.

Ample and meticulously specified quantities of ammunition for each type of weapon.

"Anything else?" the arms dealer asked as he finished writing a copy of what Lloyd had ordered.

"Shoulder holsters for the Skorpions."

Of course. The weapons merchant had listened to the list and thought this wasn't the equipment for a "recon" mission. Adding it up, there was just one possible total. This was an assassination operation. The special shoulder holsters would let the killers approach their target with the little rapid-fire Skorpions hidden from sight. These guns had to be for a hit team, the arms dealer decided.

As David Lloyd hoped.

If the thug who'd bought an Argentine passport and identity believed that just another political murder was involved, he wouldn't care that much and his prying might be a lot less intense. He would pry though. He was always looking for secrets to lever, use, abuse or sell.

If he was lucky, he wouldn't find anything.

If he wasn't, he might find an early grave.

And his hulking bodyguard would have to go too, for the Spirit Team couldn't—wouldn't—take any chances.

Next they discussed . . . bargained . . . negotiated . . . and fenced in a three minute brain game before they settled on a price. Lloyd agreed to return with half the money after Madrid's traditional late lunch . . . before four o'clock. The wanted Romanian-Argentinian agreed that the rest of the money would be paid on delivery of the shipment . . . within ten days . . . at a point the buyer would designate.

"I assume that I'll be allowed to test fire a representative sample of each weapon this afternoon," Lloyd said.

"You and your *friend* here can each try them out in my private range right now," the thug who would be Carlos Sontoya replied.

He picked up the Plexiglas phone on his desk, dialed a two digit extension and told someone they'd be "coming down" to shoot two different pistols, a rapid-fire Skorpion and an SVD sniper rifle. Then he reached under his desk to press a flush-set switch twice . . . once . . . four times.

There was no click . . . no whirring sound.

A previously invisible door in the wall behind him opened silently.

"I know it's old fashioned," he said archly, "but it works."

He led them through the opening into a brick-walled passage . . . a dozen feet straight ahead and on around a turn . . . to face a small elevator.

"I put it in for the handicapped," he lied in a mocking tone.

His sense of humor was as indecent as his life, she thought but said nothing.

His cologne was also unpleasant. She tried not to breathe in

the assertive sweet scent in the small elevator as they descended
two levels. Josephine Tan and David Lloyd never discovered
what was on the first one. The level below that housed a shooting
range.

Not big . . . not for heavy weapons . . . but private.

Some dozen yards wide . . . a hundred yards long . . . expensively and effectively soundproofed.

Well lit but without glare . . . targets at the far end . . . and the
hum of a ventilating system that would suck out the smell of
shooting.

Maybe it would pull out the odor of that cologne and the
sweating bodyguard, she told herself.

Near the elevator stood a swarthy man in a white coverall with
standard hearing-protecting "earmuffs" around his neck. He
held a Czech CZ 9 pistol in his right hand . . . a silenced Chinese
handgun in his left. He pointed the weapons at the visitors for
three seconds before he smiled and offered both pistols to Lloyd.

It didn't occur to the man in coveralls that she could shoot.

Or how close he'd come to eating a 12-gauge shotgun shell.

David Lloyd didn't think it was amusing to have weapons
aimed at him. Lloyd put down the fly-rod case that he held . . .
accepted the pistols.

"I'll bring the Skorpion and rifle now," the man who ran the
firing range said in a heavy Catalan accent. He opened a wall
locker . . . took out four sets of the oversized "earmuffs" . . . gave
one to each of them . . . and left to get the larger guns.

"Lady's choice," the leader of the Spirit Team invited and
thrust both pistols at her.

"I'll take the one I know better," she replied as she accepted
the long-barrelled Chinese handgun.

It was silenced . . . an assassin's tool.

Her dossier hadn't said a word about that, Lloyd thought.

She turned on her heel to take careful aim at a target a hundred yards away.

There were eight rounds in the Type 76's box magazine. She

fired four times at the target. The sounds were barely audible. The results were impressive. Four bull's-eyes.

The strike-force leader wondered how . . . and when . . . and where she'd become so expert with this special weapon. Lloyd had done a lot of things in battle as an SAS commando and other acts of violence, but he wasn't an assassin.

Now Lloyd put on his ear protectors, and the others slid on theirs. He raised the Czech semi-automatic, released the safety and eyed the target for scant seconds before he squeezed off the first round. Three more shots in swift succession . . . all bull's-eyes. As he finished, the man in coveralls returned with the bigger guns. She immediately reached for the sniper rifle.

She peered through the sight . . . fired three times. Bull's-eyes.

The Spirit Team commander took the Skorpion . . . braced to cope with the recoil of the rapid-fire weapon . . . aimed . . . and pulled the trigger.

Two bursts . . . very short . . . perfect.

Then he offered her the murderous little machine-pistol. It was to test the gun and Josephine Tan.

She took off her "earmuffs" and shook her head.

"It's not a woman's weapon," the arms dealer said.

Without a word, she slid on the "earmuffs" again and reached for the Skorpion. She spread her feet in the stance of an experienced shooter . . . tensed to absorb the kick . . . fired one burst before the magazine was empty. Every bullet tore the center of the target.

She handed the Skorpion to the man in coveralls, and looked at her gold wristwatch. She was extremely attractive, the renegade Romanian thought. Probably very dangerous. That made her even more interesting, he decided, as she removed her ear protectors.

The four men followed her example.

"You see? First class merchandise," the weapons merchant said.

"We'll be back with half the money this afternoon," Lloyd responded.

They took the elevator up, and Lloyd and Josephine Tan left through the garage filled with cars in for repair—the front for the armaments operation. Seated at his desk, Sontoya saw them walk towards their own vehicle. He watched on the closed circuit television system whose cameras scanned the doors to and area near the building.

"You're a good shot," Lloyd said as they entered their sedan.

She was not pleased.

"I dislike guns," she declared bitterly, "and I dislike that man in there even more. He made me lose my temper."

"People do that," he pointed out and started the car.

"*I* don't," she said. "Not if I can help it. It's *undignified.*"

Life often is, Lloyd thought, but this wasn't the time to discuss the human condition . . . or where she learned to shoot. He put the car in gear.

Sontoya saw them drive away.

He turned from the video monitor . . . looked at his bodyguard . . . and frowned.

"Who are they buying for . . . and why this stuff?" he wondered. "With newer weapons from a dozen countries flooding the market, why would *anyone* want this old Communist hardware?"

He paused . . . pondered the dangerous woman . . . sighed.

"We should know more about these people," he concluded and picked up the telephone.

26

It was sunny in Madrid as the arms dealer spoke, and he was calm.

Night held Madesh in blackness, and the soldier at the wheel of the truck was tense.

Different time zones with at least one thing in common.

Barcelona Delta could decimate both of them.

There were no lights on this road . . . no moonbeams this night. The driver of the supply truck strained to follow the narrow, twisting route from the highway to the mouth of the valley.

"Guard post ahead," the corporal seated beside him said.

With weapons pointed at them by grouchy sentries . . . always so grouchy at this hour of the night . . . the driver stopped to have their identity papers and orders checked. Then they drove ahead another mile to a second security post . . . same process.

From here on you drove with your vehicle lights off.

Orders. Nobody said whose.

The truck moved forward at three kilometers an hour . . . entered the narrow mouth of the valley. The driver didn't know what its name was. Maybe it didn't have one. Two-thirty in the morning, he thought. This is strange.

He didn't say that or anything else. He certainly didn't ask what they were delivering to this obscure valley or why it must be at this incomprehensible hour. It was better not to know, he told himself as the corporal nudged him and pointed left.

He didn't see anything except blackness, but he obeyed.

The corporal had been on previous deliveries. He knew what to do.

"Softly," the corporal said. "Softly. Tap the horn twice . . . then once."

He followed the order, and a rectangle of dim light blossomed without warning like a shell burst. It seemed to be *in* the side of the eleven hundred foot mountain . . . at its base. Then the light blinked off and on . . . twice.

"Go," the corporal ordered and pointed at the rectangle.

Now the truck moved slowly through the opening into the mountain itself. As soon as it was inside a steel door closed behind it. Bright lights almost blinded the two soldiers in the vehicle for several seconds.

"Get out," the corporal said.

As he stepped from the truck the driver saw he was in a large chamber . . . about twenty-two feet high, thirty feet wide and at least seventy feet deep. Floodlights overhead . . . men in blue coveralls in the big chamber and at two guard posts on a catwalk overhead. The ones above wore military steel helmets . . . carried automatic weapons.

There was a cement floor that looked new.

At the rear of the chamber a metal door was flanked on both sides by armed guards. For a moment the driver wondered what was beyond that door and what was going on here in such extraordinary secrecy.

The door at the back opened. The driver caught a glimpse of a well-lit passage as two men in the same coveralls pushed out a dolly. One of the wheels squeaked.

"I *told* you to oil that," a man wearing a sidearm on his hip said harshly. "A spark is the last thing we need down here. It could also be the last damn thing you'll see."

"I'll take care of it," one of the coveralled men pushing the dolly promised.

"Now."

"Yes, sir."

He hurried back up the passage to find some lubricant.

"What's the problem?" the truck driver quietly asked the corporal.

"Must be fumes."

"I don't smell any. What fumes?"

"Shut up and start unloading," the corporal responded.

He couldn't answer that question or almost any other about this hole in the mountain . . . in an uninhabited valley . . . where you came only in darkness. All he knew was the entry security ritual.

They opened the back of the Army truck, and waived to a trio of men nearby to help them move out the boxes. Each wooden or metal container had some writing in a foreign language the soldiers couldn't read. It wouldn't have mattered much if they did, for the words stencilled on the containers didn't really describe the contents or even the actual point of shipment.

When the man who had gone for the oil can returned, he lubricated the wheel. They moved the dolly close to the back of the truck. They manhandled the first crate out without much difficulty. Then the second . . . the third. They were getting good grips on the fourth when a man and a woman appeared in the rear doorway. They wore blue coveralls like everyone else here, but the truck driver noticed that they weren't like the others.

They weren't Madeshi. They seemed to be Europeans.

Then somebody lost his hold on the big box. It slipped loose. The driver screamed as it smashed his left leg. He was still gasping and crying in pain when the others lifted the weight from his ruined limb. Blood was seeping from the gash.

The bone was visible. It was shattered.

The officer in charge of portal security looked at it, and shook his head. Then he eyed the American scientists in the doorway.

Why couldn't they wait inside . . . back *there* down the passage and beyond the airlock that sealed off the "hot" area . . . as they were *supposed* to? They were probably in a hurry to inspect the new equipment, he speculated. The security officer walked over to them.

"We'll take care of this poor man," he said. "Please go back to *the facility* . . . at once."

The scientists turned and walked back towards the airlock that contained the laboratory and Barcelona Delta. This was the last shipment. Now they could go forward to earn the big bonus, and get out of here.

In the outer chamber, the security officer had something else on his mind. A dozen yards away, the injured man was still grunting and writhing in agony. Now the security officer spoke to the shaken corporal who'd just come in the truck with the driver.

"We have a problem," the captain said softly.

He was talking in a low voice so no one but the corporal could hear him.

"He has a broken leg, and we have a problem," the officer continued. "He should be taken to a hospital where they'll set his leg, but that's not possible."

The corporal nodded as if he understood, but he didn't.

"It's not possible for two reasons," the security chief said. "First, he saw something he shouldn't have seen . . . those two . . . that man and woman."

He pointed at the rear doorway.

He meant the foreigners, the corporal reasoned and nodded again.

"Second, I'm sure that you won't say anything about them or this place," the captain told him, "but how can anyone be certain . . . *absolutely* certain . . . what a man in great pain . . . confused and under anaesthesia . . . might accidentally mumble or cry out?"

"Yes, sir."

"I have to be absolutely certain he won't say a word to anyone . . . *ever.*"

The driver groaned and shook in hurt.

Finally understanding, the corporal looked over at him for several moments . . . felt his throat tighten . . . swallowed.

"I'm sorry, but it has to be done. Not here . . . not now. Put him in your vehicle, and drive him back onto the highway. When you're fifteen kilometers from here take him out and do it. Not with a bullet. It has to look like an accident . . . a hit and run thing," the captain said.

"With the truck, sir?"

"Yes, and make sure he's dead."

"Yes, sir."

The security officer paused to consider anything he might have overlooked. He had to cover every detail. Details were important.

"After they've unloaded the truck, put him in the back and start back towards the city," he instructed. "Before you do it, remove all his ID . . . including the division patch. When you get to the division HQ, give his ID to Colonel Kebeer in Counter-intelligence. I'll let him know you're coming."

"Yes, sir."

The corporal followed his orders carefully. By the time he stopped the truck, the injured man had passed out from shock. He didn't feel the pain when the corporal pulled and dragged him to the back of the vehicle, tumbled him out onto the road. It took only a minute to remove all the ID papers, dog tags and patch.

This wasn't going to be easy.

It would have been even harder if he'd known the man for some time, but this driver had only joined the unit twenty-three days ago. The corporal started the motor . . . backed over the unconscious body . . . then forward over it again . . . and back over it once more. Then he got out to examine the body.

It was mashed . . . bloody . . . ruined . . . dead.

They must be doing something very unusual back inside that

mountain, the corporal thought as he put the truck in gear. Whatever it was, it was dangerous. The corporal realized that he'd have to be extremely careful from now on . . . all the time.

If he wasn't, he might end up crushed on the highway too.

Madrid.
Paseo del Prado 8.

Just steps from the great old museum . . . a different world class collection in another fine building . . . Villahermosa Palace . . . new home to seven hundred important paintings bought from Baron Thyssen-Bornemisza.

Nourished by the Rembrandts and Titians, Manets and Renoirs and other impeccable creations, David Lloyd and Josephine Tan left the former palace and walked across the wide paseo to their hotel.

He looked at his wristwatch.

It showed 2:45 . . . half an hour before they had to leave. They separated to pack, and it was 3:05 when he recovered the envelopes of cash from the safety deposit box near the cashier's desk. He paid the hotel bill in British fifty-pound notes . . . not American money.

Automatic decision. No reflection necessary.

No credit card slips . . . no paper trail. She understood that.

No US hundred-dollar bills though he had many. They were the favored currency of international drug dealers, and might arouse suspicion. Or simply be noticed. Why run *any* risk? She understood that too.

Suitcases in the car trunk.

He didn't want the arms dealer to know they were leaving . . . or anything else. And the Romanian would want to know everything else. He was greedy as well as amoral and ruthless. Could have done well in politics, Lloyd thought as he guided the car towards Carlos Sontoya's "garage."

Politics and several other trades, he reminded himself. With his attention on the swarming afternoon traffic, he didn't see that she was watching him. She was wondering too. He didn't seem much like the usual strike-force leader though he was obviously expert in both weapons and tactics. But this man seemed more . . . the only word was *civilized* . . . and she sensed that he respected people . . . even if he had no illusions about them.

She understood what he did, but not who he was.

She realized that she wanted to know. No, *needed* to know. That was perfectly reasonable, she told herself and immediately turned her eyes from him to look out at the cheerfully imaginative drivers hurrying through the streets of the Spanish capital.

They didn't intimidate Lloyd, of course. He moved the rented sedan through them skillfully, and approached the "garage" before the time of the appointment. He drove through the neighborhood with professional wariness, and circled the block. And he studied every parked car, roof top, doorway and side street.

There . . . in the alley . . . he noticed the man on the black motorcycle.

She did too, and glanced at the fly-rod case beside her.

She told herself that she was probably overreacting.

Now David Lloyd nodded as if answering a question she didn't hear, and guided the car directly to the "garage." It wasn't far. The man on the parked motorbike could see the front door.

"Right on time," the weapons merchant said as they entered his office. "I like that."

Lloyd produced an ambiguous half-smile in response . . . put down the airline bag and the fly-rod case . . . and surveyed the room. The tall bodyguard was smirking unpleasantly and leaning against the wall off to the Spirit Team commander's left. On his right, Josephine Tan was settling into an arm chair. The top of her handbag was open again . . . just in case.

"My friends and I are very orderly people . . . very responsible," David Lloyd told the arms dealer. "We're never late, and we always pay our bills . . . in full."

"Excellent," the vicious vendor said. "You can start now."

"Let's settle a few details first," Lloyd responded. "Can you guarantee delivery nine days from today . . . at 11 P.M. . . . on the Turkish coast?"

"Where on the Turkish coast?"

Lloyd handed him a slip of paper which he studied carefully.

"Very efficient, Mr. Robinson. Latitude and longitude for the delivery and recognition signals to be exchanged by flashlight. No problem. Anything else?"

"About the night vision equipment . . . the larger units should be second generation stuff . . . the advanced model," Lloyd specified. "Light amplification of sixty-five thousand. The B-6 models with Biagish lenses."

"The Red Army's top of the line. I admire your taste, Mr. Robinson. Naturally those will each cost seven hundred dollars more, but they're worth it."

"They're worth *four hundred dollars* more," the strike-force leader pointed out, "but I won't quibble."

As he zipped open the airline bag, Sontoya spoke again.

"There's also the *standard* delivery fee. Let's see . . . for a shipment of this size . . . to the Turkish coast . . . at night . . . risky, you know . . . I'll just round it off. Because I admire you, Mr. Robinson . . . one hundred ten thousand dollars," he proposed.

"I think you're a grand chap too," Lloyd responded pleasantly, "and rounding it out is a fine idea. You said *ninety* thousand dollars? Certainly."

The rogue Romanian wasn't at all offended. He was just a bit surprised, for this Robinson had a British accent and the Brits weren't that good at bargaining. After a brief exchange of further hypocricies, they settled on ninety-two thousand dollars.

Then Lloyd reached into the airline bag and took out packages of money that he'd counted. Adding the extras agreed upon, he put the cash on the gun dealer's desk. Sontoya looked at the hundred-dollar bills.

He didn't count them.

He weighed them, using one of the delicate scales that drug dealers favored for speed and simplicity in dealing with large sums.

While he totalled the currency, the bodyguard walked several steps closer and leaned forward. He was peering into the airline bag. Lloyd smiled . . . picked up the fly-rod case . . . and pointed it in his direction.

"You like fishing?" David Lloyd asked.

There was no threat in his voice. It was in his eyes.

Angry but intimidated, the bodyguard frowned and retreated several paces. He was no sportsman, but he knew you didn't hold a fishing rod like that. He pretended that he wasn't afraid.

"I shoot," he said coldly.

Now Lloyd stood up and turned to the arms dealer.

"First quality merchandise . . . brand new," the leader of the Spirit Team specified.

"You have my word."

"Good. Our friends . . . we have so many friends . . . are very *fussy,*" Lloyd announced.

"There'll be no problem," Sontoya said and showed a lot of expensively capped teeth.

"They'll really appreciate that. Probably send you a Christmas card. *They have your address.*"

More of those gleaming teeth.

Another exchange of insincerities. Then Lloyd and Josephine Tan started to leave.

"By the way, Mr. Robinson," the weapons merchant said in an elaborately casual tone, "I spoke to those people in Algiers. They didn't seem to recall your name."

"I have a few names, like so many of your clients," Lloyd answered. "Merry Christmas."

"Merry Christmas to you," the man who'd been Nicolae Dionescu said in farewell.

Moments after they departed, he picked up his cellular phone and dialed swiftly. He whispered a few words, hung up. Some eighty seconds later, Josephine Tan looked into the side mirror as the sedan moved towards the center of the city.

"He's back there," she said.

Lloyd, who had also spotted the motorcyclist following them, nodded. He drove on for another half mile before he spoke.

"I think I'll lose him."

"There's a side street . . . sharp right two blocks ahead . . . no, *three* . . . where we can vanish through a car wash," she thought aloud.

He followed her suggestion, and it worked.

"My compliments," Lloyd said. "You know Madrid well."

"Bits and pieces," she replied. "I worked here four years ago. Played a model . . . small part . . . in an American film."

"Good one?" Lloyd asked as he studied the mirror and saw no motorcycle.

She shrugged.

"I think it was what they call *product*," she said, "and I remember that the producer kept talking about his collection of pre-Columbian artifacts. I hear that's a team sport in Beverly Hills."

"Talking or collecting?"

"I'm not sure it matters," she answered.

David Lloyd smiled before he turned the car towards the airport. When he got there and pulled up at the car rental office, he took out the luggage and put the shotgun in his suitcase. Then he looked around . . . saw no one was watching . . . and pointed at her handbag. Masking her movement with her body, she handed him the pistol which he put in his belt.

He wasn't ready to give it up yet.

He didn't until five minutes before they boarded the plane
. . . and then only after scanning the terminal a dozen times. He
bought a newspaper . . . went to a stall in the men's toilet . . .
wrapped the gun . . . and dropped it in the trash bin.

When he rejoined her, he handed her a boarding pass and
ticket. The flight was to Cairo and the ticket listed that as their
destination, but this flight was "direct" and not non-stop. Direct
was airline doubletalk meaning the flight stopped somewhere en
route, semantic magic of modern marketing.

On the way to the Egyptian capital, this flight touched down in
Athens. She noticed that there was no baggage receipt clipped to
her ticket.

"You've got other tickets too," she guessed.

"Of course."

They were under other names . . . Madrid to Athens. He was
. . . automatically and professionally . . . muddying the trail. They
boarded the jet. Fifteen minutes after it leaped into the sky, they
were sipping champagne in the first class section of the airliner.
After the second glass, she found herself thinking again about the
movie producer.

And the strike-force leader beside her.

Maybe it was the let down after the tension in the "garage"
. . . or the alcohol. She knew that she wasn't supposed to ask him
anything remotely personal, but the questions simply rose to her
lips.

"Remember what I said about the producer?"

He nodded.

"*You* don't collect pre-Columbian things, do you, Mr.
Trager?"

"I admire but I don't collect."

He didn't tell her that he had no home. She had no need to
know.

He wondered why she'd raised such an odd question, but he
didn't get to ask. She had closed her eyes, and was breathing
evenly on her way to sleep. She seemed to be smiling.

28

It was 9:40 P.M. when they cleared Immigration and Customs at the Athens airport. Lloyd looked around carefully before he led her to a public telephone to call the house in Piraeus. When the instrument rang there, the Nigerian soldier picked it up and listened warily.

Lloyd did all the speaking, and he said only two words.

"We're back," he announced and hung up the phone.

When they carried their luggage into the house twenty-one minutes later, he looked at the African heavy weapons expert he'd left in command.

"All secure, sir," Samuel Chibuku reported.

Now David Lloyd uttered another two words.

"Show time," he said and walked on towards the livingroom.

Mendoza shook his head in admiration.

"Very *cool*," he said to Josephine Tan. "How did it go?"

"Tout va bien," she replied and followed the team leader into the livingroom where he was opening his suitcase. He took out the tango video and the fly-rod case. The other three Spirits joined them by the time Lloyd inserted the cassette in the VCR player.

"It was damn boring here," the Latin sharpshooter complained.

"It won't be anymore," Lloyd promised and started the machine. "The intelligence has improved significantly."

They all leaned forward. Mendoza pointed at the VCR unit.

"We're hitting a dance school?" he asked.

"Not exactly," the team leader answered as he pressed the fast forward button.

"Good. I already know how to tango," Mendoza said.

They all stared at the screen as the tape raced ahead. When the first image of the valley appeared, Lloyd stopped the cassette and began the briefing.

"The bastards have moved their fungus operation to a new place," he said. "When I first showed you the other cassette of the corpses, I wouldn't talk about the specific target because we had no idea as to where the new place was."

He looked at the Nigerian.

"You knew that, didn't you, Samuel?" the team leader asked.

"I wasn't quite sure."

"*I* was damn sure something peculiar was going on," Mendoza volunteered, "and what's more peculiar than not knowing the site of the target?"

Now Lloyd studied the Moroccan . . . who said nothing.

"Where *is* the new target?" he questioned after a few seconds.

"No more than a mile east of the other place. It's a valley in the western part of the Islamic Republic of Madesh."

David Lloyd eyed the Moroccan for any sign that the reference to Islam might touch him. He saw no reaction at all. If there was any, it was hidden.

"Our real enemy isn't the Islamic Republic of Madesh or its people," Lloyd continued. "It isn't any Moslem fundamentalist group or lunatic terrorist outfit either. It's the very sick ruler of another country who's funding this fungus operation."

"Do we get three guesses?" Mendoza tested archly.

Lloyd ignored the question.

"He has plenty of money, and he's a homicidal son of a bitch," Lloyd told them.

That fit a score of national leaders . . . maybe two score, the Nigerian thought grimly. He didn't say that, for it was obvious. He waited for the assault-team commander to go forward with details of the target.

You could do something about the target.

Removing the murderous ruler would be much more difficult

. . . especially without the support of a major power.

"My guess is that he's bought some top people in the Madeshi government and military," Lloyd told them. "Maybe they have a common enemy. It doesn't matter. It's the fungus that counts."

He started the VCR again.

"The new site is heavily guarded by Madeshi troops," he said. "They're not the best but there are plenty of them . . . with American weapons. Sentry posts all around the one entrance to this valley."

Now the image of the truck entering the mountain appeared, and he stopped the cassette.

"Take a look," he ordered. "These people are not stupid. To prevent another slaughter in the area . . . maybe across the whole country . . . they've put the new laboratory underground. Probably an abandoned mine or ammo dump, I'd guess. Just a guess."

"Shit," Mendoza said softly.

"At least," the ex-SAS commando agreed.

"If you're just guessing," the Moroccan reasoned softly, "then we don't know the layout or interior defenses of the lab."

"We'll find out," Lloyd pledged. "We're not going in cold, and we're not going in naked. One load of equipment will be here tomorrow, and we pick up a full spread of weapons next week."

She wondered whether he'd say where.

He didn't. He'd tell them at the last minute.

This man was too careful to take chances, she thought.

"Ten to one there'll be more damn guards *inside* the mountain," Mendoza predicted.

"A hundred to one," the Spirit Team leader corrected. "I'd have them. Wouldn't you?"

Then he remembered.

"Everyone got a driver's license?" he asked.

They nodded.

"We'll need them," Lloyd said. "One more thing. We'll have two of the newest . . . most expensive . . . best protective suits for each of us."

"Do they work?" Mendoza challenged.

"I'm betting my life on it," David Lloyd answered calmly. "If you'd like to pray, I wouldn't mind that either."

Without waiting for a reply, he ran the rest of the videotape . . . rewound it all . . . answered two questions . . . and evaded another one. Then he suggested that they "break" for the night so they'd be fresh and rested when they resumed after breakfast.

He looked around the room, turning first to Mendoza to see whether the marksman was still eyeing Josephine Tan aggressively. Mendoza wasn't but he noticed the scrutiny. So did she.

"I think I'll get a beer," the team leader said and made his way to the refrigerator in the kitchen. As he took a bottle out, he saw Samuel Chibuku enter the room. Lloyd extended the chilled glass container to him in offering.

"Thank you," the Nigerian soldier said as he accepted it.

Lloyd then took out a second bottle . . . found an opener . . . handed it to Chibuku so he could use it first. Half a minute later both men were sipping the excellent lager product of a Greek brewery founded by a German master brewer many decades earlier.

"The Americans may be right about this," Lloyd said. "This cold beer isn't bad at all."

"I got used to it myself seven years ago on the Zaire border," the Nigerian replied. He opened his mouth to continue . . . stopped. Now he looked at the team leader intently.

"What is it?" Lloyd asked and swallowed another sip.

"I didn't plan it, sir."

"I probably didn't either," David Lloyd responded, "but my instinct tells me that I probably ought to know what you're talking about."

"Yes, sir," the professional soldier agreed immediately in his British-accented tones. "We're going into battle, sir. The assault force leader should have complete internal and external intelligence, sir."

"*What* didn't you plan?"

"I didn't plan to recognize your voice, sir."

The former SAS major nodded.

So much for perfection.

The man who'd created the Spirit Team thought that he'd completely changed their identities. New faces . . . new fingerprints . . . new passports . . . everything new.

Except the voices.

Whoever said the genius is in the details was right, Lloyd thought. The creator of the Spirit Team wasn't a genius . . . and he might not be right either.

"Where and when did you hear my voice before?" Lloyd asked.

"Field radio, sir. We were eavesdropping on your communications . . . seven years ago, sir."

"You were with the opposing forces," Lloyd recalled. He'd seen that when he read the heavy weapons specialist's dossier, but he hadn't paid enough attention to it.

Human error . . . an equal opportunity employer, as the Americans would say.

He was imperfect too.

"Is that it?" he asked Chibuku.

"I'm afraid not, sir. I know who you are . . . your real name. Our colonel must have met you . . . maybe served with you somewhere. He heard your voice, and told me who you were, sir."

"I won't ask you who he was," Lloyd said. "Security, right?"

"Yes, sir."

David Lloyd considered the situation, opened the refrigerator once more and took out another two bottles.

"Unless you'd prefer whiskey," he said to Chibuku.

"Beer will be fine, sir."

They drank in silence for almost a minute.

"My colonel said something else about you, sir," the Nigerian suddenly announced. "He said you were as fine a soldier as he'd ever met, and a man of high principle."

Lloyd finished his beer.

"Anything more?"

"He really admired you, sir. He said you were very fierce and unpredictable," Chibuku reported.

A strange compliment, David Lloyd reflected.

No, not so strange in the world in which he lived.

The world he'd chosen.

"I think a third bottle might be a bit much," Lloyd said.

"Yes, sir."

They looked at each other for several seconds.

"What are we going to do about this breach of security?" the strike-force leader pondered aloud.

"That's up to you, sir. It's a command decision."

"You're absolutely correct," Lloyd agreed. "While I'm thinking about it, let's keep this to ourselves."

"Of course, sir."

When Lloyd returned to the livingroom, Mendoza was speaking with the Moroccan, and Josephine Tan was nowhere in sight. Her suitcase was gone too, suggesting she might be upstairs in her bedroom. That chamber was only a few yards from the room where Lloyd slept.

He carried his own suitcase and the airline bag and fly-rod case to his room, unpacked and hung up the clothes. Then he undressed and thought about the arms delivery on the Turkish coast. First he considered the vendor. There must be millions of decent Romanians, Lloyd told himself. Unfortunately the man in Madrid wasn't one of them.

Not even half one.

He could . . . and couldn't . . . be trusted.

He'd get the shipment there because he wanted the rest of the money, and because his business future required that some kind of reputation be maintained. Even in his bottom-of-the-barrel trade, that was a necessity for survival.

And raw fear would also encourage him to fulfill the contract. Lloyd had seen the look in the weapons merchant's eyes when the threat of retaliation by *friends* was spoken. No, he'd keep his word on the delivery.

He couldn't be trusted for much else. Still the worst and most devious sort of secret policeman in his greedy guts, he was always seeking some sort of edge . . . some leverage . . . some information he could use or sell. That was why he'd sent the motorcyclist to follow them.

The compulsively cunning arms merchant didn't trust anyone else either. He wouldn't be there at the delivery . . . or within miles of it. Some secret enemies of the buyer might betray the whole transfer to the police . . . or come in themselves with guns blasting to hijack the guns and the cash. The Romanian would send someone else to collect the money and count it.

Maybe the big bodyguard.

He wasn't nearly as clever as the weapons merchant, Lloyd thought, and much more prone to violence. That could make him a serious problem for the Spirit Team, the strike-force commander reasoned as he sat on the edge of his bed and looked at the lights of the ships in the Piraeus harbor.

They must be ready to deal with him definitively.

Now David Lloyd turned his attention to other items on his mental check list . . . first draft. He'd go over it ten times, then ten times more. They would need some weapons in hand to protect themselves at the delivery, and a single shotgun wouldn't do it.

A route to the pickup . . . a way out. *Check.* Transport . . . fast but nothing that might attract the attention of Greek or Turkish coppers or coastal patrols. *Check.* Detailed intelligence on the place where they'd receive the shipment. *Check.*

He lay down on the bed. Lloyd was still adding to the list when he fell asleep.

29

By 10:05 A.M., the streets of Athens were already warm under the strong Aegean sun. So were the energetic tourists fanning out across the historic Greek capital . . . trudging up the Acropolis . . . photographing the tough "skirted" soldiers, the elite Efzones, guarding the imposing parliament building . . . and shopping in the narrow streets of the old Plaka district.

Other cheery foreign visitors . . . armed to the teeth with semi-automatic credit cards . . . were boarding one of the large white cruise ships at a dock in Piraeus. Less than a mile away, Lloyd was speaking to the men who were . . . for the moment . . . Gamal Sharif and Eugenio Mendoza.

"Let's take a drive," the team leader said.

They didn't ask where or why. They followed him out to the courtyard where Lloyd pointed first at Mendoza . . . then at the Suburu van. As the handsome marksman walked towards it, David Lloyd turned to the master burglar.

"Please come with me," the strike-force commander said, and led the Moroccan to the dark blue sedan. With Mendoza following in the other vehicle, they drove to the other side of bustling Piraeus. Then Lloyd suddenly stopped the BMW outside a large seafood restaurant.

"Three minutes," he told the Moroccan seated beside him.

He disappeared into the restaurant for no more than 110 seconds, and returned to the sedan.

"Let's go rent a truck," he said.

Eight minutes later, Lloyd stopped the BMW . . . got out . . . and gestured to Mendoza to wait there in the van. The Spirit

Team leader didn't want anyone in the rental office around the corner to connect the BMW and the van. Lloyd got back in the blue sedan, proceeded to the rental firm and arranged for a day's use of a small truck.

Though he had $9,100 in cash with him, he used a credit card. It bore . . . like his international driver's license . . . the name of James Trager. This must be a routine transaction unlikely to attract attention. A cash deposit might have done just that.

Now he led the way in the truck with the Moroccan behind him in the sedan. He had the cat burglar watch and wait in the car some seventy yards from the freight forwarder's office at the airport, a one man backup and strategic reserve. It was nearly noon by the time all the boxes from Zurich were loaded into the truck.

With the blue BMW following, Lloyd drove the truck back to the van where the three Spirits transferred half the containers to the Suburu's cargo compartment. It wasn't big enough for more. Mendoza had to make two trips to move the entire load to the house where Samuel Chibuku helped carry the boxes indoors. Across Piraeus at the rental agency, it was 1:40 by the time Lloyd returned the truck.

He didn't worry about any fingerprints.

Even if anyone did bring them up off a door-handle, the new prints Lloyd got at about the same time as the plastic surgery weren't on file anywhere.

The strike-force leader reached the house as Mendoza and the Nigerian were putting on the table cold herbed lamb, tomatoes, green beans, chunks of delicious chewy bread and Greece's exceptional yoghurt with local honey. As Lloyd looked for her the Eurasian woman emerged from the kitchen carrying a trayload of beer bottles and glasses.

Drinking from a bottle wasn't for her.

She had her own style and grace, Lloyd judged. Low-key and discreet, it was visible in many ways . . . even how she crossed the room. This woman moved like a slim and very refined cat, miles from the strut and haughty glance of so many other models.

And she thought for herself.

She was an individual . . . not a type.

But what about her skill with the assassin's gun?

Between his own bites of the simple satisfying lunch, he glanced across the table and watched her eat. When all the Spirits were finished with lunch, she got up to study the markings on the boxes from Zurich. After she found the ones she wanted, she went to the kitchen for a claw hammer to open two of them.

"Time to test these things and see if they work," she said as she began taking pieces of electronic gear from one crate.

She was as thorough as she was stylish. Step by step . . . room by room . . . floor by floor . . . she "swept" the house for camouflaged listening devices and concealed mini-transmitters. Then she checked both telephones and their lines for wiretaps. She was connecting a state-of-the-art scrambler to a remarkably compact and powerful field radio when Lloyd led Gamal Sharif out to the blue sedan again.

Lloyd drove four blocks from the house before he spoke.

"I want to acquire certain things," he said evenly, "and I think you can tell me where to get them. You're familiar with this area . . . this city."

The Moroccan shrugged noncommitally.

"You've operated here," the team leader said.

Sharif looked straight ahead silently.

"No games," the strike-force commander told him bluntly. "I *know* that you've operated here and in Turkey more than once . . . and I *know* it wasn't for the Boy Scouts."

Maybe he knew more than that, the cat burglar thought.

"What is it you want to acquire?" he asked.

"Various items. You might call them medical supplies," Lloyd answered. "Things that might be good for our health."

Then the leader of the Spirit Team spelled out his shopping list. Some three and a quarter hours and $6,715 later, they returned to the safe house with the trunk and back seat of the

BMW filled with packages. Some were big and wide . . . others thin and long. All were more than well wrapped and tied with an abundance of twine.

"You're *sure* we can get the tanks there?" Lloyd asked as they began to unload their purchases.

The master burglar nodded.

"And the wheels?"

"Yes, and the torch too," Sharif replied.

They brought the packages into the dining room . . . heaped them on the large table. The other Spirits joined them . . . waited for their commander to explain. He told them what he'd bought and why.

"We have other purchases to make tomorrow," he continued, "and a few big items to buy in Turkey."

"Soon?" Mendoza asked.

"Try the day after tomorrow."

"We'll all be in Turkey in forty-eight hours?"

"No, Mr. Mendoza," Lloyd answered. "You and Mr. Sharif will go first as the advance guard . . . point men . . . recon unit . . . and shopping squad."

The marksman's face lit up in anticipation.

"Bueno!" he said cheerfully. "I've never been to Turkey . . . or any Near East country."

"Mr. Sharif has," David Lloyd announced.

"Fine. Just give us the shopping list—" Mendoza began.

He stopped when the team leader sighed and shook his head.

It was unfortunate, Lloyd thought. Mendoza had so many gifts and valuable qualities, but he simply was not sufficiently paranoid. In this world, even a substantial skill in violence didn't necessarily make up for that character flaw.

Back to school time. Nicely.

"I hope you don't mind," Lloyd said politely, "but I'd rather not give it to you in writing. I'll just *tell* it to you and Mr. Gamal . . . when you're ready to leave."

Subtext, as college literature teachers would say.

If the list isn't written it can't fall into hostile hands.

That didn't have to be said aloud. Every Spirit "heard" it . . . including the macho shooter who wasn't about to admit the fact.

He changed the subject instead.

"How about another look at the tango cassette so we can fix the geography in our minds?" he proposed suddenly.

"Very good idea," the strike-force leader agreed.

They replayed the Madesh part of the video three times before dinner, and three times more after the meal. Lloyd ran key scenes back and forth so they could study and discuss details. Again and again he stopped the cassette to "freeze" on certain frames and images. It was essential that all the Spirits fully grasped exactly what they were seeing.

"Any questions?" Lloyd said when he turned off the machine.

"How do we get close to this valley?" Josephine Tan asked.

"By road, I'd say. I'll get a detailed map of the area," he promised.

"Could you tell us what the area is?" Mendoza tested.

"I could," David Lloyd answered evenly.

He didn't.

Still cool . . . still careful, Mendoza judged without rancor.

The others accepted Lloyd's caution with equal calm. It was, after all, *professional*.

"If you can't find a detailed map here, sir," the sensible and British-trained Nigerian soldier said, "there are some excellent map shops in London. If you know anyone in London, we could have a map in a day or two."

Lloyd wasn't admitting anything.

"Do you know anyone in London, Mr. Chibuku?" he fenced.

"Yes, sir."

"And you, Mr. Sharif?"

The burglar shook his head a moment before Josephine Tan gracefully stifled a yawn with her slim right hand.

"You're right, Mademoiselle," Lloyd said. "We've all had a long day. Let's continue this at breakfast."

Continue *what,* she asked herself as she made her way up the stairs to her room. Before she reached it, she eyed the door to his room just a few yards down the hall. She wondered what was within the room and the complex man who was still so hard to understand.

She entered her room, undressed and put on a light robe. It was too warm for anything more. Now she was thirsty, and annoyed that she'd forgotten to refill her thermos with something cold to drink. She yawned again, and decided to go downstairs for a bottle of chilled Evian. She put on her slippers before she stepped out into the corridor.

There he was . . . a few strides away.

Carrying a large bottle of Evian and smiling directly at her . . . no, *into* her, he stopped her without a word or a gesture.

"I see you're thirsty too," she finally said.

"I can get another one," he responded and offered her the bottle, "or we can share it . . . if you like."

"I'd like that," she told him and accepted the glass cylinder.

It was cold to the touch, but something inside her was starting to thaw. Aware that this chance meeting in the hall made no sense . . . and that she too was smiling, she avoided his glance for several seconds.

This wasn't the least bit romantic, she thought.

Yes it was.

"I don't want to intrude into your privacy," Lloyd said, "so I respectfully invite you into my room. You'll be entirely safe there."

As safe as I want to be, she told herself.

Why didn't men understand that?

His room had the same heavy-upper-middle-class-traditional-European furniture that her's did . . . plus an incongruous modern ice bucket, a plastic round capped by an aluminum lid. Two simple water tumblers rested on the table beside it. He opened the bottle and filled the glasses. Then he took off the lid of the ice bucket.

"I'm afraid I got the habit from the Americans," he said as he extracted a cube with a pair of tongs.

"They have some good habits," she replied.

He put ice in both tumblers, and they sipped the cold French mineral water.

"Sorry it's not champagne," he joked.

"We don't need champagne," she answered truthfully and he understood.

But he hesitated. The team leader wasn't supposed to do this. He'd bring the focus back to the mission.

"With what's waiting in Madesh," he said, "what we need is half a miracle."

She moved closer.

"I believe in miracles," she announced.

There was a beautiful view of the harbor behind her, but neither of them was looking at it. They were focused on each other.

"What do you believe in, Mr. Trager?" she asked.

Lloyd stepped back and considered the question.

"It's all right," she said after several seconds of silence. "It doesn't bother me that you hesitate. You're a very interesting man . . . though I find it hard to make a connection. You're always just a bit beyond my reach."

Now he stepped forward to within a few inches.

All he saw was her face. All he smelled was that perfume.

"This is a professional error . . . and I should have done it a long time ago," he said and cupped her face in his hands. They kissed . . . embraced . . . kissed again.

"No," she disagreed, *"this* is the right time."

They held each other very close and kissed several times more.

"You're correct," he finally said. "This is the right time."

Then the man who wasn't James Trager and the woman who wasn't Josephine Tan grasped and kissed and touched and needed . . . and went to bed. They made love twice before they fell asleep. She awoke an hour and a half later, driven by thirst to drink another glass of ice-and-Evian. She eyed the condoms on the bedtable and the handsome sleeping man who'd worn them.

He could be a prince, she thought.

Or a horror . . . or dead.

Perhaps she ought to return to her room . . . for unit morale. He might not want the others to know. She sat up in bed, trying to decide. Even if he wasn't a prince he was some kind of magician. At that moment his eyes opened and he spoke.

Not sleepily. Surely. Splendidly.

"Please don't go," he said. "We both know you should stay."

The instant he touched her face she made a strange sound. It was a deep rumble. Then he recognized it as a purr, and that was fine. It was natural for a feline animal to purr, Lloyd remembered as their passion rose again. When they were sated, they lay . . . sweaty and serene—in each others arms.

She yawned again.

"You can go to sleep now," he said softly and stroked her back.

"One question. Nothing personal."

"Fine," he agreed and kissed her neck. She shivered and pressed closer.

"How much time have we got?" she asked.

"You mean is there another woman?" he tested.

"That's not the question," she answered sleepily. "How much time before we attack that goddam laboratory? How much time for us?"

He suddenly realized what was troubling her.

"You're afraid we're going to get killed in that valley? That's it, isn't it?" he said.

He gently moved her head from its home on his shoulder, and he saw the dread in her wide black eyes. He caressed her hair.

"It's all right," Lloyd told her. "Scared is all right. This is going to be a bitch-and-a-half . . . but we're going to get into that mine, and we're coming out too."

She sighed, remembering the high walls and heavy defenses of the valley and the single entrance to the subterranean laboratory.

"Have you got a plan?" she wondered and yawned once more. David Lloyd kissed her tenderly on one eye . . . the other.

"I've always got a plan," he assured her before he kissed her warm lips. She was purring as she slid off into sleep. Her strong and tender new lover followed her into the happy darkness only a few seconds later.

30

"Plan A and Plan B," Lloyd said at breakfast as he finished his first cup of the powerful black coffee.

He didn't have to tell the others that he and the woman beside him were lovers. The glow they radiated communicated that clearly. He had no intention of discussing it anyway. Instead he spelled out the basics of Plan A and Plan B.

Each had to be executed perfectly with total teamwork. In accord with his schedule, Mendoza and Sharif left for Istanbul the next day on a midafternoon flight. They each carried $95,000 in cash and specific instructions. Samuel Chibuku had an additional $90,000 in British pounds hidden in his moneybelt and luggage the following day when he boarded the Egyptair plane to Cairo. He was on the ground beside the ancient city by the Nile for three hours the following morning as he waited for the connecting flight to Istanbul.

Lloyd and Josephine Tan sailed out of Piraeus on a chartered fifty-two-foot yacht shortly afterwards. They arrived at the rendezvous point forty-nine hours before the weapons were to be delivered and the second half of the purchase price paid.

The weapons dealer's big and beefy bodyguard entered Turkish waters an hour before the scheduled time. It was dusk, with a dazzling Near Eastern sun hanging over the nearby fishing port like a piece of fire in the sky. Enjoying his imminent humiliation of the snotty Eurasian bitch and her smug companion, the bodyguard stood on the deck of the small grimy freighter and eyed his well-armed crew.

They knew what to do. They'd carried weapons for the

Romanian all over the Mediterranean, and they were used to obeying orders. To make sure that they'd do exactly what the bodyguard said, he'd promised each of the fourteen men a thousand dollar bonus. Even if the Romanian hadn't told them to shoot down the buyers and steal the money, they'd go along with the bodyguard's scheme and swear the buyers had attacked them to grab the cargo without paying.

That would leave the bodyguard with over $144,000.

And the arms.

The bodyguard raised his binoculars to look for the small cove just a mile south of the little fishing port. Swollen with his own sense of shrewdness and an abundance of malice, he didn't even consider the possibility that someone might be watching him.

Several someones . . . all in place for hours.

Plan A and Plan B.

Weapons . . . transport . . . radios . . . frequencies and code words . . . all ready.

The sun sank and darkness ruled the coast.

That didn't bother the Spirits.

Now the bodyguard glanced at the luminous face of his gold wristwatch, and saw it was ten minutes to nine. He carefully scanned the coast in both directions . . . studied the cove a mile away . . . and listened. Then he looked up at the sky to see if any aircraft might be circling.

You couldn't be too wary. The Romanian said that twice a day.

"Ahead half-speed," the bodyguard told the one-eared captain.

The freighter moved forward slowly towards a battered jetty projecting from the sandy beach. There were two low boxy things some thirty yards back from the shore.

Trucks or vans, the bodyguard speculated.

They would come with vehicles to move the arms swiftly in the darkness.

The bodyguard . . . who'd been a noted torturer and executioner for a Colombian cocaine legion before he joined the Romanian . . . genuinely looked forward to killing the unpleasant people he'd soon face. He didn't get nearly as many opportunities to hurt and take life as he used to, and he missed that.

Would those good old days ever come back, he wondered in a silent surge of sentimental nostalgia.

Probably not, he admitted. That golden era was over, and almost everything was getting worse. These days even such simple pleasures as sex could kill you, he brooded as he raised his long flashlight and pointed it at the stone jetty.

He looked left . . . right . . . blinked out the agreed signal.

A light at the far end of the jetty flashed the right response.

Lloyd, who'd sent the answering message, looked at his watch. They'd had over half an hour. That should be enough time, he decided and spoke into the walkie-talkie he held.

"Stand by. They're coming in," he said.

He wasn't worried about the wrong people hearing. The small radios she'd picked had scramblers. Just thinking of her made him smile.

It couldn't last. It didn't. In a second it was life and death time again.

With its seventeen-year-old engine growling, the small cargo ship inched ahead in the still water of the quiet cove . . . stopped beside the tire-cushioned end of the crude jetty and dropped anchor.

On deck the bodyguard looked back over his shoulder at the hidden shooter he'd stationed on the right side . . . then at the concealed marksman lurking in the shadows on the left. The other armed crewmen would rush out blasting once the gunfire began.

He swept the shore twice more with the night-vision binoculars . . . spotted only a truck and something that appeared to be one of those self-propelled mobile homes retirees and touring families favored. He hoped that the arrogant oriental woman who shot so well was inside. He'd especially enjoy killing her.

There'd be no problem wiping them all out, he thought.

It had to be done so there'd be no survivors to tell what happened.

The aged freighter was rocking just a bit now. Someone was walking slowly down the jetty towards the ship. The bodyguard ordered the creaky gangplank to be lowered . . . gestured to the man approaching. He waved back for the bodyguard to come down onto the jetty.

No point in scaring him.

That would come before he died, the bodyguard thought and descended to the jetty to play out the charade.

There were no surprises when they met. They both knew the rules of the game. Seeing the buyer carried no case, the seller announced that all the goods were aboard and asked to see the money. The buyer answered pleasantly that he wanted to look at some of the weapons first.

It was the standard routine for arms deals, as traditional as the mating rituals of some animals or insects who circled each other and did prescribed movements or dances before they coupled. That was what David Lloyd, sweating in the body armor under his clothes, thought as he faced the bodyguard.

Lloyd also wondered whether it would Plan A or Plan B.

His gut instincts said it would probably be Plan B.

The bodyguard smiled as he ordered his men to bring down two crates and a claw hammer. He might not be so cheery, the leader of the Spirit Team thought, if he knew that Josephine Tan . . . in the blacked out mobile home . . . had him in her telescopic sight.

The first box contained Soviet AKM assault rifles.

The second Skorpion machine pistols.

Clean . . . in factory wrapping . . . new.

"Get your money and come aboard to check out another crate or two," the bodyguard invited. "We want satisfied customers, you know."

Lloyd walked to the truck.

"Stand by," he told the Nigerian. "I think it's Plan B."

The strike-force commander picked up the two airline bags. One was filled with hundred-dollar bills. The other . . . the dark sack closed with Velcro . . . had an inch of US currency atop something else. Lloyd walked back to the ship and up the gangplank.

"Ready for Plan B," Chibuku said into his walkie-talkie.

"Save us both some time," the bodyguard suggested as Lloyd stepped on deck. "Move up your truck while my men get the rest of the crates from the hold."

"It's all here?" Lloyd evaded.

"Absolutely, and your money better be too," the bodyguard said as his crew began to manhandle another crate up from below.

He pointed at one of the bags.

"I'll start counting this now," he declared roughly. "Could be a Turkish patrol boat along any minute."

Lloyd unzipped the bag heavy with US hundred-dollar bills.

He saw the unmistakable look in the bodyguard's eyes as he recognized the currency. It was much more than greed. It was danger.

"Hot night," the bodyguard said and reached up to remove his cap.

Here we go, Lloyd thought and tensed.

The bodyguard took off the dark cap. That was the signal.

The hidden gunmen had been watching him intently, facing the front of the vessel where the buyer and seller stood chatting. The two assassins leaned forward, taking careful aim. They didn't shoot Lloyd though.

They couldn't.

The missiles from two spearguns severed their spinal cords . . . at the neck . . . just under their heads. It would have been a difficult shot for most people . . . but not for Mendoza and Sharif.

They'd been sitting on the bottom of this cove for most of an hour, breathing oxygen from their tanks and holding spearguns and weapons bags. They'd made no noise as they climbed up the anchor chain . . . none as they waited to ambush the ambushers.

The spear guns had made only low coughing sounds, and the thumps of the ambushers' corpses slumping to the deck weren't much louder. Still both Lloyd and the bodyguard both heard the noises and turned towards them.

"All secure aft?" the strike-force commander asked suddenly.

"All secure," Mendoza confirmed from the shadows.

He wasn't holding the spear gun anymore. Neither was Sharif. They'd dropped the fishing gear the moment they'd fired at the ambushers . . . immediately opened their waterproof weapons bags to pull out French nine-millimeter PA-15 pistols. These semiautomatic handguns with the large magazines were part of the small arsenal Sharif had bought from "old acquaintances" in Istanbul. Lloyd's educated hunch about those shady contacts from the Moroccan's earlier operations had paid off nicely.

Nicely and usefully.

That's what the Spirit Team leader thought as he ripped open the Velcro closure of the second bag and reached under the inch of currency for a black Desert Eagle pistol. Made by Israel Military Industries . . . a powerful semi-automatic that threw devastating .50-caliber Magnum rounds . . . this Mark VII model could take off half a human head with a single shot.

The bodyguard's hand was moving towards the holstered weapon on his right hip when Lloyd produced the murderous Desert Eagle.

"Next of kin?" David Lloyd asked as he pointed it at the throat of the man who'd planned to kill him.

The bodyguard froze. He slowly raised his hands.

Then the three sailors dragging boxes onto the deck had a quasi-religious experience. They observed two ghostly pistols jutting from the darkness . . . pointing right at them . . . but the crewmen couldn't see who held the weapons. The crewmen didn't wait to find out. They put down the crates and lifted their hands too.

"Listen," the bodyguard began as he stared at the menacing metal Lloyd grasped.

"*You* listen," Lloyd broke in, "and do exactly what I tell you. I'm only going to say it once."

"I think there's been a misunderstanding," the perspiring bodyguard appealed.

"You're probably right," David Lloyd replied, "but you'll never know if I blow your brains half way to Greece."

The ex-torturer opened his mouth again . . . closed it.

"*Good,*" Lloyd said. "Now let's get social. I'd like to meet the captain . . . immediately."

"Sure."

"By the way," Lloyd added, "don't say anything unpleasant or stupid when you call him. My friend back there speaks five kinds of Spanish, and shoots bugs like you just to keep in practice."

The bodyguard called out the captain's name, and the man stepped out on deck grasping a short-barrelled Spanish assault rifle. He stopped when he saw the situation.

"Tell him to put the damn thing down or you're both dead," Lloyd ordered.

With the muzzle of the Desert Eagle looming very large, the bodyguard obeyed, and so did the captain. Lloyd then explained that he had enough grenades to convert the crew below into "dogfood." Still invisible in the shadows, Mendoza chuckled at the word but the one-eared captain took it a lot more seriously. Following Lloyd's orders, he summoned the rest of his crew . . . told them to lay down their guns and start carrying the rest of the boxes down to the jetty.

It all went quickly after that.

The Spirit Team commander summoned the truck by walkie-talkie . . . Chibuku drove it to within ten yards of the grubby freighter . . . and the crew loaded the boxes into the vehicle under the Nigerian soldier's eye . . . and twin Czech CZ Lugers.

All through this the bodyguard's humiliation and rage grew. Sweat sheeted his entire body, sticking the expensive silk shirt to his torso like cheap cotton.

"We can finish this conversation some other time," Lloyd announced as the last of the crew returned to the ship. "As you pointed out so wisely, there could be a Turkish patrol boat at any time . . . so I'll simply give you the second half of the money now."

The bodyguard wasn't certain whether this was true or a mocking joke. His anger flared even higher.

"Convey my thanks to your employer," Lloyd said and bent down to grasp the bag of money.

"You can count it if you want," he declared . . . put in on the deck . . . and pushed it towards the thug with his foot.

That was when the shamed bodyguard lost control. He twisted away from Lloyd's gun muzzle, hoping to reach the captain's assault rifle on the deck. He perished very quickly. Only a complete autopsy by an expert medical team could determine whether it was the .50 caliber slug from the Desert Eagle, Josephine Tan's bullet or the round from Gamal Sharif's pistol that killed him. The Spirit Team had neither the time nor the desire to pursue such a forensic inquiry.

"Translate this," Lloyd called out to Mendoza and turned to the shaken captain.

"There was an accident . . . after you left us . . . on the way home," Lloyd said calmly.

The captain blinked and spoke in Spanish.

"He asked, *what accident?*" Mendoza reported. "I think he's scared shitless."

The Spirit Team leader nodded.

"That's fine. Shows he's not crazy. *Crazy* could be more trouble. What accident? This poor chap," he said and pointed at the ruined corpse, "fell into the sea and couldn't swim. He'd been drinking. Most unfortunate accident."

Another exchange in Spanish.

"The captain agrees that it was most unfortunate," Mendoza said.

"He can tell that to the Romanian when he delivers the money . . . *all* the money," Lloyd said and pushed the bag of cash towards the frightened Spaniard with his foot.

More translation. The captain was blinking again.

"Every last dollar," Lloyd continued. "I'm sending word to the Romanian about exactly how many dollars, and you know what *he'll* do to you if he doesn't get it all. You can't even imagine what *we'll* do."

Mendoza relayed the message in Spanish briskly.

"Tell him we're worse than the Romanian . . . *much* worse," the leader of the Spirit Team ordered. "Tell him we're invisible, so he never saw our faces. Not one . . . not for a second. If he caught a glimpse, he forgot what he saw on this moonless night. If he says a single word about who or what he saw tonight . . . or if any of the crew does . . . we'll hunt them all down. It really will be *dogfood* time."

Lloyd could see that Mendoza was enjoying translating that message. It was also clear that the captain was acutely disturbed to hear it.

"You talked him into it," the Central American reported a minute later. "He swears on his grandmother's grave. I think it was your charm and the dogfood bit . . . mostly the dogfood . . . You know what else I think?"

"No, but you'll tell me."

"I think we ought to take them all out . . . and keep the money."

David Lloyd shook his head.

"If the Romanian doesn't get his cash, he'll try to find us . . . and we don't need that. If he's paid in full, it won't matter whether he believes this yarn about an accident. He won't do anything . . . except hire a new bodyguard."

Now the one-eared captain coughed, cleared his throat and spoke.

"He thanks you, and asks if he can go now," Mendoza said.

"Vaya con Dios," Lloyd replied.

The captain's face brightened for a moment when he heard the armed and dangerous stranger say "Go with God" in Spanish, and hurried to get his ship away before these violent men changed their minds. Sharing the same fear, the crew didn't waste a moment.

Within minutes and without a light showing, the blacked-out little freighter was moving towards the mouth of the cove and the open Aegean. The Spirits watched it head out to sea until Lloyd spoke again.

"Let's get out of here," the strike-force leader told them.

Samuel Chibuku was at the wheel of the truck when the Moroccan slid in beside him. Mendoza walked with Lloyd to the self-propelled mobile home where Josephine Tan and her rifle waited in darkness.

"That *Vaya con Dios* number was pretty good," Mendoza said.

"But you liked the *dogfood* number even more," Lloyd responded.

"How did you know?" the marksman asked as they reached the mobile home.

"Just a guess."

She opened the door for them, and the two men entered.

In the blackness David Lloyd couldn't see the tension in her face, but he heard it in her voice.

"Is it all right?" she asked urgently.

"I *think* so," the team leader . . . her lover . . . her love answered.

It would have been better if that greedy bastard hadn't tried to kill them, Lloyd thought silently. This whole episode . . . three corpses for fucking nothing . . . had been predictable . . . and stupid.

"Tell her about the whole thing," Mendoza urged.

"When we're out of here. Right now I'm driving. If you want. to sit up front with me," Lloyd said to her, "I'll fill you in."

Then he paused . . . scanned his mental check list.

"You and Gamal did well," he told Mendoza. "And you too," he said to the Eurasian woman so close to him in the darkness . . . in other ways as well.

"Anything else?" the handsome Central American asked.

"We're riding without lights till we're five miles from here."

"You got it," Mendoza said. "Now I've got a suggestion."

"Yes?"

"Tell her about the dogfood!"

Lloyd didn't. He didn't consider it either funny or important. He simply reported the failure of the attempted ambush . . . the death of three armed enemies trying to kill them . . . and his instructions to the captain.

"So Plan B worked!" she congratulated.

"I'm working on another plan now," he responded.

"I thought we already *had* a decent plan for getting into Madesh."

He nodded . . . smelled that perfume . . . let himself smile. He hadn't done that for hours.

"We do," he agreed. "Now we need one . . . a *very good* one . . . for getting *out*."

The road from the coast was not in prime condition. With no help from headlights, he drove slowly and warily . . . and silently . . . for another twenty seconds before he spoke again.

"I do have an idea," he finally admitted.

That came as no surprise at all. This strong and clever and extraordinary man always had an idea. He was as fine a problem-solver as he was a lover . . . a skilled and respectful leader.

"It could cost us half a million dollars," he thought aloud.

"We have it, don't we?"

"Yes," he acknowledged and waited for her to ask what the plan was.

When she didn't, he realized why.

She knew that he probably wouldn't tell her, so she wasn't wasting her energy . . . or his. Even though she was a professional familiar with need-to-know, she might well have another need.

The woman need.

Primeval . . . visceral . . . the essential need to trust totally and be trusted just as completely.

It was a few millennia older than need-to-know and other rational principles of the secret intelligence and covert action worlds.

He wanted to tell her, but he couldn't.

He thought of telling her something else as a sign of his admiration . . . perhaps how her long shot helped stop the homicidal bodyguard. He couldn't tell her that either, for it didn't add up to trust, and she despised shooting anyway.

She'd never said why.

That was one of her secrets, he reflected.

There were so many secrets, Lloyd told himself . . . billions of secrets . . . thousands of cloak and dagger and police organizations spending vast amounts of time and money to identify . . . steal . . . catalogue and file all those secrets.

They had to be cross-indexed and computerized too, he thought.

That's where the money was, he reasoned and looked at the mileage indicator. In a minute or two they could turn on their lights. That wouldn't really mean they were out of danger. They would be at risk until this whole operation was over . . . and they were out of Madesh.

Probably after that too.

He could hardly remember when he wasn't in danger or about to go into it . . . over seventeen years now. Without knowing why, he took his right hand from the wheel and touched her face . . . just for a moment. Then he heard her sigh.

"This plan for getting out? Is it really *very* good?" she asked hopefully.

"I'm open to other suggestions," he replied.

"It's not that good?"

"As in any plan I've ever heard, there are a dozen things that could go wrong but . . . as of now . . . it's the only plan we've got," he told her frankly. "I won't bore you with the details, but you're a key part of it."

"Me and half a million dollars?"

"Could run higher. Seven or eight hundred thousand, but I think it *might* work. I wouldn't try it if I didn't believe that."

"It's going to work, James!"

He couldn't help it. Even as he stroked her face again in the darkness, he found himself thinking about the diversion. The right diversion could improve their chances by fifteen or twenty percent.

If it succeeded.

If it didn't, David Lloyd decided as he considered the agonizing alternative, they weren't going to take him alive.

Then he turned on the lights, and they continued down the winding old road towards the rendezvous.

31

Five **days and** several hours after the freighter crew grimly
stripped the three corpses and dumped them into the Aegean,
David Lloyd and Josephine Tan sat in a poorly air-conditioned
office in the capital of Madesh. They faced the Director of Media
Affairs of the Ministry of Tourism, a chubby man with little hair
on his head . . . no interest in media . . . and a commitment to
send the president a quality birthday gift every year.

An intelligent man who joined a Master's degree in poetry
with a sensible suspicion of all foreign journalists, he was always
courteous to visitors . . . even when this senile air conditioner was
barely functioning. As a patriot, he could ignore the beads of
perspiration and he did.

He studied the paper on his desk once more.

"So you want to make a motion picture here," he said warily.
"Not one of those trashy Hollywood things, I hope."

Attitude. Lots of attitude, Lloyd judged.

That would make it easier.

"Certainly not," the strike-force leader replied righteously.
"We know your *great* nation has high moral standards, which we
respect and share. No, sir, we've never had anything to do with
those *salacious* films so full of terrible sex and immorality."

The word *salacious* suggested that this Irish person was not
wholly uneducated, the Director of Media Affairs decided and
considered mentioning his own graduate degree and five published sonnets. No, that might be vulgar.

"I'm gratified to hear that," he said instead.

"Our production will be a cultural one . . . a documentary,"

Lloyd lied earnestly. "We expect millions of people will see this high quality report on some of the many splendors of Madesh and its extraordinary contributions to civilization."

Cultural sounded fine, but the Director of Media Affairs wanted more details and assurances of proprieties. Just the usual proprieties, he explained. No women in short or sleeveless dresses. No kissing. No slums, but historic temples and palaces instead . . . the *real* Madesh.

"Precisely what we have in mind," David Lloyd assured him. "We'll bring the beauty, history and grandeur of Madesh to vast numbers of viewers, travel agents and educators in many nations. While our primary goal is culture . . . we're doing this for nonprofit and educational television networks . . . this fifty-two-minute production should also attract thousands of civilized and wealthy tourists."

"Television? Not a motion picture?" the bureaucrat asked.

"Much bigger audience . . . educated adults, not those crude teens who go to the vile things Hollywood makes to corrupt world youth."

"We're concerned about corruption too, you know," the Director replied. "Now please give me some specifics. Where do you want to tape?"

"We'll be guided by you," Lloyd told him. "In the capital and any other cultural sites or natural beauties you'd be good enough to suggest. I've heard there are two wonderful old palaces about 140 miles west of here . . . magnificent mosques in Zapor and Daribad . . . Moghul ruins near Jammur . . . great mountains on the northern border . . . the river and falls at Baliq."

The director of media affairs nodded in approval, and went on to urge "appropriate" coverage of literature and the other arts. Lloyd immediately agreed, appealing to the director to take time from his "busy schedule" to be the on-camera guide to the National Library.

That did it, and a half.

Then Lloyd wrapped up the sale.

"If I might impose on your generosity," he began, "we'd like your advice on one more thing."

Still thinking about being on camera, the Director smiled benignly.

"If there's anyone you'd be kind enough to recommend as a translator and guide?" Lloyd inquired in a very sincere voice.

"I happen to know such a young man. He'd be excellent."

"And we'd be grateful," Lloyd assured.

The pretty, young Eurasian woman sat there modest and silent. Attired in a long sleeved blouse buttoned to the neck and a skirt that went five inches below the knee, she wasn't anything like those pushy "new women" so numerous in the atheistic West. The Director hadn't met any, but he'd heard about them.

"I'll send this bright young chap over to your hotel tomorrow afternoon with the permits you'll need," he told Lloyd.

They exchanged business cards . . . compliments . . . and statements of confidence in the travel-and-culture video to come. It was 4:50 P.M. when David Lloyd and Josephine Tan left his not quite cool office and strolled down to the steamy street.

They had about seven and a half hours, and a lot to do.

32

One o'clock in the morning.

A little less hot . . . just a bit less humid in the nearly deserted streets of the capitol.

Grateful that the almost new Japanese air conditioner in her hotel room was cooling efficiently, Josephine Tan sat in the darkness looking across the square. Some fifteen minutes earlier she'd opened the window two inches. She didn't want to let in the heat. She had to.

The closed window might interfere with what she was doing.

She was doing her part in the plan. With night vision binoculars in one hand and a walkie-talkie in the other, she endured the steamy intrusion as she peered at a side street off the tree-lined square. Some forty steps down that street was the Bureau of Fuel and Minerals building erected by the British over five decades earlier when this whole area was tidy and imperial.

The plan was Lloyd's.

The building was the target.

And the criminal who was breaking in was one of the finest cat burglars in the world.

Crouching in the blacked out room, she was the lookout. Now she saw a taxi float by . . . a waiter going home on a bicycle . . . and then the Moroccan moving across the square. He was wearing dark clothes, with a dark canvas bag over his shoulder. It held his tools, a silenced pistol and a tear-gas grenade. Getting caught wasn't on his agenda.

As Sharif entered the side street, Lloyd was approaching that intersection on the pavement along the square. Seconds later he

walked into the shadows of the side street and looked in both
directions. Standing in a doorway a dozen steps from the square,
the team leader had chosen for himself the exposed post of outside backup man who'd protect the burglar from interruption or
capture.

Responsibility went with command.

He'd learned that years ago.

From this dark doorway, he'd direct the operation with the
little walkie-talkie he had in his pocket. Sharif was a world class
burglar, and Lloyd's plan made sense. The silenced machine-pistol in the shoulder holster under David Lloyd's light linen jacket
would be drawn only as a last resort.

There'd be no need for it unless something went wrong.

Lloyd knew that a lot of things could go wrong.

Unlike the arrogant, brilliant, power-mad and self-doubting
obsessive . . . a sad and common combination . . . who had created the Spirit Team, Lloyd didn't believe in perfect plans. On
paper . . . perhaps. But they didn't seem to be executed perfectly.
Bad luck. Human error.

So many dangers . . . always an inch away.

The Moroccan walked close to the buildings as he made his
way down the street. When he passed the somewhat rundown
home of the Bureau of Fuel and Minerals, six floors high and
unpainted in a quarter of a century, he caught a glimpse of an
elderly guard dozing in the lobby. Sharif saw no such protector
in the adjacent building, so he calmly circled through the alley
and picked the lock on the back door.

No sign of anyone or any security system. Pausing at each
landing to look and listen, he made his way to the top floor and
carefully crossed over to the roof of the old Fuel and Minerals
headquarters. When he couldn't detect any alarm gear on the
door, he tried the lock and found it stiff. He opened his bag, took
out a small can of oil and squirted some into the reluctant mecha-
nism.

It was low tech burglary, but it worked. He picked this lock in seconds . . . stepped inside and closed the portal behind him. He put away the oil can, took out infrared goggles and matching flashlight. Then he looked around to get his bearings . . . and to search again for any kind of alarm. He saw none, and wasn't surprised.

There was no money . . . no jewels . . . no military secrets here, just the papers that a dignified half-drowsy legion of clerks and administrators tied in red ribbons, filed in folders and forgot. Since Madesh had only a few oil wells and half of its mines were played out, the people who shuffled maps and other documents here each day were also practically forgotten.

He had no time to consider any of this. He moved swiftly down the corridor, scanning the signs on every door. Since Urdu was one of the tongues he knew, he completed his survey quickly. Then he made his way down another floor . . . still no sign of alarms or the office that was his objective.

Now he saw what he'd come for: Archives. These older files were what he needed, and the door to this space wasn't even locked. Nobody thought what was inside was worth stealing.

It was a very large room . . . scores of files . . . all organized by geography . . . by province . . . subdistrict . . . town. This practical old British system made sense, the burglar thought. If the files had been set up chronologically, he wouldn't have a chance. The Spirit Team leader, who'd planned this break-in, didn't know when the mine was dug, what sort of mine it was or other vital details.

Sharif had to work quickly but neatly.

There must be no sign that anyone had been here, nothing to make anyone in the Bureau wonder why a burglar would want to check these files. The fact that only a very few people in the Bureau knew that some secret project was in the old mine didn't mean the Spirit Team could proceed safely.

One question from one clerk or administrator.

One of the few who knew might hear it, and the defense of the valley and underground laboratory would be tripled.

With so many of the files undisturbed for years, there was dust everywhere. *Almost* everywhere. When the burglar found one with a lot less dust, he hoped.

Yes, there it was.

The right place . . . no dust . . . recently used.

He took out the drawings . . . put them on a desk . . . set up his infrared flash and pulled the camera from the canvas bag. He looked at the meticulous plans that the British coal company had filed in 1937. Experienced in the use of the little spy camera, Sharif took eighteen pictures before he put the plans back in the timeworn folder and slid it into its right place in the file.

He closed the drawer slowly and quietly.

He was half way to the door when the red light on the walkie talkie blinked. The radio was turned down low but he heard her clearly.

"Shalimar . . . Shalimar . . . Shalimar."

Sharif heard the danger signal, and so did Lloyd. The burglar hurried to the stairs to get out as soon as he could. Lloyd looked up the side street to see a uniformed policeman approaching. He was sauntering . . . clearly in no rush . . . probably patrolling his assigned patch.

The Americans would say *beat,* David Lloyd recalled from a score of films and several US television series about tough coppers who had active sex lives. The word didn't matter. This was real life, and this policeman had a real pistol. That was one of the changes introduced after the British colonial era ended.

The policeman walked right past the dark doorway in which Lloyd hid . . . continued another twenty-five steps . . . and stopped a few strides beyond the entrance to the Fuel and Minerals building. He glanced right . . . then left . . . and unzipped his trousers. He wasn't looking for intruders, the leader of the Spirit Team realized. He was emptying his bladder because he couldn't wait until his tour of patrol ended.

It wasn't only his bladder that called for relief.

His feet were sore too . . . the timeless complaint of police everywhere where patrolmen walked.

He closed his zipper, leaned against the front of the building into which Sharif had broken and reached into his pocket.

Josephine Tan couldn't see him that clearly from across the square, but she had a good view of the cruising police car that was turning up the street behind the Fuel and Minerals headquarters and the building Sharif had entered first.

"Shalimar . . . Shalimar . . . Shalimar," she said to seize the attention of both the burglar and her lover.

Then . . . in short French sentences . . . she warned that flight from the rear exit was very hazardous.

The Moroccan replied in French, asking whether he could go out the front door.

Lloyd looked up the street again, saw the policeman was lighting a cigarette. One cigarette couldn't hurt him, the officer on patrol told himself. That wasn't quite true in this place at this moment.

If he were still there when Gamal Sharif wanted to leave the building, that cigarette could get the policeman a silenced bullet between the eyes. Like so many others in his peculiar profession, the Moroccan burglar didn't like guns or violence. He'd like the horrors of a brutal Madeshi interrogation and prison even less, Lloyd guessed.

"Omar . . . Omar . . . Omar," Lloyd called over the radio to the cat burglar and advised him in French to wait for *"une minute."*

The choice of radio language was easier.

Only one Madeshi in fifteen or twenty spoke English.

One in two or three thousand knew French.

Puffing away on his cigarette, the weary policeman looked towards the square and blew a rather decent smoke ring before he turned to face the other way. A woman he knew lived two blocks up there, and her husband was often away as a night trucker.

That impure thought saved the policeman's life.

While he was considering her silken body, Lloyd came up behind him in rubber-soled shoes and dropped him with a single fierce karate blow that left him unconscious. The former SAS commando knew exactly where and how to hit him so that he'd be out but alive.

Dead would be a big mistake.

Police all around the world got agitated when one of them was killed, and they didn't let go. Dead would mean a major search and investigation that could even go inside the two adjacent buildings.

No investigation at all would be a lot better, and masking the episode as a routine street crime might be safest. Lloyd reached down to take the unconscious man's pistol, wallet and identity papers. Then the strike-force leader thought of the mini-bottle of cognac in his pocket, a trophy of the flight on Air France.

Why not . . . ?

It might confuse the issue even further, and might shame the policeman into not reporting the attack at all. After all, alcoholic drinks were forbidden in this devout Islamic nation.

Lloyd emptied the small bottle over the unconscious man, swallowed the last few drops and raised the walkie-talkie to tell Sharif it was safe to come out. The Moroccan gave Lloyd the camera, stepped around the policeman without a word of comment and walked away towards his hotel . . . not the one where Lloyd and the Eurasian woman were staying . . . properly . . . in separate rooms. The cat burglar had in his pocket a ticket on the 9 A.M. flight to Cairo.

Lloyd wasn't thinking about travel as he made his way back to the hotel across the square. Peering through the night-vision binoculars from her blacked out room, she watched him walk towards the hotel . . . towards her. She closed the window, ending the unwanted flow of humid air.

She began to undress.

She was finishing as he entered her room.

"I was worried," she said. "Is it all right?"

"It's all right," he answered and took her in his arms.

After that neither of them said anything for a while. They made love to each other instead, and that was more than all right.

Things weren't going nearly as well for Heinz Gimpel in Dortmund, a city of 575,000 in Germany. There was a real lack of romance and affection in the existence of Herr Gimpel, owner of a small firm that made a variety of electrical and kitchen appliances.

Though he was never rude and always *reasonably* honest in both his personal and business relationships, at least one person didn't love him at all. There wasn't anything that Gimpel could have done about it, for he'd never met that individual and had no idea that the stranger actively disliked him.

And could get people killed anywhere . . . easily.

Heinz Gimpel, who always charged competitive prices and delivered very reliable products from the firm his grandfather founded, had made one small mistake several weeks earlier. It was a casual remark to a customer. Gimpel didn't even remember saying it.

He asked the buyer, a swarthy man who said he was Brazilian, what he'd do with the seventy-two top-of-the-line timing devices that the stranger had just purchased . . . in cash. The man had replied that he'd resell them in his shop in Rio, and he'd remembered the question.

He'd mentioned it to another man who wasn't Brazilian either, and that person told someone else who thought it was amusing and passed it along. The anecdote reached a prominent individual who didn't find this . . . or anything else . . . funny.

So it was that this morning . . . as Heinz Gimpel finished his regular breakfast and gave his wife her regular kiss and prepared to leave for the plant at the regular time . . . that a fourth man who couldn't even spell Rio de Janeiro delivered a package.

Right through the window beside the breakfast table in the kitchen.

It hit the floor, and exploded into flames.

It also hurled bits of glowing phosphorus in a wide arc, setting curtains, dish towels and both Herr and Frau Gimpel ablaze. The time had been picked with the daily routines of both Gimpels in mind.

Someone had reasoned that Gimpel might have discussed the "Brazilian" sale with his spouse, so both of them must be permanently silenced. Both Gimpels had to die in this "house fire."

They did.

The man who delivered the package left Dortmund within the hour.

He had other people to silence.

The irritable and implacable Supreme Leader for Life of Fozira was cleaning up the loose ends.

33

Nephew or son-in-law?" Lloyd challenged as they walked across the hotel lobby towards the beaming young man in the crisp white suit.

It was 2:50 P.M., and the Spirit Team leader and Josephine Tan had enjoyed a leisurely lunch while waiting. The man in immaculate white who stood at the front desk held a large manila envelope in his right hand. Maybe it contained what they needed.

"Nephew or son-in-law?" Lloyd repeated.

He was confident that his effort to "sweeten" the Director of Media Affairs had succeeded, and that the official had . . . as would bureaucrats around the world . . . probably across the galaxy . . . sensibly selected some relative to work with the television crew as guide and translator.

That he'd be overpaid by the foreigners was beyond question.

What was in question was *which* relative.

"It's even money," Lloyd reminded cheerfully. "Take a guess."

The Eurasian woman smiled . . . and surprised him.

"Cousin," she said and she was right.

His name was Ibrahim. He had a degree in geography and ecology, but there weren't any jobs right now and he'd always been *very* interested in television. Not just for himself. For his beloved country, which he knew extremely well. To help the visitors he'd make time to show them the many wonders of Madesh. Assisting this television documentary could be his small contribution to his native land.

He said all this with genuine sincerity and an honest smile. His warmth remained undiminished after Lloyd offered him a weekly wage that the team leader thought was three times the going rate for a guide-translator. It was actually four times the norm, which the Director of Media Affairs' cousin . . . *first* cousin . . . took as a good omen for the project.

Then he remembered the envelope.

"You'll see what a wonderful country this is," the youthful patriot vowed and presented the permits.

Lloyd eyed them at scanner speed.

Very impressive-looking . . . very official-looking . . . adorned with an elaborate red wax seal over an indecipherable signature.

Not a word in English.

"You're on the payroll now," Lloyd said and gave the three pages to his new aide to translate.

"These are very complete," the twenty-six-year-old Madeshi told him. He went on to read a general authority to videotape for a television documentary at "significant sites" in the capital, the other locations Lloyd had mentioned "and additional scenic, historic and cultural places and institutions."

"They're signed by the Minister of Tourism himself," earnest Ibrahim Salim said proudly. "We can start immediately."

Perfect, Lloyd thought as they left to rent a car at the Kemwel agency around the corner.

Free access everywhere with a government official's relative as cover.

Paying two weeks salary in advance wouldn't hurt either, the pragmatic strike-force leader reasoned. Encouraged by this gesture and frequent compliments, the well-educated and enthusiastic guide showed the foreigners to fourteen sites . . . in and near the capital . . . during the next three days. Then Lloyd announced that he and his assistant had to leave for a short time to check on the crew's cameras, sound gear and vehicles.

They'd all drive into Madesh next Saturday afternoon at five.

Since the guide was now an *important* member of the unit, he

should meet them at the frontier crossing outside Jundabad with
the rented car. The young Madeshi should bring toilet articles
and several changes of clothes for a two-and-a-half- to four-week
"shoot." When Lloyd gave him another wad of local currency to
cover expenses while they were away, Ibrahim Salim took off his
new sunglasses . . . put his right hand over his heart . . . and
vowed to be there exactly on time with a full tank of petrol.

He repeated this at the airport as they waited to board the
Pakistani airliner heading west. As he did so, David Lloyd's attention seemed to wander for a few moments and he appeared to
be looking over the guide's shoulder at an assortment of commercial transports from four countries and several Madeshi military helicopters on the tarmac.

Josephine Tan noticed that Lloyd was only half-listening.

When their flight was airborn, she asked why.

"Just thinking," he said.

"You're always thinking."

Then she saw that glow in his eyes, and remembered.

"*Almost* always," she corrected evenly.

"I was thinking about our *next* departure from Madesh,"
Lloyd told her.

"Is there a problem?"

"Let's say that what I had in mind could be improved," he
replied. "I'd like to do something more contemporary . . . more
with-it. We're a media firm in the Nineties, and we should be
aware of our *customers.*"

She understood immediately.

The Madeshi frontier police . . . the whole infantry division
and the planes at the air base between the mine and the border.

"We should learn from the advertising chaps and special ef-
fects people," he continued. "They know people see what they
think they see, and they respect what they're supposed to. We
need a *lot* of respect for our production."

He paused for several seconds before he nodded.

"We'll get it," he predicted cheerfully.

Then he sighed as he remembered this airline didn't serve liquor.

In Washington the next morning, Thomas James Maccarelli was even more discontented. The best-dressed Secretary of State since Warren Christopher felt that he was . . . as he often said in his fine Floridian accent . . . "between a rock and a hard place." Last week he'd told the president how well things were going in talks with Madesh on additional military assistance, and now *this*.

"Please bring him in," Maccarelli told his senior aide.

Within half a minute the uneasy ambassador of the Islamic Republic of Madesh entered warily. He hadn't received the usual diplomatically polite invitation to visit the Secretary of State. Instead there had been a surprisingly blunt telephone call.

It wasn't the least bit friendly.

Neither was the Secretary of State as the ambassador saw the moment he stepped into the large office.

Maccarelli was visibly angry about something, but there had been no clue on the phone as to what it was. The ambassador took a deep breath, forced himself to smile as protocol required and walked forward with his hand extended.

The Secretary of State ignored it.

"Thank you, Sidney," he said to his aide who'd ushered in the Madeshi.

Maccarelli was throwing out his right hand man.

What didn't he want the aide to hear?

Sidney Frank left, and Maccarelli still wouldn't shake hands.

"My government has received some extremely disturbing information," the Secretary of State announced.

He was dumping the traditional amenities of international discourse out the window, the ambassador thought. It wasn't supposed to happen this way. In the Youssef Khan's twenty-three years as a diplomat in four major capitals, he'd never met this before.

"I have some photographs to show you," Maccarelli said and pointed to a large coffee table beside a couch.

Then the chief foreign affairs officer of the most powerful country on the planet picked up a big envelope from his desk and started towards the coffee table. The envoy to Washington of a minor Third World nation that had long professed friendship towards the United States swallowed and joined him beside the table.

"My government views this as a blatant breach of an important international agreement, and a significant threat to the security of the region," Maccarelli declared.

Now he was speaking in the familiar diplomatic jargon that the ambassador knew.

But what was he talking about?

"This is *not acceptable*," Maccarelli said. "It will be impossible to renew the military assistance agreement . . . or to consider one penny of economic aid until this matter is rectified."

Youssef Khan had a degree in mathematics, but he didn't need that expertise to add up the numbers. He knew them by heart.

Ninety-five million dollars a year in weapons . . . for five years.

That came to four hundred eighty million dollars.

And the economic help and loan guarantees could be nearly as much.

Total: nearly a billion dollars.

Losing *that* was definitely *not acceptable*.

"Mr. Secretary," the ambassador began, "I can assure you—"

Maccarelli dropped the envelope on the coffee table in a most undiplomatic way, and glared.

"Take a look at *those* before you assure me of anything," he said hostilely.

The ambassador realized this was no time to discuss the

amenities. He pulled from the envelope six big and very clear color photographs. He'd never seen anything like them . . . blue bodies of humans and animals. The ambassador blinked uncertainly.

The pictures puzzled him.

No one in his government had told him or any other Madeshi ambassador anything about the entire Barcelona Delta project.

The mass murder fungus wasn't their business.

They had no real need to know.

"What is this?" Youssef Khan asked.

"This is the result of the illegal bacteriological warfare weapon being made in *your* Torat Valley!" the Secretary of State replied accusingly.

All the photos were of the Torat Valley.

There wasn't one of the nearby valleys or the truck entering the mine where the new laboratory was about to start production.

Maccarelli hadn't been informed about that. The Army's practical Chief of Staff and the Director of Central Intelligence had agreed that it might be risky to do so. They couldn't take the slightest chance of somehow leaking to the Madeshi that the location of the new lab had been discovered.

That it wasn't safe.

That it could be attacked.

If the Madeshi and Pariah didn't suspect that, they wouldn't increase the number and strength of security units protecting it.

And if the Secretary of State didn't know, he couldn't possibly tell anyone. That would preserve deniability for the president . . . and leave the Army and CIA with their options open.

So the secretary of state who didn't know . . . because the CIA and Army didn't think he needed to . . . told the shocked ambassador who didn't know . . . because his country's military leaders were sure he didn't need to . . . that the United States was demanding immediate and total demolition of the deadly fungus project.

This was nonnegotiable.

The Islamic Republic of Madesh had seventy-two hours to reply affirmatively . . . or face the consequences.

34

How could the Americans have found out?" the tense Madeshi military attache asked urgently.

He was perspiring . . . frightened.

General Hassan was neither.

The Supreme Leader for Life was in excellent spirits for several reasons. First, he'd just enjoyed reports that another two of the vendors had been silenced. Tinkering with the brakes of a Brazilian supplier's big Mercedes had killed him . . . and some other people who didn't matter. The money-hungry American who'd helped recruit the Rosebud experts had fallen ten floors from a window . . . with a little help. His corpse had crushed a dog.

Hassan didn't mind that.

He hated dogs.

Second, the news from the mine an hour ago was that production would begin in six days . . . or seven at the outside.

A week, he thought.

In a week he'd be the greatest military power on Earth. Of course, the population of the planet would be a bit smaller. There would be a million or two less Jews. Israel was the target he'd chosen so carefully.

It was the perfect target. Whipped up by decades of propaganda, the self-serving rhetoric of cheap demagogues and shrill slogans of some naive religious leaders, many millions of Hassan's brethren . . . women too, though they hardly counted . . . hated the Jews and their little country.

Their *tough* little country. Hassan had a secret respect for them and their break-all-rules defense forces, but that wouldn't stop him from unleashing the blue spores. Then he would be the feared one. He'd let the other countries in the region know . . . very quietly . . . that he held the weapon.

And the stupid blustering Americans would do nothing.

They didn't know . . . couldn't prove . . . this fungus was his.

Those people in the mine were no threat. There was going to be a serious accident in the subterranean facility within an hour after the fungus shipment was on its way. Small cylinders of deadly gas and more than a dozen camouflaged explosive charges were in place. No survivors.

A terrible accident in an old abandoned mine.

Such things happened everywhere, Hassan thought contentedly.

The third reason that he felt good was that it was now a race. He was in a race against time with a fat, old, major power that had so much muscle and so little brains. Hassan was a compulsive competitor, and the competition couldn't get much bigger or better than this.

"What are we to do?" the Madeshi colonel appealed.

Hassan considered the problem and possible scenarios.

"Stall," he said. "Delay."

"How can we possibly stall the United States?"

"You'll have to divert too," Hassan told him and went on to explain how to do both . . . simply . . . specifically. He also gave the colonel a twenty-inch canvas suitcase that contained an additional four million dollars "for your colleagues' expenses."

"We *certainly* don't want to cause any tensions between our brothers in Madesh and Washington," Hassan continued. "You have my word. That entire operation will be terminated within . . . ten days."

"Stall for ten days?"

"Do your best, friend," Hassan urged.

Following his advice, the Foreign Minister of Madesh issued a strong statement about yesterday's terrible event in Nepal.

Somebody . . . it wasn't entirely clear who . . . had attempted a coup. The prime minister had been seriously wounded, and there was speculation that the Chinese could have been behind it.

Madesh had no interest at all in Nepal, but Washington had supported the new prime minister. Awareness that the possibility the Chinese were involved might trouble the US authorities . . . or at least confuse them . . . made sense of Hassan's suggestion. Madesh strongly denounced the "heinous assault" on the prime minister as a threat to "an emerging democracy."

And the Madeshi delegate repeated this at the United Nations. Two South American countries that also wanted to curry favor with Washington "strongly supported" the Madeshi statement, and the BBC began planning a documentary about women in Madesh.

Four hours before the ultimatum would expire, the Madeshi ambassador returned to the office of the Secretary of State. There was a "frank exchange of views"—diplomatic jargon for "no blows were struck." As soon as the ambassador left, Maccarelli spoke to Sandra Jefferson Lynes on a secure line for ten minutes.

After the conversation ended, she sat thinking . . . silent . . . trying to make up her mind. Then she phoned Maccarelli back . . . on another secure line. Despite her carefully worded efforts, he was confident that diplomacy was solving the problem.

"With Madesh on our side . . . one of our few friends out there . . . it would be a mistake to rock the boat. That's what he said," she told Carling half an hour later.

The deputy director of operations frowned uncertainly.

"Just what does that mean?" he asked.

"The Madeshis have said that this whole thing with the fungus was a rogue operation by a small group of irresponsible militants who are being severely punished for this idiotic . . . unauthorized . . . and very hazardous adventure. That's exactly what their ambassador swore to our honorable secretary of state."

"And he believes that?" Carling wondered.

"He *wants* to believe it. He was also told no senior official had the slightest idea this was going on . . . that the illegal operation basically ended after the *awful accident* . . . and the sealing of the Torat Valley proves it."

"What did the ambassador say about the other valley?" Carlin challenged. "What did he and Maccarelli say about the pictures of the damn truck going into the side of the mountain?"

She took a pack of cigarettes from her desk drawer . . . looked at them . . . took control and put them back in the drawer.

She shook her head.

"Neither the ambassador nor the Secretary of State has *seen* those sat photos or knows they exist," she said.

"T. J. Maccarelli will blow his stack when he finds out we've only told him part of the story," Carling predicted.

"If he doesn't then," she replied and thought about the damn cigarettes again, "he surely will when he learns that the fungus and scientists are both born in the USA. He'll go ballistic!"

Silence. Five seconds. Ten.

"Is that it?" Carling asked.

"That was the *good* news," Sandy Lynes said bitterly. "The *bad* news is that Maccarelli was so pleased with his own diplomacy that he spoke to the President about the Madeshi situation . . . and the President told him he was doing the right thing."

"He doesn't know the facts either," Carter Carling protested.

"That's right," she agreed. "We've been working hard to keep the damn facts from him, and we've been brilliantly successful."

"Can we stop this fungus *without* telling Maccarelli and the President?"

She considered this for several seconds.

"Maybe I ought to tell someone else about the present mess first," she reasoned. "Maybe it's time to call in the cavalry."

Since the US hasn't had cavalry for approximately half a century, the Director of Central Intelligence reached out to another branch of the Army. Brigadier General Paul J. Sherman and his bright-eyed aide, Major Sara Velez, of Military Intelligence, were in the DCI's office within forty-five minutes of her telephone summons.

"That's all of it," the DCI said when she'd brought it up to date through Maccarelli's talk with the president. "Since your wizards invented this horror and are now cooking up more, I thought you'd like to know . . . and might have some suggestions."

Velez glared . . . opened her lips to speak . . . closed them.

"Whatever you were about to say, say it," the director of Central Intelligence declared.

Velez glanced at General Sherman . . . saw him shrug.

Now the young major looked directly at the DCI.

"I was going to say it was one of *your* wizards who illegally created this rogue unit that might get us into an even worse mess."

"Or save the world," Sandra Jefferson Lynes speculated.

The DCI turned to Sherman.

"Does she always talk like this to Cabinet officers?" Lynes asked.

"I think she was brought up to think clearly and express herself freely," the general answered. "Major Velez is a very fine officer . . . an exceptional one."

"She looks as if she wants to shoot me," the Director of Central Intelligence observed.

"I hope not," Sherman replied. "Major Velez is an outstanding shot."

The Texan major was loyal to the Army, and her commanding officer was loyal to her. The DCI wondered how much loyalty Sandy Lynes could count on in this complicated, levantine, Old Boys' agency she headed.

"We don't have a lot of time," the Director of Central Intelligence told them, "so we'd better find some alternative solutions . . . some other scenarios. With all due respect for the wisdom of our Secretary of State, I'm not convinced that the diplomatic approach will cut it. I don't believe we can trust the Madeshis . . . and I'm sure we can't trust that bastard Pariah."

Sara Velez's face brightened in approval.

Hearing the cool DCI call Hassan a bastard showed a lot of sense . . . a lot of promise.

"My people will be working on alternative solutions too," the director of Central Intelligence promised. "The ideal solution would be a peaceful one . . . a quiet one that wouldn't embarrass our country or Madesh."

"And would put those renegade scientists out of business," Velez proposed.

The DCI nodded.

"That could be especially tricky," she said. "I'm not sure that the Madeshi or Pariah would give them up. All right, let's attack this problem right away and put our ideas on the table here tomorrow afternoon at . . ."

She paused to press a key on her computer . . . then another.

She saw her schedule on the screen immediately.

"Tomorrow at four."

Sherman and Velez returned to his office in the Pentagon, and went to work immediately.

The general assigned her to create a high-priority team . . . small for obvious reasons of secrecy . . . herself, a former Rosebud leader and two of his most imaginative G-2 officers. He'd be attacking the problem too . . . putting everything else aside.

He did.

Sherman sat at his desk with a yellow pad . . . then rose to pace . . . filled his pipe and smoked a whole bowl of the aromatic rough-cut tobacco. Then he made some notes on the pad . . . realized they were useless . . . swore and tore the page to bits.

He burned the bits in his large ashtray.

He made some more notes.

When Sara Velez came in with two cartons of that merciless Pentagon coffee, Sherman was talking to someone on scrambler-phone.

"Those are the coordinates," the G-2 general said. "It's an exercise, of course, but an important one. Some guys with a lot of stars are on my butt about this. Can you get back to me by 0930 tomorrow? Thanks a million, Tim."

He hung up the phone, and closed his eyes for several moments.

"Tim Knowlton?" she asked.

"You're a witch!" Sherman replied.

"Not really. Tim Knowlton is the best damn target controller in the Strategic Air Command . . . Number One with long range missiles. One of the possible scenarios is to zero in an ICBM with a hydrogen warhead to melt that valley and everything for a mile around," she said.

"It's just an idea," he answered. "We need a whole range of them. Anyway she said the *ideal* solution would be a peaceful one. She didn't say the *only* solution."

She put the carton of coffee on his desk, walked to a chair and sat down. After a moment she lifted her own container of coffee to her lips and sipped.

"I thought about a missile too," she told him. "Maybe we could make that Plan F."

"F?" the general asked as he reached for the carton of hot liquid on his desk. "Why F?"

"Because there must be five better plans," she replied and sipped more of the bitter brew.

"You know you're a fine officer," Sherman said, "but you can be a . . ."

She finished the thought.

"A pain in the ass. I know I can be a pain in the ass, sir. I'm not sure I want to stop being a pain in the ass," she announced.

"You're very good at it," the general said gloomily and swallowed some of the hostile coffee. He didn't even notice the harshness. He was used to it, and a number of much more unpleasant things.

She couldn't or wouldn't let go of it.

"General," she pressed, "have you considered that the Spirit Team . . . people *we* sent in there . . . might be in the kill zone when the warhead toasts the whole neighborhood?"

He thought for a few seconds before he took another gulp of the liquid insult.

"I hope not," the general said and began writing on his pad again.

35

It was after midnight.

Friday was gone.

In violation of her firm decision, Sandra Jefferson Lynes was finishing her second pack of cigarettes since the crisis management meeting had begun in her office at four o'clock. It had run until nine . . . adjourned briefly for food from downstairs . . . and resumed an hour ago.

No progress. Not one of the plans would do the job.

And no one in the US government except two decent middle-aged and basically intelligent men who were (1) Secretary of State, and (2) President, chief executive and commander-in-chief, believed that the fungus project would stop.

It was probably going forward right now.

The DCI and everyone else in her office were tired, worried and frustrated. Almost sullen . . . worn and silent . . . stuck and stubborn, they eyed each other through the haze of cigarette and pipe smoke. Neither health nor the environment were on this meeting's agenda.

"Maybe we should take a ten-minute break," the director of Central Intelligence suggested. "Stretch our legs . . . and our heads. Then we can come back and figure out what to do."

"I know one thing to do right away," Major Sara Velez said, and explained.

The DCI was impressed by the practical and excellent proposal. Sherman's aide had a lot of mouth, the DCI thought, and a lot of brains too.

"Do it," Lynes told Carling.

Reed was pleased by the telephone call.

Something must be happening, he reasoned as he steered his car from the highway onto the CIA turnoff and drove on to the security post where he showed his credentials.

Something was happening, and he wanted to know what that was. Carling wouldn't summon him at this hour unless it was something significant. There were few cars in the parking lots. Reed smiled at his small success as he guided his sedan into a choice spot.

It could be a trick, he thought as he got out and locked the door.

A trick or a trap.

What kind?

He had to be ready for anything. They'd already tried many tactics to rattle, fool or intimidate him. They hadn't had a chance, he told himself proudly. And they didn't now.

More security at the building's main door . . . then up to Carter Carling's office. Reed carried the case with the jamming device to thwart any recording. There was no telling what they might try to trick or force him into saying.

Carling looked tired and troubled.

That suited serene and sure Edward Reed nicely.

The strong one had the psychological advantage in these mini-wars.

"Any word from your Spirit Team?" Carling asked urgently.

Showing weakness, Reed judged. No way to play the power game.

You had to be strong . . . alert . . . flexible . . . to win.

Reed knew that it was his time to win . . . big.

"They've picked up the sat photos of the valley and mine entrance," he replied, "and they're on their way."

"Stop them."

What was Carling up to?

"The DCI says stop them . . . now . . . immediately."

It wasn't supposed to happen like this.

"Why?" Reed blurted.

"It's complicated," Carling responded.

"Explain it in small words," Reed snapped.

Carling took a deep breath.

"New players in the game," Carling began. "They don't want to alienate our good friends, the Madeshis."

"The damn Madeshis would be Godzilla's friends if the money was right!" Reed erupted.

Carling nodded.

"I think you're correct, but State and the White House don't. The Madeshis swear the fungus thing was a small rogue operation that they're closing down right away."

"How did State and the White House get into this?"

"The DCI felt she ought to tell Maccarelli, and he covered his butt by telling the president," Carling explained.

There was no point in denouncing Carling for telling the DCI. The damage was done. Recriminations would only create more problems, Reed thought quickly. He needed good relations to sell the alternative plan. It wasn't as pretty but it would take care of Reed's future. He could still outwit them all.

"The DCI was very impressed by your initiative and creativity," Carling continued. "Good idea . . . bad luck. The political picture's changed, so we have no choice now. DCI says it's time to pull the plug on this. Send the recall signal . . . immediately."

Reed had long envied and despised Carling.

It would be a pleasure to see him sweat now.

Sweat? He'd *bleed.*

"There isn't any recall signal," Reed replied.

Carter Carling . . . in shock . . . had no idea of what to do or say.

Edward Reed did. He spoke with skill and assurance. Tonight all of them . . . even the DCI and the President . . . needed Edward Reed. He had something they wanted desperately . . . something no one else possessed.

"But we can still stop the operation," Reed added calmly.

"Thank God!" the deputy director sighed.

Reed couldn't help smiling when he thought of the money. Then he forced an earnest expression onto his face so Carling wouldn't suspect the slick trick that was coming.

"Before I say *how,*" Reed announced, "I'll tell you *why* . . . why there's no recall signal. I didn't forget. I didn't want any type of communication . . . any connection . . . that could be traced back to the Agency."

"Good thinking," Carling lied. The deputy director didn't really care, of course. Bigger things than Reed's ego were on the line. "How can we stop your team?"

"Not *we. I.* I'm the only one who can," Reed said arrogantly.

"Of course," Carling agreed with swift and utterly counterfeit sincerity. "You invented them."

"More important, I *know* them and they *know* me," Reed reminded. "I'll have to go to Madesh to find them and abort the mission. Face to face, it's the only way."

Carling considered the proposal.

"How can you find them?" he worried.

"They'll be near the new lab. The Madeshis will help me find them. I'll describe them . . . five foreigners . . . four men, one African and a Eurasian woman . . . traveling together close to the Torat Valley. Not many foreigners in the neighborhood," Reed pointed out, "so it shouldn't be that hard for the local police to spot them."

"You'll go to the local police?"

"Why not? You said the Madeshis are our friends, and they're deeply embarrassed by this whole situation. They'll want to help end this entire mess."

"What about the Spirits?" Carling asked.

"We've got to retire them," Reed answered. "Too bad, but the secret's out so they're useless to the Agency from now on."

"It could be awkward later if any of this leaked out," the deputy director warned.

"There'll be no leak," Reed promised and thought about the money as he left for his home.

Millions of dollars.

He deserved it . . . and he would enjoy every penny of it.

While he waited for an answer, he considered what he might do . . . and what they might do . . . if his plan was rejected. No, they couldn't do that. They had surrendered both reason and might to the unrealistic logic of politics that had put the Agency . . . and the whole government . . . into so many whirlpools and cesspools for years . . . but *they* could do nothing to stop the Spirit Team.

There was a clear choice.

Either they accepted Reed and his plan as a way to avoid immediate conflict with a "friend" . . . or they began the destruction of Edward Reed who'd defied their mediocrity and authority. They might smash him later . . . either bureaucratically or perhaps one of those car crashes once so popular . . . anyway.

They were afraid of him now . . . which meant they probably hated him, he reasoned. It might be prudent to prepare to leave. The four perfect passports and the rest of the stolen money were waiting for him in safety deposit boxes opened under other names.

He could travel light . . . flee swiftly.

He took out a loaded pistol and three extra clips from the safe he knew the Agency's experienced burglars had opened and inspected. The weapon was wholly legal, for Reed had a proper pistol permit issued in Virginia. Then he pulled a canvas suitcase from the closet . . . rechecked it for any miniature electronic beacons the Agency's gifted technicians might have covertly implanted . . . and found it was "clean."

He began to pack.

He'd be going either to Madesh . . . which was no picnic . . . or someplace a lot worse. It could be the unemployment office or perhaps prison, he thought as he put in a favorite shirt.

Or it could be a mortuary.

Now the suitcase was full, and he zipped it shut.

He was ready to go.

36

Lloyd **peered through** his sunglasses into the late afternoon
glare. He was driving the self-propelled vehicle, the standard
rolling office . . . equipment hauler . . . and mobile home used by
film and television crews around the world. Josephine Tan sat
beside him.

Another Spirit Team mobile unit was behind him.

The Madeshi border lay ninety yards directly ahead.

It was only a short time after Reed had promised there'd be no
leaks . . . and it was hot. This was usual for 5 P.M., and that was
the reason the ex-SAS commando had chosen this time. Baked
by the whole day's heat and bored by the dreary routine at this
frontier checkpoint where nothing happened, the guards here
would be tired and indifferent by this time of day.

The weapons and communications gear were well hidden.

Some fifty yards beyond the border the rented car waited, as
scheduled.

David Lloyd stepped on the gas pedal . . . then trod briefly on
the brake three times. The blinking tail light was the signal to the
mobile unit behind him.

At the wheel in that vehicle, Gamal Sharif nodded.

"We're going in," he said to the Nigerian.

Still the disciplined soldier, Chibuku scanned the area on each
side of and beyond the border post for any sign of troops or armored vehicles. Out of habit he was checking the lay of the land
for defensible positions or escape routes. So was Lloyd.

The team leader glanced at her again.

With a scarf over her head . . . no makeup . . . long-sleeved shirt and not-too-tight slacks, she didn't seem very glamorous or sexy or offensive to the dress code that local custom required. There was no reason for an unsophisticated border guard to suspect that one of the lipsticks in her large bag was a camouflaged Mace spray or that there was a .32-caliber pistol in a holster on her left ankle.

The other Spirits also had immediate access to hidden weapons, but they weren't supposed to use them unless Lloyd pulled out his first.

"Low-key and easy," Lloyd reminded Josephine Tan, and Mendoza who sat behind them. "And let's be damned careful with our guide who's waiting for us. We can't do or say anything that could make him suspicious. He's our ticket in . . . our pass to the valley."

"You said that three times," Mendoza observed.

"I'm telling you again. He's a decent young man, and we can't get him involved. If he gets one bloody clue," Lloyd warned, "that could be be very dangerous for us."

"And him," Mendoza added as Lloyd pulled the vehicle up at the customs post.

She saw the team leader nod, and she understood.

"James, he's practically a boy," she appealed.

"If we all play it right, he'll grow into a fine man," Lloyd answered.

Now the guards strolled from the shade of their small hut. Some had pistols in holsters on their hips. All of them had sweat-stained shirts and the gait of men whose feet hurt. One who had a couple of stripes on a shoulder patch and a US M-16 rifle seemed to be in charge.

He approached the first vehicle . . . gestured with his gun muzzle for the driver to open the window. Lloyd obeyed at once, rolling it down and thrusting out the permits signed by the Minister of Tourism.

Lloyd recognized the patch. He'd made sure the whole team memorized the insignia of Madesh's police, frontier units and army. This border patrolman with the M-16 was a sergeant. From the way he handled, studied, turned and pondered the passes, it appeared that he was also barely literate. Actually he'd finished the sixth grade. The problem was he'd never seen this kind of pass before.

Gamal Sharif got out of the second vehicle to help . . . and at just the right time. The uncomfortable sergeant had ordered his men to search the two mobile homes. The weapons and ammunition were cleverly concealed, but the frontier guards could get lucky.

Or unlucky, the Moroccan thought as he addressed the sergeant in Urdu.

If they found any of the guns, the Spirits would cut them down. They'd have to. Facing this, the practical burglar decided to end the search before it went too far.

Gamal Sharif switched to another tongue . . . a lingua franca . . . a language understood in many lands.

Cigarettes, the international currency more widely accepted in many countries than the dollar, pound, yen or deutschmark. In some of the former Soviet states it was Marlboros. In others a different American brand. Here in Madesh which had been part of Britain's empire, the preferred brand was London's crisp State Express 555.

The Moroccan opened a fresh pack, took out one and lit it. As he puffed, he casually offered the pack to the sergeant who accepted it as his due. After igniting the tip of a State Express 555 with a lighter "contributed" by a previous traveler, the sergeant put the pack in his pocket. The wages were poor and there were no bribes from smugglers who preferred more southern routes, so small "donations" . . . intended or not . . . were routine.

They were a modest price for border crossers who wanted quicker service and a shorter stop in the broiling sun . . . and the dust. There was a lot of dust here . . . and not nearly enough "donations," the sergeant thought as he coughed and inhaled some of the fine smoke.

At this moment the guide walked up through the burning afternoon. He introduced himself to the bored sergeant who seemed a bit more alert when Ibrahim Salim mentioned who his *first* cousin was.

And pointed out that the taping passes had been signed by The Minister. Mention of The Minister had a positive effect. Just as one of the other customs men was about to open a video equipment box that had a sniper rifle in among the gear . . . moments before Mendoza might have shot him dead with a silenced pistol hidden inches from the marksman's left hand, the sergeant made a shrewd decision.

Studying the pretty Eurasian woman and wondering what she looked like naked, he decided not to run the risk of some stupid complaint to The Minister or any other distant politician.

"That's *it,*" he said to the other guards, who immediately stopped their inspection. He eyed the passes again for several seconds, not warily but as a curiosity. This wasn't exactly a border crossing for VIPs, and he'd never seen such documents before.

He returned the passes to Lloyd who thanked him in English . . . which the translator converted into thirty seconds of flowery Urdu. After perfunctory examination of the Spirits' passports, the perspiring sergeant grunted and gave them to the first cousin of somebody who was a director of something in the capital.

The two mobile homes crossed into Madesh. When the guide urged the "producer" and Josephine Tan to ride with him in the more comfortable car so he could start describing the sights, Lloyd yielded the wheel in the mobile unit to Mendoza and walked to the rented sedan with the Eurasian woman. The air-conditioning was on "high" and it was startlingly cold in the car.

Now Ibrahim Salim waved to the sergeant.

After blowing a ragged smoke ring, the sergeant waved back.

"Nice man," the guide declared as he put the sedan in gear.

Lloyd decided not to mention that the sweaty and unwashed sergeant urgently needed a bath. Such a candid comment might seem inappropriate for an honored visitor, and disturb the guide.

"Charming," David Lloyd lied effortlessly and looked ahead at the stunted hills. He saw more rock than greenery, but trees and shrubs . . . even some courageous and colorful flowers . . . dotted the horizon. When the guide found it a strain to describe all this and the area's history of invasions and migrations . . . Mongol hordes and tribal armies and the kilted Scottish battalions London had marched through here a century ago . . . and still drive, Lloyd agreed to take the wheel.

Now Ibrahim Salim unfolded a map, tapped it energetically.

"Marvelous . . . marvelous," he said in a loud voice. "Great things ahead. We're on our way to a great sixteenth-century palace . . . about forty-eight miles from here. Straight down the road."

The two lane road twisted like a corkscrew, but Lloyd was prudent . . . and silent. He smiled and said nothing.

"It's a famous palace! I told you about it! Splendid for television! Walls, gardens, turrets and some fine birds. The prince used them for hunting . . . when there was a prince. We're a republic now," the young guide celebrated. "Yes, the democratic and Islamic Republic of Madesh."

He really believed that his country was a democracy, Josephine Tan realized. Was it youth or patriotism? Both admirable . . . both hazardous. She elected to concentrate on the landscape and the energetic guide's tales and running nature talk. He knew a great deal. Ibrahim Salim's education had not been wasted.

As the sun began to set he suddenly pointed ahead . . . and to the left. It was the long abandoned palace, as dramatic and magnificent as he'd promised.

And it was time to put on a show . . . to do a "shoot" that would fit and confirm their role. Lloyd pulled to the side of the road, and the two mobile homes came to a stop behind him.

It didn't take long to unload and set up one of the Ikegami video cameras that had cost fifty-one thousand dollars apiece. As a prelude to what they'd "shoot" up close the next morning . . . as an "establishing" shot to frame this sequence, they panned across the remarkable palace . . . then did both sides and the ruined gardens in front of it as well.

"Hawk!" the guide called out abruptly. "Black hawk!"

He pointed at a bird circling and gliding between their vehicles and the historic princely estate.

"It is good luck," Ibrahim Salim told the Spirits. "In my country this is tradition. We believe a black hawk brings good fortune."

"I won't argue with that," replied Lloyd who knew better than to challenge anyone's folk beliefs. "I welcome this omen of good fortune," the team leader said. "Let's hope we see more black hawks and our project is a success."

"Inshallah," the Moroccan added.

"If Allah wills it," Ibrahim Salim translated. "Yes, *Inshallah.*"

That night while they camped half a mile from the palace, Mendoza took from the mobile units' refrigerators some of the fresh food purchased before they crossed into Madesh and put together a creditable meal on the butane stove. The air was clean and the night was cool . . . well, cooler. After they ate and talked about the next day's shooting, some went to the tents they'd put up. Others bedded down in the bunks in the mobile units.

They didn't all go to sleep.

Lloyd wouldn't permit that.

Someone had to be on guard at every moment . . . because somebody, a bandit or a squad of security police, might attack in the night. It might even be deserters from some army unit ready to kill for their vehicles, other equipment, wallets or wristwatches. Each member of the Spirit Team wore a different kind, and none was heavy gold or bejewelled. Any one of them was worth six or eight weeks of a Madeshi soldier's salary.

The team leader took the first shift. While he looked and listened in the moonlit silence, he thought about Josephine Tan. Then he heard the distant call of a wild dog . . . somewhere out there calling to its mate.

* * *

Far away . . . across a continent and a wide ocean . . . Edward Reed was listening to a different kind of dog. As far as Reed was concerned, Carter Carling was definitely a son of a bitch. If the unimaginative, overcautious, treacherous deputy director hadn't told the DCI, Reed wouldn't be living on the edge of a knife.

His brilliant Spirit Team would be allowed to strike.

And they would succeed . . . *he* would succeed.

Reed would never forgive Carling for selling him and them out.

"State will be briefing the Madeshi ambassador in the morning," Carling announced. "Maccarelli will let them know you're coming to Jammur to help identify a covert action group that's operating near their new lab . . . the one they didn't mention because they didn't know an unauthorized splinter group was still in the fungus business."

Each side would know it was a lie.

Both sides would know that the other realized it was a lie, but they'd pretend that they didn't.

Everyone would save face and avoid the awkwardness of principles.

Rules of the game.

The old game . . . the new game . . . the always game that was now being played by tall children with hydrogen bombs and nation-killing fungus.

"What am I supposed to say about this covert action group?" Reed tested.

"Whatever will get the Madeshi to work with you in rounding them up," Carling replied carefully. "There's a real community of interest here. In one word, quiet. The Madeshi want to keep it quiet that this fungus was being developed there, and we'd prefer to keep the existence and mission of the Spirit Team even more quiet . . . a complete secret."

Carling hesitated for several seconds.

"We must suppress the fact that Barcelona Delta was cooked

by our people after we signed the treaty," he continued. "There's no good reason to identify the Spirits as ours either. They've got Russian weapons, you say. They *could* be Russians."

And they could be dead very soon.

That had always been Reed's back up plan . . . a last resort . . . one in a trade where last resorts came very quickly and easily.

"Or someone else on a recon mission for another power . . . maybe the damn Israelis," the deputy director said. "They're running *hot* operations in all the Arab countries, you know."

Then he said what Reed had been waiting for him to say.

"These Spirits aren't even Americans," he pointed out. "Never were, right?"

The unspoken message was clear and brutal.

To avoid political problems . . . to obliterate all traces of the operation . . . to bury the dirty secret of Barcelona Delta . . . to guarantee no future leaks, the Spirits could be sacrificed.

Destroyed.

"We have to consider *the national interest,*" Carling declared righteously.

Reed thought about the convenient, puffy, all-purpose phrase that governments around the world used to justify everything from gang rape to starving hordes of children . . . from naked betrayal to mass murder. The tragic joke was that the national interest could change at any time, and public servants had to pretend the past had never been.

Edward Reed didn't mention that to the deputy director.

Reed didn't care who lied or betrayed. He hadn't for many years.

Now he simply said what Carling wanted to hear.

"I'll leave for Madesh as soon as State has alerted our friends there that I'm coming to help them," Reed told him with a straight face.

With the usual stumbling and foot dragging of the bureaucracies of the two countries, a day and a half passed before Reed boarded the transatlantic flight on the first leg of his journey to Madesh. The whole thing was coming to a head, he told himself, and he couldn't help smiling.

It was working out remarkably well . . . for Edward Reed.

He could easily accomplish the three things on his agenda.

The personal one . . . the one that mattered.

As Carling wished, he would betray the Spirit Team . . . once his "children" but now more trouble than they were worth.

Then he would expertly and happily betray Carling and the other fools who'd never recognized Edward Reed's extraordinary talents.

Having done that, he'd gradually fake a growing depression and talk about being burned out. Glad to bury all embarrassing questions about the Spirit Team and any stolen money, they'd be glad to see this troublemaker go. He'd leave with a routine scroll of commendation and a modest pension.

And $4,176,000 of their money.

He'd have the last laugh on all of them.

Just thinking about it in the plane, he giggled.

37

After a day of taping at the sixteenth-century palace, they climbed into their vehicles at 4:50 and headed east. Lloyd had worked out the route and schedule after a long discussion with the enthusiastic guide, an energetic young man who seemed to excel at long . . . often interesting . . . discussions. He knew a lot, and was delighted to share it.

East was what mattered to the Spirit Team leader.

His simple plan was to start from the frontier and schedule tapings in twelve or thirteen places as they moved east. He never intended to do more than three before the "crew" reached the trio of ancient temples that just happened to be near the Torat Valley.

Not too near.

That could catch the attention of the Madeshi security units protecting the valley with the new laboratory.

These temples weren't close to the heavily guarded valley entrance. The historic shrines were on the blind side . . . behind the end of the valley sealed by nine-hundred-foot stone peaks.

Located in a bleak and arid area almost four miles from the back of the target valley, they'd been sadly unused since the last priests of that once great faith died or left two centuries ago. What hadn't been stolen from these once lavish centers by invading armies or assorted brigands had been thoughtfully looted by entrepeneurial local folk. A number of fine items from these temples had been sold to museums in London, Berlin, Tokyo and New York.

The young guide explained this as Lloyd led the small convoy

east again after the second day of taping at a famous royal tomb,
so prominent that it had its own gift shop. Actually it was more
of a hut and seemed to sell more bottles of nearly chilled cola
than color postcards or terra-cotta medalions bearing portraits
of the dead king. The cotton T-shirt Mendoza bought wasn't bad
at all.

Rolling on towards night and Jammur, Lloyd noticed an occa-
sional army truck . . . then a large military helicopter moving at
cruise speed overhead as if on some routine road patrol. Now he
saw another truck and a khaki-colored vehicle that could be a
staff car.

"Is there a military base near here?" Lloyd asked casually.

"Two," the guide replied proudly. "There's one for ground
soldiers . . . I passed it driving to meet you . . . and an airfield too.
Several kinds of modern planes . . . all gifts from the Americans. I
hear they're very rich but can't play rugby. Is that true?"

"That's what some people say," Lloyd answered.

"We have fine rugby teams in Madesh," the first cousin declared.

As he resumed his running report on the flowers and shrubs
along the road, Lloyd slowed to avoid running over a bullock
and cart and silently wondered where the air base might be. In
the mobile unit behind the rented car, the Nigerian soldier was
considering the same question. He'd seen his soldiers cut down
by fighter planes and gunships more than once. After the attack
on the laboratory . . . if they got in through the security units
. . . and somehow made it out, the strike force would still have to
go 140 miles to the border.

What kind of Madeshi air power would they face?

JAMMUR = 28.

The sign was in kilometers, of course. Lloyd's mind flashed a
map on his mental screen, and he realized that they'd pass the
army base at any moment. It was just around the next turn . . . a
sprawling installation ringed by barbed wire. That didn't bother
the team leader much.

The armored cars did.

He saw two of them . . . and a light tank . . . inside the gate.

Would there be any armored vehicles at the valley?

Now Lloyd turned on the car radio, and the sedan was filled with the sounds of a strings and percussion quintet playing vibrant Madeshi music that reminded the team leader of a concert by Ravi Shankar's group. Lloyd's head moved to the music, so the guide didn't notice his meaningful nod to Josephine Tan.

In swift response, she announced that she wanted to check one of her tape machines in the mobile unit behind them. Lloyd stopped the sedan at the side of the road, halting the small convoy. She made her way to the second vehicle, and she turned on a tape recorder.

After she'd slid out a concealed short-wave and wideband radio that could pick up many frequencies . . . including those of the army base and the not-so-distant military airfield . . . she thought about the other scanner. Not now. Not here. This close to a military installation some electronics person might wonder why a mobile home would need the kind of telescope antenna she'd have to raise.

In the dark . . . far from here . . . she'd get the frequencies.

They were vital for the escape.

In the car ahead of her, the young guide was giving it a rest. Pleased to see that Lloyd enjoyed Madesh's music which not many foreigners appreciated, Ibrahim Salim had fallen silent. The team leader enjoyed that nearly as much, for the first cousin had been pouring out facts and chat with nonstop gusto for hours.

As they neared the city of Jammur, the guide began to speak about its history and the famous poet who'd lived there. And that mosque had been the spiritual base of a remarkable spiritual leader who'd attracted students from as far as Lahore and Tashkent. Even though it meant deferring a visit to the place where a fountain with healing powers had been in a wonderful garden long deceased, Lloyd told the guide that he'd skirt the city so they might get to the ruins . . . their next site for taping . . . sooner.

That wasn't the real reason, of course.

Few tourists came to the backwater that was Jammur, and a convoy of three vehicles filled with foreigners might be noticed.

With the guide talking about the nineteenth-century victory— only ten kilometers *that* way—of Britain's Third Lancers under a very great general, David Lloyd directed the Spirit Team in a loop that barely touched Jammur. This route took them out to the east on the road that passed the Torat Valley.

The Moroccan had also memorized the map and satellite images. He knew that the fifth turnoff on the left led to the Torat Valley, and the seventh to the fungus laboratory's new home. Immediately after passing the fourth turnoff he took a video minicam from its plastic case. A few minutes later when he spotted the Torat sign, he aimed the compact camera and began taping.

And he looked, too . . . intently . . . carefully.

The cat burglar saw no guards or security post at this turnoff, nothing to suggest to drivers on the modest main road that there was anything significant here. At the next turnoff a mile away, however, Gamal Sharif and the camera both registered something else . . . something more.

Tire tracks. Wide tread . . . not a car but a truck.

Several such tracks that some security man had overlooked.

There had been a number of trucks. Deep tracks meant they'd carried heavy loads. It wasn't a lot to report, the cat burglar thought, but it was something. Somethings could add up or tear down, ruin a security plan that hadn't been meticulously executed.

Lloyd drove three miles beyond the valley where the blue murder was being readied . . . then turned left at a crossroads as the guide advised. The ruins they wanted for the documentary were on the far side . . . the sealed-by-nature rear side of the valley that housed the mine. Nature had built the walls tall behind these seven valleys, piling her stone from eight hundred to nine hundred fifty feet high.

The Spirits looked at this rocky barrier for several seconds when they got out of their vehicles. It wasn't simply that the back faces of the valleys were tall. They were steep . . . hostile.

"Very impressive," David Lloyd said loudly.

He was facing the other way. He had his back to the valleys, looking at the ancient ruins some four hundred yards away. The other Spirits followed their leader's example, showing the guide their interest in and admiration for the twelfth century site they were here to tape.

This evening it was Lloyd who cooked dinner, delivering a tasty French bistro menu that delighted Josephine Tan. The others liked it too, even the guide who complimented the mutton *daube* extravagantly before he ate the last bite on his plate . . . excused himself . . . and adjourned at 8 P.M. to his tent to sleep. The sedative that Lloyd had put in the young man's food had worked nicely.

He was snoring softly by 8:15, ten minutes before Josephine Tan opened the sun roof in her mobile unit and pressed the button that raised the telescopic antenna. Within minutes, she was recording radio conversations from the military air base and from Jammur's small civilian airfield. At the same time, the other scanner was locating and identifying the radar frequencies of the old fashioned equipment the military were using.

At 9:10 the Spirits heard a plane growl by almost directly overhead. It sounded like a turboprop . . . not a jet . . . more than one engine. She was puzzled, for both of the daily flights to the civilian airport were before 4 P.M., and the military weren't at all keen on night flights which they felt taxed their pilots' skills and the base's navigational gear and landing lights.

She handed the headset to the Moroccan.

He listened to the Urdu, and reported.

A special flight from the capital.

There was a VIP aboard, and the elderly turbo-prop transport was arriving at the military field in seven minutes. A staff car and driver were to be ready.

It was just over ten minutes before the plane touched down, and five minutes more before the VIP and the general who commanded the counterintelligence operations of the army got into the staff car. Since the vehicle went out to the runway where the transport halted . . . instead of moving up to the control tower as was usual, very few people caught more than a glimpse of the nameless VIP.

Just two or three noticed that he was Western.

Edward Derry Reed had arrived in Madesh to betray the Spirits.

38

While they were taping the historic wonders the next morning, Lloyd shocked her with a single sentence. He spoke quietly so none of the others would hear.

"We've got to get rid of Ibrahim . . . this afternoon," the strike-force leader told her.

"Wait a minute," she protested.

"How about three hours?" Lloyd answered. "I don't mean get rid of this fine young patriot *permanently.* I want him away from us for a while during active flying hours so you can go ahead with your scan of radio and radar frequencies."

It was a good idea and a tactical necessity.

She was sorry . . . said so.

"I misunderstood, James," she apologized.

"I probably should have phrased it differently," he replied.

She had leaped . . . no, fallen . . . to the conclusion that her fine new lover was a casual killer, and he was making it worse by being reasonable. She reconsidered a moment later. Not worse . . . better. That was how she felt now too.

Just before 11 A.M. Lloyd put the deception into motion.

"Ibrahim," he said confidentially. "Gamal insists on cooking us a grand Moroccan . . . or is it Egyptian . . . dinner tonight. He really needs your help. Would you do me a favor and go into town with him to buy the food? You know the town and the language a lot better."

They left at half past one in the rented car. The guide was tactful, kind and effective as he showed the burglar to an assortment of shops and stalls in the food section of the bazaar. The smiling first cousin was courteous, discerning about quality and politely picky about freshness.

He wasn't too bad at bargaining either, the Moroccan judged, though the burglar knew he himself might do better since he had more experience. This intelligent and innocent young man made the ritual process of food purchasing a pleasant interlude, after which he insisted on taking Sharif to an outdoor tea house where they sipped and talked about Madeshi cooking for twenty minutes.

"Tomorrow *I* will create the dinner . . . a Madeshi feast," he promised as they got into the car for the drive back. Moving through the middle of the city in crawling traffic, Sharif was concentrating on the tangle of cars, trucks, bicycles and horse-drawn vehicles when the guide suddenly pointed to the left.

"Central Police Station," he identified.

The Moroccan turned his head in automatic response, and saw four men entering the sturdy two-storey building.

Three were in the uniform of the army of the Islamic Republic of Madesh. They were dark and trim, stern faced and soldierly.

Gamal Sharif didn't recognize Colonel Kebeer, and didn't know he'd commanded the massacre of the blue people fleeing the Torat Valley. He'd never seen the counterintelligence general or the major with him.

But the fourth man . . . a civilian foreigner . . . was no stranger.

The burglar looked twice . . . then again . . . to make sure.

"Son of a bitch!" Lloyd said when the burglar returned and told him.

With the guide in the latrine in one of the mobile units, the strike-force leader waved to all the Spirits to gather round.

"He's *here,*" Lloyd said. "The man in the bow-ties . . . the man who recruited us . . . he's here. Gamal saw him with some army officers . . . one a general . . . going into the Central Police Station."

For a few seconds Josephine Tan wondered why he was here.

Then she understood and gasped.

"That's right," David Lloyd said grimly. "There's only one reason he'd be here . . . with senior officers . . . entering a bloody police station."

"He's here to *finger* us," said Mendoza who saw all the American gangster movies.

"He's the only one who can," Lloyd declared. "He's the only one who knows what we look like. This bastard can point out every one of us."

The Nigerian heavy weapons specialist frowned.

"You think he's here to sell us, sir?" he asked Lloyd.

"I think we're in fucking mortal danger," Lloyd answered harshly, "and I'm not ready to die."

Then he looked at her.

"I'm not ready either, James," she said.

"Why would he come to betray us?" Samuel Chibuku wondered.

"Because somebody or something has changed . . . or somebody's *perception* of something has changed," Lloyd replied. "There's been no solid fixed truth in this from the beginning."

"Russian scientists in American clothes and eyeglasses," the cat burglar recalled.

"And a lot of other triple-talk and bloody games," Lloyd agreed. "Right now that bastard may be showing them pictures of us or working with some police sketch artist. We don't have a lot of time, my friends."

"He doesn't either," Mendoza said.

"We'll take him all right," Lloyd responded. "We'll take him out because we have to. We'll *never* be safe while he's alive."

The Moroccan nodded.

"If he tried to sell us once, he'll try again," Gamal predicted.

"We'll take him *after* we do the lab," Lloyd told them. "Those blue corpses were real . . . I think. If I'm right, the fungus is real. Our plan to destroy the lab and wipe out the damn fungus is no fantasy either. It's a gamble, but it's real."

Mendoza leaned forward.

"What about the money we were promised?" he asked.

"First we'll do this lab," Lloyd answered. "And if we don't get killed we'll go after the money. I've got a plan for that. Then we'll take care of this bastard."

Mendoza shook his head.

"We'll never see the money," he predicted.

"Let's see the lab first. We'll have to move up the attack," Lloyd told them. "We'll have to do it tonight. Recon at 11:30 . . . strike an hour later."

He gestured to Josephine Tan, and they walked several steps before he spoke to her.

"If we hit at 12:30, it has to be *in* and *out*. No more than fifteen minutes down there. We make it or we don't. If it runs more than fifteen minutes, we're dead," he said. "If we're not dead, we're coming out the front door at 12:45 or 12:46. Probably under heavy fire. It has to go like bloody clockwork. You know the plan."

"I'll be waiting for you, James."

"Ready to move. We won't have a second to spare."

"Entendu," she said and went into the mobile unit which housed her hidden electronics gear. She had a lot to do. After checking the electronic record of local radar activity, she called in the Moroccan to audit the voice tapes of radio transmissions from the military airfield.

He listened for twelve minutes before he suddenly pulled off the headset, stood up and sprinted out to tell Lloyd.

"I think the *laboratoire* may have already started production," the Moroccan said urgently. "Radio message to the air base. A priority flight is touching down shortly after midnight for refueling. Be prepared to fill the tanks with full load of JP-4 jet fuel. The plane's carrying a cargo of toys for the poor children of Bangladesh. Nice gesture, huh?"

"I'll take a guess," the team leader announced. "It's a Fozira Airways plane, right?"

"Precisely, and it will only be on the ground for seventy min-

utes. And if someone loads a box or two aboard in that time . . .
perhaps more toys . . . no one would mind," Sharif said.

"It's a pickup," Lloyd reasoned. "Has to be, and you must be
right. We're running out of time, my friend."

"As always," the veteran cat burglar said.

"As always," Lloyd agreed.

In divisional headquarters on the other side of Jammur, Colonel Kebeer reread the freshly decoded message. All hospitality
should be extended to the visitor who'd come to see the "medical
service project." He should be taken through the clinic to see the
research unit that was being closed as the "fever research" work
ended.

There was a message buried beneath these words.

Kebeer understood it, and knew what he was to do.

He was to fool the gullible foreigner by showing him the underground facility they were starting to dismantle so carefully.
Unaware that the blue fungus was ready for shipment, the visitor
would leave with the image of complete Madeshi cooperation as
the ambassador in Washington had solemnly pledged.

There was more in the message.

With the inspection and deception completed, Kebeer would
leave the laboratory with the visitor. The same helicopter flight
from the guarded valley would also take out a small bio-box containing the fungus. The special container would be delivered to
the Foziran jet transport that was refueled and ready for immediate takeoff.

The joke would be on the arrogant Americans who tried to tell
the whole world what to do. The message . . . like all the others
about this fungus project . . . didn't indicate who'd ordered this
or who was in control. That made Kebeer uncomfortable. The
masked chain of command . . . the thought that someone outside
Madesh was in control . . . made the colonel even more uncomfortable.

Pleased that the fungus project was leaving Madesh, the colonel was glad that he'd soon be back to normal work that didn't

involve hundreds of blue corpses . . . that didn't force him to kill his own officers. He hadn't forgotten Aziz, and he knew he never would.

The blue women and children.

The screaming and then the smell when the blazing jet fuel ate the flesh. Those memories didn't go away either.

This whole thing was an industrial process, Kebeer thought. It wasn't soldierly at all. He looked at his watch, and thought about the foreigner who'd come to identify the Russian saboteurs. Why would Moscow send commandos here now? Were they really here to steal the fungus as the man from Washington said . . . or was it something else?

It was usually something else in these feuds between nations. Eastern or Western . . . large or small . . . whatever color or faith, it always seemed to come to something else, the colonel told himself. Then he found the man from Washington and told him something different.

Not entirely different.

It was another lie . . . another trick . . . another deed that had nothing to do with a soldier's honor. Kebeer explained that they'd be going out to the laboratory later. The American could see for himself that the rogue group's entire installation was being dismantled.

The man with the bow-tie pretended to believe him. He was enjoying all this intensely. He was back in the field . . . back in the action and exciting danger . . . and the best was yet to come. Within a day or two . . . three at the most . . . the Spirits would be found.

Power.

He had the God power in this.

He'd created them, and he would destroy them.

The Spirits were superb fighters, but he was greater. It pleased him that they wouldn't be taken alive.

And the renegade scientists were also doomed, Reed thought happily. They had no place to go, and they'd soon be there. Like the Spirits, they'd get no trial . . . no appeal . . . no deal. At first the greedy death-makers would be surprised. Then they'd be corpses . . . anonymous in unmarked holes. Nobody . . . not Washington . . . not Pariah . . . not the Madeshi could let them survive.

"We're flying out to the *facility* in one of those fine Blackhawks you gave us," Colonel Kebeer announced. "We can eat dinner at the base mess first."

For the second time today Edward Reed was depressed.

He'd had Madeshi food for lunch.

He didn't care for it at all.

39

The afternoon sun was beginning to fade when Lloyd and his crew got into their vehicles. Having finished their taping here, they started east towards the next site nineteen miles away.

Just in time.

Eight minutes after they left, one of the Madeshi Army's helicopter gunships swept over the valley that hid the laboratory . . . circled for a dozen miles . . . and radioed back that the search of the area had provided no sign of the Russian commandos.

Josephine Tan and the cat burglar heard the report, and she whispered it to Lloyd later while Sharif was preparing dinner at the new site—a collection of dramatic domed tombs of the dynasty that followed the Moghuls. The young guide stood twenty yards away talking with Mendoza, explaining . . . with gestures . . . how *he* would frame the shot if he were directing.

The marksman nodded in feigned approval.

He had no idea whether Ibrahim Salim would pursue a directing career . . . or be alive by dawn.

The Eurasian woman was also thinking about the guide's survival. Even if the Spirit Team might perish in tonight's strike at the security-ringed lab, Ibrahim Salim didn't *have* to die. To make it clear that he was a dupe and not an ally of the assault force, she did two things. With Lloyd's assent, she made sure that the guide received an even stronger dose of sleeping potion than he'd gotten the previous evening. And when he was unconscious she and the burglar bound and gagged him. They were especially careful in fixing the gag, looking and listening several times to make sure that he continued to breathe easily.

He did.

If he died tonight, it wouldn't be at the hands of the Spirit Team.

Having taken him out of play, they drove back warily in the warm night to the base of the tall stone barrier that protected the rear of the valley. Not the heavily guarded one where an abandoned mine hid a maniac's lethal dream . . . *another* next to it. Nobody lived in either now. Kebeer had cleared out everyone.

Small valleys.

Semi-arid. Lots of rocks. Few people. No questions.

No problem for a colonel and truckloads of armed soldiers.

The Spirits got out of their blacked-out vehicles . . . looked up at the crest. It was a daunting sight. Mendoza didn't describe the nearly sheer walls quite like that.

"Mother!" he whispered.

"The whole family . . . and former school friends," David Lloyd agreed. "It's recon time. Party of two. Me . . . because I'm an experienced climber and I do my own recon anyway. Gamal because he's done a lot of up-and-down work in his brilliant career as a break-in artist."

"How about breaking *out?*" Mendoza asked.

"How about helping us with the bloody gear?" the team leader responded.

The hidden weapons . . . climbing equipment . . . bacteria-proof garb . . . light body armor . . . walkie-talkies . . . black jump-suits . . . and explosives were extracted from concealment. As the Spirits donned the armor, jump suits and climbing gear, Lloyd turned to Chibuku. A veteran soldier with ample battle-field experience and substantial skills in long-range reconnaissance, he was an expert reader of maps and charts. He was the one who'd pointed out another possible entrance to the target.

Not the guarded valley.

The even more protected subterranean laboratory.

He'd seen it in the photos of the mine plans . . . the pictures the burglar had taken at the archives. He'd noticed that a second

shaft had been dug into the back of the same low mountain from
the adjacent valley. The British entrepreneurs had made another
effort to find more coal. On the old chart this later shaft *seemed*
to intersect with the lower recesses of the mine where ruthless
people were growing the fungus.

There were questions . . . life-and-death ones.

Did that second shaft still exist?

Had it collapsed years earlier . . . or was the long unused second shaft waiting to crush them now?

It was their only hope of getting in . . . and breaking out would
be even harder.

"Hope you're right on this, Samuel," Lloyd said and grasped
the African soldier's hand. Next the team leader shook the cat
burglar's hand too.

"Piece of cake," Lloyd said like a ritual mantra or prayer.

"Piece of cake," Gamal Sharif replied automatically.

Josephine Tan wasn't quite as cool or nearly as confident.

She wasn't part of any macho SAS or commando tradition.

She didn't shake David Lloyd's strong hand as a comrade-in-
arms. She looked directly into his eyes, and she kissed him. There
was no reason for them to be discreet anymore. It was too late for
that.

Lloyd and Sharif flashed thumb's up salutes, and picked up
their gear. They packed it—checked it—hooked it . . . looked at
the crest . . . and started up the rocky wall. The surface was steep
and unforgiving. It was a war right from the start.

Few handholds . . . even fewer places for their climbing boots
. . . many difficult outcroppings . . . place after place where they
had to turn and cut back to a different route. Suppressing curses
to save breath . . . they ascended slowly.

Aware of the threat of time.

Always aware of that and their rage against Reed.

They were half way up when they heard the distant clatter.

It was overhead . . . to the west . . . a mile . . . maybe two.

Then her calm voice came from the walkie-talkie that Lloyd

wore around his neck like some electronic talisman.

"Aircraft approaching. Speaking local on a military frequency. Signal stronger. Closing fast."

Lloyd and the agile Moroccan pressed themselves into the shadows as the noise grew louder. It didn't sound like a high-speed jet. They heard it slowing down . . . wondered why. If it was on night patrol protecting the area around the laboratory, it might start a searchlight sweep of the ground at any moment. The climbers and their allies below were in grave danger.

Caught out in the open, they'd be hunted down like game.

They held their breath . . . waited.

No hostile searchlight stabbed from the sky.

The aircraft was a helicopter, and the people in it had something in common with the Spirit Team. They didn't want any attention either. They were coming to an ultra-secret installation, and a powerful beam from the sky might be seen miles away.

Now the noise from the engines and rotors was deafening.

Lloyd looked up . . . then away. In the split second his trained eye and computer-memory had identified the craft as an American-made UH-60L, a powerful and reliable Sikorsky machine he knew well. He'd flown a dozen times in this tough and ready "bird" the US Army had designated the Blackhawk, a prime player in the Gulf War blitzkrieg

There could be armed soldiers in the machine.

The Blackhawk could move a fully equipped squad of infantry, 11 men and their weapons.

Now the helicopter slowly moved on, and stopped over the adjacent valley near the entrance to the laboratory. There it hovered for half a minute until somebody turned on a circle of ground lights to define a landing area. Then the Blackhawk descended . . . out of sight.

Lloyd and the Moroccan started up the cliff again.

Both of them were fit . . . strong . . . skilled in this work. They were also both panting when they finally pushed and muscled themselves over the crest. Lloyd mopped his brow . . . put on the

Red Army night goggles . . . turned on the infrared beam . . . and scanned the valley cautiously.

No one. No living thing of any kind.

And no surprise either.

Lloyd expected that special measures would be taken to protect the privacy and security of the subterranean death factory in the adjacent valley. It was both logical and tactically sound to move the few residents and their animals to another place six miles away . . . as Kebeer had done months earlier. This helped those defending the laboratory.

It also assisted anyone attacking from the rear.

Lacking time to enjoy the irony, Lloyd and Sharif looked around again before they drew silenced pistols from their gear bags and started down to the valley floor. It was much easier descending, but one thing didn't change. There were still dozens of opportunities to break a leg or a neck.

Or make a noise that would betray them.

Four times loose rocks fell clattering beneath their weight. Four times they froze, tense with pistols ready. Four times there seemed to be no reaction from any defenders.

It looked as if there were no sonic alarms in place.

You couldn't be sure, Lloyd thought. Bells might be ringing in some underground command post. Guards could already be on the way.

The two Spirits reached the valley floor . . . looked left and right slowly and methodically . . . moved out across the flat terrain almost soundlessly. It was more than a talent. It was a skill honed by a lot of experience in the staying-alive trade. They eyed the ground very carefully as they advanced. Some bastard could have seeded the whole floor with maiming anti-personnel mines.

The moon kept kept sliding and gliding in and out behind the clouds. They advanced cautiously, expecting everything and anything. Now they approached the place where the second shaft *should* be . . . where the old chart showed it *would* be.

There was no sign of it.

Some careless fool had erred in drawing a map over half a century ago, and soon a million people . . . maybe two million . . . might die for it.

Two million and five, including the Spirit Team.

Anger flared in the team leader. Cold and hard. Anger against the damn map-maker and Pariah and the man who'd come to betray them to the Madeshi. Lloyd *knew* . . . in his blood and bones . . . that this war couldn't end here or now.

Neither could David Lloyd.

He didn't speak. Neither did Sharif. They looked at each other . . . saw shared determination . . . and eyed the rocky floor of this semi-arid valley again. Here and there they saw heaps of crude brick and stones from small, ruined houses . . . some wrecks of what had been shelters for farm animals . . . several amputated tree trunks and a few shattered wooden fences . . . no opening of a shaft. No hope.

Suddenly Lloyd stepped back and pointed.

Not away, but at a low mound of stones almost at their feet.

They began to pull rocks and rubble from the heap. They ripped out scraggly weeds and stubborn bushes that bound the mound together. Then they resumed tugging aside and lifting many more stones . . . large and small . . . packed together beneath the stunted growth.

There wasn't anything here.

The cat burglar didn't say that though. In a minute or two the team leader would recognize this, and they'd try another heap. Then another.

Suddenly they both saw it. There was a rough rectangle of worn grey planks . . . the weathered lid of the shaft . . . hidden and waiting for decades. Time and rain that had penetrated through the upper rocks had rotted some of the aged wood. That made it easier to pull and wrestle the old planks apart.

Lloyd and Sharif paused . . . smiled at each other.

The war against the fungus and the bastards . . . *all* the bastards . . . wasn't lost yet.

Now the lid was demolished. Lloyd and the Moroccan stared at the black hole. Then they closed their eyes to recall the details on the chart. After a dozen seconds, they opened their eyes and pointed their infrared beams down into the darkness. They couldn't see very far . . . but they couldn't wait either. The team leader pointed into the opening, and they entered.

The shaft was nearly seven feet wide . . . six high . . . and had an odd, nasty odor. As they moved forward warily they discovered what it was. The earthen floor was littered with the skeletons of rats . . . hundreds of them . . . that had died and rotted here.

Both men had smelled death before. They kept going.

Here the tunnel narrowed for several yards. *There* they almost stumbled into a wide hole where a big chunk of the floor had collapsed. At several places the wooden supports along the walls of the passage were visibly dry-rotted, and fallen rocks nearby forced the two intruders to turn sideways so they might . . . barely . . . inch through.

Some three hundred ten yards away, Colonel Kebeer led Edward Reed and a taciturn Foziran officer from the outer area of the mine, where supplies were unloaded, up to the massive airlock. The Foziran major, who'd come in the civilian airliner, was in a business suit. Kebeer had introduced him to Reed as an inspector from the Ministry of Health.

"We're investigating this entire project," Kebeer lied. "The whole operation was shut down as soon as we learned about it. Fortunately it never got into production."

Reed didn't believe a word of it, but he played the insane game he knew so well. He nodded gravely, and silently wondered when he'd meet the Rosebud renegades. They were an *interesting* minority. The large majority of the Rosebud men and women had rejected corruption and dishonor, two of Edward Reed's favorite preoccupations. He hoped that he'd find out why this group had yielded to temptation.

Was it only the money . . . or something else?

Reed realized that they wouldn't want to tell him. Perhaps

they didn't even know themselves . . . didn't want to know. It was too bad so many people shunned the dark places within them, Reed thought. Then his attention abruptly moved to other things as Kebeer guided them through the airlock into a different world.

Everything was white and brilliantly lit.

It looked almost sterile, reminding Reed of the terrible fungus.

This immaculate, modern, scientific looking place could kill you, the CIA executive thought. It was cool down there and frightening . . . but exciting too. Following Kebeer, Reed eyed the unmarked doors on both sides of the long passage.

These doors were made of steel, he realized.

And there was something unspeakable . . . lethal . . . and intriguing behind one of them.

Which one?

Would the scientists be as menacing as their creation . . . or simply boring like so many other people? That intellectual Jewish woman in New York . . . something Arendt . . . had won fame writing about the Holocaust and the *banality* of evil. Reed wondered whether these world-threatening renegades would be banal and mediocre too.

Kebeer suddenly stopped beside an intercom unit mounted on the wall beside a door. He said something in Urdu into the squawk box, and inserted a plastic ID card into a slot beneath it. Five seconds later they heard a click, and the door opened.

Not very far away . . . in the other shaft . . . the long-abandoned one that was neither clean nor white nor brightly lit . . . the space that was dark and dirty and dangerous in a different way . . . the Spirits advanced.

No time. No choice. They had to.

Silently . . . stubbornly . . . Lloyd and the slim burglar moved through the blackness. Everything looked strange in the unreality of the infrared beams. In some places the Spirits had to bend low to get through . . . in others they sucked in breath and body . . . always wary not to touch anything that might trigger a cave-in.

As they pressed ahead, one thing remained constant. It was the stench of the rats. Some of them must have died recently, Lloyd calculated. That was promising.

To survive the rats had to eat something . . . drink something. This meant they must have access to the other shaft that housed the laboratory and its staff. In that place there would be food and water for the people . . . and a way out to the other valley.

David Lloyd led the way forward for another sixty yards. He stopped abruptly when he spotted the narrow beam of light from a small opening low in the side of the tunnel . . . not far above the floor. When he reached it, he slid up the night goggles and crouched down to take a look.

He saw Reed with some other people. It was difficult to count how many for Lloyd's peep-hole was not large. One of the others was a tall man in the uniform of a Madeshi colonel. There was also a man and a woman whom the team leader recognized from the video cassette he'd been given in San Juan . . . two of the "Russian" scientists.

To hear what was being said, Lloyd shifted and pressed his ear to the opening. The Madeshi colonel thanked the scientists for their "contributions to agricultural research," and wished them a safe voyage home. When they replied, both the man and woman sounded absolutely American.

That didn't bother Lloyd at all, for he'd expected it. What troubled him acutely was the sight of Reed. The cool professional team leader had to suppress an impulse to shoot him down on the spot. Lloyd didn't like the surge of emotion. It wasn't supposed to happen.

It was dangerous for all of them . . . and the mission.

He forced himself to concentrate on the next step in the assault. Lloyd stood up, took a small electronic device from his bag. This very sensitive eavesdropping instrument was equipped with a short-range transmitter. He flicked the "on" switch before he placed it in the opening.

Now the team had an "ear" to listen for them.

Lloyd and Sharif started back to the surface. When they finally emerged, clouds obscured the moon and the valley was dark. The team leader looked through his light-magnifying goggles towards the rear of the valley . . . then up to the top of the cliff over which he and the Moroccan had entered.

The others should be on the crest by now.

Lloyd's eyes moved back and forth slowly, searching for them but they were nowhere in sight.

It was time for the strike force to assemble and go on together to the attack. There was hardly a minute to spare.

Where were they?

40

Some twenty-five yards outside the valley, Josephine Tan tried not to worry about her lover. Seated before the radio in the mobile unit where the drugged guide slept, she was systematically and expertly sweeping the frequencies used by the military air field and army base.

There was an automatic weapon beside the radio.

Every forty or fifty seconds she eyed her gold wristwatch. It was clear that the final battle was at hand, and minutes would count as much as bullets. The man about whom she cared so much and knew so little had told them that when he spelled out his plan.

Like this remarkable man, it had no margin for error.

What was he doing now?

At that moment, Chibuku and Mendoza were still almost one hundred ten feet below the crest of the cruel wall. Using gear and methods similar to those that had brought Lloyd and the cat burglar to the top, they fought their way up . . . hand over hand . . . as if in man-to-man combat. Bearing larger equipment bags than the two Spirits who'd gone ahead to scout, they finally made it over the highest point.

Breathing hard, they took off climbing gloves and put on the Red Army's finest night goggles.

After several seconds of tension, they spotted two small figures about five hundred feet away on the valley floor.

Lloyd saw them at the same time.

"Come right down, but be damned careful," he ordered over

his walkie-talkie. "Steep slope. Loose rocks. Repeat, loose rocks."

When they met near the shaft opening, Lloyd came right to the point.

"Our lucky night," he said. "The bastard who's here to sell us is down in the laboratory. There are soldiers there too . . . with a full colonel . . . and those not-so-Russian scientists."

"Troop strength?" the practical Nigerian officer asked.

"I don't know, and I don't know where the guard posts are either."

"Location of the fungus?" Mendoza questioned.

The team leader shrugged.

"I wish I could tell you," he replied. "Our intelligence is *far* from complete. From a professional point of view, it wouldn't be sensible to press this attack."

Mendoza recognized the steel and anger in his voice.

The sharpshooter decided to take a chance.

"You feeling sensible?" he challenged.

"Not very," David Lloyd answered, "and not safe either . . . and I don't like it."

The Spirits looked at their leader . . . then at each other.

For a few moments they thought about the fungus . . . and Reed, who threatened their future . . . and the rogue scientists who threatened the whole world.

"I don't like it myself," Mendoza announced. "Maybe the attack isn't exactly sensible, but I say *let's do it.*"

Lloyd saw the others nod and shoulder their weapons bags.

"Any questions?" the team leader asked.

"What about the germ-proof suits?" Chibuku said.

"We'd never get through this shaft's narrow tunnels with the suits intact," Lloyd answered, "and a surprise attack from the rear . . . through these tunnels . . . is our *only* chance."

Now the clouds parted and the team leader looked up at the sky.

He saw the full moon. Was it some sort of sign?

"From here on, no talking except in emergencies," he ordered. "Follow me."

As they stepped up to the entrance of the shaft, Josephine Tan glanced at her watch again and sighed. Then she spoke seven words into the microphone of her scrambler-equipped transmitter.

From somewhere, somebody responded with four words.

The Spirits didn't utter even one as they trailed David Lloyd . . . very carefully . . . into the shaft. Putting on their infrared goggles, they remained silent as they descended . . . eyed the old tunnel . . . and tried not to choke on the vile odor of the legion of rotted rat corpses.

The team leader drew a silenced Chinese pistol from his bag, and pointed straight ahead. In single file, they followed him as he made his way back towards the place where he'd placed the listening device and minitransmitter. The Spirits were eighteen yards away from it when Lloyd's walkie-talkie suddenly picked up what the eavesdropping unit was hearing.

Two voices . . . both male.

Since their native tongues differed, they spoke to each other in a third language . . . a common one they'd learned at school.

English.

English English. They'd both had teachers educated in England or teachers who'd learned from other teachers who studied there.

The two men addressed each other as colonel and major. One was Kebeer . . . the other the Foziran officer who'd come in a business suit on a civilian airliner to bring the fungus to General Hassan. The colonel and the major were easy to understand as they spoke crisply and clearly in the fine and starchy BBC tradition.

Half an hour.

That was all the Spirits had.

They heard the major say that "the box" would fly out with him and the unsuspecting American in thirty minutes. Then while the porky fool from Washington was working with the sketch artist and military police to trap the foreign raiders, "the box" would be en route to the Foziran capital.

"Then on to Israel a few days later," the Foziran chuckled.

"Are you *sure?*" Kebeer asked.

"I wasn't *told* that, but I heard we're collecting data on air currents there for next week. That's *Top Secret.*"

"I won't tell anyone," Kebeer pledged and he meant it. He was aware that offending Fozira's ruler could be a fatal error.

In the nearby tunnel, Lloyd saw the impact of the conversation in the cat burglar's face. He'd been born in Morocco of Jewish parents who moved to Tel Aviv from the Atlantic port of Essaouira, once home to a large Jewish community. Self-employed in recent years, the man who currently called himself Gamal Sharif had been . . . for a decade . . . a master thief for Israel's world-class Mossad cloak-and-dagger organization.

He was more than one of the best burglars on the planet.

He also had very good ears and an excellent memory.

"It's *Hassan,*" he said. "This box is going to Fozira, and under that refined English speech the major has a definite Foziran accent. This whole operation . . . it's all Hassan!"

David Lloyd nodded in agreement.

Mendoza's response to the name was less restrained.

"Road kill!" he said contemptuously.

The team leader looked at Chibuku and Sharif . . . saw the hard hostility and resolve in their eyes. They'd decided.

"Hassan isn't going to get this fungus," Lloyd promised and lifted the walkie-talkie to his lips again.

"Weather report. Weather report," he said.

"Wind from the west, seven. Repeat, *seven,*" Josephine Tan replied.

He understood. Then he led them to the eavesdropping unit,

gently and noiselessly pulled it free and pointed at the small hole.

"Quick and quiet," he ordered and tapped his silenced pistol. "We kick it in on the count of three."

In addition to weapons, ammunition and the light body armor under their jumpsuits, each member of the assault carried an extra climbing rope. The Spirits now tied these to wooden beams behind them, hoping the aged tunnel supports wouldn't immediately crack or crumble under pressure.

Ten seconds.

Maybe a dozen.

That was all the time the beams had to hold.

If they didn't stand up that long, the strike force would be pulped under tons of rock and earth in the collapse of the old shaft and the "dead" Spirits would be buried permanently.

Lloyd peered down through the small opening again . . . a final check of the target. He saw the Foziran in civilian clothes following the Madeshi colonel towards the doorway. The Spirit Team leader glanced at his wristwatch, and saw that the key number . . . the survival number . . . had shrunk to six.

It wasn't a race anymore. It was a desperate sprint.

Six minutes to do the nearly impossible or die.

"Set your timers for five plus," he told the Nigerian.

"Five plus," Samuel Chibuku confirmed in a firm even voice.

Battle time . . . and Lloyd felt a familiar surge of anticipation . . . almost exhilaration. He knew that it was neither adult nor rational, but for the moment he didn't care. For at least the next five plus minutes, he couldn't afford to care.

The team leader checked his assault team, and saw that they'd all drawn silenced weapons and hooked their climbing ropes to their harnesses. Lloyd raised his right boot several inches above the tunnel floor. They all understood.

"Maximum speed. Maximum effort. All we care about is the Goddam fungus," he said. "One . . . two . . . *three!*"

The combined impact of their climbing boots broke open a much wider hole in an instant. They swiftly smashed it even larger with a second simultaneous salvo of fierce kicks . . . then a third. Suddenly the team leader could see the whole room for the first time.

The Madeshi colonel was gone.

He couldn't be far, but that didn't matter.

Here and now was what counted. Everyone *here* in this chamber must be silenced *now* before any of them could sound the alarm. There were four human targets. Three were uniformed guards carrying M-16 semi-automatic rifles that the US had given to its loyal anti-Communist ally. The fourth was a swarthy male in civilian clothes . . . just a step from the doorway.

He was leaving, which made him more dangerous than the men with the guns.

He had a better chance of escaping to sound the alarm.

Lloyd computed and picked his target in a split second. He swung the silenced pistol and fired twice at the man in civilian clothes. Having just heard the hole being kicked open wider, the Foziran was turning in automatic reaction when the first slug tore off most of his left ear. The searing pain and shock knocked him off balance a moment before the second bullet went right through his neck.

He staggered out into the corridor, gasping and trying to scream. No sounds came from his ruined throat. Bubbles of blood billowed from his lips as more crimson dripped from what had been an ear.

The team leader was the first down the ropes to the floor. The silence in the room ended abruptly when the uniformed guards began firing at the other three Spirits as they swiftly descended with practiced ease. Mendoza held an automatic weapon that put three rounds into one Madeshi soldier's forehead. Another guard was taking aim at Mendoza when Sharif knocked him over with a shot in the heart.

The Nigerian was the last one down, silenced pistol in one fist and grasping his sack of explosive charges in the other. Lloyd was already at the doorway in urgent pursuit of the Foziran major when he heard an awful grinding sound behind him. He recognized it at once.

The other Spirits would know what to do, he decided.

He kept running.

His back was to the room now, and one of the guards raised his M-16 to shoot him down. The Madeshi soldier was interrupted when the tunnel that the Spirits had just left rumbled even louder . . . began to collapse . . . and hurled down a five foot section of beam that impaled the guard as if it was a javelin. He stared at the awful wooden thing in his abdomen in disbelief for several seconds before he died.

With the tunnel above caving in and only seconds before the room they'd invaded would be devastated, the three Spirits sprinted out into the passageway. Looking in one direction . . . then the other . . . they saw Lloyd running down the corridor to the left. The reason he'd chosen that route was obvious. There were crimson stains on the white floor marking the trail of the wounded man who spoke with a Foziran accent.

Simple logic. He was a Foziran major . . . a soldier.

Even hurt, he'd rush to protect what he'd come for . . . he'd do his duty.

If he did, he'd lead them to the fungus . . . unless he dropped from loss of blood first.

Now there was a deafening roar, and the room they'd left didn't exist. Clouds of dust and a barrage of rock and wood fragments exploded into the corridor as if a large bomb had detonated. For several seconds the Spirits were enveloped . . . almost blinded . . . in the fallout from the tunnel collapse.

It didn't stop them.

They coughed . . . cursed . . . grunted . . . and ran unhesitatingly after the team leader.

As the Spirits charged down the corridor to catch up with him, a door opened on the right side . . . then two others on the left. The people inside had heard *something* . . . felt *something* too. The thing that every one of them feared . . . and none dared mention . . . was an obliterating cave-in. They'd been told that wasn't possible. Still they had to know.

They opened the doors to find out what happened.

The Spirits saw them.

Urgent threat. Extremely dangerous.

That was how the strike force instantly categorized them. It didn't matter that they carried no guns. They had other deadly weapons. Their expertise in producing the blue fungus made their brains weapons of mass destruction. That was why the Spirits . . . quite deliberately . . . shot them all in the head.

It was take-no-prisoners time.

Some other amoral renegades might make this fungus or something worse next year . . . but not these. Only one of them was on the video they'd watched so many times. That left seven "Russian" scientists, and the bastard who'd come to betray them . . . and the fungus . . . to be destroyed.

How could they kill the fungus without terrible risk?

The team leader would know. He undoubtedly had a plan, they told themselves.

Around the corner in the passage, Lloyd first saw another crimson smear and guessed he was on the right route. Then he looked ahead. He caught a glimpse of the tall Madeshi colonel helping the bleeding Foziran. When the man Lloyd had wounded pointed back, the colonel looked in that direction.

He saw a stranger in a black jumpsuit . . . holding a silenced pistol.

Lloyd saw him; and swung the gun.

Kebeer had reacted immediately, dragging the injured Foziran around the next turn barely two seconds before Lloyd fired. The muted Chinese weapon made a soft "plop," but Kebeer's service pistol was much louder. Though he couldn't see Lloyd, the colonel fired three rounds to arouse the guards . . . to warn everyone that the impregnable secret base had been penetrated.

He helped-pulled the bleeding man . . . those red bubbles at his lips were *awful* . . . a dozen steps to a transparent box attached to the wall. Kebeer didn't waste time groping for a key. He smashed the Plexiglas cover with the butt of his gun, reached in and pressed the red button.

One push would trigger the fire alarms.

Three was the signal for an attack.

He pressed the attack warning . . . repeated it. Seconds later jarring klaxons were blaring insistently as Kebeer hurried the half-dazed Foziran towards Room 8, the scientific heart of the laboratory. They had to get there before the men in the black jumpsuits. There'd be more than the one he'd seen, the colonel thought, and they'd be merciless . . . as Kebeer would if he led the assault.

How many of them were there?

Did they know that the fungus was in Room 8?

As a security professional, Kebeer urgently wondered which traitor had helped them penetrate his defenses. As a practical soldier who even more urgently wanted to live to see the dawn, he grabbed the bleeding Foziran and ran for survival.

At the entrance to the mine and five other guard posts, uniformed men with semi-automatic weapons also ran. They fanned out in groups of three to cover each tunnel and the corridor intersections.

The "dead" intruders were running too. Only a dozen strides behind their team leader, they moved swiftly around the corner into the next passageway. The ugly klaxons were sounding loudly here too. Ignoring specific instructions to stay behind their locked doors if the attack signal sounded, the men and women who heard the tunnel collapse and then the shocking klaxons reacted instinctively and opened their doors to flee.

They didn't get very far.

With the element of surprise and need for silenced guns audibly gone, the Spirits blasted their way forward with automatic weapons, scything down everyone they saw and tossing grenades through each open door. When they paused before rushing around the corner, Chibuku pulled a prepared Semtex charge from his bag and set the timer in one move.

Five minutes.

Now the first trio of security guards faced them as they turned the corner. There was a firefight. Two of the Madeshi soldiers fell, and the third . . . seeing he was outnumbered and outgunned . . . fell back shouting for reinforcements.

Another passageway . . . another firefight . . . this time with two teams of guards and the survivor of the first one. The Madeshi were no cowards, but they were young conscripts with no combat experience trying to stop an elite unit of battle-tested veterans in body armor . . . men who were much cooler and much better shots.

The surprise assault . . . one they'd never thought possible . . . had shaken the guards, and the efficiency and ferocity of the frightening invaders in black hit the Madeshi like an earthquake. Five of the seven guards were down within seconds. Stunned by what seemed to be overwhelming force, the other two fled.

Another corridor . . . another time bomb.

This one was set for four minutes.

Lloyd was moving swiftly down another passage, following the crimson trail. A soldier stepped suddenly from a doorway, pointing his M-16 at the team leader. In reflex reaction, Lloyd shot first and he didn't miss. Now someone appeared in a doorway on the other side of the corridor.

As the team leader pulled the trigger, he recognized the face of a scientist in the video. Lloyd had no idea that this man was a forty-two-year-old US citizen named Harold F. Rice . . . a former employee in a Top Secret project codenamed Rosebud . . . a man who'd never had a traffic ticket and each month sent twenty-three hundred dollars to a nursing home near Tampa to take care of his beloved seventy-nine-year-old mother.

When the man appeared in the doorway, Lloyd fired at this enemy . . . if he worked with these bastards he must be an enemy . . . in preemptive self-defense. Rice toppled to his knees, tried to reach out for the dead guard's rifle. Lloyd shot him again.

The silenced pistol was empty. Lloyd put it in his bag, pulled out a machine gun and looked for the bloody trail on the floor again. He couldn't find it. The wounded man couldn't vanish without a trace.

He hadn't.

When Lloyd reached the intersection of two corridors, he glanced right . . . then left. There wasn't a drop of blood on the floor. No reason and no time to panic. The team leader began to scan the walls on the left.

A red smear . . . five and a half feet above the floor.

The wounded man had staggered, reeled against the wall before the colonel could support him. Left. They'd gone left.

Pain . . . fear . . . tension . . . death flooded the tunnels, but Edward Reed was smiling. He'd heard the klaxons and the shooting and muffled sounds of grenades, and they didn't trouble him at all. He was delighted, as he always was when he was right. These sounds had to mean that *his* Spirit Team . . . the people *he'd* chosen as the very best . . . had arrived. It was inconceivable that a small assault group could penetrate this heavily guarded place with a single entrance . . . but they'd done it.

He was proud of them . . . even prouder of himself.

Even if Madeshi troops wiped them out now . . . as must be . . . the Spirit Team had already proved that Reed was right in his vision. It was vision and imagination that made *him* greater than any of them . . . including the fools in Langley, Reed thought exultantly.

His smile grew bigger.

The man who was with him thought Reed had lost his mind in battle panic. That had to be it. The young captain . . . assigned by Kebeer to keep the American busy and away from anyone who might tell him what he shouldn't hear . . . certainly saw nothing amusing in a surprise attack by an unidentified force of unknown strength. With the gunfire and grenade blasts growing louder and nearer, the practical escort officer tasted fear in his mouth.

Not of the enemy strike force.

Of what might happen to friend and foe alike if a stray bullet or explosion released the thing that the foreign scientists were making . . . the thing the colonel wouldn't even name. No one but a maniac could grin with that stuff less than forty yards away in the place called Room 8.

Whether this smiling visitor was insane or not, the escort officer knew he must protect the American and guide him away from danger. It would be embarrassing to Madesh . . . and costly to the young captain's career . . . if Reed were hurt in any way.

"Colonel Kebeer said he'd meet us at the airlock," the security officer lied and looked at his watch.

Not far away, Lloyd was eyeing his own wristwatch.

Four minutes.

The red stains weren't as close together anymore, he noticed. That meant the wounded Foziran didn't have as much blood left to lose, the team leader calculated as he rushed forward. Too bad. Lloyd wasn't feeling sympathy for Hassan's envoy. He just hoped that the man didn't die before he'd led Lloyd to the fungus.

While he followed the trail, Madeshi guards stepped out twice to shoot him but Lloyd cut them down first with short, efficient bursts. He didn't even break stride as he put in a new magazine without looking. He didn't need to look. He knew this weapon . . . and many others . . . by heart as well as by eye.

Now a grenade rolled out into the passage.

That stopped him. He had to spring back ten steps and hurl himself around the corner before the grenade exploded. The episode cost him time he didn't have . . . couldn't spare. And he still didn't know where the fungus was.

Only sixty yards away, Kebeer saw the sign.

Room 8.

There were extra guards on either side of the door. Kebeer pointed to two of them . . . gestured for them to defend the passage behind him . . . the one with drops of blood on the floor. Not many drops, for the Foziran was barely able to walk anymore.

Kebeer used his ID card to open the door. Signaling to the other two guards to hold up the Foziran, Kebeer strode swiftly into the large laboratory to face a cluster of visibly agitated scientists and technicians. Though they didn't worry about the enormous number of people their blue fungus would kill somewhere . . . later, they were acutely disturbed by the klaxons signalling an attack . . . now . . . that might threaten their own lives.

One of the Rosebud people in the room seemed calm, however.

Kebeer was surprised to see it was the woman scientist.

While the others babbled questions and appeals, she stood coolly near the counter on which a small hard-sided suitcase rested. Reading the question in the colonel's eyes, she pointed to it.

"Is it ready?" he asked.

She nodded.

Kebeer began to reach for it. She grasped the handle first.

"I'm coming with you," she announced.

"You'd be safer here. We'll have them wiped out in a few minutes," he lied.

"I'd rather not wait," she replied firmly.

He had no time or need to argue with her.

"Certainly," he said.

While the others were pleading, she picked up the suitcase and started towards the exit. After promising the others that no one could break in, Kebeer walked quickly after her. Frightened and uncertain, the others begged . . . one wept . . . as the colonel and the woman left the big chamber.

The gunfire was louder now.

And Lloyd was getting nearer.

The team leader glanced at his watch.

Three minutes now . . . 180 seconds. It would be bloody close, he thought.

As he did so, Samuel Chibuku put another charge in place.

In the mobile unit outside the valley, Josephine Tan stood up and turned off her radio gear. She bent over to make sure that the gagged guide was breathing before she picked up her machine gun.

Then she left the vehicle, and turned her perfect-model face up to the stars to look and listen. Nothing . . . nothing but the beauty of the heavens. She shook her head . . . checked the magazine in her weapon. Next she reached into her gear bag to make certain that she had the two extra magazines of ammunition.

As her lover had told her to do in routine precaution.

He *couldn't* be dead, something deep inside her insisted fiercely.

Outside Room 8, one of the guards supporting the wounded Foziran spoke loudly to be heard over the noise of battle.

"He's out, colonel," he told Kebeer. "Going to be hard to move."

"He'll slow us down," the woman warned bluntly. "We can come back for him later."

She was shrewd enough to guess Kebeer wasn't coming back, the colonel reasoned dispassionately, and she was right about the unconscious Foziran. He *would* slow their escape, and he wasn't needed anyway. It was the fungus . . . not the messenger . . . that mattered to Hassan. Kebeer could deliver it to the Foziran airliner himself.

Another burst of gunfire . . . not more than fifty yards away.

Kebeer pointed at the woman . . . then the two guards.

"Follow me," he ordered and started towards the airlock.

As he turned right for the final twenty yards, Lloyd saw him. The team leader was entering the other end of the passage to Room 8 when . . . from behind . . . he caught a glimpse of the colonel, the pair of uniformed guards and a woman carrying a small suitcase.

Lloyd's finger froze on the trigger of his machine gun.

His gut instincts said . . . *loudly* . . . that there was a very strong chance that the fungus was in that suitcase. Under attack, she wouldn't be fleeing with her makeup. It would be something extremely valuable . . . crucial.

Three seconds to decide. Maybe four.

With about two and a half minutes left, he *had* to go with his instincts. That meant he couldn't shoot at her or the Madeshi officer. If a bullet hit the suitcase, the spores might be loose and everyone in this whole complex would die horribly.

Now two other Madeshi guards . . . much closer to him . . . were taking aim. Staring at the intruder in the black jumpsuit, they were a little scared . . . a little slow. He was neither. He shot them first.

Short bursts . . . both fatal. They dropped their weapons as they fell. Now Lloyd charged ahead to catch up with the suitcase. He was after the suitcase . . . not the woman. Aside from a fanatical female terrorist of the July 9th Brigade who'd been trying to blow him up at an airport, Lloyd had never slain a woman, and he wasn't looking forward to this shoot-out.

"Leader! Leader!"

It was the other three Spirits. They'd fought their way through half a dozen mini-battles with Madeshi soldiers, blowing up eleven offices and storage places on the way. In one of the shootouts a Madeshi bullet had grazed Mendoza's forehead, opening a small gash he was covering with a bandana that made him look like a gypsy.

Lloyd raised one hand to wave at them, stopped in mid-gesture.

"Drop! Drop!" he shouted.

Without an instant's hesitation, they hurled themselves to the floor. Lloyd swung his automatic weapon as they did so, pouring bullets over them at three uniformed guards who were about to shoot them in the back.

"Party's over," he said. "Let's go."

Mendoza, Chibuku and Sharif got up . . . looked at the one

dead and two badly wounded guards sprawled behind them . . . and turned to the team leader.

"Come on, dammit!" he called impatiently. "We've got about two fucking minutes!"

At the airlock, Kebeer used his ID card to open it. As it swung open, he suddenly pointed back down the corridor behind them. The woman and the two soldiers automatically spun to see what the threat was.

That was a mistake.

That was when Kebeer smashed his pistol butt into the back of her head. She was crumpling to the floor when he took the suitcase from her. Then the colonel pointed again . . . this time at one of the guards.

"I'm going through to get help," Kebeer said. "Cover the corridor."

"Yes, sir."

Kebeer gestured to the other soldier to come with him . . . turned to enter the airlock.

"Colonel," the guard standing beside the semi-conscious woman called out. "What about *her,* colonel?"

Kebeer looked down at her. He had "the box," and his flank was secure. There was no way the men in black could get through the airlock to pursue him. They didn't have one of the coded ID cards. They were trapped inside, and they die there.

The colonel smiled.

"Kill her," he said coolly and led the other soldier into the airlock.

The heavy door closed behind him a moment later.

He'd won.

41

There was Reed and the young captain escorting him.

Kebeer saw them as soon as he stepped from the airlock. The klaxon was still sounding harshly, but the colonel smiled as he closed the heavy door behind him.

Excellent.

The noise didn't bother him. Kebeer had "the box" and the gullible CIA official whom they had to get back to Washington alive. He could report that the Madeshi had cooperated fully and the project was shut down completely . . . it really was.

"All the records we'll need to punish the people who set up this rogue operation," Kebeer lied briskly and tapped the suitcase. "Let's get out of here."

As they walked towards the exit to the valley, a dozen other Madeshi soldiers looked at the colonel uncertainly. The klaxon kept repeating the loud warning that the installation was under attack, but these members of the perimeter defense unit had no idea of who the enemy was or what was happening *inside*.

"It's all right," Kebeer assured them. "We have contained the intruders, and they're just about wiped out. Maintain your positions."

Dubious but disciplined, these "good soldiers" asked no questions. They did what this full colonel told them to do, and he guided Reed, the captain and the guard he'd led through the airlock across the large outer chamber. He walked quickly, for there might be another force of men in black preparing a second attack.

"Hurry," he urged and opened the camouflaged door to the valley.

Some ninety-five yards away . . . on the other side of the airlock . . . the guard Kebeer left behind was following orders. After peering down uncomfortably at the woman on the floor for some time, he heard her groan and decided it would be better to get it over with now. Wondering whether it was true that Western women were promiscuous and insatiable, he raised his M-16 to shoot her in the head.

Two things happened simultaneously.

She opened her eyes and saw the rifle pointed at her.

David Lloyd and Mendoza appeared at the end of the corridor. Registering enemy soldier . . . armed . . . about to shoot woman, Mendoza squeezed off a burst that hardly left enough of the guard for any autopsy.

The Spirits ran forward, looked at the woman and every one of them recognized her immediately.

Another face from the video . . . another mercenary and very dangerous rogue scientist . . . another essential target.

She groaned . . . feebly pointed at the airlock.

"Get them! Kill them!" she gasped.

Lloyd looked at the door carefully . . . shook his head.

"Electronic lock," he said. "Heavy steel. Might be blast proof."

He eyed his wristwatch.

"One minute plus," he announced.

They'd come very close, he thought.

The charges the Nigerian had placed would be going off soon. At least they'd be spared having to kill this corrupt woman. She'd die with them.

She was clutching . . . clawing at the neckline of her blouse.

"Kill them! Kill them!" she insisted . . . and pulled something from inside the garment. It was a chain. Attached to it was her own coded ID card, an electronic key to the airlock . . . a card that Kebeer couldn't and didn't see.

While Samuel Chibuku was quietly placing another explosive charge, Lloyd deftly opened the chain's catch . . . pulled free the electronic key . . . pushed it into the lock. Then the Spirits ran into the airlock.

"They'll probably be waiting for us," Sharif warned as Lloyd prepared to open the door on the other side.

"It's a sure thing," Lloyd agreed. "Grenades . . . ready?"

He swung open the door, and the Spirits threw out four anti-personnel grenades. Half a dozen of the guards were sent flying. Seconds later the Spirits erupted from the airlock into the outer chamber . . . firing their machine guns as they came.

Some of the soldiers fought bravely, shooting back until they fell. Two of the wounded kept firing, but one guard simply fled for the exit and pushed his way out to the valley. The Spirits raced after him. As they emerged, the first of Chibuku's timed charges exploded deep inside.

The noise of the helicopter rotors was much louder. The Blackhawk with Madeshi Air Force markings was barely fifty yards away. Four men . . . three in army uniforms of the Islamic Republic of Madesh . . . were preparing to get aboard. One of the trio was carrying a small suitcase.

It had to be *the* suitcase, Lloyd calculated.

It had to be stopped.

"That's it!" the team leader shouted. "That's the box!"

The four men at the helicopter saw the Spirits running towards them. Colonel Kebeer rushed up into the rotorcraft, leaned down to pull in Reed.

"Shoot them!" Kebeer ordered and slammed the door.

As the rotors spun faster and louder in preparation for take-off, the captain and the guard began firing at the charging men in black. One of them was several strides ahead of the others, and the captain decided that he might be the leader.

The Spirits were all shooting at the helicopter when the Madeshi captain took careful aim and shot David Lloyd twice. The team leader fell. Now a crewman aboard the Blackhawk opened fire with one of the two 7.62mm machine guns, pouring out long bursts that made the other Spirits drop for cover.

They kept shooting from the valley floor as the helicopter ascended.

They didn't know if Lloyd was dead or alive, but they were certain about something else.

The bastards had escaped with "the box."

The unstoppable blue fungus was on its way to Hassan.

42

With its two turbo-jet driven rotors picking up speed, the Blackhawk climbed swiftly. It was over the edge of the valley when the Spirits heard a rapidly building screetch and rattling roar.

It sounded exactly like the helicopter that just rose.

It was.

Racing out of the night was another Blackhawk with the colorful insignia of the army of Madesh. Two of the surviving guards who'd emerged from the side of the mountain in courageous pursuit saw it, and cheered the arrival of reinforcements.

They stopped cheering when the Spirits drove them back with grenades. Then the men in black cheered, picked up their fallen leader and carried him to where this second rotorcraft was landing.

Lloyd opened his eyes . . . winced.

The impact of the two bullets was still more than painful, but the body armor had saved his life. His stomach hurt . . . and his chest felt as if he'd been clubbed with a large hammer. When he breathed, a rib . . . maybe two . . . hurt intensely. Probably broken, he thought and coughed.

That hurt too . . . a lot.

"You all right, sir?" Chibuku asked.

"Everything hurts," he answered.

"He's fine," Mendoza said cheerfully. "He's too mean to die."

The time bombs would be going off inside now, collapsing every tunnel . . . crushing every person and thing. All those greedy rogue scientists would be corpses, Lloyd thought and

286

winced again. That wasn't enough. The fungus was still alive.

They were at the helicopter, a powerful noisy machine whose overhead rotor could decapitate an elephant. The Spirits weren't afraid. They knew it didn't contain hostile soldiers or any enemy unit. The Madeshi markings were a fake.

This was the Spirits' own air force.

The team leader had planned the deception and timing . . . the entire escape. The country across the border also got Black-hawks six years earlier from those generous Americans, and one of the pilots flying them was bored with his job, his wife and his modest salary.

He wasn't at all bored when Lloyd and Sharif had offered him the equivalent of ten years pay . . . plus a nicely forged Turkish passport . . . to steal the fine Sikorsky machine and fly it to the place just outside Madesh where the false insignia were painted on with great care.

At the right time.

When the schedule for the Spirits' attack was set by coded radio signals from Josephine Tan's transmitter, the pilot brought the Blackhawk in over the border and came straight to this val-ley. He was a minute late, but none of the Spirits mentioned that as they hurried into his machine.

"Go! Go! Go!" Lloyd ordered and pointed up in the direction the other helicopter had taken.

As the stolen Blackhawk rose, the team leader spoke bluntly.

"That other chopper . . . we've got to knock it down!" he told the pilot. "Another ten thousand if you catch it!"

"You've got it!" promised the pilot who enjoyed using phrases he'd learned from American flight instructors.

He gave it full throttle. Now Lloyd spotted the other Black-hawk silhouetted against the moon. Unaware that he was being pursued, the man flying it was proceeding at a normal cruise speed. Sharing that ignorance, Kebeer didn't tell him to go any faster.

That was the colonel's second mistake of the night.

Behind Lloyd and the hired pilot, the other Spirits were opening weapons bags and boxes containing armaments Sharif had bought from a black market dealer in Istanbul. Suspecting that they might well have to fight their way out, David Lloyd had instructed him to "buy some insurance for the trip."

Now Kebeer looked at the suitcase . . . then back at the valley. He saw the other helicopter . . . closing fast.

What was another rotorcraft . . . it looked like a Blackhawk . . . doing here?

Taking no chances, he ordered the pilot to take evasive action which he checked with the air base by radio. He also told the two machine gunners to man their weapons.

"What is it?" asked Reed who watched the gunners prepare.

"I'm not quite sure," Kebeer replied and gestured towards the unidentified aircraft. It kept gaining. Fifteen seconds later, the pilot told Kebeer that the air base had no knowledge of another helicopter in this sector.

"Shoot them down," he ordered.

"As soon as they're in range, sir," the pilot replied and immediately alerted the machine gunners behind them to be ready.

In the other helicopter a mile away, Lloyd was in the co-pilot's seat beside the skilled aviator he'd hired.

"We're getting nearer," the team leader said.

"I think they're slowing down," the veteran pilot told him.

Ambush.

He didn't utter the word, but that's what all his instincts called out to him. He turned to warn the others.

"You ready back there?" he asked loudly over the rush-roar of the rotors.

"Just about," Mendoza answered.

"How's the toy kit, Samuel?" Lloyd pressed.

The Nigerian made a final adjustment before he replied.

"I'm ready, sir," he announced.

"Ready on the other machine gun," Sharif said.

At that moment, the Madeshi pilot saw that he was within range. He suddenly swung his machine in a tight arc and accelerated rapidly. One of his machine gunners sprayed the rear compartment of the stolen Blackhawk . . . then put another burst into the cockpit before the Madeshi pilot swung his helicopter away to get out of range of the other machine's guns.

Both of the rotorcraft were at about seventeen hundred feet . . . but that changed when the pilot beside David Lloyd slumped forward with three 7.62mm bullet wounds. Seconds after he fell forward on the controls, the Blackhawk went into a steep dive. He was mortally wounded, and the helicopter was also on its way to oblivion.

One thousand one hundred feet . . . nine hundred . . . six hundred.

It would be scrap in a few moments, Reed thought as he watched it drop. Maybe there'd be a fine explosion when it hit, he hoped. Then a fire. They'd be incinerated so they could never be identified . . . and that would also be quite appropriate. A blazing Viking's funeral . . . ceremonial farewell of the medieval Norse warriors. A burning aircraft would do just as well as the burning ships the Vikings used for their fallen heroes.

In their own way they were heroes, he told himself.

His heroes. Too bad about the Eurasian woman. It was a shame that such intelligence and beauty had to be cremated, but Edward Reed didn't need her anymore and neither did any government.

In another ten seconds the Spirits would be only memories.

Lloyd was pulling . . . fighting . . . dragging the unconscious pilot back off the controls. The team leader finally dragged him away as the altimeter showed four hundred feet. Now it was two hundred.

The falling Blackhawk was down to eighty feet when David Lloyd struggled and hauled the controls to level the aircraft. It shuddered and shook. It might have broken apart under the mas-

sive stress if not for the excellent engineering and workmanship
of a small army of men and women in Stratford, Connecticut,
where the burly beast was born.

Lloyd had no time to consider this. He was guiding a type of
aircraft he hadn't flown in four years . . . barely in control . . .
flying sixty feet above rocky terrain he didn't know. He was
under attack by enemies who were ruthless and evil . . . a reality
that made everything a lot better. Being under attack seemed to
clarify and simplify every awful aspect of this situation. It was
almost as if this was his natural environment.

Attack and counterattack . . . instant logical sequence.

All his human faculties . . . seeing . . . hearing . . . thinking
. . . were intensified, magnified, accelerated. He was operating at
top speed on educated instinct.

Dead ahead . . . two hundred yards . . . a small mountain. He
twisted the controls sharply, and missed it by a good thirty yards.
A very good thirty yards, he thought as the sweat coated his body
and he began the Blackhawk's climb to a safer altitude.

Eight hundred . . . one thousand two hundred . . . one thousand six hundred feet.

Now Mendoza came up to the cockpit.

"Jeezus," the sharpshooter said.

"And all the Apostles. We can talk religion later," the team
leader declared. "Tell Samuel to stand by with the toy kit. The
bastards are coming back to finish us off."

This time the Madeshi pilot approached more cautiously. He
knew that in fifteen or twenty seconds he'd be within range of the
other helicopter's machine guns, and he'd have to fly evasively.

That wasn't quite right. While the stolen Blackhawk's automatic weapons couldn't reach him yet, the toy kit could. Built as
an air defense weapon for ground troops, the Stinger had more
range and other important features.

Like a heat-seeking head. That's what guided the supersonic
infrared missile straight as an arrow to the rear engine of the
Madeshi helicopter. The passive combined infrared and ultravio-

let homing system rammed the rocket precisely into the target, blasting off the 1,870-horsepower propulsion unit . . . back rotor . . . and the Blackhawk's tail.

Now it was the Madeshi chopper that was in trouble.

The dry-throated pilot was struggling to control his maimed machine as it began to circle . . . as if it had a mind of its own . . . in a wide, lazy curve. Like some injured dog, the Blackhawk seemed to be making its way "home" to where it had picked up Reed, the young captain, Kebeer and "the box."

With one rotor gone, its speed was falling. It was limping along at barely one hundred five miles an hour . . . then less . . . and it was losing altitude. Smoke was trailing from a small fire in the broken rear.

Down below on the ground, Josephine Tan heard the sounds of a helicopter and looked up at the sky. A rotorcraft was drifting closer. Now she saw the yellow flames. Which Blackhawk was it?

Another one appeared. As the injured aircraft wobbled ahead and down, the second Blackhawk flew behind it . . . one hundred fifty feet higher. Which one had the fungus? Which held her lover and the other Spirits?

With great skill and enormous physical exertion, the Madeshi pilot barely managed to clear the outer wall of the valley and ease his crippled craft down. It wasn't a gentle landing. The machine hit the rocky floor of the valley with an impact that broke off another six feet of the rear. If the helicopter wasn't built with extra strength and materials to survive hostile fire, everyone on board would have perished in the crash landing.

A gunner and the co-pilot did, but Kebeer, Reed, the escort captain and the pilot managed to stumble out of the ruined metal thing. Cut and bruised . . . gasping and more than a little shaken . . . they walked and staggered from the wreck.

The men in black had found the invisible laboratory . . . penetrated the impregnable underground installation . . . and brought through Madesh's air defenses a surprising helicopter with an equally surprising weapon. And they'd knocked down Kebeer's own chopper, but they hadn't won . . . and they wouldn't.

Kebeer had the suitcase.

The Foziran plane would wait.

There would be more Madeshi military aircraft here soon, and they'd drive off or destroy the other Blackhawk.

Then the colonel would bring the suitcase to the Foziran transport, which would fly home under the cover of darkness.

There'd probably be a medal in this for him, Kebeer told himself. Maybe a promotion to general. He certainly deserved it. The enemy had been *very* good, he admitted, but he'd been better. A medal and maybe a large gift from the very rich ruler of Fozira, Kebeer thought.

He glanced at the American. The CIA official's clothes were ripped, and he seemed somewhat dazed.

"Are you all right?" Kebeer asked.

The man from Washington shook his head silently.

It wasn't supposed to go like this.

His stomach was knotted and curdled with fear, and he *hated* it.

The sound of the other Blackhawk was growing louder.

It was sweeping in . . . perhaps for the kill. Holding the handle of the suitcase in his right hand, Kebeer took Reed's elbow with his left.

"They may be coming in to strafe," the colonel warned. "Let's get away from the plane and take cover."

Reed recognized that this was a sensible precaution, but neither of them took cover. The flames in the burning tail clawed higher, and suddenly reached out to touch the fuel tank. The powerful explosion threw the crash survivors through the air like projectiles, hurling them in an arc of violence.

The pilot was tossed a dozen yards, dropping on a low stone wall that broke both his legs. Kebeer was slammed into the ruin of a well. Edward Reed had his left shoulder shattered when he dropped on a jagged outcropping of rock.

The pain was terrible, but it could have been a lot worse he thought. Broken shoulders heal, he told himself as he stood up moments later. Then he saw another shoulder . . . a leg . . . two skulls.

All human . . . all bleached by sun and wind.

Bones . . . human and animal . . . were scattered all around him.

Suddenly Reed realized where he was.

The Torat Valley. He was trapped in the Torat Valley, the one that Madeshi troops had sealed after the Barcelona Delta massacre.

There must be some way out. There had to be. He'd climb out with the tall Madeshi colonel. Reed turned to find Kebeer . . . didn't see him but noticed the suitcase broken open by the explosion and impact when it hit a boulder. He could hear the other helicopter hovering overhead, and in reflex reaction peered up to see where the enemy was.

In the jagged circle of light cast by the burning wreck of the Madeshi rotorcraft, he saw something else first. It was a fine blue mist. Puzzled, he stared at it for several seconds before he realized what it was.

These were the fungus spores that so many had died for.

The wonderfully sophisticated . . . totally illegal . . . utterly amoral . . . and completely untreatable Barcelona Delta.

The impressive scientific horror that would soon cover and murder him.

In the helicopter overhead, The Spirits were too high above the valley floor to see the look of terror that distorted Edward Derry Reed's face. They couldn't hear him howling either.

They flew lower, machine guns ready as they turned on the Blackhawk's searchlight. Burning fuel from the rotorcraft was spreading. Now Lloyd spotted the broken suitcase, and he reacted immediately.

He pulled back on the controls, sent the helicopter rising rapidly and away from the danger. As the Blackhawk raced away to pick up Josephine Tan, Reed walked over to the young captain who'd been his escort and protector. The Madeshi officer had lost half his uniform and most of the hair on his head to fire. He sat on the ground among the bones, barely conscious.

He simply stared when Reed walked over and took the pistol from his holster. He didn't say a word when the American turned . . . slowly strode a few yards away . . . and put the gun muzzle in his mouth.

43

In the great tradition of international diplomacy, Madesh and the United States lied to each other shamelessly during the next three days.

Madesh's ambassador in Washington reported "with regret" that Reed and military officers escorting him had died in a helicopter accident after inspecting the "totally terminated" agricultural "research project." When two satellite scans showed the mine entrance collapsed . . . plus the wreckage of a burned Blackhawk with several fresh human corpses in the Torat Valley boneyard, the Department of State decided to accept the tale even if it was probably neither the whole story nor entirely true.

Secretary of State Maccarelli responded by thanking the Madeshi government for its cooperation. He added the automatic request that his condolences be transmitted to the families of the dead escort officers and helicopter crew. There was no request that Reed's remains be sent home.

Both the Army and the CIA had made it unpleasantly clear that bringing the corpse back might raise even more unpleasant questions. It really wasn't practical anyway. First of all, it would be almost impossible to determine which of the ghastly blue bodies had been Reed. Second, no one employed by either the US or Madesh would go anywhere near any of the fungus-covered corpses.

Each government was tacitly relieved that *it* seemed to be over. Since the proprieties of prevarication had been mutually observed . . . from a respectful distance, both governments could go back to the normal charades, oratorical obfuscations and ritual deceptions that helped pass the time.

The Spirits didn't think it was over.

They weren't nearly as relaxed about the past . . . present . . . or future.

Assembled in the hotel room in Zurich, they were furious.

The glare in the eyes of the cat burglar and the Nigerian soldier was rich in rage, and Mendoza spit out a curse that sounded lethal even in mellifluous Spanish.

"*Merde! Merde! Merde!,*" Josephine Tan agreed indignantly. "First this *bête* tries to sell us out, and then this *rape!*"

With Reed dead, it was highly unlikely that his unidentified associates would pay each of the Spirits the half million dollars he'd promised as completion fee for the mission. That was more than bad enough, but it wasn't all. On his way to Madesh to betray them, the computer-cunning father of the Spirit Team had managed to empty their special Swiss, Bahamian and Panamanian bank accounts into which he'd been paying their earnings every month.

"It is a rape," Lloyd said, "but not entirely a surprise. I never quite trusted that man. In our trade, devious is normal and tricky is fine . . . but he always seemed just a bit *too* devious . . . a bit *too* bloody tricky."

"This won't get us our money," Mendoza declared bitterly. "Talk won't do it."

David Lloyd walked to the bar . . . poured two small balloon glasses of elegant Delamain cognac . . . and gave her one.

"Talk is *exactly* what will do it," David Lloyd disagreed and sipped the golden pleasure. "Not *our* talk. *His.* Every time I spoke with that man I was wired. I have it all on tape."

Chibuku and Sharif nodded in admiration.

Now the team leader looked at her.

"What about you?" he asked.

"I didn't trust him either," she replied and tasted the fine cognac. *"Oui,* I was wired every time too . . . You knew that, didn't you?"

He smiled . . . sampled the cognac again.

"Just a guess," he said. *"Lucky* guess."

She shook her head. She didn't mind his modesty, but she didn't believe it either.

"There was *something* about that man," she recalled with a frown. "He was what the Americans call *spooky."*

"That makes sense," Lloyd told her amiably. "He was a spook,"

The other Spirits recognized the word. It was standard usage in Washington and among media across the US for an employee of the much-criticized Central Intelligence Agency.

"Our money?" Mendoza reminded.

"I have a plan," Lloyd told them quietly.

"Of course," she said and beamed. He always had a plan . . . as the unit commander should.

"And there's something else to take care of in addition to the money," David Lloyd announced.

"Something or *someone?"* the cat burglar tested.

"Both," the team leader replied. "I'm thinking about that thug in Fozira."

"So am I," Sharif said. "Do you have a plan?"

"Yes," the team leader acknowledged, "but something in the way you just asked suggests you have one too. I'd like to hear it."

There was anger in Sharif's short hard-edged sentences.

There was also considerable intelligence and logic.

The other Spirits all nodded in approval.

"That's a *fine* plan," Samuel Chibuku judged.

"It could work," Mendoza agreed.

"What do you think?" Sharif asked the team leader.

David Lloyd smiled . . . sipped the aged cognac again.

"Brilliant," he replied. "Do it."

Four days later, a senior technician in the State Security orga-

nization of the zoo that was the government of Fozira finished
his seventh rechecking of the package with X-ray machine,
magnetometer, explosives detector and a sniffing dog trained to
identify bombs or drugs. Then he repeated all the tests again.

You couldn't be too careful with packages going to the Supreme Leader for Life . . . not if you valued your own.

General Hassan had so many enemies. They were so devilish.

The technician finally got up the courage to start unwrapping
the parcel. He knew there were bombs that went off when the
outer string was cut. Taking no chances of some ingenious new
trick he hadn't detected, he put the package in the "bomb room"
with thick walls and no window. Using the closed-circuit television and remote-controlled "fingers" patiently and carefully, he
severed the string.

There was no blast.

Then he looked at the gauge on the air analyzer.

No poison gas.

It took him thirty-one minutes to remove . . . layer by layer
. . . the materials that shielded the innermost contents. He didn't
see them clearly until he adjusted the lens of the video camera.

Close-up. A round plastic thing . . . an inch high and five
inches in diameter like some unusual compact for a woman's face
power. It was bright blue . . . an unusual shade of bright blue.

Close Up. A square envelope . . . about six by six inches . . . the
sort that might enclose a birthday card. There were three words
printed in block letters.

General Hassan.

Personal.

The technician informed his supervisor who notified a colonel
When word reached Fozira's cruel and cautious leader, he appeared to be uneasy when he heard about the bright blue plastic
container. He looked even more concerned when he asked where
the box had come from and was told that the return address on
the outer wrapper was the Final Mining Company . . . Torat Valley . . . Madesh.

Above General Hassan's name on the outer wrapper was a block of stamps from Madesh, but they hadn't been cancelled. Wondering how the package came through the mail . . . and fearing some lethal trick, Hassan sent his chief security officer into the "bomb room" to open the square envelope.

Hassan watched on the closed-circuit television system.

He looked at the man . . . then at the plastic "compact" whose color exactly matched that of Barcelona Delta . . . back to the man again. Now the loyal colonel was removing from the envelope a single sheet of paper. The seconds flickered away. He showed no sign of either poisoning or the fungus.

There could still be something deadly in there, Hassan thought. It might be slow acting, he told himself.

A sincere believer in homicide as a method of social change, Fozira's president had been extremely suspicious . . . even more than usual . . . about plots and deceptions since the Madeshi reported the total destruction of the underground laboratory and its entire staff.

It was hard to believe this could happen at the *last* minute.

And it was just too convenient that the major he'd sent to bring back the fungus was also buried there with all the US scientists . . . leaving no survivor who might tell a different story.

The same Madeshi politicians and generals he'd bribed could have sold his expensive and irresistible weapon of mass destruction to another nation for a higher price, Hassan thought as he watched the colonel step towards the television camera. Yes, it was just the sort of thing those damned Iranians would try.

And the Iranians or somebody else might have contaminated the letter . . . it didn't matter how. Since it might be lethal, Hassan wasn't going to touch it. That's why the colonel was now holding it up two inches from the camera.

Extreme close-up.

Dear General Hassan:

As you've undoubtedly noticed, the color of the plastic

case is precisely that of the fungus. Inside the case are
photos of the foreign scientists we buried in the laboratory
in Madesh.

We realize that you've been worried about them and
when you'll get delivery. Since we have the fungus, your
worries are over. You can be certain that we'll deliver it immediately after you resume *any* efforts to acquire any bacteriological or biological weapon or other mass destruction
system.

We'll deliver it all over Fozira.

That includes your command bunker.

This is your only warning.

We'll be watching you.

              The Spirit Team

Stunned, Hassan couldn't speak for several seconds.

Then he began to recover his control.

"Open the plastic case," he said over the intercom to the man
holding the letter. "I want to see what's inside."

In the next minute and a half, Hassan looked at the nine things
the colonel took from the blue case. Six were small pictures . . .
head shots . . . of the rogue scientists. The seventh was a folded
piece of thin paper covered with a chart of air currents to and in
Fozira.

They *knew,* the Supreme Leader for Life realized.

Who were they? Where were they? How many?

How could he hurt them . . . kill them . . . if he didn't know?

Choked with frustration and rage, he had to smash someone
or something. He barely fought down an impulse to draw his pistol and blow the closed-circuit screen to bits. Aware that he
shouldn't let his staff see him go berserk, he controlled himself. If
he "lost it" his commanders might read this as a sign of weakness, and he could lose everything.

Holding on to his hate, he managed to make his way back in
silence to his soundproofed inner office. He closed the heavy

door . . . eyed the life-sized painting of himself in the gold-leafed frame . . . and studied his image in the big wall mirror.

He still looked presidential . . . looked like pure power.

Reassured by the strength of his image in this world in which image counted so much, the Supreme Leader for Life felt less threatened . . . less impotent . . . less of a failure. He'd get to the Spirit Team later.

He could still go forward towards domination without the fungus. All he had to do was eliminate the competition . . . intimidate or destroy the leaders of other countries who might challenge him. He studied the map on the stand beside his huge desk.

Which countries first?

Egypt and Iran. *Definitely* Iran.

That would be a very good start.

44

The Director of Central Intelligence was wearing a beige linen suit and had a cold bitter look in her eyes. Brigadier General Paul J. Sherman noticed both as he entered her office.

"Sit down," Sandra Lynes told him. "We've got a *unique* little multimedia presentation, and I'd like your input."

The G-2 officer nodded and glanced over at the CIA director of operations and the deputy director seated on the couch. Both were frowning, and each shrugged . . . barely . . . in acknowledgment.

Bad news time, Sherman thought.

"Unique?" he tested without much hope.

"I'll let you judge," she replied in a voice that made him feel he'd been threatened. Then she pressed a button on a console built into her desk.

"You may know these people," she said as a large-screen television set slid from a wall panel and the concealed VCR began to roll.

Sherman recognized the faces at once.

They belonged to the eight rogue Rosebud scientists and technicians.

The general nodded again, wondering what was going on here.

"I gave those pictures to your man Reed," Sherman told her as if disclaiming responsibility for whatever was bothering her. He didn't know what it was, but he wanted no part of it.

"There are other pictures on this cassette . . . the blue corpses *your* fungus left in the Torat Valley," she announced.

Sherman winced, and waited warily for her next words.

"Since you've seen them," she continued, "I think we can go on to the other items that came with it. This morning . . . in an air-express package from Paris . . . addressed to me and marked *personal.*"

She took from her desk drawer four audio cassettes.

Microcassettes, the little ones used in very small recorders.

The kind used for secret taping.

When she moved aside a handsome white Arabia vase filled with yellow tulips Sherman saw the compact tape machine. The cassettes were numbered 1 . . . 2 . . . 3 . . . 4. She chose to play them in that sequence.

"Look at the video first," a man with a slight English accent said. "You'll recognize the contents, and understand who we must be. The only people who could have it are those you sent to Madesh to destroy . . . permanently . . . the blue fungus threat.

"We are those people . . . legally dead . . . very much alive.

"In accord with the agreement, we have destroyed the laboratory and the blue fungus threat. We respected the contract, and you didn't. You've behaved dishonorably. You sent him to betray us, and you haven't paid us what we were promised despite our full performance.

"Because of that, we are now threatening you. The audio and video contents of this package contain important evidence that American scientists have developed an extremely lethal biological weapon in direct violation of the international treaty . . . and that their continuing work on this blue fungus killed hundreds of civilian men, women and children within the past few months.

"There is also strong evidence that an armed illegal invasion and covert assault was executed to destroy property, civilians and military personnel in a friendly power that is an ally of the United States.

"In addition, we can provide evidence that the friendly power was collaborating with a third country condemned by the United Nations for state terrorism and the US government knew it.

"We are ready to send the already duplicated packages of evidence to major newspapers and broadcast networks in the United States, Britain, Europe, the Middle East and Asia. What this would do to the reputation of your agency and the entire US intelligence and defense communities is obvious.

"The damage would also affect significantly the international perception of US diplomatic and political leadership at the highest level. This demonstration of incompetence and immorality would fuel a global scandal.

"That is our threat. Here are our terms. On the twenty-first of this month at 4 P.M., a courier . . . unarmed and unescorted . . . is to deliver high quality diamonds in stones of three to five carats with a wholesale value of ten million dollars.

"If you place an advertisement reading Hanover College reunion on campus August 6th . . . all welcome . . . in the *International Herald Tribune* . . . all editions around the world . . . on the eighteenth of this month, the site of delivery and further instructions will be given to a US military attache at noon on the nineteenth. Our identification and authentication phrase will be Dr. Jay Botchman.

"Our threat is real. The terms are non-negotiable.

"The choice is yours."

Sherman looked down . . . considered what he'd heard . . . and raised his head to face the DCI again.

"What about the other three cassettes?" he asked.

"One conversation between Reed and some woman with a French accent . . . two between Reed and the man with the English accent who delivered the threat," she replied. "There's enough in them to cause us all . . . that includes the Army . . . an enormous amount of trouble. The whole damn strike on Madesh is spelled out, and you can guess what Congress would do if it heard the not-too-subtle suggestion that *all* the Rosebud mercenaries be eliminated."

"It wouldn't be hard to hear," Carling added bitterly. "Very good for covert recordings. They've got the tradecraft down cold."

"Too bad Reed didn't," the broad faced director of operations said. "An experienced field agent wouldn't let himself be taped so easily. These people are cute. Giving us only two days notice of where to deliver is *real* cute."

Carling sighed in agreement.

"They'll have the place under surveillance," he predicted. "They'll be watching to see that we don't flood it with agents."

The G-2 general took out his pipe . . . paused . . . and looked at her.

"Go ahead. Smoke," she said impatiently. "Smoke and talk. I could use that input right now."

He packed in the tobacco and lit it before he spoke.

"On the basis of what these people have already done," he began, "I'd say that this threat is real and we'd better take it seriously. These people are damn good."

"The *best,* according to Reed," Sandra Lynes said.

"Our people are pretty good too," the director of operations declared righteously.

"Of course," she agreed with the obligatory sincerity—the mechanical kind she'd offer a Senate committee. "Go on, general."

"Good and *tough,"* he continued. "What they pulled off in Madesh is awesome. Recognizing this, the question isn't one of anybody in Washington's blame or ego or ass but whether we deal or fight."

He puffed on the pipe again.

"Fight who? Who the hell are these people to threaten the entire US intelligence community?" he thought aloud. "We simply don't know. We don't know the size of this Spirit Team . . . their weapons . . . or where they are. We only know three things. First, they're *not* in Paris. If they're this good, they probably left town before the package did."

"Maybe we can track down this Botchman," Carling argued.

"Not a fucking chance," Sherman answered and glanced at the DCI apologetically.

"I've heard the word before," she said and thought about how often the president used it . . . in private . . . to trusted friends.

"Not a chance because they're smart enough to pick a name from some phone book," Sherman explained. "They'd never leave tracks to anyone they knew. That's the second thing. Don't waste time looking for Botchman."

This general was pretty good himself, she judged. A lot of the Old Boys in the Agency looked down on Military Intelligence officers as hacks and dullards, but Sherman didn't fit that mold at all.

"What's the third thing?" she asked.

"I'm a soldier," he answered. "I'm not trained to back down. I'm trained to fight. As a senior officer, I also know that the objective is the national interest of the United States. These people are literally out of sight . . . and they have the capacity and will to hurt the national interests of the United States if we don't deal."

"Will?" she said. "You believe they'd do it?"

"We played hardball with them . . . the hardest. We tried to have them killed," Sherman reminded grimly. "Now they're playing hardball with us. In their position, I'd probably do the same goddam thing. Wouldn't you?"

The Director of Central Intelligence didn't answer. She didn't have to and she didn't want to. If she did, it could be extremely embarrassing later if some of those virtuous bastards in Congress or the media asked the wrong questions.

She had to protect herself and the president.

She knew about deniability too.

"I know our government's official policy is we don't give in to terrorist blackmail," the general said. "I also know that our government and a lot of others do plenty of things unofficially when they believe they have to. Some of our noblest allies give in to terrorists regularly on so-called humanitarian grounds. We don't have to claim that. If we pay the Spirits, it'll be secret . . . if we're lucky."

"Lucky?" she asked.

"If we don't fuck it up . . . and if they keep their word," Sherman replied.

"You're saying we should deal?" she pressed.

"The lesser of two evils," he answered.

She thanked him. Aware that she didn't want him to hear the decision or debate that would follow, he played the game. He said something polite and correct, and he left.

"I guess we have to pay them," she said slowly.

Carling and the director of operations tried . . . carefully and respectfully . . . to talk her out of it. They failed, and started to walk back to the director of operations' office.

"How do we know they'll keep their word?" Carling worried.

"How do we know they won't keep coming back for more money?" the head of CIA operations responded.

Neither man spoke for the next ten seconds.

"It might help if we could talk to them . . . to see how they feel," Carling suggested.

"Talk to them or take them out," his boss replied. "We can't have them running out there loose. No slipups, Carter."

"No slipups," Carling promised.

There shouldn't be any problem with the DCI, he reasoned. They'd tell her that the Spirits opened fire first.

45

At 4 P.M. on the twenty-first, Mr. Carl Hunt and a score of other people entered the main terminal of Rome's large Leonardo da Vinci International Airport. He had a US diplomatic passport that identified him as a courier for the Department of State, and a brown leather attache case chained to his left wrist.

His real name was Charles Bisciglia, and he was actually employed not by State but by what with-it Washingtonians called "another agency of the government." It was the one run by Sandra Lynes, but he wouldn't admit that even under rigorous questioning. He carried the diplomatic passport to shield him from any sort of interrogation, delay or other inconvenience by Italian authorities.

Anything could happen in the next thirty minutes, he thought.

Bisciglia was an able field agent who spoke Italian well and had twelve years of operational experience outside the United States. He realized that something could go wrong at any moment. Despite Carling's very carefully shaped and professional plan . . . the cautious reconnaissance of the terminal . . . the eighteen armed CIA agents inside the building and ten others outside . . . there *might* be a problem.

This hand-picked CIA force of veteran field agents could handle problems, Bisciglia told himself loyally as he eyed the airline check-in counters that faced him. He knew this terminal from half a dozen previous visits. That gave him additional confidence. It was also one reason he'd been chosen by Carling.

The precise place for delivering the brown case hadn't been chosen by Carling. Neither had the garb that Bisciglia wore. Tan pincord suit . . . yellow shirt . . . green tie with golden floral pattern . . . black half-boots and gold-rimmed eyeglasses.

They had specified all that.

And the exact route Bisciglia should follow from entering the terminal to delivery at the phone booth downstairs on the lower level.

Neither Carling nor the CIA's able Rome "station chief" had said who *they* were. That had made Bisciglia uneasy. The tension diminished when he heard he'd be guarded every step of the way by a strong security team . . . and *they* were highly unlikely to do anything but accept the case. Then he was to deliver the oral message.

Bisciglia hadn't been told that there might be shooting.

He carried no weapon.

He took a few steps from the automatic door . . . looked around . . . saw three of the security agents protecting him . . . and felt better. He also saw an extraordinary number of priests and nuns, even more than he'd observed on his two visits to the Vatican.

There were over one hundred . . . maybe one hundred and thirty . . . in this hall.

Now he saw fifty or sixty more emerging from two buses that had just pulled up outside.

And Lloyd saw him.

Wondering about all the clergy, Bisciglia almost bumped into a young nun. Yielding to his curiosity, he politely asked the slim woman . . . she seemed to be Asian . . . why there were so many "servants of God" in the terminal now. He inquired . . . first in Italian and then in English when she didn't respond . . . whether this was some special occasion.

"Very special," she replied enthusiastically. She explained that a cardinal was returning from two weeks in central Africa where the Holy Father *himself* had sent him to carry hope and faith.

The cardinal had risked his life to go into plague areas, the beaming nun reported, and the Holy Father *himself* had sent this delegation of three hundred priests and nuns and a monsignor to honor his courage and devotion.

Now Mendoza . . . off left near the TWA counter . . . saw him.

Down to the right, Samuel Chibuku was watching him too.

Bisciglia thanked Josephine Tan, and walked away with real respect for her obvious religious fervor. So that's why all the clergy were here, he thought. He hadn't known of the cardinal's mission or that he'd return this afternoon . . . at 4:25 . . . to Leonardo da Vinci International Airport. The CIA "station chief" hadn't known either, the courier reasoned. Otherwise he would have mentioned it.

David Lloyd had known.

That was why he'd set the delivery for this place . . . at this time.

That was why Josephine Tan wore the habit of a nun, and the male Spirits were dressed as priests. So was the cat burglar who was outside at the wheel of the car.

Sorry that he wouldn't see the cardinal being welcomed, the courier now followed the instructions *they* had sent. He turned left . . . made his way to the pharmacy . . . and examined the window displays. Then he walked back past the automatic doors to the entrance of Alitalia's private Club Freccia Alata where First Class and other VIP passengers were coddled.

The upscale little oasis had ample amenities. This afternoon it also had an armed CIA field agent in the bulky uniform of a maintenance worker sweeping the floor near its doorway. He was rated as a sharpshooter . . . like the three men in the van outside.

As Bisciglia approached the entrance to the club Rome's affluent called the CFA, the courier was looking ahead to the next part of his designated route. Outside to the escalator . . . then to the lower level where he'd exchange passwords with the woman in the grey pantsuit and yellow shoes . . . and hand over the case.

He had the key to unlock the wrist-chain, and he had memorized the passwords. He also had the sense of well being that came from knowing all those security men waited to protect him downstairs.

He didn't get downstairs.

He didn't even reach the escalator.

It all happened very quickly.

Everyone in the arrival hall . . . the legion of priests and nuns and scores of other passengers and employees of the terminal and various famous airlines . . . was stunned. They were gasping too, and many were weeping.

"Everyone" didn't include four people. These exceptions were a sweet-faced nun and three Franciscan priests. They had thrown the smoke bombs and incendiary grenades that set off the noisy fire alarms. They were the ones who tossed a dozen tear-gas cannisters around the courier, enveloping and blinding him in seconds.

He couldn't see anything. He could hardly breathe.

David Lloyd, Josephine Tan, Samuel Chibuku and Eugenio Garcia Mendoza had no such problems. In accord with Lloyd's assault plan, they put on respirators as soon as they began the attack.

They'd come with other special equipment too.

With fire alarms sounding loudly . . . hundreds of decent and God-loving people and dozens of atheists coughing and crying in shared distress . . . scores retching, staggering or collapsing . . . and mass confusion escalating into panic, Lloyd moved in swiftly on the dazed and no-longer-so-confident courier.

The large hall was filled with screams, curses, prayers and more than a little fear of a terrorist massacre. Ignoring this uproar and chaos which he'd expected, Lloyd took an expensive-but-worth-it wire cutter from under his somber brown Franciscan attire.

It was a matter of timing and teamwork now.

Just before the attack he'd spotted a pair of Italy's tough and black booted anti-terrorist police with automatic weapons and gas mask cases. These two professionals and others who'd be racing towards the audible assault wouldn't panic like civilians. Well trained, they'd be putting on their gas masks at any moment.

The Spirits had twenty seconds . . . maybe thirty.

They didn't waste one of them.

Each Spirit had an assignment. Chibuku and Mendoza were the screening unit to cover Lloyd. The team leader hit the near helpless courier at the back of the head, stunning him with a pistol butt. As the man with the case sagged, Chibuku and Mendoza ambushed the two police and knocked them unconscious.

Before they hit the floor, Lloyd cut the chain to the courier's wrist . . . grabbed the leather case . . . and tore it open with the wire cutter's pointed nose. Simultaneously, Josephine Tan reached under her skirt to produce a nylon sack that had a hook on it.

Seven seconds.

There were a dozen small bags in the case.

Ten million dollars in diamonds. Carling had played it safe. He'd provided the precious stones so he could comply with the DCI's instructions . . . never expecting to lose them. Now Lloyd found them.

The team leader scooped them up in four movements . . . shoved them into the mouth of the bag she held ready. He immediately pressed shut the Velcro strips on the mouth. She raised her skirt at the same moment, and he placed the hook over a sturdy money belt she wore under the garment.

Sixteen seconds.

Hit and run.

It was time to run.

They walked instead. It would attract less attention. They pushed their way through the turbulent unseeing throng, discarding the gas masks just before they reached the automatic doors. Mingling in the panicky crowd that was stumbling out, they emerged from the terminal. Pretending to cough and choke like the others, they rubbed their eyes and gasped realistically as they wandered "groggily" from the building.

A dozen anti-terrorist cops charging to blast the terrorists ignored them as simply some of the unfortunate victims . . . pious clerics who deserved respect.

The CIA security team covering the outside of the terminal didn't really see them in among the other hurting priests and nuns emerging from the building.

No one made any effort to stop them as they made their way to the car where Sharif waited behind the wheel. As they entered the inconspicuous Italian sedan, the chaos continued inside the terminal. The CIA operatives assigned to protect the courier and terminate the threat of the Spirit Team took advantage of the continuing fumes and confusion to collect their dazed agent and the wreck of his attache case.

They carried both out to the command van.

There the mission supervisor . . . a capable and thinking sandy-haired professional named Kenneth Dixon who was "control" for this operation . . . looked at the courier and ruined case. Dixon was the only person whom Carling had trusted enough to tell the basics about the Spirit Team.

Not about Barcelona Delta. Not a word.

The fungus was none of Dixon's business.

Now Dixon had to return to Washington to report.

The courier groaned . . . coughed several times and opened his red and swollen eyes.

"What . . . what happened?" he whispered.

"I wish I knew," Dixon answered candidly.

"The case?"

"They took it," Dixon told him. "It wasn't your fault. They're the best."

The battered courier gasped and coughed again.

"Best what?" he wondered.

"Best clandestine operators . . . best strike force in the world," Dixon replied. "They may be the best Goddam *everything*, but that's not all."

He looked down at the courier who'd done his job well . . . but not well enough.

"What else?" the hurting courier whispered.

"They're not only the best . . . but they hate us . . . for a reason. More than one. We don't know who they are . . . or what they look like . . . or what they'll do next."

"What do you think they'll do?" Bisciglia gasped.

"Whatever they want," Dixon answered grimly. "We have a real problem here. They're the best. They can do anything!"

46

Four priests and a nun.

The guards at the exit from the airport took one look . . . nodded respectfully . . . and waved the car through immediately.

"We did it! We did it!" Mendoza exulted a hundred yards down the road.

"With a little luck," Lloyd said.

The woman seated beside him in the back seat . . . the woman who wondered why he was so modest . . . shook her head.

"Fortune favors the bold," she quoted.

"Vergil," Lloyd recalled. "So my dear friend read Vergil . . . in Latin, I'd bet."

"French classical education," she replied with a smile. "It was much more than luck. We're a fine team, and we had a brilliant plan."

The Nigerian, who was seated on her right, nodded in accord.

"I'd call it brilliant, sir," he announced.

"There's enough glory for all of us," Lloyd told them. "There has been from the moment we met in Athens. Every person in this car has performed with distinction. We did it because each of us played a crucial part in our joint effort. We're alive because we're a natural team."

"There's a fit," the burglar behind the wheel agreed.

She reached under her garment and took out the bag of diamonds. Then she tugged down her skirt and put the ten million dollar sack in her lap.

"That was uncomfortable," she said as she smoothed the skirt. "Diamonds are for the neck."

"Or the wrist . . . or the finger," Lloyd suggested.

She waited for him to continue, but Mendoza broke in with a question.

"What do you think we'll get for these stones in Amsterdam or Tel Aviv?"

"Not quite what they're worth wholesale," Sharif answered. "Not ten. Maybe six. At least five."

"A million bucks each," Mendoza celebrated. *"Not* bad."

"Not bad for us," the cat burglar pointed out soberly. "About a thousand people died for this. Not so great for them."

Seated next to him, the marksman turned and glared.

"Easy on the guilt trip," he admonished. *"We* didn't bust any treaties . . . and *we* didn't invent the blue shit . . . and *we* didn't try to wipe out a whole damn country. Governments did that, Babes. And it wasn't *our* idea to destroy that mine . . . and kill the scientists . . . and all the other people down there. You can pin those stiffs on a government too."

"He's right," Lloyd said.

"We just did a job," Mendoza insisted, "with everyone out to bury us. We beat 'em all . . . all the suits . . . all the generals . . . all the public servants in white shirts. You know, *they* don't feel the least bit guilty. They'd do it again tomorrow."

And twice on Sunday, the team leader thought. Despite the smug and popular global paranoia about the CIA, it wasn't just the Americans who did these viciously virtuous things. Not by a long shot.

"As I see it," Mendoza continued, "we did the good stuff. We took out the lab and saved a lot of lives. They didn't. I say leave it. We can take our diamonds and walk. It's over."

"It isn't over," Lloyd disagreed. "At least fifteen other countries are getting ready to wage biological war."

"And make nerve gas . . . and who knows what else?" Chibuku asked.

"A lot else," Lloyd said, "and a lot of governments are playing the game . . . not just gangsters like Fozira. They're getting plenty of help from businessmen and scientists all over the world. Many governments . . . from the pious democracies to dirty tyrannies . . . are selling missiles and chemicals and bio-horrors to the biggest monsters and head cases around."

He stopped and faced the woman beside him.

"I don't mean it's hopeless. There are some wonderful people around too," he said and looked into her wide eyes.

Something stirred inside her. She had to tell him.

"James," she began.

He shook his head.

"My name . . . my *real* name . . . is David," he told her.

He was risking his life for her, she realized.

"My name is Emilie," she replied proudly.

"It suits you," he declared and silently took her hand.

Moved and unwilling to intrude on their moment, Chibuku stared out the window.

In the front seat, Sharif and Mendoza glanced at each other and instantly considered what they'd heard. Should they risk it too?

"No way!" Mendoza announced abruptly.

"Maybe later," the master burglar equivocated.

Then the Nigerian soldier spoke suddenly in a strong voice.

"Alfred. That's *my* name," he said.

They all looked at each other, and laughed as the car rolled on to safety. They were alive and almost rich . . . and no one was trying to kill them at the moment. They could build on that.

The End

WALTER WAGER

Walter Wager is the bestselling author of more than twenty thrillers, which have been published in twelve languages. Three of his novels have been adapted for film: *58 Minutes* (the basis for *Die Hard II*), *Viper Three* (filmed as *Twilight's Last Gleaming*), and the classic *Telefon*. Other novels include *Otto's Boy*, *Designated Hitter*, *Sledgehammer*, and *Time of Reckoning*.

Wager's articles on travel and the performing arts are published everywhere: *The New York Times*, *The Los Angeles Times*, *The Denver Post*, *The Baltimore Sun*, *The San Francisco Chronicle*, *The Houston Chronicle*, *Playbill* magazine, and *Performing Arts* magazine.

Wager has been Special Assistant to the Israeli Director of Civil Aviation, a senior editor at the United Nations Secretariat, a radio and TV scriptwriter for CBS, and a writer-producer at NBC. Wager's interest in the performing arts led to positions as the editor in chief of *Playbill*, the nation's premier theater guide, as communications director of the Julliard School, and as publicity director for ASCAP.

Walter Wager sits on the boards of directors of the Mystery Writers of America and the National Academy of Popular Music. He held a Fulbright fellowship at the Sorbonne after his graduation from Columbia, and holds degrees in law from Northwestern and Harvard.